CALLAHAN

Once, it was just another Irish name (and also a tunnel in Boston), but since 1972, when Spider Robinson started writing stories about the bar called Callahan's Place, the name has brought to mind a number of thoughts in the minds of his readers. Here's a brief sampling:

"Tall tales . . . fine and funny. . . . A significant achievement for light humor!"

—*Houston Post*

"What you're reading is truly unique, because the man who wrote [it] is truly unique . . . Enjoy."

—*Ben Bova*

"A master!"

—*Locus*

"Robinson's creative imagination is admirable."

—*Publishers Weekly*

"Robinson is the hottest writer to hit science fiction since Ellison, and he can match the master's frenetic energy and emotional intensity, arm-break for gut-wrench."

—*Los Angeles Times*

But you don't have to take their word for it. See for yourself. Turn the pages till you get to the Backword (page xi), and see if you can stop. Betcha can't read just one!

BOOKS BY SPIDER ROBINSON

*denotes a Tor Book

THE
CALLAHAN
CHRONICALS

SPIDER ROBINSON

TOR®

A TOM DOHERTY ASSOCIATES BOOK.
NEW YORK

This is a work of fiction. All the characters and events portrayed in this book are either products of the author's imagination or are used fictitiously.

THE CALLAHAN CHRONICALS

Cover art by James Warhola
Edited by James Frenkel

A Tor Book
Published by Tom Doherty Associates, LLC
175 Fifth Avenue
New York, NY 10010

www.tor.com

Tor® is a registered trademark of Tom Doherty Associates, LLC.

ISBN: 0-812-53937-0

First Omnibus edition: October 1997

Printed in the United States of America

0 9 8 7 6

CONTENTS

THE CALLAHAN CHRONICALS

BACKWORD

by Spider Robinson

Yes, I know. They're usually called Forewords. Especially when, like this one, they are found at the front of the book. You can think of it as a Foreword if you like. But I expect these may be the last words I will ever write about Callahan's Place, and so for me, this is a Backword.

Dignum et justum est. It is somehow appropriate that this volume should begin with a Backword—for these are the collected tales (pun intended, of course) of Callahan's Place, as backassward a tavern as you're likely to find.

Just *how* backassward, I am reluctant to try and explain here. If you don't already know The Place, just skip this Backword and go on to the stories themselves. Since almost all of them were designed to be sold first to magazines, then collected in book form later, I have had to think up *dozens* of ways to explain Callahan's Place to a newcomer, without repeating myself. The increasing difficulty of this trick over the years has, in fact, something to do with why these are the last words I plan to write about the joint.

Suffice it to say that in a world which was slowly evolving the concept of "cocooning," Mike Callahan was backward enough to believe that good fellowship and shared merriment are worth more than a VCR and a CD player. In a society where tolerance has waxed and waned as arbitrarily as skirt lengths, Mike was backward enough to serve booze to any entity capable of ordering it (with one notable exception). In a culture where pessimism has metastasized like slow carcinoma, that crazy Irishman was backward enough to try and raise hopes, like hothouse flowers. In an era during which even judicious use of alcohol has been increasingly bad-rapped, the man who has come to be known as The Mick of Time was backward enough to think that sometimes the world can look just that essential tad better when seen through a glass, brightly. (As long as you let someone else drive you home afterward.) Above all, he—and his goofball customers—believed that shared pain is lessened, and shared joy is increased.

Now he is gone. Gone back whence he came, and we are all the poorer for it. But I refuse to say that we will not see his like again. Or his love again.

Witness the fact that this volume exists. The seeds Callahan planted seem to be germinating nicely. The books in which these stories originally appeared, *Callahan's Crosstime Saloon*, *Time Travelers Strictly Cash*, and *Callahan's Secret*, were all paperback originals—that is to say, loss leaders. The covers given to the second volume and all reissues of the first (until Tor came along) were . . . well, less than wonderful. The combined advertising budgets of all three books would not have sufficed to purchase a copy of the word-processing program with which I'm typing this.

Yet somehow the three books are all still in print, a full quarter of a century later—and still generating more reader mail and fan comment than all twenty-two of my other books put together. *Saloon* was named a Best Book for Young Adults by the American Library Association. All the Callahan books have been published in several languages around the globe. They have been optioned for TV and movies for over a decade (by a succession of folks who creep ever closer to actually getting something produced). One of the stories herein, ''Dog Day Evening,'' was a finalist for science fiction's top honour, the Hugo Award. There are at least six lines of Callahan's Place T-shirts in existence (none of which brings me a dime). The hideous custom called Punday Night, created by Mike Callahan, has become a regular feature (or is it a bug?) at Boston's Boskone and other regional science fiction conventions. (I understand Boston has even named a municipal *tunnel* after Callahan's.)

Fans have produced and sent me Callahan stories, poems, plays, paintings, and songs, many of them wonderful. Steve Jackson Games put out a wonderful Callahan's role-playing game a few years back, well designed by Chris McCubbin. Everywhere I go, people seem to know that I like Old Bushmill's. And they pour me some . . .

And finally, sagacious publisher Tom Doherty and canny editor Jim Frenkel have perceived a demand for this edition you hold in your hands (or paws, or whatever you use): the first-ever mass-market omnibus of all the Callahan stories in a single volume. Without distractions (*Cash*, for inadequate reasons confessed in its Foreword, was partly non-Callahan stories). With a Warhola cover. The kind of edition you lend to a trusted friend, or give to a loved one, or leave to your grandchildren, or just spend a lot of time with.

It would seem that Mike Callahan has left something of himself behind.

And now we come to the real reason why this is called a Back-word. In looking back over this book, I am looking back over the whole of my professional life. "The Guy With The Eyes," the first of the stories you are about to read, was the first attempt I ever made to write something for money—lo, these twenty-five years past. And the last piece you'll read is my most recent short story, previously "published" only on the Internet.

I have a lot to look backward to.

If I had not had the incredible good fortune to sell that first Callahan story (on its first submission!) to Ben Bova at *Analog*, I honestly do not believe I would ever have written another word for sale. I would not have had the courage to quit my job guarding a sewer (don't ask), and move from New York to Nova Scotia. Which means I would never have met my darling Jeanne, would never have fathered my darling Terri! Instead of shrinking and dropping away, the scabs of New York life might have calcified into horny, heavy armor.

And here's the punchline: just a few months ago, thanks to Callahan's Place, I finally managed to achieve—by about the most back-assward route imaginable—the secret lifetime dream I gave up twenty-five years ago to become a writer!

What I really *wanted* to be when I grew up, you see, was a folk-singer/songwriter—only they stopped *having* them just about the time I entered the business, back at the end of the Sixties. Science fiction was my booby-prize, for never getting to cut a record. It's been a pretty good one, all things considered . . . but it just ain't music, you know?

Then a year ago, a computer-game designer named Josh Mandel of Legend Entertainment bought the right to create a CD-ROM game based on Callahan's Place—and asked if by any chance I might be willing to record some of my original songs for the game's soundtrack. Professionally. In a real studio. With real pro players backing me up.

So I told him what Donald Trump is alleged to have said to the gorgeous blonde stranger who offered to perform an intimacy upon him in a crowded elevator. What's in it for me? I said, and a budget was agreed upon.

Wait, we're not done yet. That night I went out to a local club called the Yale. I do this exactly twice a year, when Amos Garrett passes through town. Amos is my favorite musician in all the world, a guitarist of awesome lyricism; you will find him mentioned at least once in this very volume (in "The Blacksmith's Tale"), and I have written the liner notes for two of his albums. That night when he came down off the stand on his break, I told him, rather shyly, of my silly little invitation to cut an almost-record, and asked if he could recommend a good producer. He did: Danny Casavant. And then he dropped the bomb. "Got a lead guitar player yet?"

That's right, friends: if you purchase the 1997 Legend Entertainment computer-game CD-ROM *Callahan's Crosstime Saloon*, click on Fast Eddie, and ask him for some music, you will be given a choice of four songs, all written and sung by me (lyrics for two of them appear in this book; Jake even lent me Lady Macbeth to play rhythm guitar), all backed by a killer band, and all featuring the greatest living wizard of the Telecaster, Amos Garrett, on lead!

Even when I was a professional musician, I never dared dream so high: I am happier than a pig in Congress.

(Josh's game itself is splendid, by the way: ingenious, hilarious, intricate, visually stunning, and most important, infused throughout with the *feeling* I've tried to give Callahan's Place. By which I mean, it is an environment in which shared pain is lessened, shared joy is increased, and the puns really suck.)

* * *

Jeanne, Terri, writing, and music. The four pillars on which my happiness stands—and I owe all four to Callahan's Place. When I think of how different, how bleak and desolate my life could have been if I hadn't happened to pay attention, a decade and a half ago, to the drunken ramblings of a broken-down fellow folk-singer named Jake Stonebender, lab-quality freon drips into my veins.

What Mike Callahan has done for me cannot be undone by anything as trivial as his disappearance. His Place was more than a collection of wood and nails.

Some years back I got a phone call at 4 A.M. from a total stranger in California. God knows how he got my unlisted number. He declined to give his name or even his town. His voice was flat. He said he was on the verge of suicide—he didn't want to talk about why. And the deciding factor would be this: would I tell him, please, if Callahan's Place really existed, and if so how to get there?

I've been asked that question hundreds of times in the last decade and a half. I gave it my best shot. I don't think what I said pleased him. I think he was expecting highway directions and perhaps a secret password. But all I could tell him was the truth. I hope he believed me.

"You're standing in it," I told him.

And so are you. And so am I.

As long as we remember that, it will always be true. I used to live on Long Island; trust me: if it could happen in Suffolk County, it can happen anywhere. I have received several dozen letters from readers, triumphantly informing me that they have found the real Callahan's Place. No two have the same location: none has yet named a bar I've ever entered or heard of.

Nonetheless, all of them are correct.

Furthermore—as you will find out when you get to the end of this book, and encounter the first and only new Callahan's short story I've written since 1985—some readers apparently couldn't be bothered pub-crawling all the way across Long Island looking for the joint . . . so they created their own. That's right: the damn Place has actually metastasized, without any help or encouragement from me, onto the Internet!

So let's get to it. Belly up to the bar and place your order, and bless you for asking: I'll have a Bushmill's. Listen to that little son of a bitch play that piano. Merry in here, ain't it? Hey, *Jake!* Leave off polishing that bartop a minute, will you? Come on down here and tell us one more time about the night the whole thing got started . . .

—Vancouver, British Columbia
January, 1997

PART I

CALLAHAN'S CROSSTIME SALOON

To Ben Bova

SPIDER ROBINSON: THE SF WRITER AS EMPATH

by Ben Bova

When *Analog* magazine was housed over at the Graybar Building on Lexington Avenue, our offices were far from plush. In fact, they were grimy. Years' worth of Manhattan soot clung to the walls. The windows were opaque with grime. (What has this to do with Spider Robinson? Patience, friend.)

Many times young science fiction fans would come to Manhattan and phone me from Grand Central Station, which connected underground with the good old Graybar. "I've just come to New York and I read every issue of *Analog* and I'd like to come up and see what a science fiction magazine office looks like," they would invariably say.

I'd tell them to come on up, but not to expect too much. My advice was always ignored. The poor kid would come in and gape at the piles of manuscripts, the battered old metal desks, and mountains of magazines and stacks of artwork, the ramshackle filing cabinets and bookshelves. His eyes would fill with tears. His mouth would sag open.

He had, of course, expected whirring computers, telephones with TV attachments, smoothly efficient robots humming away, ultramodern furniture, and a general appearance reminiscent of a NASA clean room. (Our present offices, in the spanking new Condé Nast Building on Madison Avenue, are a little closer to that dream.)

The kid would shamble away, heartsick, the beautiful rainbow-hued bubble of his imagination burst by the sharp prick of reality.

Still, despite the cramped quarters and the general dinginess, we managed to put out an issue of *Analog* each month, and more readers bought it than any other science fiction book, magazine, pamphlet, or cuneiform tablet ever published.

And then came Spider Robinson.

Truth to tell, I don't remember if he sent in a manuscript through the mail first, or telephoned for an appointment to visit the office. No matter. And now he's off in Nova Scotia, living among the stunted trees and frost heaves, where nobody—not even short-memoried editors—can reach him easily.

Anyway, in comes Spider. I look up from my desk and see this lank, almost-cadaverous young man, bearded, long of hair, slightly owlish behind his eyeglasses, sort of grinning quizzically, as if he didn't know what to expect. Neither did I.

But I thought, *At least he won't be put off by the interior decor.*

You have to understand that those same kids who expected *Analog*'s office to look like an out-take from *2001: A Space Odyssey* also had a firm idea of what an *Analog* writer should look like: a tall, broad-shouldered, jut-jawed, steely-eyed hero who can repair a starship's inertial drive with one hand, make friends with the fourteen-legged green aliens of Arcturus, and bring the warring nations of Earth together under a benignly scientific world government—all at the same time, while wearing a metallic mesh jumpsuit and a cool smile.

Never mind that no SF writer ever looked like that. Well, maybe Robert A. Heinlein comes close, and he could certainly do all of those things if he'd just stop writing for a while. But Asimov is a bit less than heroic in stature; Silverberg shuns politics; Bradbury doesn't even drive a car, much less a starship.

Nevertheless, this was the popular conception of a typical *Analog* writer. Spider Robinson was rather wider of that mark than most.

He had a story with him, called "The Guy With The Eyes." There wasn't much science fiction in it. But it was one helluva good story. About a crazy bunch of guys who get together at a truly unique place called Callahan's.

We went to lunch, and Spider began telling me how he worked nights guarding a sewer 'way out on Long Island. Far from being a dropout, he was writing stories and songs, as well as sewer-sitting. He's a worker, and he knows science fiction very well, a fact that surprised a lot of people when he started reviewing books for *Galaxy* magazine. He's also a guitar-strummin' singer, and I found out how good he is at many a party. But that was later.

I bought "The Guy With The Eyes." When it came out in *Analog*, it caused a mild ripple among our readers. I had expected some of them to complain because it wasn't galaxy-spanning superheroic science fiction. Instead, they wrote to tell me that they got a kick out of Callahan's Place. How about more of the same?

Now, an editor spends most of his time reading lousy stories. John Campbell, who ran *Analog* (née *Astounding*) for some thirty-five years, often claimed to hold the Guinness Book of Records championship for reading more rotten SF stories than anyone else on Earth. (Most likely he could have expanded his claim to take in the entire solar system, but John was a conservative man in some ways.)

So when you spend your days and nights—especially the nights— reading poor stories, it's a pleasure to run across somebody like Spider: a new writer who has a good story to tell. It makes all those lousy stories worthwhile. Almost.

It's a thrill to get a good story out of the week's slushpile—that mountain of manuscripts sent in by the unknowns, the hopefuls, the ones who want to be writers but haven't written anything publishable yet.

But the *real* thrill comes when a new writer sends in his second story and it's even better than the first one. That happens most rarely of all. It happened with Spider. He brought in the manuscript of "The Time-Traveler," and I knew I was dealing with a pro, not merely a one-time amateur.

We talked over the story before he completed the writing of it. He warned me that he couldn't really find a science fiction gimmick to put into the story. I fretted over that (*Analog* is, after all, a science fiction magazine), but then I realized that the protagonist was indeed a time traveler; his "time machine" was a prison.

Just about the time the story was published, thousands of similar time travelers returned to the U.S. from North Vietnamese prisons. Spider's story should have been required reading for all of them, and their families.

Sure enough, we got a few grumbles from some of our older readers. One sent a stiff note, saying that since the story wasn't science fiction at all, and he was paying for science fiction stories, would we please cancel his subscription. I wrote him back pointing out that we had published the best science fiction stories in the world for more than forty years, and for one single story he's cancelling his subscription? He never responded, and I presume that he's been happy with *Analog* and Spider ever since.

Callahan's Place grew to be an institution among *Analog*'s readers, and you can see it—and the zanies who frequent Callahan's—in all their glory in this collection of stories. What you're reading is something truly unique, because the man who wrote these stories is a unique writer. It's been my privilege to publish most of these stories in *Analog*. Several others are brand new and haven't been published anywhere else before.

It's also been a privilege, and a helluva lot of fun, to get to know Spider personally. To watch him develop as a writer and as a man.

He went from guarding sewers to working for a Long Island newspaper. When that job brought him to a crisis of conscience—work for the paper and slant the news the way the publisher demanded, or get out—his conscience won. He took the big, big step of depending on nothing but his writing talent for an income. But Spider *writes*; he doesn't talk about writing, he works at it.

It wasn't all that easy. He had personal problems, just like everybody else does. Not every story he put on paper sold immediately. Money was always short.

One summer afternoon he met a girlfriend who was coming into town from Nova Scotia. She had never been to New York before. Spider greeted her at Penn Station with the news that his lung had just collapsed and he had to get to a hospital right away, he hoped she didn't mind. The young lady (her name is Jeanne) not only got him to a hospital; she ended up marrying him. Now they both live in Nova Scotia, where city-born Spider has found that he loves the rural splendor of farm life. (Me, I stay in the wilds of Manhattan, where all you've got to worry about is strikes, default, muggings, and equipment failure. Nova Scotia? In winter? Ugh!)

Meanwhile, Spider's stories kept getting better. He branched out from Callahan's. He turned a ludicrous incident on a Greyhound bus into a fine and funny science fiction story. He wrote a novel with so many unlikely angles to it that if I gave you the outline of it, it would probably drive you temporarily insane. But he made it work. It's a damned good novel, with bite as well as humanity in it. We'll publish a big slice of it in *Analog*, and it will come out both in hardcover and paperback later on.

And his stories were being noticed, appreciated, enjoyed by the science fiction fans. At the World Science Fiction Convention in 1974 he received the John Campbell Award as Best New Writer of the Year. At that time he had only published three or four stories, but they were not the kind that could be overlooked.

What does it all add up to? Here we have a young writer who looks, at first glance, like the archetypical hippie dropout, winning respect and admiration in a field that's supposed to admire nobody but the Heinleins and Asimovs.

It just might be that Spider Robinson represents the newest and strongest trend in science fiction today. He's a humanist, by damn. An empath. He's sensitive to human emotions: pain, fear, joy, love. He can get them down on paper as few writers can.

The SF field began with gadgeteers and pseudoscience. It developed in the Thirties and Forties with writers such as Heinlein and Asimov, who knew and understood real science and engineering, and could write strong stories about believable people who were scientists and engineers. In the Fifties and Sixties we began to get voices such as Ted Sturgeon, Fred Pohl, Harlan Ellison—writers who warned that not everything coming from the laboratory was Good, True, and Beautiful.

Now here's Spider Robinson, writing stories that are—well, they're about *people*. People in pain, people having fun, people with problems, people helping each other to solve their problems. Spider is a guy who can feel other people's emotions and help them to deal with them. He's like a character out of an early Sturgeon story—kind, down-to-earth, very empathic. Literarily, he is Sturgeon's heir.

That's the good news. He is also an inveterate punster. You'll see his puns scattered all through the Callahan stories. In fact, there are whole evenings at Callahan's devoted to punning contests. Nobody's perfect.

I remember getting a newspaper clipping from Spider which showed a NASA drawing of the design for a toilet to be used under zero gravity conditions in the Skylab satellite. (NASA has problems that thee and me can't even guess at.) The cutaway drawing of this engineering marvel showed that there was a rotating blade inside the toilet bowl, to "separate the liquid from the solid wastes," as NASA's engineers euphemistically put it.

Spider, in his scrawly handwriting, had scribbled across the top of the clipping a brief note, followed by an arrow that pointed unerringly to the bowl and the separator blade. The note said, "Ben: Near as I can figure, the shit is *supposed* to hit the fan!"

As I said, nobody's perfect. But Spider comes pretty damned close. Read about him and his friends at Callahan's Place. Enjoy.

April, 1976
New York City

FOREWORD

by Spider Robinson

Books get written for the damndest reasons. Some are written to pay off a mortgage, some to save the world, some simply for lack of anything better to do. One of my favorite anecdotes concerns a writer who bet a friend that it was literally impossible to write a book so B*A*D that no one could be found to publish it. As the story goes, this writer proceeded to write the worst, most hackneyed novel of which he was capable—and not only did he succeed in selling it, *the public demanded better than two dozen sequels* (I *can't* tell you his name: his estate might sue, and I have no documentation. Ask around at any SF convention; it's a reasonably famous anecdote).

This book, as it happens, was begun for the single purpose of getting me out of the sewer.

I mean that literally. In 1971, after *seven years* in college, with that Magic Piece of Paper clutched triumphantly in my fist, the best job I was able to get was night watchman on a sewer project in Babylon, New York—guarding a hole in the ground to prevent anyone from stealing it. God *bless* the American educational system.

What with one thing and another, I seemed to have a lot of time on my hands. So I read a lot of science fiction, a custom I have practiced assiduously since, at the age of six, I was introduced to Robert A. Heinlein's *Rocket Ship Galileo*. One evening, halfway through a particularly wretched example of Sturgeon's Law ("Ninety percent of science fiction—of *anything*—is crap"), I sat up straight in my chair and said for perhaps the ten thousandth time in my life, "By Jesus, *I* can write better than this turnip."

And a lightbulb of about two hundred watts appeared in the air over my head.

I had written a couple of stories already, and had actually had one printed in a now-defunct fanzine called *Xrymph*. (Hilariously enough, one of the crazies who produced *Xrymph* was the editor who bought this book that you hold in your hands: Jim Frenkel.) But my entire output at that time could have been fit into a business envelope, and its quality might be most charitably described as shit-ful. On the other hand, I had never before had the motivation I now possessed: I Wanted Out Of The Sewer.

It was time to become a Pro.

I realized from previous failures that as a tyro, it behooved me to select a subject I knew thoroughly, as I was not yet skillful enough to bluff convincingly. Accordingly, I selected drink. Within a week I had completed the first chapter of this book, "The Guy With The Eyes."

Looking in a library copy of *Writer's Guide*, I discovered that there were four markets for my masterpiece. I noted that Ben Bova paid five cents a word and everyone else paid under three, and that's how my lifelong friendship with Ben was begun. I mailed it and he bought it, and when I had recovered from the shock of his letter of acceptance, I gathered my nerve and rang him up to timidly ask if editors ever condescended to waste a few minutes answering the naive questions of beginning writers. Ben pointed out that without writers, editors couldn't exist, and invited me to lunch. And when I walked into the *Analog* office (stumbling over the occasional Hugo), very nearly the first thing he said was, "Say, does that Callahan's Place really *exist*? I'd *love* to go there."

Since that day I estimate I have been asked that question about $5,372 \times 10^{10}$ times, by virtually every fan I meet. One gentleman wrote to me complaining bitterly because I had said in "The Guy With The Eyes" that Callahan's was in Suffolk County, Long Island, and he wanted me to know that he had by God spent six months combing every single bar on Long Island without finding the Place.

I seem to have struck a chord.

Well I'm sorry, but I'll have to tell you the same thing I told those $5,372 \times 10^{10}$ other people: as far as I know, Callahan's Place exists only between a) my ears, b) assorted *Analog* and *Vertex* covers, and of course c) the covers of this book. If there is in fact a Callahan's Place out there in the so-called real world, and you know where it is, I sincerely hope *you'll* tell *me*.

'Cause I'd really like to hang out there awhile.

February, 1976
Phinney's Cove, Nova Scotia

"There is nothing which has been contrived by man by which so much happiness has been produced as by a good tavern or inn."

—Samuel Johnson

THE GUY WITH THE EYES

Callahan's Place was pretty lively that night. Talk fought Budweiser for mouth space all over the joint, and the beer nuts supply was critical. But this guy managed to keep himself in a corner without being noticed for nearly an hour. I only spotted him myself a few minutes before all the action started, and I make a point of studying *everybody* at Callahan's Place.

First thing, I saw those eyes. You get used to some haunted eyes in Callahan's—the newcomers have 'em—but these reminded me of a guy I knew once in Topeka, who got four people with an antique revolver before they cut him down.

I hoped like hell he'd visit the fireplace before he left.

If you've never been to Callahan's Place, God's pity on you. Seek it in the wilds of Suffolk County, but look not for neon. A simple, hand-lettered sign illuminated by a single floodlight, and a heavy oaken door split in the center (by the head of one Big Beef McCaffrey in 1947) and poorly repaired.

Inside, several heresies.

First, the light is about as bright as you keep your living room.

Callahan maintains that people who like to drink in caves are un-stable.

Second, there's a flat rate. Every drink in the house is half a buck, with the option. The option operates as follows:

You place a one-dollar bill on the bar. If all you have on you is a fin, you trot across the street to the all-night deli, get change, come back and put a one-dollar bill on the bar. (Callahan maintains that nobody in his right mind would counterfeit one-dollar bills; most of us figure he just likes to rub fistfuls of them across his face after closing.)

You are served your poison-of-choice. You inhale this, and con-front the option. You may, as you leave, pick up two quarters from the always-full cigarbox at the end of the bar and exit into the night. Or you may, upon finishing your drink, stride up to the chalk line in the middle of the room, announce a toast (this is mandatory) and hurl your glass into the huge, old-fashioned fireplace which takes up most of the back wall. You then depart without visiting the cigarbox. Or, pony up another buck and exercise your option again.

Callahan seldom has to replenish the cigarbox. He orders glasses in such quantities that they cost him next to nothing, and he sweeps out the fireplace himself every morning.

Another heresy: no one watches you with accusing eyes to make sure you take no more quarters than you have coming to you. If Callahan ever happens to catch someone cheating him, he person-ally ejects them forever. Sometimes he doesn't open the door first. The last time he had to eject someone was in 1947, a gentleman named Big Beef McCaffrey.

Not too surprisingly, it's a damned interesting place to be. It's the kind of place you hear about only if you need to—and if you are very lucky. Because if a patron, having proposed his toast and smithereened his glass, feels like talking about the nature of his troubles, he receives the instant, undivided attention of everyone in the room. (That's why the toast is obligatory. Many a man with a hurt locked inside finds in the act of naming his hurt for the toast that he wants very much to talk about it. Callahan is one smart hombre.) On the other hand, even the most tantalizingly cryptic toast will bring no prying inquiries if the guy displays no desire to uncork. Anyone attempting to flout this custom is promptly black-jacked by Fast Eddie the piano player and dumped in the alley.

But somehow many do feel like spilling it in a place like Cal-lahan's; and you can get a deeper insight into human nature in a week there than in ten years anywhere else I know. You can also quite likely find solace for most any kind of trouble, from Callahan himself if no one else. It's a rare hurt that can stand under the advice, help, and sympathy generated by upwards of thirty people that *care*. Callahan loses a lot of his regulars. After they've been coming around long enough, they find they don't need to drink any more.

It's that kind of a bar.

I don't want you to get a picture of Callahan's Place as an agonized, Alcoholics Anonymous type of group-encounter session, with Callahan as some sort of salty psychoanalyst-father-figure in the foreground. Hell, many's the toast provokes roars of laughter, or a shouted chorus of agreement, or a unanimous blitz of glasses from all over the room when the night is particularly spirited. Callahan is tolerant of rannygazoo; he maintains that a bar should be "merry," so long as no bones are broken unintentionally. I mind the time he helped Spud Flynn set fire to a seat cushion to settle a bet on which way the draft was coming. Callahan exudes, at all times, a kind of monolithic calm; and U.S. 40 is shorter than his temper.

This night I'm telling you about, for instance, was nothing if not merry. When I pulled in around ten o'clock, there was an unholy shambles of a square dance going on in the middle of the floor. I laid a dollar on the bar, collected a glass of Tullamore Dew and a hello-grin from Callahan, and settled back in a tall chair—Callahan abhors barstools—to observe the goings-on. That's what I mean about Callahan's Place: most bars, men only dance if there're ladies around. Of one sex or another.

I picked some familiar faces out of the maelstrom of madmen weaving and lurching over honest-to-God sawdust, and waved a few greetings. There was Tom Flannery, who at that time had eight months to live, and knew it; he laughed a lot at Callahan's Place. There was Slippery Joe Maser, who had two wives, and Marty Matthias, who didn't gamble any more, and Noah Gonzalez, who worked on Suffolk County's bomb squad. Calling for the square dance while performing a creditable Irish jig was Doc Webster, fat and jovial as the day he pumped the pills out of my stomach and ordered me to Callahan's. See, I used to have a wife and daughter before I decided to install my own brakes. I saved thirty dollars, easy . . .

The Doc left the square-dancers to their fate—their creative individuality making a caller superfluous—and drifted over like a pink zeppelin to say hello. His stethoscope hung unnoticed from his ears, framing a smile like a sunlamp. The end of the 'scope was in his drink.

"Howdy, Doc. Always wondered how you kept that damned thing so cold," I greeted him.

He blinked like an owl with the staggers and looked down at the gently bubbling pickup beneath two fingers of scotch. Emitting a bellow of laughter at about force eight, he removed the gleaming thing and shook it experimentally.

"My secret's out, Jake. Keep it under your hat, will you?" he boomed.

"Maybe you better keep it under yours," I suggested. He appeared to consider this idea for a time, while I speculated on one of life's greatest paradoxes: Sam Webster, M.D. The Doc is good for a couple of quarts of Peter Dawson a night, three or four nights a week. But you won't find a better sawbones anywhere on Earth, and those sausage fingers of his can move like a tap-dancing centipede when they have to, with nary a tremor. Ask Shorty Steinitz to tell you about the time Doc Webster took out his appendix on top of Callahan's bar . . . while Callahan calmly kept the Scotch coming.

"At least then I could hear myself think," the Doc finally replied, and several people seated within earshot groaned theatrically.

"Have a heart, Doc," one called out.

"What a re-pulse-ive idea," the Doc returned the serve.

"Well, I know when I'm beat," said the challenger, and made as if to turn away.

"Why, you young whelp, aorta poke you one," roared the Doc, and the bar exploded with laughter and cheers. Callahan picked up a beer bottle in his huge hand and pegged it across the bar at the Doc's round skull. The beer bottle, being made of foam rubber, bounced gracefully into the air and landed in the piano, where Fast Eddie sat locked in mortal combat with the "C-Jam Blues."

Fast Eddie emitted a sound like an outraged transmission and kept right on playing, though his upper register was shot. "Little beer never hoit a piano," he sang out as he reached the bridge, and went over it like he figured to burn it behind him.

All in all it looked like a cheerful night, but then I saw the Janssen kid come in and I knew there was a trouble brewing.

This Janssen kid—look, I can't knock long hair, I wore mine long when it wasn't fashionable. And I can't knock pot for the same reason. But nobody I know ever had a good thing to say for heroin. Certainly not Joe Hennessy, who did two weeks in the hospital last year after he surprised the Janssen kid scooping junk-money out of his safe at four in the morning. Old Man Janssen paid Hennessy back every dime and disowned the kid, and he'd been in and out of sight ever since. Word was he was still using the stuff, but the cops never seemed to catch him holding. They sure did try, though. I wondered what the hell he was doing in Callahan's Place.

I should know better by now. He placed a tattered bill on the bar, took the shot of bourbon which Callahan handed him silently, and walked to the chalk line. He was quivering with repressed tension, and his boots squeaked on the sawdust. The place quieted down some, and his toast—"To smack!"—rang out clear and crisp. Then he downed the shot amid an expanding silence and flung his glass so hard you could hear his shoulder crack just before the glass shattered on unyielding brick.

Having created silence, he broke it. With a sob. Even as he let it out he glared around to see what our reactions were.

Callahan's was immediate, an "Amen!" that sounded like an echo of the smashing glass. The kid made a face like he was somehow satisfied in spite of himself, and looked at the rest of us. His gaze rested on Doc Webster, and the Doc drifted over and gently began rolling up the kid's sleeves. The boy made no effort to help or hinder him. When they were both rolled to the shoulder—phosporescent purple I think they were—he silently held out his arms, palm-up.

They were absolutely unmarked. Skinny as hell and white as a piece of paper, but unmarked. The kid was clean.

Everyone waited in silence, giving the kid their respectful attention. It was a new feeling to him, and he didn't quite know how to handle it. Finally he said, "I heard about this place," just a little too truculently.

"Then you must of needed to," Callahan told him quietly, and the kid nodded slowly.

"I hear you get some answers in, from time to time," he half-asked.

"Now and again," Callahan admitted. "Some o' the damndest questions, too. What's it like, for instance?"

"You mean smack?"

"I don't mean bourbon."

The kid's eyes got a funny, far-away look, and he almost smiled. "It's . . ." He paused, considering. "It's like . . . being dead."

"Whooee!" came a voice from across the room. "That's a powerful good feeling indeed." I looked and saw it was Chuck Samms talking, and watched to see how the kid would take it.

He thought Chuck was being sarcastic and snapped back, "Well, what the hell do you know about it anyway?" Chuck smiled. A lot of people ask him that question, in a different tone of voice.

"Me?" he said, enjoying himself hugely. "Why, I've been dead is all."

"S'truth," Callahan confirmed as the kid's jaw dropped. "Chuck there was legally dead for five minutes before the Doc got his pacemaker going again. The crumb died owing me money, and I never had the heart to dun his widow."

"Sure was a nice feeling, too," Chuck said around a yawn. "More peaceful than nap-time in a monastery. If it wasn't so pleasant I wouldn't be near so damned scared of it." There was an edge to his voice as he finished, but it disappeared as he added softly, "What the hell would you want to be dead for?"

The Janssen kid couldn't meet his eyes, and when he spoke his voice cracked. "Like you said, pop, peace. A little peace of mind, a little quiet. Nobody yammering at you all the time. I mean, if you're dead there's always the chance somebody'll mourn, right? Make friends with the worms, dig *their* side of it, maybe a little poltergeist action, who knows? I mean, what's the sense of talking about it, anyway? Didn't any of you guys ever just want to run away?"

"Sure thing," said Callahan. "Sometimes I do it too. But I generally run someplace I can find my way back from." It was said so gently that the kid couldn't take offense, though he tried.

"Run away from what, son?" asked Slippery Joe.

The kid had been bottled up tight too long; he exploded. "From what?" he yelled. "Jesus, where do I start? There was this war they wanted me to go and fight, see? And there's this place called college, I mean they want you to care, dig it, care about this education trip, and they don't care enough themselves to make it as attractive as the crap game across the street. There's this air I hear is unfit to breathe, and water that ain't fit to drink, and food that wouldn't nourish a vulture and a grand outlook for the future. You can't get to a job without the car you couldn't afford to run even if you were working, and if you *found* a job it'd pay five dollars less than the rent. The TV advertises karate classes for four-year-olds and up, the President's New Clothes didn't wear very well, the next Depression's around the corner and you ask me what in the name of God I'm running from?

"Man, I've been straight for seven months, what I mean, and in that seven god damned months I have been over this island like a fungus and there is *nothing* for me. No jobs, no friends, no place to live long enough to get the floor dirty, no money, and nobody that doesn't point and say 'Junkie' when I go by for seven *months* and you ask me what am I running from? Man, *everything* is all, just everything."

It was right then that I noticed that guy in the corner, the one with the eyes. Remember him? He was leaning forward in rapt attention, his mouth a black slash in a face pulled tight as a drumhead. Those ghastly eyes of his never left the Janssen kid, but somehow I was sure that his awareness included all of us, everyone in the room.

And no one had an answer for the Janssen boy. I could see, all around the room, men who had learned to *listen* at Callahan's Place, men who had learned to empathize, to want to understand and share the pain of another. And no one had a word to say. They were thinking past the blurted words of a haunted boy, wondering if this crazy world of confusion might not after all be one holy hell of a place to grow up. Most of them already had reason to know damn well that society never forgives the sinner, but they were realizing to their dismay how thin and uncomforting the straight and narrow has become these last few years.

Sure, they'd heard these things before, often enough to make them into clichés. But now I could see the boys reflecting that these were the clichés that made a young man say he liked to feel dead, and the same thought was mirrored on the face of each of them: *My God, when did we let these things become clichés?* The Problems of Today's Youth were no longer a Sunday supplement or a news broadcast or anything so remote and intangible, they were suddenly become a dirty, shivering boy who told us that in this world we had built for him with our sweat and our blood he was not only tired of living, but so *un*scared of dying that he did it daily, sometimes, for recreation.

And silence held court in Callahan's Place. No one had a single thing to say, and that guy with the eyes seemed to know it, and to derive some crazy kind of bitter inner satisfaction from the knowledge. He started to settle back in his chair, when Callahan broke the silence.

"So run," he said.

Just like that, flat, no expression, just, "So run." It hung there for about ten seconds, while he and the kid locked eyes.

The kid's forehead started to bead with sweat. Slowly, with shaking fingers, he reached under his leather vest to his shirt pocket. Knuckles white, he hauled out a flat, shiny black case about four inches by two. His eyes never left Callahan's as he opened it and held it up so that we could all see the gleaming hypodermic. It didn't look like it had ever been used; he must have just stolen it.

He held it up to the light for a moment, looking up his bare, unmarked arm at it, and then he whirled and flung it case and all into the giant fireplace. Almost as it shattered he sent a cellophane bag of white powder after it, and the powder burned green while the sudden stillness hung in the air. The guy with the eyes looked oddly stricken in some interior way, and he sat absolutely rigid in his seat.

And Callahan was around the bar in an instant, handing the Janssen kid a beer that grew out of his fist and roaring, "Welcome home, Tommy!" and no one in the place was very startled to realize that only Callahan of all of us knew the kid's first name.

We all sort of swarmed around then and swatted the kid on the arm some and he even cried a little until we poured some beer over his head and pretty soon it began to look like the night was going to get merry again after all.

And that's when the guy with the eyes stood up, and everybody in the joint shut up and turned to look at him. That sounds melodramatic, but it's the effect he had on us. When he moved, he was the center of attention. He was tall, unreasonably tall, near seven foot, and I'll never know why we hadn't all noticed him right off. He was dressed in a black suit that fit worse than a Joliet Special, and his shoes didn't look right either. After a moment you realized that he had the left shoe on the right foot, and vice versa, but it didn't surprise you. He was thin and deeply tanned and his mouth was twisted up tight but mostly he was eyes, and I still dream of those eyes and wake up sweating now and again. They were like windows into hell, the very personal and private hell of a man faced with a dilemma he cannot resolve. They did not blink, not once.

He shambled to the bar, and something was wrong with his walk, too, like he was walking sideways on the wall with magnetic shoes and hadn't quite caught the knack yet. He took ten new singles out of his jacket pocket—which struck me as an odd place to keep cash—and laid them on the bar.

Callahan seemed to come back from a far place, and hustled around behind the bar again. He looked the stranger up and down and then placed ten shot glasses on the counter. He filled each with rye and stood back silently, running a big red hand through his thinning hair and regarding the stranger with clinical interest.

The dark giant tossed off the first shot, shuffled to the chalk line, and said in oddly-accented English, "To my profession," and hurled the glass into the fireplace.

Then he walked back to the bar and repeated the entire procedure. Ten times.

By the last glass, brick was chipping in the fireplace.

When the last, "To my profession," echoed in empty air, he turned and faced us. He waited, tensely, for question or challenge. There was none. He half turned away, paused, then swung back and took a couple of deep breaths. When he spoke his voice made you hurt to hear it.

"My profession, gentlemen," he said with that funny accent I couldn't place, "is that of advance scout. For a race whose home is many light-years from here. Many, many light-years from here." He paused, looking for our reactions.

Well, I thought, *ten whiskeys and he's a Martian. Indeed. Pleased to meet you, I'm Popeye the Sailor*. I guess it was pretty obvious we were all thinking the same way, because he looked tired and said, "It would take far more ethanol than that to befuddle me, gentlemen." Nobody said a word to that, and he turned to Callahan. "You know I am not intoxicated," he stated.

Callahan considered him professionally and said finally, "Nope. You're not tight. I'll be a son of a bitch, but you're not tight."

The stranger nodded thanks, spoke thereafter directly to Callahan. "I am here now three days. In two hours I shall be finished. When I am finished I shall go home. After I have gone your planet will be vaporized. I have accumulated data which will ensure the anni-hilation of your species when they are assimilated by my Masters. To them, you will seem as cancerous cells, in danger of infecting all you touch. You will not be permitted to exist. You will be *cured*. And I repent me of my profession.''

Maybe I wouldn't have believed it anywhere else. But at Calla-han's Place *anything* can happen. Hell, we all believed him. Fast Eddie sang out, ''Anyt'ing we can do about it?'' and he was serious for sure. You can tell with Fast Eddie.

''I am helpless,'' the giant alien said dispassionately. ''I contain . . . installations . . . which are beyond my influencing—or yours. They have recorded all the data I have perceived in these three days; in two hours a preset mechanism will be triggered and will transmit their contents to the Masters.'' I looked at my watch: it was eleven-fifteen. ''The conclusions of the Masters are foregone. I cannot pre-vent the transmission; I cannot even attempt to. I am counterprogrammed.''

''Why are you in this line of work if it bugs you so much?'' Callahan wanted to know. No hostility, no panic. He was trying to *understand*.

''I am accustomed to take pride in my work,'' the alien said. ''I make safe the paths of the Masters. They must not be threatened by warlike species. I go before, to identify danger, and see to its neutralization. It is a good profession, I think. I thought.''

''What changed your mind?'' asked Doc Webster sympatheti-cally.

''This place, this . . . 'bar' placc we are in—this is not like the rest I have seen. Outside are hatred, competition, morals elevated to the status of ethics, prejudices elevated to the status of morals, whims elevated to the status of prejudices, all things with which I am wearily familiar, the classic symptoms of disease.

''But here is difference. Here in this place I sense qualities, at-tributes I did not know your species possessed, attributes which everywhere else in the known universe are mutually exclusive of the things I have perceived here tonight. They are good things . . . they cause me great anguish for your passing. They fill me with hurt.

''Oh, that I might lay down my geas,'' he cried. ''I did not know that you had love!''

*   *   *

In the echoing stillness, Callahan said simply, "Sure we do, son. It's mebbe spread a little thin these days, but we've got it all right. Sure would be a shame if it all went up in smoke." He looked down at the rye bottle he still held in his big hand, and absently drank off a couple ounces. "Any chance that your masters might feel the same way?"

"None. Even I can still see that you must be destroyed if the Masters are to be safe. But for the first time in some thousands of years, I regret my profession. I fear I can do no more."

"No way you can gum up the works?"

"None. So long as I am alive and conscious, the transmission will take place. I could not assemble the volition to stop it. I have said: I am counterprogrammed."

I saw Noah Gonzalez' expression soften, heard him say, "Geez, buddy, that's hard lines." A mumbled agreement rose, and Callahan nodded slowly.

"That's tough, brother. I wouldn't want to be in your shoes."

He looked at us with absolute astonishment, the hurt in those terrible eyes of his mixed now with bewilderment. Shorty handed him another drink and it was like he didn't know what to do with it.

"You tell us how much it will take, mister," Shorty said respectfully, "and we'll get you drunk."

The tall man with star-burned skin groaned from deep within himself and backed away until the fireplace contained him. He and the flames ignored each other, and no one found it surprising.

"What is your matter?" he cried. "Why are you not destroying me? You fools, you need only destroy me and you are saved. I am your judge. I am your jury. I will be your executioner."

"You didn't ask for the job," Shorty said gently. "It ain't your doing."

"But you do not understand! If my data are not transmitted, the Masters will assume my destruction and avoid this system forever. Only the equal or superior of a Master could overcome my defenses, but I *can* control *them*. I will not use them. Do you comprehend me? I will not activate my defenses—you can destroy me and save yourselves and your species, and I will not hinder you.

"Kill me!" he shrieked.

There was a long, long pause, maybe a second or two, and then Callahan pointed to the drink Shorty still held out and growled, "You better drink that, friend. You need it. Talkin' of killin' in my

joint. Wash your mouth out with bourbon and get outta that fireplace, I want to use it.''

"Yeah, me too!'' came the cry on all sides, and the big guy
looked like he was gonna cry. Conversations started up again and
Fast Eddie began playing "I Don't Want to Set the World On Fire,''
in very bad taste indeed.

Some of the boys wandered thoughtfully out, going home to tell
their families, or settle their affairs. The rest of us, lacking either
concern, drifted over to console the alien. I mean, where else would
I want to be on Judgment Day?

He was sitting down, now, with booze of all kinds on the table
before him. He looked up at us like a wounded giant. But none of
us knew how to begin, and Callahan spoke first.

"You never did tell us your name, friend.''

The alien looked startled, and he sat absolutely still, rigid as a
fence post, for a long, long moment. His face twisted up awful, as
though he was waging some titanic inner battle with himself, and
cords of muscle stood up on his neck in what didn't seem to be the
right places. Doc Webster began to talk to himself softly.

Then the alien went all blue and shivered like a steel cable under
strain, and very suddenly relaxed all over with an audible gasp. He
twitched his shoulders experimentally a few times, like he was making sure they were still there, and then he turned to Callahan and
said, clear as a bell, "My name is Michael Finn.''

It hung in the air for a very long time, while we all stood petrified,
suspended.

Then Callahan's face split in a wide grin, and he bellowed, "Why
of course! Why yes, yes of course, Mickey *Finn*. I didn't recognize
you for a moment, Mr. Finn,'' as he trotted behind the bar. His big
hands worked busily beneath the counter, and as he emerged with
a tall glass of dark fluid the last of us got it. We made way eagerly
as Callahan set the glass down before the alien, and stood back with
the utmost deference and respect.

He regarded us for a moment, and to see his eyes now was to
feel warm and proud. For all the despair and guilt and anguish and
horror and most of all the hopelessness were gone from them now,
and they were just eyes. Just like yours and mine.

Then he raised his glass and waited, and we all drank with him.

Before the last glass was empty his head hit the table like an anvil, and we had to pick him up and carry him to the back room where Callahan keeps a cot, and you know, he was *heavy*.

And he snored in three stages.

THE TIME-TRAVELER

Of course we should have been expecting it. I guess the people at Callahan's read newspapers just like other folks, and there'd been a discotheque over on Jericho Turnpike hit three days earlier. But somehow none of us was prepared for it when it came.

Well, how were we to know? It's not that Callahan's Place is so isolated from the world that you never expect it to be affected by the same things. God knows that most of the troubles of the world, old and new, come through the door of Callahan's sooner or later—but they usually have a dollar bill in their fist, not a .45 automatic. Besides, he was such a shrimpy little guy.

And on top of everything, it was Punday Night.

Punday Night is a weekly attraction at Callahan's—if that's the word. Folks who come into the place for the first time on a Tuesday evening have been known to flee screaming into the night, leaving full pitchers of beer behind in their haste to be elsewhere. There's Sunday, see, and then there's Monday, and then there's Punday. And on that day, the boys begin assembling around seven-thirty, and after a time people stop piddling around with drafts and start lining up pitchers, and Fast Eddie gets up from his beat-up upright piano and starts pulling tables together. Everyone begins ever-so-casually jockeying for position, so important on Punday Night. Here and there the newer men can be heard warming up with one another, and the first groans are heard.

"Say, Fogerty. I hear tell Stacy Keach was engaged to the same girl three times. Every time the Big Day come due, she decided she couldn't stand him."

"Do tell."

"Yup. Then the late Harry Truman hisself advised her, said, 'Gal, if you can't stand the Keach, get out of the hitchin.' "

And another three or four glasses hit the fireplace.

Of course the real regulars, the old-timers, simply sit and drink their beer and conserve their wit. They add little to the shattered welter of glass that grows in the fireplace—though the toasts, when they make them, can get pretty flashy.

Along about eleven Doc Webster comes waddling in from his rounds and the place hushes up. The Doc suffers his topcoat and bag to be taken from him, collects a beer-mug full of Peter Dawson's from Callahan, and takes his place at the head of the assembled tables like a liner coming into port. Then, folding his fingers over his great belly, he addresses the group.

"What is the topic?"

At this point the fate of the evening hangs in the balance. Maybe you'll get a good topic, maybe you won't—and the only way to explain what I mean is by example:

"Fast Eddie," says Callahan, "how 'bout a little inspirational music?"

"That would bring the problem into scale," says Doc Webster, and the battle is joined.

"I had already noted that," comes the hasty riposte from Shorty Steinitz, and over on his right Long-Drink McGonnigle snorts.

"You've cleffed me in twain," he accuses, and Tommy Janssen advises him to take a rest, and by the time that Callahan can point out that "This ain't a music hall, it's a bar," they're off and running. Once a topic is established, it goes in rotation clockwise from Doc Webster, and if you can't supply a stinker when your turn comes up, you're out. By one o'clock in the morning, it's usually a tight contest between the real pros, all of them acutely aware that anyone still in the lists by closing gets his night's tab erased. It has become a point of honor to drink a good deal on Punday Night to show how confident you are. When I first noticed this and asked Callahan whose idea Punday had been in the first place he told me he couldn't remember. One smart fella, that Callahan.

This one night in particular had used up an awful lot of alcohol, and one hell of a lot of spiritual fortitude. The topic was one of those naturals that can be milked for hours: "electricity." It was about one-fifteen that the trouble started.

By this point in a harrowing evening, the competition was down to the Doc, Noah Gonzalez, and me. I was feeling decidedly punchy.

"I have a feeling this is going to be a good round Fermi," the Doc mused, and sent a few ounces of Scotch past an angelic smile.

"You've galvanized us all once again, Doc," said Noah immediately.

"Socket to me," I agreed enthusiastically.

The Doc made a face, no great feat considering what he had to work with, and glared at me. "Wire you debasing this contest with slang?" he intoned.

"Oh, I don't know," interceded Noah. "It seems like an acceptable current usage to me."

"You see, Doc?" I said desperately, beginning to feel the strain now. "Noah and I seem tube be in agreement."

But Doc Webster wasn't looking at me. He wasn't even looking in my direction. He was staring fixedly over Noah's right shoulder. "I regret to inform you all," he said with the utmost calm, "that the gent at the bar is *not* packing a lightning rod."

About thirty heads spun around at once, and sure enough, there was a guy in front of the bar with a .45 automatic in his hand, and Callahan was staring equably into the medicine end. He was holding out a saltshaker in his huge horny fist.

"What's that for?" the gunman demanded.

"Might as well salt that thing, son. You're about to eat it."

Now your run-of-the-mill stickup artist would react to a line like that by waving the rod around a little, maybe even picking off the odd bottle behind the bar. This fellow just looked more depressed.

He didn't look like a stickup artist if it came to that; I'd have taken him for an insurance salesman down on his luck. He was short, slight, and balding, and his gold-rimmed glasses pinched cruelly at his nose. His features were utterly nondescript, a Walter Mitty caricature of despair, and I couldn't help remembering that some of our more notable assassins have been Walter Mitty types.

Then I saw Fast Eddie over at the piano slide his hand down to his boot for the little blackjack he carries for emergencies, and began trying to remember if my insurance was paid up. The scrawny gunman locked eyes with Callahan, holding the cannon steady as a rock, and Callahan smiled.

"Want a drink to wash it down with?" he asked.

The guy with the gun ran out of determination all at once and lowered the piece, looking around him vaguely. Callahan pointed to the fireplace, and the guy nodded thanks. The gun described a lazy arc and landed in the pile of glass with a sound like change rattling in a pocket.

You might almost have thought the gun had shattered a window that kept out a storm, but the *whoosh*ing sound that followed was really only the noise of a couple dozen guys all exhaling at the same time. Fast Eddie's hand slid back up his leg, and Callahan said softly, "You forgot the toast, friend."

I expected that to confuse the guy, but it seemed he knew *something* about Callahan's Place after all, because he just nodded and made his toast.

"To progress."

I could see people all up and down the bar firing up their guessers, but nobody opened his trap. We waited to see if the guy felt like telling us what his beef with progress was, and when you understand that you will have gone a long way toward understanding what Callahan's Place is all about. I'm sure anywhere else folks'd figure that a man who'd just waved a gun around owed 'em an explanation, if not a few teeth. We just sat there looking noncommittal and hoping he'd let it out.

He did.

"I mean, progress is something with no pity and no purpose. It just happens. It chews up all you ever knew and spits out things you can't understand and the only value it seems to have is to make a few people a lot of money. What the hell is the sense of progress anyway?"

"Keeps the dust off ya," said Slippery Joe Maser seriously. Now Joe, as you know, has two wives, and there sure as *hell* ain't no dust on him.

"I suppose you're right," said the clerical-looking burglar, "but I'd surely appreciate a little dust just at the moment. I was hip-deep in it for years, and I didn't know how well off I was."

"Well, take this to cut it with," said Callahan, and held out a gin-and-gin. As he handed it over, his other hand came up from behind the bar with a sawed-off shotgun in it. "I'll be damned," said Callahan, noticing it for the first time. "Forgot I had that in my hand." He put it back under the bar, and the balding bandit swallowed.

"Now then, brother, pull up a chair and tell us your name, and if you've got troubles I never heard before I'll give you the case of your choice."

"Make it I. W. Harper."

"Pleased to meet you, Mr. Harp-oooooooch!" said Doc Webster, the last rising syllable occasioned by Long-Drink McGonnigle's size nines having come down hard on the Doc's instep. Pretty quick on the uptake, that Long-Drink.

"My name is Hauptman," the fellow said, picking up the drink. "Thomas Hauptman. I'm a . . ." He took a long pull. "That is, I *used* to be a minister."

"And then God went and died and now what the hell do you do, is that it?" asked Long-Drink with genuine sympathy.

"Something like that," Hauptman agreed. "He died of malaria in a stinking little cell in a stinking little town in a stinking little banana republic called Pasala, and his name was Mary." Ice cubes clicked against his teeth.

"Your wife?" asked Callahan after a while.

"Yes. My wife. No one dies of malaria any more, do you know that? I mean, they licked that one years ago."

"How'd it happen?" Doc asked gently, and as Callahan refilled glasses all around, the Time-Traveler told us his story.

Mary and I (he said) had a special game we played between ourselves. Oh, all couples play the same game, I suppose, but we knew we were doing it, and we never cheated.

You see, as many of you are no doubt aware, it is often difficult for a man and a woman to agree (sustained audience demonstration, signifying hearty agreement) . . . even a minister and his wife. Almost any given course of action will have two sides: she wants to spend Sunday driving in the country, and he wants to spend it watching the football people sell razor blades.

How is the dilemma resolved? Often by histrionics, at ten paces. She will emote feverishly on the joys of a country drive, entering rapture as she portrays the heart-stopping beauty to be found along

Route 25A at this time of year. He, in turn, will roll his eyes and saw his hands as he attempts to convey through the wholly inadequate vocabulary of word and gesture how crucial this particular game is to both the History of Football and the Scheme of Things.

The winner gets, in lieu of an Oscar, his or her own way.

It's a fairly reasonable system, based on the theory that the pitch of your performance is a function of how important the goal is to you. If you recognize that you're being out-acted, you realize how important this one is to your spouse, and you acquiesce.

The not-cheating comes right there—in not hamming it up just to be the winner (unless, rarely, that's the real issue), and in admitting you've been topped.

That's why when Mary brought God into the argument—a highly unfair, last-ditch gambit for a minister's wife—I gave in and agreed that we would spend my vacation visiting her sister Corinne.

I had given up a congregation over in Sayville, not very far from here. Frankly Mary and I had had all the Long Island we could take. We hadn't even any plans: we intended to take a month's vacation, our first in several years, and then decide where to settle next. I wanted to spend the month with friends in Boulder, Colorado, and Mary wanted to visit her sister in a little fly-speck banana republic called Pasala. Corinne was a nurse with the Peace Corps, and they hadn't seen each other for seven or eight years.

As I said, when a minister's wife begins to tell him about missionary zeal, it is time to capitulate. We said good-bye to my successor, Reverend Davis, promised to send a forwarding address as soon as we had one, and pushed off in the winter of 1963.

We divided the voyage between discussing the growing unpleasantness in a place called Vietnam, and arguing over whether to ultimately settle on the West or East Coast. We both gave uncertain, shaky performances, and the issue was tabled.

Meeting Corinne for the first time I was terribly struck by the dissimilarity of the sisters. Where Mary's hair was a rich, almost chocolate brown, Corinne's was a decidedly vivid red. Where Mary's features were round, Corinne's were square, with pronounced cheekbones. Where Mary was small and soft, Corinne was long and lithe. They were both very, very beautiful, but the only characteristic they shared was a profundity of faith that had nothing to do with heredity, and which went quite as well with Corinne's fiery sense of purpose as with Mary's quiet certainty.

Pasala turned out to be a perfect comic-opera Central American country, presided over by a small-time tyrant named De Villega. The hospital where Corinne worked was located directly across the Plaza de Palacio from the palace which gave the square its name. De Villega had built himself an immense mausoleum of an imitation castle from which to rule, at about the same time that the hospital was built, with much the same sources of funding. Pasala, you see, exports maize, sugar cane, a good deal of mahogany . . . and oil.

As Corinne led us past the palace from the harbor, I commented on the number of heavily armed *guardias*, in groups of five each of which had its own *comisario*, who stood at every point of entry to the huge stone structure with their rifles at the ready. Corinne told us that revolution was brewing in the hills to the north, under the leadership of a man named Miranda, who with absurd inevitability had styled himself *El Supremo*. Mary and I roared with laughter at this final cliché, and demanded to be shown someone taking a siesta.

Without cracking a smile, Corinne led us around behind the hospital, where four mule-drawn carts were filled with khaki figures taking the siesta that never ends. "You cannot deal with the problems of Pasala by changing the channel, Tom," she said soberly, and my horror was replaced by both a wave of guilt and a wistful, palpebral vision of Boulder in the spring—which of course only made me feel more guilty.

We dined that night in a miserable excuse for a cafe, but the food was tolerable and the music quite good. Considering that the two women had not seen each other for years, it was not surprising that the conversation flowed freely. And it kept coming back to *El Supremo*.

"I have heard it said that his cause is just," Corinne told us over coffee, "and I certainly can't argue otherwise. But the hospital is filled with the by-products of his cause, and I'm sick of revolution. It's been worse than ever since De Villega had Miranda's brother shot."

"Good God. How did that come about?" I exclaimed.

"Pablo Miranda used to run this cafe, and he never had a thing to do with revolution. In fact, an awful lot of militant types used to drink in a much more villainous place on the other side of town, rather than embarrass Pablo with their presence. But after *El Supremo* blew up the armory, De Villega went a little crazy. A squad of *guardias* came in the door and cut Pablo in half.

"Things have been accelerating ever since. People are afraid to travel by night, and De Villega has his thugs on double shifts. There are rumors that he's bringing in trucks, and cannon, and a lot of ammunition from the United States, for an expedition to clean out the hills, and the American Embassy is awfully tight-lipped about it.''

"What kind of a ruler is De Villega?" Mary asked.

"Oh, an absolute thief. He robs the peons dry, rakes off all he can, and I'm sure the country would be better off if he'd never been born. But then, there are some conflicting reports about *El Supremo* too: some say he's a bit of a butcher himself. And of course he's a Communist, although God only knows what that means in Central America these days.''

I began to reply, when we heard an ear-splitting crash from outside the cafe. Glasses danced off tables and shattered, and pandemonium broke loose. Three men scrambled to the door to see what had happened; as they reached the doorway a machine-gun spoke, blowing all three back into the cafe. They lay as they fell, and Mary began to scream.

"Tom," Corinne shouted above the din of gunfire and panic-stricken people, "*we've got to get to the hospital.*"

"How do we get out?" I yelled back, rising and lifting Mary from her seat.

"This way."

Corinne led us rapidly through the jabbering crowd to a back exit, at which were gathered a good number of people too frightened to stick their heads out the door. I was inclined to agree with them, but Corinne simply walked out into the night. I glanced at Mary, she returned my gaze serenely, and we followed.

There were no sudden barks of gunfire; the revolutionaries were not really interested in anyone within the cafe, they were simply shooting anything that moved back in the plaza.

As I helped Mary through the dark streets behind Corinne I tried to figure the way back to the hospital, but I could not recall where the back door of the cafe lay in relation to the door through which we had entered. But it seemed to me that we would have to cross the plaza.

I called to Corinne and she halted. As I came up to her a volley of gunfire sounded off to our left, ending in a choking gurgle.

"Considering what you've told us about Miranda's egregious charm," I said as softly as a heaving chest would let me, "hadn't

I better get you two ladies to the America Embassy? It's built like a fort." And it lay on this side of the Plaza.

"The hospital is very short-staffed, Tom," was all Corinne replied, with a total absence of facial expression or gesture. But I knew I could never equal a performance like that in a lifetime of trying. As she spun on her heel and continued walking, Mary and I exchanged a long look.

"And she's a rank amateur," I said, shaking my head sadly.

"She and I used to do summer stock together," she said, and we followed Corinne's disappearing footsteps.

Crossing the plaza turned out to be no more difficult than juggling poison darts; the few who shot at us were terrible marksmen. By the time it was necessary to cross open space, most of the fighting had centralized around the palace itself, and both sides were in general much too busy to waste good bullets on three civilians running in the opposite direction. But as we reached the hospital, I glanced over my shoulder and saw trucks pulling around the corner of the building into the plaza, towing cannon behind them. As we raced through white corridors toward the Emergency Room I heard the first reports, then nothing.

The artillery provided by the U.S. State Department got off exactly three rounds. At that point, we later learned, a bearded man appeared on the palace balcony, overlooking the carnage in the square, and heaved something down onto the trampled sward. It was De Villega's head. Sensing the political climate with creditable speed, the uniformed cannoneers worked up a ragged cheer, and the revolution was over.

But not for us. The maimed and wounded who continued to be brought in through the night gave me my first real understanding of the term *waking nightmare*, and until you have spent a couple of hours collecting random limbs and organs for disposal I will thank you not to use the term yourself. I had rather naively assumed that the worst would be over when the battle stopped, but that turned out to be only the signal for the rape and plundering and settling of ancient grudges, which got a good deal uglier. I tried to get Mary to take a few hours of sleep, and she tried to get me to do the same, and although we both put on the performance of a lifetime neither of us would concede defeat.

It was about three the next afternoon when I heard the scream. I left one of De Villega's *rurales* to finish sewing up his own arm and sprinted down a crowded hall toward the surgery where Mary and Corinne had been for the past thirteen hours. It sounded as though the scream had come from there . . .

It had. As I burst in the door I saw Mary first, in the impersonally efficient grip of the largest man I've ever seen in my life. Then I saw Corinne, struggling with a broad-backed revolutionary who was throttling a uniformed patient on the operating table. The crossed bandoliers over his shoulders rose and fell as he strangled, as though he wanted there to be more to it than simply clenching his fingers. Corinne's flailing fists he noticed not at all.

She was undoubtedly stronger than I—I wasted no time in tugging at the madman's shoulder. I picked up the nearest heavy object, a water pitcher I believe, and bounced it off the back of his skull as hard as I could. He sighed and crumpled, and I whirled toward the giant that held my Mary.

"You should not have done that, *señor*," he said in a deep, soft voice. "The man on the bed, he once did a discourtesy to Pedro's wife. A grave discourtesy."

"Get out of this room at once," Corinne snapped in her best drill sergeant voice, shaking with rage.

The big man shook his head sadly. "I am afraid not, *señorita*," he rumbled. Hands like shovels tightened around Mary's biceps, and she still had not uttered a sound since I burst in. "*Señor*," the giant said to me, "you must please put down that pitcher, or I will be forced to do your own wife a small discourtesy." I started. "Ah, you see? I know who you are; and I would not wish to be discourteous to the wife of a man of God."

The gorilla on the floor began to stir, and the huge man sighed. "I am afraid it is all over for you, *Padre*. Pedro, he is a most unreasonable man when he feels his honor is at stake. You hit him from behind."

Corinne snarled and leaped at him, and I followed suit. Even together we could not budge him or his iron grip, but we kept him too busy to hurt Mary, and I think we might eventually have prevailed. But suddenly something large and heavy smashed into my left kidney, and I fell to the floor gasping with pain. Through the haze I saw Pedro, his tangled hair soaked with blood on the side, step over me and reach for Mary, and my soul died in my chest.

Then my ears rang with a shot, and I twisted about on the floor to see a tall man with a bristling mustache framed in the doorway, a smoking automatic in his hand. He wore the shapeless khakis of the mountains and there was an easy arrogance in the smile with which he regarded all of us.

Behind me there was thud as a body hit the floor. Half-blind with pain, I contrived to roll over again and saw that the pistol shot had taken off the top of Pedro's skull.

"There is that about martial law," said the man in the doorway with sardonic amusement. "It is addictive."

I finally managed to sit up, bracing myself against a large oxygen bottle. "Who are you?" I managed.

The lean, mustached man bowed low. "Permit me to introduce myself, *Padre*. I am *El Supremo e Illustrisimo Señor* Manuel Conception de Miranda, the current ruler of this republic. You in turn, are the Reverend Hauptman, and I must assume that the charming lady there—release her at once, Diego—is your wife Mary."

His excellent English bespoke an unusual degree of education, and his bearing was a studied claim to nobility. I began to believe that we three might survive the afternoon for the first time in what seemed like hours.

"How do you all seem to know who we are?" I asked. "We only arrived yesterday, and I don't think we've spoken to more than a handful of Pasalans. Yet that monster over there knew us . . . and I'm *sure* I'd remember him."

"I know all about the comings and goings of all American nationals in Pasala," he said smugly. "Your country has been a source of much inconvenience to me, and I am a thorough man, as are my lieutenants. Diego is one; Pedro there was another. I cannot abide a lieutenant who loses his head." He holstered his gun and entered the room, and I struggled to my feet with Mary's help. We clung together, and she trembled violently.

El Supremo looked about, failed to find a place to sit. He strode to the operating table, shoved the wounded and unconscious soldier off onto the hard floor quite casually, and sat down with his legs dangling over the edge.

Corinne went for him, but before she covered three feet the giant Diego intercepted her and lifted her clear off her feet. She struck at his face with balled fists, but he appeared not to notice. She was sobbing with rage.

"Diego," said Miranda with a grin, "since you do not seem to be content unless you have a woman in your hands, why don't you take the young lady to my apartments and keep her there until I come, eh?"

Mary and I both cried out.

"My friends," said Miranda, still grinning, "this is only justice. I had a woman, Rosa, and she was heart of my heart. She was killed last night, by an American cannon shell. Because of your country, I have no woman. It seems only fair that America give me a woman. I prefer an unmarried woman, and I do not think the sister of a minister's wife will disappoint me." He laughed, a gay laugh that froze my blood.

"There is that about martial law," I heard myself say. "It is selective."

"Explain," *El Supremo* barked.

"I believe the man on the floor over there was shot for attempted rape," I said quietly.

"*Padre*," said the tall revolutionary, drawing his gun again, "in the absence of a lawful constitution for Pasala I must do the best I can myself. Occasionally I may be inconsistent, as I am now in sentencing you and your wife to ten years' imprisonment for disturbing the peace.

"But you will find that there is *this* about martial law: it is effective."

The next twenty minutes were the last free minutes I would spend for ten years, and the last free minutes of Mary's life, but I don't remember one of them. *El Supremo* marched us at gunpoint across the plaza to the palace, down many flights of stairs, to the lowest of the three basement floors which made up the palace's dungeons. There he locked us personally into a nine-by-twelve stone cell, and left.

We were there for nine years, and I will not speak of those years. After Mary died, I was alone there for eleven months longer, and I will not think of those months. I will only say that in the first weeks, I thanked God for giving Miranda the spark of humanity which caused him to put both Mary and me in the same cell . . . but soon, as I began to see the subtlety and horror of his true intent, I came to curse him with a black hatred. Ten years inside a stone cube with no heat, no ventilation and a pail for a toilet can do much to a marriage, and that Mary and I survived as long as we did was, I assure you, due only to the depth and strength of her character. And even she couldn't keep me from losing my faith in God . . .

*   *   *

The minister was silent, staring into his glass as though he read there a strange and terrible secret which he could not quite believe. The stillness was absolute; no flames danced in the fireplace. I caught Doc Webster's eye, and he seemed to come back from somewhere else with a start.

"What happened to Corinne?" he asked hoarsely.

Hauptman put down his glass suddenly, and looked around at us incuriously. "I've been told she died that night," he said conversationally, "and I rather hope it's true. Miranda was . . . an animal."

"Couldn't the American Embassy do anything to get you out?" asked Long-Drink quickly, and I saw Callahan nod approval.

"The American Embassy," replied Hauptman bitterly, "neither had the slightest knowledge of our incarceration, nor cared to know. If anyone at all was aware of our presence in Pasala, he must have assumed we had been killed in the uprising, and he undoubtedly heaved a great sigh when he realized he had no idea who to send condolences to." His words came like machine-gun bullets now.

"We were listed in the prison records as 'Hidalgo, Tomaso and Maria, subversives,' and that was quite good enough for the State Department, if they checked at all. *El Supremo* was quite an embarrassment to the United States, and when they had him assassinated two years later, the puppet *presidentes* they installed were far too busy entertaining American oil executives to be bothered inspecting the palace dungeons. The only human we saw for nine years was a perpetually drunken jailer who brought such of our food as he didn't eat himself. I'd be there now, except that when . . . when Mary died, th-they . . ." He broke off, got a fresh grip on himself and continued, "Someone noticed her body being removed for burial, and became curious as to why Maria Hidalgo looked like an American. It was a year before I was released, owing to, let me see now, 'political complications of an extremely delicate nature in the Middle East,' I think they said . . . my God, I just realized what they meant! It sounded insane at the time, and I hadn't thought about it since." He laughed bitterly. "Well, what do you know? Anyway, for the last six months I was there I had Red Cross food and a blanket, so that was hunky-dory. Turned out there was a man from Baltimore four cells down, part of the hospital staff, and he was released too. If Mary hadn't died we'd both still be there." The minister laughed again, gulped down the rest of his gin-and-gin and made a face. "She was always getting me out of scrapes."

More gin appeared before him; he gulped it noisily.

"You know," he said with a dangerous high note in his voice, "in all the nine years the prayers never stopped rising from that filthy little cell. For the first three years we prayed that someone would depose *El Supremo*. For approximately the next three years, Mary prayed constantly that my faith in God would return. Then, for about a year, I prayed to I-don't-know-who that Mary would live. And after malaria took her, I spent my time praying to anyone who would listen for a chance to kill *El Supremo* with my own hands.

"I mean to say, isn't it ironic? All that prayer, and none of it did the slightest good. *El Supremo* was dead all the time, I never seemed to get that belief back, and Mary . . ." He broke off short and began to laugh softly, a laugh that got shriller and shriller until the glass burst in his hand. He then just sat and looked at his bleeding palm until Doc Webster came over and gently took it away from him.

"Well, at least this damned thing is disinfected," the Doc grumbled. "Don't ever pull that with an empty glass." Someone fetched his battered black bag, and he began applying a dressing.

Along about that point, everyone in the place got real interested in the floor or the ceiling. It somehow didn't seem as though there was a single intelligent thing that could be said, and it was slowly becoming necessary that somebody say *something*.

Callahan was right there.

"Reverend," he rumbled, hooking a thumb in his belt, "that's a right sad story. I've heard an awful lot of blues, and I can't say I ever heard worse. But what I would like to have explained to me is how, if you follow me, the *hell* does all this bring you into my joint with a heater in your fist?" There was steel in his voice, and the minister looked up sharply, guilt replacing the agony on his features. *Bravo, Callahan*, I thought.

See, I knew what the preacher couldn't: that when there's anger in Callahan's voice, it's just got to be theatrics, because when Callahan is good and truly pissed off he don't bother to talk at all.

The little minister was a while finding words. "You see," he said finally, as the Doc finished bandaging his hand, "it was ten years. Ten *years*. I . . . I don't know if you can understand what I mean. I know it's been two years since Mary died—it's not just that. But you see, she was all I knew for such a long time, and now I don't know anything at all.

"You must understand, in all that time we never saw a newspaper or a magazine or a TV broadcast, never heard so much as a radio.

We had utterly no communication with the outside world; we were as isolated as two human beings can be.''

"Hell," said Tommy Janssen, "that sounds like what I could use to straighten out my head once and for all." I was thinking about a Theodore Sturgeon story called "And Now The News," and I kind of agreed with Tommy, which shows how well I'd read the story.

"Straighten your head out!" Hauptman exploded.

"Now, you know perfectly well what the boy means," Long-Drink interceded. "No one is saying those years weren't nightmares for you, but you know, they were nothing to write home to mother about for *us*. You missed a lot of turmoil, a lot of bad times and trouble, and maybe in that at least you were better off. I know most of us here have probably wished we could get away from everything for a long spell, and you did it. What's wrong with isolation?"

"Nothing, *per se*," Hauptman said quietly. "The problem is this: the world won't wait for you. You drop out for more than a short time, and brother, the world goes on without you."

"I think," said Callahan slowly, "I begin to see what you mean."

"You don't even begin," Hauptman said flatly. "You can't. You're too close to it. The whole world turns upside down in ten years, but you turn upside down with it, and so to you it's right side up. It all happens over days and weeks and months, and most people can adapt that fast. But I don't recognize the first thing about this world—I didn't live through it.

"Let me give all you good people a history lesson."

He got up, walked to the bar and put out his hand. Callahan put a glass of gin in it. He turned, faced us all, took a long swallow, and cleared his throat pedantically.

"Mary and I left for Pasala in February of 1963," he said. "I've since had occasion to supplement my own memories with references from *The New York Times*, and you may find some of them interesting.

"On the day of our departure, for instance, there had been a total of thirty-three Americans killed in Vietnam since the start of U.S. involvement. Not that anyone was aware of it: it wasn't until a few days after we left that Senator Mansfield's study group issued a warning that the Vietnam struggle was becoming an 'American War, that cannot be justified by present U.S. security interests in the area.' Why, the godforsaken place was costing us a whole four hundred million dollars a year!

"Of course, General O'Donnell replied the next day that all those combat pilots among the 'advisers' were there to train the Vietnamese, not to take part in the war themselves.

"Lot happened since then, hasn't it?

"How about another area, my friends? In November of 1962, Dean Munro of Harvard University warned undergraduates against use of 'the stimulant LSD that depresses the mind,' and censured Professors Alpert and Leary for promoting its use. Dr. Leary replied that hysteria could only hamper research, and pointed to the absence of any evidence that the drug was harmful.

"In California, meanwhile, authorities were sounding a similar warning note concerning a newly-discovered drug which was beginning to appear on the streets. It was called Methedrine.

"The New American Church was still fighting unsuccessfully for the right to continue using peyote in its religious ceremonies, a practice which predated white settlement of America. Harry Anslinger had just retired as head of the Federal Narcotics Agency, and there was some talk of controlling the sale of airplane glue to those under eighteen.

"Incidentally, while Leary and Alpert (who I understand calls himself Ram Dass lately) found little difficulty in preserving their academic autonomy, others were not so lucky. Professor Koch was fired from Illinois University for daring to suggest in print that premarital sexual relations should in some cases be condoned. By the time Mary and I got on the boat, the efforts of the American University Professors' Association to have him reinstated had been entirely fruitless. A month after we left, the Illinois Supreme Court declined to intervene. Whatever Masters and Johnson were doing, they weren't talking about it. The sexual revolution was still being vigorously, and apparently successfully, ignored.

"Hard to remember back ten years, isn't it? How about the space race? The latest news I've heard puts us quite a few moon landings and space probes ahead of the Russians, and most people I've spoken to seem to assume it was always that way. America has felt pretty cocky about the Big Deep for quite a while now. Did you know that by February of 1963, the Russian Vostok series had racked up 130 orbits, a total of 192 hours in space, while the U.S. had a total of 12 orbits and 20 hours? A couple of years earlier, President Kennedy—remember him?—had publicly committed us to putting a man on the moon in the next decade, and he was widely pronounced deranged. Eight years later, Armstrong took the first lunar walk, and the nation yawned. *Oh, you people are so damned blasé about it all!*

"I could go on for hours. When I dropped out, assassination had not yet become commonplace; J. F. K. had not yet been canonized, and R. F. K. was just arguing his first case in any court, as Attorney General of the United States. Cinerama was just getting started, hailed as the wave of the future, and the New York World's Fair had not yet opened. Two months after we left, *Cleopatra* premiered, and Twentieth Century Fox stock dropped two dollars a share—"

Hauptman broke off, began to laugh hysterically. Callahan reached across the bar and gripped his shoulder with a hand like a steak, but the minister shook his head.

"I'm all right," he managed, choking with laughter. "It's just that I haven't told you the funniest joke of all. Nearly killed me at the time, and I didn't dare break up.

"You see, when I was finally released, they brought me directly to Washington, where some very cheerless men wanted to ask me a number of questions and help me memorize what had officially happened. But first they decided to compensate me for my troubles with the thrill of a lifetime. I was conveyed before the President of the United States for a hearty handclasp, and I thought I was going to faint from holding in the laughter.

"I hadn't thought to ask who the President was, you see. It didn't seem especially important, after all I'd been through, and I didn't expect I'd recognize the name. But when Richard Nixon held out his hand, I thought I'd die.

"—You see, three months before I left, Nixon lost the race for governor of California, and assured the press with tears in his eyes that they wouldn't have Dick Nixon to kick around any more . . ."

This time the whole place broke up, and Doc Webster almost lost his tonsils trying to whoop and swallow at the same time. Fast Eddie tried to swing into "Don't Make Promises You Can't Keep," but he was laughing so hard he couldn't find the keys, and a barrage of glasses hit the fireplace from all around the room.

Which was fine for catharsis. But as the laughter trailed off we realized that this catharsis was not enough for Tom Hauptman. As his impassioned words sank in it began to dawn on all of us that we had adapted to an awful lot in ten years, and in some crazy way this confrontation with a man who was forced to try and swallow a whole new world in one gulp seemed to drive home to all of us just how imperfectly we *had* adapted, ourselves.

"You know," Long-Drink drawled in the sudden silence, "the little man has a point. Been a lot goin' on lately."

"It occurs to me," Tommy Janssen said softly, "that ten years ago I'd never heard the word *heroin*," and he gulped at his beer.

"Ten years ago," Doc Webster mused, "I thought that heart transplants were the province of science fiction writers."

"Ten years ago," Slippery Joe breathed wistfully, "I was single."

I was thinking that ten years ago, I wore a crewcut and listened to Jerry Lee Lewis and Fats Domino. "Christ," I said, as the impossible burst over me. "Nobody'd ever heard of the *Beatles* in 1963!" The whole electric sound, the respectability of rock and its permeation of all other forms of pop music, had taken place while Hauptman was rotting in a cell, listening to his fingernails growing. What must the music of today sound like to him? Jim McGuinn of the Byrds had pointed out in the late Sixties that the Beatles had signaled a change in the very sound of music. He compared pre-Beatles music to the bass roar of a propellor plane, and the ensuing post-Beatles rock to the metallic whine of a jet engine. From what I hear on the radio, it seems that we're already up to the transonic shrieking of a rocket exhaust, and Hauptman was getting it all at once. From Paul Anka to Alice Cooper in one jump! Why, the sartorial and tonsorial changes alone were enough to boggle the mind.

We all stared at him, thinking we understood. But he looked around at us and shook his head, and took another drink.

"No," he said. "You still don't understand. What you are all just beginning to see is what I would, if I were a science fiction writer, call the Time-Traveler's Dilemma: *future shock*, I believe they're calling it now. But my problem is the Time-Traveler's Second Dilemma: *transplant shock*.

"You see, you're all time-travelers too, traveling through time at a rate of one second per second. In the past few minutes, you've all been made acutely aware of just how much time you've passed through in the last ten years, and it's made you think.

"But I've traveled ten years all at once, and I don't have your advantages. Strange as this particular time is to you, you have roots woven into its fabric, you have a place in it however tenuous, and most important of all, you have a *purpose*.

"Don't you understand? I was a *minister*.

"I was charged with responsibility for the spiritual development of other human beings. I was trained to help them live moral lives, to make right choices in difficult decisions, and to comfort them when they needed comfort. And now I don't even begin to grasp their *problems*, let alone the new tools that people like me have been jury-rigging over the past ten years to help them. Why, I went to a fellow cleric for advice, and he offered me a marijuana cigarette! I called an old acquaintance of mine, a Catholic priest, and his wife answered the phone; I told her I had a wrong number and hung up. This whole Watergate affair is no revelation to anyone who was in Pasala in 1963; it's been a long time since I believed Uncle Sam was a virgin. But I used to be in the minority.

"Gentlemen, how can I function as a minister when I don't even begin to comprehend *one single one* of the moral issues of the day? When I can't, because I haven't lived through the events that gave them birth?"

He finished off his gin, left the glass on the table, and began tracing designs in the moisture it had left there.

"I've looked for other work. I've looked for other work for nearly six months now. Are any of you here out of work?"

Which was a shame, him saying that, because it caused me to pitch a perfectly good glass of Bushmill's into the fireplace.

Hauptman nodded, and turned to the red-haired mountain behind the bar.

"And that, Mr. Callahan," he said quietly, "is the long and short of why you find me in your establishment with a pistol I bought in an alleyway from a young man with more hair than Mary used to have. I simply didn't know what else to do."

He looked around at all of us.

"And now that didn't work either. So there's only one thing left I can do." He heaved a great sigh, and his shoulders twitched. "I wonder if I'll get to see Mary again?"

Now, we're a reasonably bright bunch at Callahan's (with some notable exceptions), and nobody in the room figured that the one thing Hauptman had left to do was start up a chain letter. But at the same time, we're a humane bunch, with a fanatical concern for individual liberty, and so we couldn't do any of the conventional things, like try to talk him out of it, or call the police, or have him fitted for the jacket that's all sleeves. Truth to tell, maybe one or two of us agreed with him that he had no alternative. We were pretty shaken by his story, is all I can say in our defense.

Because we just sat there, and stared at him, and felt helpless, and the silence became a tangible thing that throbbed in your temples and made your eyes sting.

And then Callahan cleared his throat.

"To be or not to be," he declaimed in a voice like a foghorn. "Is that the question?"

Like I said, we're a bright bunch, but it took us a second. By the time I got it, Callahan had already lumbered out from behind the bar, swept a pitcher and three glasses to the floor, and wrapped the tablecloth around him like a toga. Doc Webster was grinning openly.

"Listen, ya goddamn fathead," Callahan declaimed in the hokey, stentorian tones of a Shakespearean ham, " 'tis damn well *nobler* to suffer the slings and arrows of outrageous fortune, than to take arms against a sea of troubles, and by opposing, let 'em lick ya. Nay, fuck that . . ." His eyes rolled, his huge hands sawed the air as he postured and orated.

Hauptman stared blankly, his mouth open.

Doc Webster heaved himself up onto a chair, *harummph*ed noisily and struck a pose.

"Do not go gentle into that good night," he began passionately.

Suddenly Callahan's Place became a madhouse, something like a theater might be if actors "tuned-up" as cacophonously as do orchestras. Everyone suddenly became the Ghost of Barrymore, or thought he had, and the air filled with praises of life and courage delivered in the most impassioned histrionic manner. I unpacked my old guitar and joined Fast Eddie in a rousing chorus of "Pack Up Your Sorrows," and I guess among us all we made a hell of a racket.

"All right, all right," Callahan bellowed after a few minutes of pandemonium. "I reckon that ought to do, gents. *I* think we took the Oscar."

He turned to Hauptman, and tossed the tablecloth on the floor.

"Well, Reverend," he growled. "Can you top that performance?"

The little minister looked at him for a long spell, and then he began to laugh and laugh. It was a different kind of laugh than we'd heard from him before: it had no ragged edges and no despair in it. It was a full, deep belly-laugh, and instead of grating on our nerves like a knife on piano wire it made us feel warm and proud and relieved. Kind of a tribute to our act.

"Gentlemen," he said finally, clapping his hands feebly, still chuckling, "I concede. I've been out-acted fair and square; I wouldn't try to compete with a performance like that."

Then all at once he sobered, and looked at all of us. "I . . . I didn't know people like you existed in this world. I . . . I think that I can make it now. I'll find some kind of work. It's just that . . . well . . . *if somebody else knows how tough it is, then it's all right*." The corners of his mouth, lifting in a happy smile, met a flood of tears on their way down. "Thank you, my friends. Thank you."

"Any time," said Callahan, and meant it.

And the door banged inevitably open, and we spun around to see a young black kid, chest heaving, framed in the doorway with a .38 Police Positive in his hand.

"Now everybody be quiet, an' nobody gonna get hurt," he said shrilly, and stepped inside.

Callahan seemed to swell around the shoulders, but he didn't move. Everybody was frozen, thinking for the second time that night that *we should have been expecting it*, and of all of us only Hauptman refused to be numbed by shock any more, only Hauptman kept his head, and only Hauptman remembered.

It all happened very quickly then, as it had to happen. Callahan's shotgun was behind the bar, out of reach, and Fast Eddie had been caught with both hands in sight. The minister caught Doc Webster's eye, and they exchanged a meaningful glance across the room that I didn't understand.

And then the Doc cleared his throat. "Excuse me, young man," he began, and the black kid turned to tell him to shut up, and behind him Hauptman sprang from his chair headlong across the room and headfirst toward the fireplace.

He landed on his stomach, and his hands plowed straight into the welter of broken glass. As he wrenched over on his back, his right hand came around with that big .45 in it, and the kid was still turning to see what that noise behind him was.

They froze that way for a long moment, Hauptman sprawled in the fireplace, the kid by the bar, and two gun-muzzles stared unblinking across the room at each other. Then Callahan spoke.

"You'll hurt him with a .38, son, but he'll kill you with a .45."

The kid froze, his eyes darting around the room, then flung his gun from him and bolted for the door with a noise like a cross between a sneeze and a sob. Nobody got in his way.

And then Callahan spoke up again. "You see, Tom," he said conversationally, "moral issues never change. Only social ones."

One thing I'll say for the boys at Callahan's: they can keep a straight face. Nobody cracked a smile as Callahan fed the cops a perfectly hilarious yarn about how the minister had disarmed a thief with a revolver he had only that afternoon taken from a troubled young parishioner. Some of us had even argued against involving the police at all, on general principles—I was one of them—but Callahan insisted that he didn't want any guns in his joint, and nobody else really wanted them either.

But when I was proudest of the boys was when the police asked for a description of the thief. None of us had given any thought to that, but Doc Webster was right in there, his dragon-in-the-shower voice drowning out all others.

"Description?" he boomed. "Hell, nobody was ever easier to describe. The guy was six-four with a hook-nose, blonde hair, blue eyes, a scar from his right ear to his chin, and he had one leg."

And not one of us so much as blinked as the cop dutifully wrote that down.

Perhaps that kid would have another chance.

Tom Hauptman, however, didn't come off so well in the aplomb department. As one of the cops was phoning in, Long-Drink called out, "Hey, Tom. One thing I don't understand. That cannon you had was in the fireplace for a good hour or so, and that hearth is plenty warm even when the fire's been out a while. How the hell come none of the cartridges went off?"

The minister looked puzzled. "Why, I have no idea. Do you suppose that . . . ?"

But the second cop was making strangling sounds and waving the .45. At last he found his voice. "You mean you *didn't know?*"

We looked at him.

He tossed the gun to Callahan, who one-handed it easily, then suddenly looked startled. He hefted the gun, and his jaw dropped.

"There's no clip in this gun," he said faintly. "The damned thing's unloaded."

And Tom Hauptman fainted dead away.

*   *   *

By the time we recovered from that one, Callahan had decided that Doc and Noah and I were Punday Night Champions, and we were helping ourselves to just one more free drink with Tom Hauptman when Doc came up with an idea.

"Say, Mike," he called out. "Don't you think a bunch of savvy galoots like us could find Tom here some kind of job?"

"Well, I'll tell you, Doc," said Callahan, scratching his neck, "I've been givin' that some thought." He lit a cigar and regarded the minister with a professional eye. "Tom, do you know anything about tending bar?"

"Huh? Why, yes I do. I tended bar for a couple of summers before I entered the ministry."

"Well," Callahan drawled, "I ain't getting any younger. This all day and all night stuff is okay for someone your age, but I'm pushing fifty. Why I hit a man last week, and he got up on me. I've been meaning to get myself a little part-time help, sorta distribute the load a little. And I'd be right honored to have a man of God serve my booze."

A murmur of shock ran through the bar, and expression of awe at the honor being accorded to Tom Hauptman. He looked around, having the sense to see that it was up to us as much as it was to Callahan.

"Why the hell not?" roared Long-Drink and the Doc together, and the minister began to cry.

"Mr. Callahan," he said, "I'd be proud to help you run this bar."

About that point a rousing cheer went up, and about two dozen glasses met above the newly-relit blaze in the fireplace. Toasts got proposed all at once, and a firecracker went off somewhere in the back of the room. The minister was lifted up onto a couple or three shoulders, and the most god-awful alleycat off-key chorus you ever heard assured him that he was indeed a Jolly Good Fellow.

"This calls for another drink," Callahan decreed. "What'll it be, Tom?"

"Well," the minister said diffidently, "I've had an awful lot of gin, and I really haven't gotten back into training yet. I think I'd better just have a Horse's Ass."

"Reverend," said Callahan, vastly chagrined, "whatever it is, you're gonna get it on the house. 'Cause I never heard of it."

All around the room conversations chopped off in mid-sentence as the news was assimilated. The last time in my memory when Callahan got taken for a drink was in 1968, when some joker in a pork-pie hat asked for a Mother Superior. Turned out to be a martini with a prune in it, and Callahan by God went out and bought a prune.

Hauptman blinked at the commotion he was causing, and finally managed, "Well, it, uh, won't set you back very much. It's just a ginger ale with a cherry in it." He paused, apparently embarrassed, and continued just a shade too diffidently, "You see, they call it that be—"

"—CAUSE ANYONE WHO'D ORDER ONE IS A HORSE'S ASS!" chorused a dozen voices with him, and a shower of peanuts hit him from all over the room. Tommy Janssen heaved a half-full pitcher at the fireplace, and Fast Eddie snatched it out of the air with his right hand as his left picked up "You Said It, Not Me" in F sharp.

Hauptman accepted his drink from Callahan, and he had it to his lips before he noticed the remarkably authentic-looking plastic fly which Callahan had thoughtfully added to the prescription. The explosion was impressive, and I swear ginger ale came out his ears.

"Seemed like a likely place to find a fly," said Callahan loudly, and somehow Fast Eddie managed to heave the pitcher at him without interrupting the song. Callahan fielded it deftly and took a long drink.

"That's what I like to see," he boomed, replacing his cigar in his teeth. "A place that's *merry*."

THE CENTIPEDE'S DILEMMA

What happened to Fogerty was a classic example of the centipede's dilemma. Served him right, of course, and I suppose it was bound to happen sooner or later. But things could have gone much worse with him if he hadn't been wearing that silly hat.

It was this way:

Fogerty came shuffling in to Callahan's Place for the first time on the night of the Third Annual Darts Championship of the Universe, an event by which we place much store at Callahan's, and I noticed him the moment he walked in. No great feat; he was a sight to see. He looked like a barrel with legs, and I mean a big barrel. On its side. On top of this abundance sat a head like a hastily peeled potato, and on top of the head sat—or rather sprawled—the most ridiculous hat I'd ever seen. It could have passed for a dead zeppelin, floppy and disheveled, a villainous yellow in color. From the moment I saw it I expected it to slide down his face like a disreputable avalanche, but some mysterious force held it at eyebrow level. I couldn't estimate his age.

Callahan served him without blinking an eye—I sometimes suspect that if a pink gorilla walked into Callahan's, on fire, and ordered a shot, Callahan would ask if it wanted a chaser. The guy inhaled three fingers of gin in as many seconds, had Callahan build him another, and strolled on over to the crowd by the dart board, where Long-Drink McGonnigle and Doc Webster were locked in mortal combat. I followed along, sensing something zany in the wind.

Some of us at Callahan's are pretty good with a dart, and consequently the throwing distance is thirty feet, a span which favors brute strength but requires accuracy along with it. The board is a three-foot circle with a headshot of a certain politician (supply your own) on its face, concentric circles of fifty, forty, twenty, ten, and one point each superimposed over his notorious features. When I got to where I could see the board, Doc Webster had just planted a dandy high on the right cheek for forty, and Long-Drink was straining to look unconcerned.

"What's the stakes?" the guy with the hat asked me. His voice sounded like a '54 Chevy with bad valves.

"Quarts of Scotch," I told him. "The challenger stakes a bottle against the previous winner's total. Last year the Doc there went home with six cases of Peter Dawson's." He grunted, watched the Doc notch an ex-presidential ear (you supplied the same politician, didn't you?), then asked how he could sign up. I directed him to Fast Eddie, who was taking a night off from the piano to referee, and kept half an eye on him while I watched the match. He took no part in the conversational hilarity around him, but watched the combat with a vacuous stare, rather like a man about to fall asleep before the TV. It was reasonably apparent that wit was not his long suit. Doc Webster won the match handily, and the stein that Long-Drink disconsolately pegged into the big fireplace joined a mound of broken glass that was mute testimony to the Doc's prowess. One of my glasses was in that pile.

About a pound of glass later, Fast Eddie called out, "Dink Fogerty," and the guy with the hat stood up. The Doc beamed at him like a bear being sociable to a hive, and offered him the darts.

They made a quite a pair. If Fogerty was a barrel, the Doc is what they shipped the barrel in, and it probably rattled a lot. Fogerty took the darts, rammed them together point-first into a nearby tabletop, and stood back smiling. The Doc blinked, then smiled back and toed the mark. Plucking a dart from the table-top with an effort, he grinned over his shoulder at Fogerty and let fly.

The dart missed the board entirely.

A gasp went up from the crowd, and the Doc frowned. Fogerty's expression was unreadable. The champ plucked another dart, wound up and threw again.

The dart landed in the fireplace fifteen feet to the left with a noise like change rattling in a pocket.

"It curved," the Doc yelped, and some of the crowd guffawed. But from where I stood I could see that there were four men between Doc Webster and the fireplace, and I could also see the beginnings of an unpleasant smile on Fogerty's thick features.

None of the Doc's remaining shots came close to the target, and he left the firing line like a disconsolate blimp, shaking his head and looking at his hand. Fogerty took his place and, without removing that absurd hat, selected a dart.

Watching his throw I thought for a second the match might turn out a draw. His wind-up was pitiful, his stance ungainly, and he held the dart too near the feathers, his other arm stiff at his side. He threw like a girl, and his follow-through was nonexistent.

The dart landed right between the eyes with a meaty *thunk*.

"Winner and new champeen, Dink Fogerty," Fast Eddie hollered over the roar of the crowd, and Fogerty took a long, triumphant drink from the glass he'd set down on a nearby table. Fast Eddie informed him that he'd just won thirty-five bottles of Scotch, and the new champ smiled, turned to face us.

"Any takers?" he rasped. The '54 Chevy had gotten a valve job.

"Sure," said Noah Gonzalez, next on the list. "Be damned if you'll take us for three dozen bottles with one throw." Fogerty nodded agreeably, retrieved his dart from the target and toed the mark again. And with the same awkward, off-balance throw as before, he proceeded to place all six darts in the fifty-circle.

By the last one the silence in the room was complete, and Noah's strangled "I concede," was plainly audible. Fogerty just looked smug and took another big gulp of his drink, set it down on the same table.

"Ten dollars says you can't do that again," the Doc exploded, and Fogerty smiled. Fast Eddie went to fetch him the darts, but as he reached the target . . .

"*Hold it!*" Callahan bellowed, and the room froze. Fogerty turned slowly and stared at the big redheaded barkeep, an innocent look on his pudding face. Callahan glared at him, brows like thunderclouds.

"Whassamatter, chief?" Fogerty asked.

"Damned if I know," Callahan rumbled, "but I've seen you take at least a dozen long swallows from that drink you got, and it's *still full*."

Every eye in the place went to Fogerty's glass, and sure enough. Not only was it full, all the glasses near it were emptier than their owners remembered leaving them, and an angry buzzing began.

"Wait a minute," Fogerty protested. "My hands've been in plain sight every minute—all of you saw me. You can't pin nothin' on me."

"I guess you didn't use your hands, then," Callahan said darkly, and a great light seemed to dawn on Doc Webster's face.

"By God," he roared, "a telekinetic! Why you lowdown, no-good . . ."

Fogerty made a break for the door, but Fast Eddie demonstrated the veracity of his name with a snappy flying tackle that cut Fogerty down before he covered five yards. He landed with a crash before Long-Drink McGonnigle, who promptly sat on him. "Tele-what?" inquired Long-Drink conversationally.

"Telekinesis," the Doc explained. "Mind over matter. I knew a telekinetic in the Army who could roll sevens as long as you cared to watch. It's a rare talent, but it exists. And this bird's got it. Haven't you, Fogerty?"

Fogerty blustered for awhile, but finally he broke down and admitted it. A lot of jaws dropped, some bouncing off the floor, and Long-Drink let the guy with the hat back up, backing away from him. The hat still clung gaudily to his skull like a homosexual barnacle.

"You mean you directed dem darts wit' yer mind?" Fast Eddie expostulated.

"Nah. Not ezzackly. I . . . I make the dart-board *want darts*."

"Huh?"

"I can't make the darts move. What I do, I project a . . . a state of wanting darts onto the center of the target, like some kinda magnet, an' the target attracts 'em for me. I only learned how ta do it about a year ago. The hard part is to hang on to all but one dart."

"Thought so," growled Callahan from behind the bar. "You make your glass want gin too—don't ya?"

Fogerty nodded. "I make a pretty good buck as a fisherman—my nets want fish."

It seemed to me that, given his talent, Fogerty was making pretty unimaginative use of it. Imagine a cancer wanting X-rays. Then again, imagine a pocket that wants diamonds. I decided it was just as well that his ambitions were modest.

"Wait a minute," said the Doc, puzzled. "This 'state of wanting darts' you project. What's it like?"

And Fogerty, an unimaginative man, pondered that question for the first time in his life, and the inevitable happened.

There's an old story about the centipede who was asked how he could coordinate so many legs at once, and, considering the mechanics of something that had always been automatic, became so confused that he never managed to walk again. In just this manner, Fogerty focused his attention on the gift that had always been second nature to him, created that zone of yearning for the first time in his head where he could observe it, and . . .

The whole half-dozen darts ripped free of the target, crossed the room like so many Sidewinder missiles, and smashed into Fogerty's forehead.

If he hadn't been wearing that dumb hat, they might have pulped his skull. Instead they drove him backward, depositing him on his ample fundament, where he blinked up at us blinking down at him. There was a stunned silence (literally so on his part) and then a great wave of laughter that grew and swelled and rang, blowing the cobwebs from the rafters. We laughed till we cried, till our lungs ached and our stomachs hurt, and Fogerty sat under the avalanche of mirth and turned red and finally began to giggle himself.

And like the centipede, like the rajah whose flying carpet would only function if he did *not* think of the word "elephant," Fogerty from that day forth never managed to bring himself to use his bizarre talent again.

Imagine getting a netfull of mackerel in the eye!

TWO HEADS ARE BETTER THAN ONE

As usual, it was a pretty merry night at Callahan's when the trouble started.

I don't want to give the impression that every time us Callahan's regulars (Callahanians?) get to feeling good, there's drama around the corner. The reason it seems that way is probably that, barring disaster, merriment is the general rule at Callahan's Place. Most of us have little better to do than get happy in another's company, and we're not an unimaginative bunch, so we keep ourselves pretty well amused.

Being a Wednesday, it was Tall Tales Night (as opposed to Monday, the Fireside Fill-More singalong night, or Tuesday, which we call Punday). Along about eight-thirty, when most of the boys had arrived, and the level of broken glass in the fireplace was still rather low, Callahan dried his big meaty hands on his apron and cleared his throat with a sound like a bulldozer in pain.

"All right, gents," he boomed, and conversations were tabled for the night. "We need a subject. Any suggestions?"

Nobody spoke up. See, the teller of the tallest tale on a Wednesday night gets his drinking money refunded, and most folks like to lie low until they've had a chance to examine the competition and come up with a topper. Not that the first tale told never wins, but it has to be pretty memorable.

"All right," Callahan said when no one took the lead. "People, places, or things?"

"We did t'ings last week," Fast Eddie pointed out from his seat at the upright. True enough. I'd had everybody beat with a yarn about a beer-nut tree that used to grow in my backyard until I watered it, when Doc Webster wiped me out with the saga of a '38 Buick of his that understood spoken English, which would have been just fine except that it took on a rude highway cop one day and chased him across six lanes of traffic. Doc claimed to have buried it in his backyard after it expired from remorse.

"Ain't nothing says we have to be consistent," Callahan replied. "We can do things again."

"Naw," Doc Webster called out. "Let's do people."

"All right, Doc. What kind? You sound like you got something in mind."

"Wal . . ." drawled the Doc, and people checked to see that their drinks were fresh. Those who needed a refill put a dollar bill on the bar and were refueled by Callahan, who did not need to ask what they wanted.

". . . I was just thinking," the Doc continued, his own drink as magically full as always, "of my Cousin Hobart, the celebrated Man With The Foot-Long Nose." ("Oh, relatives tonight," someone muttered.) "Hobart's mother died in childbirth, naturally, and his father succumbed to acute embarrassment shortly thereafter. As a child Hobart was a born showman, keeping the orphanage in stitches with incredibly accurate woodpecker imitations, and upon attaining the age of seven he ran away, to form the nucleus of a traveling road company which played *Pinocchio* in every theater in the country, and some in the city too. This kept him in Kleenex until he outgrew the role, and *Cyrano de Bergerac* was not popular at the time, so he struck off on his own and in short order became something of an old stand-by on the vaudeville circuits, where his ability to identify the perfume of ladies in the last row and his prowess on the nose-flutes (as many as five at one time) were a never-failing draw. He might have lived on in this way for a good many years, for he was a fanatically hygienic man, and although there were dark rumors about his sex life, he was invariably discreet. The young ladies he visited were for some reason equally reticent, even with their best girl friends—let alone their husbands.

"No, it was not a cuckold's knuckles (say that three times fast with ice cubes in your mouth and you can have this drink) that finally put an end to Cousin Hobart's career, though it might have been. It was by his own hand that, if I may put it this way, The Nose was blown. One night he retired early with only a slight head cold for company, a yard-long handkerchief knotted to the bedstead (Hobart went through a lot of laundresses before he found one with a strong stomach). Thrashing in his sleep; he rolled over and contrived to wedge the end of his nose in his right ear. Sensing some obstruction, the mighty proboscis sneezed—and damned near blew his brains out.

"When his head had stopped ringing, a wide-awake Hobart settled down to some cold hard thinking. The incident could happen again at any time—the miracle was that so likely a phenomenon had taken so long to first occur—and next time the airseal might be better. Only by chance had Hobart survived at all. He reached his decision reluctantly, but he was a brave man: he followed through. He had his nose entirely amputated the next day, repudiating all nose-hood and installing a suction cup in the middle of his glasses. Within a week he had landed a job with some moonshiners, and he works their still there still."

The Doc took a long gulp of Peter Dawson's and looked around expectantly, blinking.

There was a silence, not much thicker than an elephant's behind.

"A moonshiner with *no nose*?" snorted Long-Drink, who keeps a still in his garage for Sundays when Callahan's is closed. "That's ridiculous. How did he smell?"

"Terrible," the Doc replied placidly.

A general groan began, but Callahan held up a hand. "What's the moral, Doc?"

The Doc blinked again. "No nose is good nose."

The sky rained peanuts, and very few missed the Doc, his more-than-ample upholstery making him an excellent target. Callahan, maddened beyond endurance, seized up a seltzer bottle and was restrained with some difficulty. Me, I was worried. This would be hard to beat. I decided against another Bushmill's.

As I recall, the next one up was Shorty Steinitz, with the story of his uncle Mort D. Arthur the magician, who walked down the street one day and turned into a drugstore. But three of us shouted the punchline before he got to it and he pitched his glass into the fire in disgust, toasting "To weisenheimers" first and putting his shoulder behind it. Then Tommy Janssen did a creditable job, W. C. Fields-style and better done than Fields usually is, about a Cousin Alex Ameche who used to hang from a hook on his kitchen wall and claim to be a telephone.

"Obviously a masochist," Tommy intoned nasally. "The amount of abuse that man absorbed was simply incredible. Folks'd try to humor him, put a dime in his left ear, pick up his right hand from where it hung in his other ear, dial his nose in a circle and listen to his hand. But when nothing transpired, they would inevitably beat him about the head and shoulders until the dime came out of his mouth, dislocate his arm at the shoulder and leave the premises in a great rage, cursing prodigiously." This was pretty good stuff, but Tommy's moral, "A chameleon would do well to imitate objects of a species with which Man is not at war," had no pun in it, and it seemed the Doc still (the Doc's still) had the edge. Noah Gonzalez's effort, a one-joke story about an overaggressive uncle who customarily turned on the TV with such ferocity that one day the TV turned on him, was an obvious loser. For some crazy reason as each tale-teller realized he'd blown it and would thus be paying his night's tab, he invariably pitched his glass into the fireplace—which costs you your fifty cents change. Callahan had raked in a fortune in dollar bills by the time I was ready to make my move, and I decided for the hundredth time that Callahan is no fool, even if he does have to sweep out that fireplace every morning.

"All right," I said at last, "it's time to tell you good people about my Grandfather Stonebender." I decided my country drawl would serve best.

"You stole that from Heinlein," shouted Noah, the only other SF freak in the room. "One of the characters in 'Lost Legacy' had a Grandfather Stonebender who could do anything better than anyone. No fair lifting stories."

"Heinlein must of heard about the real Grandfather Stonebender from my grandmother," I said with dignity, "and at that he toned him down for a cynical public. I'm talking about the *real* Stonebender—the man who built the pyramids, freed the slaves, invented the prophylactic, cured yaws—that Stonebender."

"What's yaws?" Callahan asked injudiciously.

"Why thanks, Mike. I'll have a beer."

A cheer went up, and Callahan made a ferocious face at me as he drew a draft Bud. "Not that Grandfather Stonebender's legendary success was surprisin'," I continued smoothly, "as he was born with three heads. His mother was frightened by a pawn shop while she was carrying him. Doctor was so startled he swore off the sauce, and the child raised up such a fuss cryin' three ways at once that they sent him home early, where he caused his mother some unforseen and unprecedented difficulties with nursing.

"Fortunately, he matured quickly and found early employ as the 'before,' 'during,' and 'after' for hair-tonic commercials. Which anyway kept him in hair-tonic. 'Fore too long, though, his combined IQ had brought him the prominence he deserved in several unrelated fields, and he passed his weekends doing a trio at the local ginmill for relaxation. *His* sex life was something incredible, his prenatal trauma also having left him with three . . . but that's neither here nor anywheres I should be talkin' about. Point is, he wasn't no loser like Doc's cousin Hobart, reduced to geekin' in sideshows for a livin'. Grandfather Stonebender lived entirely off his wits—had to, to keep himself in neckties.

"But the same strange fate that provided him with three times the brains and earning power of a normal man carried with it the seeds of his destruction. He fell prey to the Committee Syndrome.

"One day he was debating Free Silver with himself. It was a burnin' issue at the time, and sad to say, he lost. This made him so mad he punched hisself right in the mouth, and broke several teeth and a knuckle. Bein' a gentleman, he had no alternative: he challenged hisself to a duel. Next mornin', acting as second for both sides so as to keep it in the family, he shot hisself in the right eye from point-blank range and died. Papers were full of it at the time. 'Course, if you read the only daily around you know the papers are still full of it, but anyhow that's how my Grandfather Stonebender passed on, from the past on.''

Doc Webster's mouth hung open in astonishment, but Callahan again called for the moral before the general outrage could begin.

"Just goes to show," I explained, "that three heads are bitter, then none." I closed my eyes and waited for the holocaust, smugly sure that I wouldn't have to rely on cheap gags to get free beer any more tonight.

But the silence was broken not by groans, but by a single groan, and the pain in that groan was not put-on at all. It came from the open doorway across the room, and as we all spun around we beheld a sandy-haired young man, shockingly disheveled, leaning against the door-frame and sobbing. As we watched, frozen, he slid from its support and fell full-length into Callahan's, landing on his face with a crash.

Somehow I knew intuitively that I was not a winner tonight after all.

For all his bulk, Doc Webster was the first to reach the newcomer. He rolled him over and began doing doctor-things almost before the rest of us had started to move, and swung his great black bag in a lethal circle when we crowded too close. Nobody ignores pain in Callahan's Place, but I guess sometimes we're a hair too eager to help.

The kid wasn't much older than Tommy Janssen, maybe twenty-five or so, but you had to look past the haunted lines of his face to see it. At first glance he might have been thirty or better, and the expression he'd worn before he passed out would have looked more at home on a man eighty years old and tired of living. His eyes were set in close against a hooking nose, and his cheeks were broad enough to make his mouth seem a shade too small. His lips were the kind of full that isn't especially sensual, and his frame had just a bit more meat than it needed. His clothes seemed to have been pulled on in the dark in a hell of a hurry, fly unzipped, shirt only partially tucked in, and buttons mismatched with holes. Furthermore he was dressed for June—and it was a particularly rainy March out. He was soaked clear through, hair that looked usually brushed back lying limply across half his face.

It looked like he'd gotten to Callahan's just about in time.

His upper cheeks and temples were livid with purple bruises, and his knuckles were swollen. Doc Webster searched his hair and found more contusions beneath. "Looks like somebody gave this poor bastard an awful beating," the Doc announced.

The kid's eyes opened. "That was me," he said feebly, swallowing something foul.

Someone fed the Doc a glass of straight rye, and he tipped a little of it into the kid's mouth. It seemed to help. Color came back to his pasty face, and he tried to get up. The Doc told him to lie quiet, but the kid shook him off and made it as far as the first table, where he fell into a chair and looked around groggily. He didn't seem to notice us, but whatever he was expecting to see scared him silly.

It wasn't there; he relaxed some. Callahan was already piling corned beef sandwiches in front of him, and the table happened to have a pitcher of somebody's beer already on it. Throwing us all a grateful glance, *seeing* us this time, he fell on the food like the wolves upon the centerfold, and got outside of three sandwiches in short order, washing them down with great draughts of beer.

When he was done he looked Callahan squarely in the eye. "I don't have any money to pay you," he said.

"I didn't figure you did," Callahan agreed. "Go on, eat up. They were getting stale—these bums here don't eat, far as I can tell. You can owe me." He produced more food.

"Thanks. I'm OK now. I think. For a while."

The Doc wanted to get something straight. "You put them bruises on your own head, young feller?"

"Jim MacDonald, Doctor. Yes, I put most of those there."

"I'll bet it felt good when you stopped," Long-Drink said, and immediately regretted it. I wouldn't want Doc Webster's mass balanced on my toe either.

"If it did, I might stop more often," MacDonald said with a ghost of a grin, wincing at the sudden pain in his temples. "Lately it's the most fun I have."

"Want to talk about it?" Callahan suggested delicately.

"Sure, why not? You'll never believe me anyhow. No one would." MacDonald's grin was gone now.

Callahan drew himself up and registered wounded dignity. "Son, this here is Tall Tales Night at my place, and I am prepared to believe anything you can say with a straight face. Hell, I sometimes believe the Doc over there, and his face ain't never been straight. Come on, spit it out. Maybe you won't owe me for them sandwiches and beer after all." The big Irishman put a fresh light on his ever-present El Ropo and gave the kid a fresh beer to lube his mouth with.

I looked around; the boys were reverting to their favorite listening postures as naturally and gracefully as Paladin used to go into that gunfighter's crouch of his. *The hell with the budget*, I decided, and slapped another single on the bar, helping myself to a shot of Irish uisgebagh from the bottle labeled, "Give Every Man His Dew."

"It started with my brother Paul," MacDonald began, and I groaned inside. The perfect shaggy-relative story, shot to hell. "He was ten years older than me, and he was really only my half-brother. Dad divorced and remarried when Paul was only three, and that's why I had some hope for a while.

"You see, Paul was a mutant.

"Not in any gross physical sense—his body was not malformed in any detectable way. But he was an Instantaneous Echo.

"You've probably heard of them, maybe seen one on TV or read about 'em in places like Charles Fort. From the age of twelve Paul could mimic anything you said—at the instant that you said it. The voice and inflection were different, but he never stumbled, even when he didn't comprehend the words he was parroting. No noticeable time-lag—he simply said what you were saying, as you said it. Sometimes he actually seemed to jump the gun by a hair, and *that* was really strange.

"Around the time that I was five, a couple of fellows from Duke came around with a truckful of equipment and put Paul through a series of tests. At first they were quite excited, but as the testing continued their excitement wore off, and eventually they told my father that Paul was just like all the other Instant Echoes they'd studied, simply a man who'd learned how to hook his mouth in parallel with his ears. According to their newest findings, he could not, in fact, 'jump the gun' as he sometimes seemed to, and while the actual lag was small, they claimed to be able to measure it. They were unhappy. They'd hoped to prove that Paul was a telepath.

"Me, I think he got cagey.

"Paul had always been an introspective kid and about that time he became moodier than ever. He seldom left the house, and when he did he was quite likely to return in tears, claiming a migraine as the cause. My father got our doctor to prescribe some strong stuff for the migraines, but it didn't seem to help for too long. Paul, having finished high school at fifteen with excellent grades, showed no interest whatever in college, a job, or girls. He seemed to be the typical loner, with a bit of hypochondria thrown in.

"It was about then that the trouble started between my father and mother (Paul's stepmother, you understand). She felt that Paul had to earn a living regardless of his headaches, and insisted that he should do so at sideshows and on nightclub stages, doing his instant echo routine. Dad was having none of it; he'd made a good deal of money with a good deal of hard work, running a used-car chain, but he was perfectly willing to indulge a temperamentally infirm son, rather than set him on a stage to be gawked at by yokels.

Mother was . . . not a very nice person, I'm afraid, and I suspect she thought of the child she had inherited as an untapped gold mine scant years from his majority. I think she wanted Paul to make a bundle while she could still get at it; she'd always had some of the Backstage Mother Complex. How I managed to remain neutral I don't know. But then, nobody asked my opinion.

"When Paul was twenty and I was nine and a half, I got my first big scare.

"It was all an accident, for by this time Paul had become uncannily adept at avoiding people, leaving the house only after dark and never straying far. The only spot he showed any affection for was the abandoned gravel pit a few miles from home, a place so gloomy at night that even the area's love-struck teenagers avoided it. I went there with him two or three times—Paul seemed to accept my company more often than anyone else's, particularly when I was younger. I didn't especially care for the place myself—it seemed to me the loneliest place I'd ever imagined—but I suppose a kid will follow his big brother just about anywhere he's invited.

"I think that must be where he met the girl.

"Mom and Dad were out that night at a PTA meeting or some such. I was watching TV, and if you want to know the truth, I was eating some stolen jelly beans from the horde Mother used to hide away for herself. So when Paul came crashing through the front door, I jumped a foot in the air before I even saw him. When I got downstairs, my first crazy thought was that the migraines had finally split poor Paulie's head open. He looked . . . well, I guess I've given you a pretty fair imitation tonight, crashing in here the way I did. His scalp was laid open around the sides of his head, his forehead was dripping blood in lines that streamed crazily over his face, his fingers were raw and bleeding, and his eyes held so much agony that even at nine years old I was more terrified by them than by anything else.

"He was babbling incoherently, swinging his arms wildly as if to ward off some closing demon, and sobbing as though his heart would break. I'd never seen anyone his age cry like that, you know? I rushed to his side and got him to sit down, and without thinking about it I went to the bar and mixed him a martini, just as Mother had taught me to do for her. Little enough of it went down his throat, but it calmed him some, and the rest at least got some of the blood off his chin.

"Of course, when he'd calmed down a little I asked him what

had happened. 'She looked so nice, Jimmy,' he raved, 'so *nice*. I thought it would be all right. I mean, I knew it would be bad, but I thought I could take it. *She looked so goddamned nice,*' he shrieked, trembling like a leaf. Finally I got the story out of him in bits and pieces.

"It seems my brother was a telepath, after all.

"A latent telepath, at any rate. From age five to fifteen, his only telepathic manifestation was his instant-echo bit, and that was done unconsciously. Subvocalized thoughts must be closest to the surface. During that time he never received thoughts except those about to be verbalized, never sensed emotions, and never had any conscious volitional control of his wild talent.

"But about midway through puberty the picture began to change. His power was still beyond his control, but it *grew*. With no warning, he would suddenly find himself inside someone else's head, with increasing frequency and for increasing lengths of time. The first time he plugged in was for a split-second only, just enough to scare him silly, and it didn't reoccur for a couple of months. By now, he told me, telepathy came to him every week or so, for as much as five or ten minutes at a time.

"You must understand, this was nothing like the traditional 'telepathy' of science fiction stories. It was not the ability to send messages without speech; Paul had never succeeded in sending anything. Nor was it the ability to receive such messages. It was, rather, a process of entering the skull of another, receiving its entire contents and perceiving them as a gestalt.

"I wonder if you can imagine what that's like? Perhaps, if you've ever thought of telepathy at all, you've thought of how terrible it would be if someone were inside your strongest defenses, privy to all your secrets and desires and shameful memories and frustrated lusts and true feelings. Well you might—but have you ever considered how terrible it would be to find yourself in someone *else's* head, with all that unsought and unwanted knowledge? As long as people remain locked in their own skulls, they should be—because as most people intuitively realize, the things that grow and fester in a sealed skull aren't always fit to share.

"On top of that, there's the sheer shock of directly confronting a naked ego as strong as your own, and Paul told me that night that it doesn't help a bit that the other ego is unaware of you. Most people never get over believing that they're the center of the Universe, even when they know it isn't so—to have your nose rubbed in it is unsettling.

"And so, Paul told me between sobs, he began avoiding people the best he could as his strange and terrifying power grew in him. Repeated exposure made the minds of his immediate family tolerable to him, and his telepathy seemed to be sharply limited by distance, with an effective radius of about a hundred feet or so. By keeping strangers beyond that limit, Paul could achieve peace of a sort, the flashes of telepathy bringing him only glimpses of Dad, Mother, and myself. Dad he pitied with an intensity heretofore unknown to that emotion; Mother he hated beyond all understanding; and me he often found soothing, until I grew up enough to start having dark secrets of my own. He told me some things about myself then, that . . . but that's irrelevant.

"The point is, that night, communing with himself in the moonlit gravel pit, he met a girl, about his age or a little older. One of the strange things about out-of-the-way places is that, while you almost never meet anyone there, anyone you do run into is somehow very liable to be friend-material. At any rate, she seemed to Paul the nicest and most gentle girl he'd ever seen in his life, not at all like any other girl he'd ever met. She spoke softly, and only when she had something to say, and he felt in her a *difference* that he could not explain to me in words.

"Whatever the reason, he let down his guard for once. Instead of running away or driving her from him with rudeness, as he had learned to do with strangers, he stayed to talk. Before too many minutes had passed, he began to lose the usual terrifying fear that his wild talent would strike, began to believe that it might be all right if it did, began finally to almost hope that it would.

"And it did.

"I'm sure she was a lovely girl, but the best of us harbor dark secrets—sometimes even from ourselves. I don't know specifically what shattered Paul that night, but I'm sure it was nothing that a bishop on his deathbed would have felt compelled to confess. Maybe it was nothing more dishonorable than her lifetime's accumulation of pain, for one's own sorrow may be bearable by its familiarity and yet staggering to a stranger.

"In any event, it hit Paul even harder than usual, because he had dared to hope. Now, if your ears are overloaded, you can stuff your fingers into them; if your nose is outraged, you can hold it; if your eyes are blinded you can shield them with your arm. But when your brain itself is overwhelmed by direct input, all you can do is smash at it with a rock, hoping to drive the other consciousness away with your own. Sometimes, if you're lucky, it works.

"For Paul, that night, it hadn't worked.

"Now you must understand that I was very young. I barely comprehended the things that Paul was telling me, and if I understood what had happened, I surely didn't understand why it had hit him as hard as it obviously had. Being able to read minds had no drawback that my nine-year-old mind could see; I sure didn't know much about human nature. But I was trying hard to empathize with my big brother.

"That's the only explanation I have for what occurred. Because as Paul reached the terrible climax of his story, for one split second a shutter opened—and like a camera plate, my child's mind was imprinted with the total contents of the mind of my brother.

"It lasted only that split second, and it faded about as fast as a flashbulb-burst from two feet away; the impact was over quickly, but the blinding afterimage seared my brain for many seconds more. I screamed. Several times. Instantly our positions were reversed, and Paulie was holding me, restraining my hands. He knew at once what had happened, and the grim set of his jaw said that he had been expecting it for years now.

" 'It's over,' he barked, 'Jimmy listen to me, it's over. It won't happen again for months, maybe years.'

"It wasn't what he said but the pure joyous relief of how *far away* his voice sounded that cut through my child's terror and brought me back from the edge of hysteria. Why, Paulie was *miles* away—at least a foot! And there were comforting walls of bone, cartilage, and skin—and blessed empty air!—between us. I calmed down, and Paulie held me tightly in his arms and in savage whispers explained to me what I was, what had happened to us, and what I could expect from now on. He had hoped, he said, that I would be spared because my maternal genes were different from his; he explained genetics to me, as well as it can be explained to a nine-year-old, and he told me what a mutant was. He told me how much easier to bear the telepathic flashes would become, and he told me how much easier they would not become. He told me how often to expect the onslaught ('flashing,' he called it), and advised me on how to avoid flashing by avoiding sentient beings as much as possible. I suppose you could say it was the end of my childhood. I know that four years later, when my father haltingly undertook to explain the Facts of Life to me, they came as a helluvan anticlimax.

"I suppose that next landmark in the story is the night my father and I found Paul collapsed across my mother in the living room, the lamp that had crushed her skull still clenched in his hand, but I don't think I want to talk about that now. They took Paul away that night, like a sack of sugar, and hauled him off to King's Park, completely catatonic. He's been that way ever since, and as far as I can tell he never flashed again. Or anything.

"That was fourteen years ago."

Callahan had been refilling his glass as he talked, but MacDonald spilled this one over half the table. He drank the rest as fast as it could pour and shut up.

"I get it," Fast Eddie said after a while. "Yer afraid de same t'ing is gonna happen ta you."

"Jesus," Doc Webster said in an undertone behind me, "he's just about due." I did some rapid mental calculation, and turned pale.

"No, Eddie," I said aloud. "Jim's overdue. Unless . . ." I let it trail off.

MacDonald grinned hideously, shook his head. "No, friend, I haven't killed anyone yet . . . though I wouldn't care to make any predictions for tomorrow. No, my pattern didn't follow Paul's after all. Not precisely, that is. For one thing, I never was an Instant Echo.

"I waited all through adolescence for the next flash, and when it hadn't come by the time I graduated high school I dared to begin to hope that I was different. By sophomore year of college, I'd shoved the fear back into the far corners of my mind, and convinced myself that my one fleeting experience had been a freak, perhaps Paul sending instead of receiving for once.

"In junior year it hit again, in the middle of a party. I was paralyzed. There were *twenty-one people* there, and for one awful second I was sure my head would burst from overcrowding. I learned more about human nature that night than I had in the previous twenty years, and I very nearly died. I passed out eventually, but not before I'd gained an undeserved reputation as an acidhead, and lost my girlfriend.

"From that point on, they started coming again and again. The next flash was six months later, the next four and a half, then five, then three, then I stopped keeping track. Right now I'd guess they hit every day or so, but I'm not sure. I can't tell you an awful lot about the time between them.'' His head dropped.

"Why do you suppose your pattern was different from your brother's, Jim?" Doc Webster asked.

"I'm not sure," MacDonald repeated without looking up. "Maybe the different heredity, maybe random chance."

"Perhaps," I put in, "it was getting your first jolt so much younger than Paul did. Maybe the trauma hit you so young you hadn't come to accept limits on your mind yet, and your subconscious whipped up some kind of defense that lasted as long as the trauma did."

"Maybe so," MacDonald said, glancing up at me with hopeless eyes. "But if it did, it's forgotten how to do it again. And my conscious doesn't know the trick." He giggled. "I haven't even improved on Paul's trick with the rock." The giggle dissolved into hysterical laughter, the table danced, and his glass shattered on the floor.

Callahan's broad hand caught him open-palm across the cheek, rocking him in his chair. His laughter cut off, and his shoulders slumped for a second. Then he sat up very straight and stuck his hand out soberly. Callahan shook it gravely and produced a full glass of beer from nowhere; MacDonald took a grateful sip.

"I suppose I should say, 'Thank you, I needed that,' Mister . . . uh . . ."

Callahan told him his name.

". . . Mr. Callahan, but to tell you the truth I almost think I'd rather do it myself." He looked around at the rest of us and his face went all to pieces and he buried his head in his arms. "Oh, *Jesus!*"

"Listen, Jim," Tommy Janssen spoke up quickly, "what the hell did you do after that party? I mean, dig, you couldn't stay in school, right? Too many people, flip you right out. What did you do, go home and become a loner like Paul?"

MacDonald spoke listlessly. "I tried, brother, I tried. I went home and told my father everything—why his second wife had died, and what Paul was, and what I was—and that night he got up to get a drink of water and dropped dead in the bathroom.

"Thank God I didn't flash that.

"I got out fast after that—I got a flash of the man who ran the funeral home that almost did make me a murderer. So I took off, and got myself the only job I was suited for.''

''Lighthouse?'' Chuck Samms guessed.

''Nope. No openings; there almost never are. But the Forestry Service can always use fire-lookouts who don't mind isolation. Miles from anybody in a well-stocked cabin with nothing to do but watch the forest spread out below you. I even got lucky; the area I drew averaged thirty-five days of rain every summer, so I got to sleep late a lot. On hot days in Oregon you get to stand a twelve-hour watch.

''God, it was peaceful.'' He was talking freely now. ''I think I got a flash from a bear once, but it must have been at the extreme limit of my range. Then one day I flashed a bluejay as it sailed about six feet over my head, and that was . . . just beautiful!'' He shivered. ''Almost worth the rest of it.''

''What brings you this way?'' Callahan wanted to know.

''What else? The expected: a forest fire in my zone. Called it in fast, and then got too close to a firefighter who was trapped by a widowmaker and roasting slowly. My boss figured me for an epileptic and fired me as gently as he could. I didn't argue the point. I had a little money saved up. I came back east.''

''Why?'' Callahan asked.

''To see Paul. To visit him.''

''Have you?''

''No, damn it, I couldn't get near the place. I flew right into MacArthur, doped up with sleeping pills so I'd be asleep when we went over New York City, and rented a car with the last of my bankroll when I landed. I intended to drive on through and hope for the best, but halfway out of Islip I flashed a guy in the next lane. He . . . he was a drug dealer. Heroin and cocaine.''

Tommy Janssen's face went hard as a rock, and he gripped his beermug like a bludgeon.

''I was very, very lucky,'' MacDonald continued. ''Any crash you walk away from is a good one, and that's what I did: just left the wreck married to a tree, climbed up the embankment and walked away. I walked for *hours,* and not too long ago the supervisor of this town we're in drove past me in his big limousine and I flashed him. The next thing I knew I was in here, talking a blue streak. Hey, how come you guys believe all this?''

We looked around at each other, shrugged. ''Dis here is Callahan's Place," Fast Eddie tried to explain, and somehow MacDonald seemed to understand.

"Anyway," he went on, "that's the whole story. King's Park is a long way from here, and frankly, gentlemen, I don't think I can make it any further. Any suggestions?"

There was a long silence.

Fast Eddie opened his mouth, closed it, opened it again, and left it that way. Shorty scratched where it itched. Doc Webster sipped thoughtfully at his drink. I racked my brains.

Callahan spoke. "One."

MacDonald started, turned to face him. He looked Callahan up and down from his thinning red hair to his outsized brogans, and sat up a little straighter. "I would very much like to hear it, Mr. Callahan," he said respectfully.

"Contact Paul from here," Callahan said flatly.

MacDonald shook his head violently. "I *can't*. I told you, this thing can't be controlled, dammit."

"You said 'no' a little too loud, old son," Callahan grinned. "Maybe you can't do it—but you think you can."

MacDonald shook his head again. "No. I don't want to flash him. Don't you understand? He's catatonic. A vegetable. I just want to see him, to try and speak with him."

"Why use words?" I asked.

"They're less dangerous, damn you," he snapped. "If you fail with words you can say to yourself, 'Gee, that's sad,' and go do something else."

"What else?" Doc asked. "What did you plan to do after you saw Paul?"

"I . . . I don't know."

"Well, then."

"Look, what could it possibly accomplish?" MacDonald barked.

"Maybe a lot," Callahan said quietly. "Here's how I figure: Paul found a way to block the flashes out—a defense. But he found it at the end of his rope—so he just threw it up and slapped ferrocement over it, and he's been huddling inside it ever since." Callahan took the cigar out of his mouth and rubbed his granite jaw. "Now you're in sorry shape, but old son I don't judge you to be at the end of your rope yet. Paul was continuously telepathic by the time he killed his stepmother, wasn't he?"

"Yes, I believe he was," MacDonald admitted. He was thinking hard.

"Well, there you are. If you can reach him, remind him of what it's like to be hooked into reality without flashing, maybe you can talk him into coming out from behind that shield, and using it only when he needs it. In return, maybe he can teach you how to build the shield.

"What do you say, son?"

MacDonald grimaced. "I can't flash at will. The distance is too great. Our maximum fields of sensitivity don't reach each other by several miles. I'm not due to flash again for at least a day or two, and Paul . . . doesn't flash any more."

"All right," Callahan agreed. "Those are the reasons why it can't possibly work. Now, why don't you try it?"

"Because I'm afraid, dammit!"

Doc Webster spoke up softly. "No reason to fret, son. We'll keep you from hurting yourself."

MacDonald looked around at us, started to speak and paused. His eyes were terrible to see.

"That's not what scares me," he admitted at last, in a voice like a murdered hope. "What scares me is that I may establish contact with my brother and *not* be able to kill myself."

Callahan lumbered around behind the bar, brought his shotgun from beneath it and laid it on the bartop.

"Son," he said firmly, "I don't like violence in my joint. And suicide usually strikes me as a coward's solution. But if you need to die, I'll see that you do."

A couple of jaws dropped, but nobody objected.

Except MacDonald. "What about the police?"

"That's my problem, burglar."

MacDonald's eyes seemed to see a far place, and I hope to God I never see it myself. I suppose he was examining his guts. The suspense hung in the air like the electric calm before a cyclone, and nobody made a sound.

After a long, timeless moment he nodded faintly. "All right. I'll try, Mr. Callahan."

We relaxed a trifle in our chairs, and then tensed right back up again. Callahan put out his cigar and laid a hand on the shotgun, unobtrusively waving Chuck and Noah out of the line of fire.

MacDonald sat bolt upright, put his hands over his ears. He

opened his eyes real wide, looked around one last time, and closed them tight. His brow knotted up.

Now, I don't know quite how to explain just what happened next, because it doesn't seem to jibe with what Jim MacDonald had told us. But I figure that if he was a telepath, some of us at Callahan's are pretty fair empaths. Maybe he was tapping us himself, maybe not. All I know for sure is that all at once the lights were gone and I wasn't in the bar any more, and Callahan and the Doc and Fast Eddie and Tommy and Long-Drink and Noah and Shorty and Chuck and I were all crowded together somehow, *touching*, like we were rubbing shoulders in back of a truck we had to push-start. We didn't waste time wondering, we put our backs into it.

That's crazy, there was no truck, not even a hallucinatory one, but I guess it describes the sort of thing we did as well as words can. We . . . *pushed,* and just like with a truck there came a time when the thing we were pushing gave a hell of a shudder and took off, leaving us gasping far behind.

The thing we were pushing was Jim MacDonald.

The lights came back and the familiar sights of Callahan's Place came back and I was alone in my skin again, looking around at Callahan and the rest of the boys and realizing with surprise that I hadn't been the least bit scared. They were looking around too, and it was a few seconds before we saw MacDonald.

He was sitting rigid in his chair, trembling like a man with a killing fever. Doc Webster started for him like an overweight white corpuscle but pulled up short and looked helpless. The air around MacDonald's head seemed to shimmer like the air over a campfire, and we heard his teeth gnashing.

Then, not suddenly but gradually, almost imperceptibly at first, he began to relax. Muscles unknotted, joints unlocked, his face began to soften. He . . . I don't know how to say this either. He *wore his face differently*. The MacDonald he loosened into was changed, somehow older.

He had won.

"Our deepest thanks, gentlemen," he said in a more resonant voice than he had used before. "I think we'll be all right from here on."

"What will you do now?" Callahan rapped, and I wondered at the cold steel in his voice.

MacDonald considered for a moment. "We're not really sure," he decided finally, "but whatever we do, we hope we can find a way to help other people the way you've helped us. There must be lots of things we can do. Maybe we'll finish school and become a psychiatrist like I planned once. Imagine—a telepathic head-shrinker."

Callahan's hand came away from the trigger of the scattergun for the first time; Jim/Paul didn't catch it, but I did. I was rather glad to know that the intentions of the world's only two telepaths were benign, myself.

Callahan looked puzzled for a second, then his face split into a huge grin. "Say, can I offer you fellas a drink?"

And MacDonald's new voice echoed him perfectly.

"Don't mind if we do," he added, laughing, and got up to take a chair at the bar.

"Hey," Fast Eddie called out, ever one to remember the important details, "wait a minute. De cops'll be lookin' for youse fer leavin' dat accident. Whaddya gonna tell 'em? Fer dat matter, how d'ya get yer udder body outa King's Park?"

"Oh, I dunno," Callahan mused, putting a careful double-shot of Chivas Regal in front of MacDonald. "It seems to me a telepath could dodge him a lot of cops. Or a lot of witchdoctors. Wouldn't you say, gents?"

"We guess so," MacDonald allowed, and drank up.

And they were right. All three of them.

I haven't heard much from either of the MacDonald brothers yet, but then it hasn't been that long, and I'm sure they've both got a lot of thinking and catching up to do. I wonder if either of them is thinking of having kids. One way or another, I expect to be hearing good things of them, really good things, any day now.

It figures. I mean, two heads are better than one.

THE LAW OF CONSERVATION OF PAIN

There's a curious kind of inevitability to the way things happen at Callahan's. Not that we wouldn't have managed to help The Meddler out *some* way or other even if it had been, say, Thursday night that he came to us. But since it was Monday night, I finally got to learn what it is that "heavy metal" music is good for.

After ten years as a musician, it was about time I found out.

Monday night is Fill-More Night at Callahan's Place, the night Fast Eddie and I do our weekly set on piano and guitar. But don't let the name mislead you into thinking we play the kind of ear-splitting music the Fillmore East was famous for. Although I do play an electric axe (a Country Gent Six) and have an amplifier factory-guaranteed to shatter glass, these are the only remnants of a very brief flirtation with rock that occurred in much hungrier times than these. I don't *like* loud noises.

No, the name derives from the curious custom we have at Callahan's of burying our dead soldiers in the fireplace. You can usually tell how good a night it's been by how many glasses lay smashed on the hearth, and after one particularly tasty session Doc

Webster nicknamed Eddie and me the Fireside Fill-More. To our intense disgust, it stuck.

This particular Monday night, things was loose indeed. Eddie and I had held off our first set for half an hour to accommodate a couple of the boys who were playing a sort of pool on the floor with apples and broomsticks, and by the time Callahan had set up the two immense speakers on either side of the front door, the joint was pretty merry.

"What're you gonna play, Jake?" the Doc called out from his ringside seat. I adjusted the mikestand, turned up my axe just enough to put it on an equal footing with Fast Eddie's upright, and tossed the ball right back to the Doc.

"What would you like to hear, Doc?"

"How about, 'There Are Tears In My Ears From Lying On My Back And Crying In The Evening Over You'?"

"Naw," drawled Long-Drink from the bar, "I want to hear 'He Didn't Like Her Apartment So He Knocked Her Flat,'" and a few groans were heard.

Doc Webster rose to the occasion. "Why not play the Butcher Song, Jake?"

I resigned myself to the inevitable. "The Butcher Song?"

"Sure," boomed the Doc, and conducting an invisible band, he sang, "Butcher arms around me honey/hold me tight . . ." Peanuts began to rain on his head.

Callahan shifted the right speaker a bit, and turned around with his hands on his hips. "Play the Camera Song, Jake."

"Hit me, Mike."

With a voice like a foghorn undergoing root-canal work, Callahan began, "Lens get together 'bout half past eight/I'll ring your Bell & Howell . . ." and a considerable number of glasses hit the fireplace at once. One or two had not been emptied first; the crackling fire flared high.

In the brief pause that ensued, Fast Eddie spoke up plaintively. "Hey, Jake. I got an idea."

"Be gentle with it," the Doc grinned. "It's in a strange place."

"What's your idea, Eddie?" I asked.

"How about if we do de one we been rehoisin' all afternoon?"

I nodded judiciously, and turned to face the house. "Regulars and gentlemen," I announced, "for our first number we would like to do a song we wrote yesterday in an attempt to define that elusive essence, that shared quality which brings us all together here at

Callahan's Place. In its way it is a song about all of us.

"It's called the Drunkard's Song."

And as Eddie's nimble piano intro cut through the ensuing cat-calls, I stoked up my guitar and sang:

> *A swell and wealthy relative of mine had up and died*
> *And I got a hundred thousand from the will*
> *So a friend and I decided to convert it into liquid form*
> *The better our esophagi to fill*
> *So we started in the city, had a drink in every shitty*
> *Little ginmill, which is really quite a few*
> *And a cabbie up in Harlem took us clean across the river*
> *Into Brooklyn, where he joined us in a brew*
> *We was weavin' just a trifle as we pulled into Astoria*
> *At eighty miles an hour in reverse*
> *But it was nothin' to the weavin' that we did as we was*
>   *leavin'*
> *And from time to time it got a little worse*
>> *Well there's nothin' like drinkin' up a windfall*
>> *We was drunker than a monkey with a skinfull*
>> *We wuz so goddamn drunk it was sinful*
>> *And I think I ain't sober yet*

As we finished the chorus, Fast Eddie tossed up a cloud of gospel chords that floated me easily into my solo, a bit of intricate pickin' which I managed to stumble through with feeling if not precision. When it was Eddie's turn I snuck a look around and saw that everyone was well into his second drink, and relaxed. There were smiles all around as I slid into the second verse:

> *We was feeling mighty fine as we crossed the city line*
> *Suckin' whiskey and a-whistlin' at the girls*
> *But the next saloon we try someone wants to black my eye*
> *'Cause he doesn't like my long and shaggy curls*
> *So then a fist come out of orbit, knocked me clean across*
>   *the floor*
> *But I was pretty drunk and didn't even care*
> *And I was pretty disappointed when the coppers hit the joint*
> *As I was makin' my rebuttal with a chair*
> *But the coppers came a cropper 'cause I made it to the*
>   *crapper*

And departed by a ventilator shaft
Met my buddies in the alley as they slipped out through the
   galley
And we ran and ran and laughed and laughed and laughed
   Yeah there's nothin' like drinkin' up a windfall
   We was drunker than a monkey with a skinful
   We wuz so goddamn drunk it was sinful
   And I think I ain't sober yet

This time Fast Eddie jumped into the gap with a flurry of triplets. I could tell that he knew where he was going, so I gave him his head. As he unfolded a tasty statement, I looked around again and saw wall-to-wall grins again.

No, not quite. Tommy Janssen, sitting over by the mixer, was definitely not smiling. A pot-bellied gent in an overcoat, who I didn't recognize, was leaning over Tommy's shoulder, whispering something into his ear, and the kid didn't seem to like it at all. Even as Eddie's solo yanked my attention away again I saw Tommy turn around and say something to the overcoated man, and when I looked back the guy was standing at the bar with his nose in a double-something.

I put it out of my mind; verse three was a-comin'.

Halfway out of Levittown we got our second wind
In a joint so down it made you laugh
So I had another mug, and my buddy had a jug
And the cabbie had a pitcher and a half
When we got to Suffolk County we was goin' into overdrive
The word had spread and crowds began to form
We drank our way from Jericho on down 110 to Merrick
   Road
A-boozin' and a-singin' up a storm
I lost my buddy and the cabbie in the middle of the
   Hamptons
We was drunker than it's possible to be
But there finally came a time when I just didn't have a dime
I sat on Montauk Point and wept into the sea

And everybody in the joint joined in on the final chorus. All except the guy in the overcoat . . . who was already on his second double-something.

Yeah there's nothin' like drinkin' up a windfall
We was drunker than a monkey with a skinfull
We wuz so goddamn drunk it was sinful
And I think I ain't sober yet!

A storm of glasses hit the fireplace, and Fast Eddie and I went into our aw-shucks routine at about the same time. When the cheers and laughter had died down somewhat, I stepped back up to the mike and a-hemmed.

"Thank you for your sympathy, genties and ladle-men," I said. "We'll be passing the eleven-gallon hat directly," I tapped the huge Stetson on my head significantly and grinned.

"Well now . . ." I paused. "We only know two songs, and that was one of them, so we're real glad you liked it." I stopped again. "What do you think we ought to play now, Eddie?"

He sat awhile in thought.

"How 'bout de udder one?" he asked at last.

"Right arm," I agreed at once, and hit a G.

Doc Webster beheaded a new bottle of Peter Dawson's and took a hearty swallow.

"Okay, folks," I continued. "Here's a medley of our hit: a sprightly number called, 'She Was Only A Telegrapher's Daughter, But She Didit-Ah-Didit.' " I started to pick the intro, but the sound of glass smashing in the fireplace distracted me, and I bungled it.

And in the few seconds before I could take another stab at it, the fellow in the overcoat burst noisily and explosively into tears.

Fast Eddie and I were among the first to join the circle that formed immediately around the crying, pot-bellied man. I didn't even stop to unplug my guitar, and if anyone had trouble stepping over the stretched-out telephone cord they kept it to themselves.

Paradoxically, after we had rushed to encircle him, nobody said a word. We let him have his cry, and did our best to silently share it with him. We offered him only our presence, and our concern.

In about five minutes, his sobs gave way to grimaces and jerky breathing, and Callahan handed him a triple-something. He got outside of half of it at once, and set the remaining something-and-a-half down on the bar. His face as he looked around us was not ashamed, as we might have expected; more relieved than anything else. Although there was still tension in the set of his lantern jaw and in the squint of his hazel eyes, the knot in his gut seemed to have eased considerably.

"Thanks," he said quietly. "I . . . I . . ." He stopped, wanting to talk about it but unable to continue. Then he must have remembered the few toasts he'd seen earlier in the evening, because he picked up the rest of his drink, walked over to the chalk line in the middle of the room, drained the glass and announced, "To meddlers." Then he pegged the glass into the exact geometrical center of the fireplace.

"Like me," he added, turning to face us. "I'm a meddler on a grand scale, and I'm not sure I've got the guts. Or the right."

"Brother," Callahan said seriously, "you're sure in the right place. All of us here are veteran meddlers, after a fashion, and we worry considerable about both them things."

"Not like this," the Meddler said. "You see, I'm a time-traveler too." He waited for our reaction.

"Say," piped up Noah Gonzalez, "it's a shame Tom Hauptman's off tonight. You two'd have a lot to talk about."

"Eh?" said the stranger, confused.

"Sure," Callahan agreed. "Tom's a time-traveler too."

"But . . . but," the guy sputtered, "but I've got the only unit."

"Oh, Tom didn't use no fancy equipment," Noah explained.

"Yeah," agreed Callahan. "Tom did it the hard way. Never mind, friend, it's a long story. You from the past or the future?"

"The future," said the time-traveler, puzzled at our lack of reaction. I guess we're hard to startle. "That is, the future as it is at present . . . I mean . . ." He stopped and looked confused.

"I get it," said Noah, like me a veteran SF fan. "You're from the future, but you're going to change that future by changing the past, which is our present, right?"

The fellow nodded.

"How's that again?" blinked Doc Webster.

"I am from the year 1995," said the man in the overcoat with weary patience, "and I am going to change history in the year 1974. If I succeed, the world I go back to will be different from the one I left."

"Better or worse?" asked Callahan.

"That's the hell of it: I don't know. Oh kark, I might as well tell you the whole story. Maybe it'll help."

Callahan set 'em up, and we all got comfortable.

*   *   *

Her name (said the stranger) was Bobbi Joy, and you couldn't say there'd never been anyone like her before. Lots of people had been like her. April Lawton, for instance, was nearly as good a guitarist. Aretha had at times a similar intensity. Billie Holiday surely bore and was able to communicate much the same kind of pain. Joni Mitchell and Roberta Flack each in their own way possessed a comparable technical control and purity of tone. Dory Previn was as dramatic and poignant a lyricist, and Maria Muldaur projected the same guileless grace.

But you could have rolled them all together and you still wouldn't have Bobbi Joy, because there was her voice. And it was just plain impossible that such a voice could be. When a Bobbi Joy song ended, whether on tape or disc or holo or, rarest of good fortune, live, you found your head shaking in frank disbelief that a human throat could express such pain, that such pain could be, and that you could hear such pain and still live.

Her name was the purest of irony, given to her by an employer in a previous and more ancient profession, a name she was too cynically indifferent to change when her first recordings began to sell. I've often wondered what her past customers must feel when they hear her sing; I'm certain every nameless, faceless one of them remembers *her*.

They surely appreciate as well as anyone the paradox of her name—for while God seemed to have given her every possible physical advantage in obtaining joy, it never got any closer to her than her album jackets and the first line of her driver's license. Although many pairs of lips spoke her name, none ever brought its reality to her.

For the scar on her soul was as deep and as livid as the one that ran its puckered, twisted way from her left cheekbone to her right chin.

The Woman With The Scar, they called her, and many, seeing only a physical wound, might have wondered that she did not have it surgically corrected—so easy a procedure in my time. But she sang, and so we understood, and we cried with her because neither of her scars would or could ever be erased, and that, I suppose you'd say, was her genius. She represented the scars across the face of an entire era; she reminded us that we had made the world in which such scars could be, and that we—all of us—were as scarred as she. She . . .

This is absurd. I'm trying to explain sex to a virgin, with a perfectly good bed handy. Lend an ear, friends, and listen. This holo will tell you more than I can. God help you.

The stranger produced a smooth blue sphere about the size of a tennis ball from one of his pockets, and held it out toward the fireplace. The shimmering of the air over the crackling fire intensified and became a swirling, then a dancing, and finally a coalescing. The silence in Callahan's was something you could have driven rivets into.

Then the fireplace was gone, and in its place was a young black woman seated on a rock, a guitar on her lap and starry night sky all around and behind her. Her face was in shadow, but even as we held our breath the moon came out from behind a cloud and touched her features. It gave an obsidian sheen to her skin, a tender softness to a face that God had meant to be beautiful, and made a harsh shadow-line of the incredibly straight slash that began an inch below her left eye and yanked sideways and down to open up lips that had been wide already, like a jagged black underline below the word "pain." She was black and a woman and scarred, and as the thought formed in our minds we realized that it was a redundancy. Her scar was visible externally, was all.

We were shocked speechless, and in the stillness she lifted her guitar slightly and began to play, a fast, nagging, worrisome beat, like despairing Richie Havens, an unresolved and maybe unresolvable chord that was almost all open string. An E minor sixth, with the C sharp in the bass, a haunting chord that demanded to become something else, major or minor, happy or sad, but *something*. A plain, almost Gregorian riff began from that C sharp but always returned unsatisfied, trying to break free of that chord but not succeeding.

And over that primevally disturbing sound, Bobbi Joy spoke, with the impersonal tones of the narrator behind all art:

> *Snow was falling heavily on U.S. 40 as the day drew to a close. This lonely stretch of highway had seen no other movement all day; the stillness was so complete that the scrub pines and rolling hills by the roadside may have felt that the promise*

given them so long ago had come to pass, that man had finally gone and left them in peace forever. No snakes had swayed forth from their retreats that day, no lizards crawled, no wolves padded silently in search of winter food. All wildlife waited, puzzled, expectant, caught in the feeling of waiting . . . for what?

Gradually, without suddenness, each living thing became aware of a curious stuttering drone to the far east, which became audible too slowly to startle. It swelled, drew nearer, and small muscles and sinews tensed, then relaxed as the sound was identified as familiar, harmless.

A pale green 1960 Dodge, with no more than three cylinders firing, crept jerkily into view through the shrouds of snow. Wipers blinking clumsily, the great machine felt its way along the road, its highway song hoarse and stuttered. With a final roar of mortal agony, it fell silent: wipers ceased their wiping, pistons ceased driving, lights winked out, and the huge car coasted gracefully off the road and rolled to a stop with its nose resting on a snow-laden mesquite.

Stillness returned to U.S. 40 . . . and still, on either side of it, the animals waited.

Even as she finished speaking, the walking bass line with which she was underpinning her mournful chord returned to that dysharmonic C sharp. Then with breathtaking ease it slid down two tones to B, became the dominant of a simple E minor, and as bass, organ, and drums came in from nowhere she began to sing:

Snow fallin' gentle on the windshield
Sittin' on the side of the road
Took a ride—my engine died and left me
Sittin' on the side of the road
In a little while I'll get out and start a-walkin'
Probably a town pretty near
But it just occurs to me that I ain't got no
More reason to be there than to be here
But I'll be leavin'
(sudden key shift)
Soon as I find me a reason to
Right now it's nice just to watch the snow
Coverin' the windshield and windows . . .

She finished on a plaintive A minor, toppled off it back into that ghostly mosquito-biting E minor sixth again, and the other instruments fell away, leaving her guitar alone. Again, she spoke:

Snow now completely covered the windshield and windows, forming a white curtain which hid the interior of the car, and any activity within—if there was any to be seen. No sound issued from the car, no vibration disturbed the snow on its doors. The animals were puzzled, but delighted: perhaps a human understood at last.

The C sharp walked down to B again, but this time it belonged to a clean, simple G chord, supported by a steel guitar and the trapping of bluegrass, a comparatively happy sound that only lasted for the first four lines as that voice—that voice!—picked up the song again, etching us with its words:

Don't worry now. I'm goin'
Any minute now, I'll be goin'
Leave the car
—It isn't far to walk now
Any minute now, I'll be going
(slowing now, an electric guitar leading into an achingly repeated
    C-E A-minor progression that went nowhere . . .)
Soon as I can find a place I want to go
Soon as I can find a thing I want to do
Soon as I can find someone I want to know
Or think of something interesting and new
(a sudden optimistic jump into the key of F . . .)
I mean, I could make it easy to the next town
(twisting crazily into E flat . . .)
But what am I to do when I get there?
(inexorably back to C . . .)
That's what I made this odyssey to find out:
Two thousand miles and still I just don't care . . .
(a capella:)
Is it worthwhile to go on looking?

We wanted to cry, wanted to shout, wanted to run forward with a hundred reasons for living, find some way to heal the hurt in that voice, and no one made a sound. Alone again with her guitar, Bobbi

Joy wove that dysharmonic tapestry of hurting notes that was already becoming as familiar to us as the taste that a bad dream always has in the cold morning; and as she began to speak again, not a muscle flickered in her ebony face, as though her scar was all the expression she would ever need or be allowed.

> *The snow began to drift.*
> *In a minute—or an hour—the car was half-buried in a heavy white winter coat of wet snow. The animals were already beginning to forget about the car. It had not shown movement in so long that they were coming to regard it as part of their environment—of less interest than the tattered 1892 edition of* The Denver Record *pinned under a rock, which at least still fluttered occasionally in the wind.*
> *For the memory of the animals is short, and the years are long, and they have found that very little is worth puzzling over for very long.*
> *And still, the snow fell . . .*

This time she stayed with the C sharp, built an A chord around it, and was joined only by harpsichord and bass. There was no ambiguity to this part: a simple, mournful melody that had no change-ups, no surprises, just the quiet calm of resignation, of unheeded defeat.

> *Sort of friendly here inside the car*
> *Even though it's gettin' kinda cold*
> *Haven't stirred, or said a word, in hours*
> *I believe it's gettin' awful cold*
> *In the glove compartment, there's a small flask:*
> *Little Irish whiskey for the soul*
> *But reachin' out to get it seems a great task*
> *And anyway, it isn't all that cold*
> *It might keep me warm*
> *But it just ain't worth the trouble . . .*

Her shoulders seemed to slump, and the droning background of her guitar took on a terrible finality.

> *There was no longer a Dodge by the side of U.S. 40; just a drift like many others, peaceful and horribly cold. A faint*

illumination began to expose mysteries of snow-sculpture, hummocks and valleys of white. But for the swirling haze, you might have said it was dawn.

The car was completely hidden from sight—and so, in caves, holes, and shelters, were the animals. But they no longer remembered the car . . . and at least in their dwellings were some signs of life.

And with shattering unexpectedness she slammed into E major, driving with horns and bass and moog and drums in a frenzied hallelujah chorus that dared you to begin hoping again. Surely that throbbing beat was a heart starting to beat, surely that energy was purposeful!

We sat up straighter, and crossed our fingers.

I've got it!
There's something that I want to do
A thing that seems to have some kind of point
I've got some grass, enclosed in glass
Here inside my shirt
Think I'm gonna roll myself a joint
(the bottom fell out of voice and arrangement, scared away by solemnity and a trembling echo . . .)
A complicated operation—might disturb the peace
But it ought to warm me just as well as drink
So it's something worth the trouble and it's gonna help me find
A reason to get out of here
I think
(a capella)
Now where did I put all those Zig-Zags?

Again that C sharp rang out, shocking return to inevitability, and the droning guitar cut the rug out from under us. Helpless, not knowing whether the music or the words frustrated us more, we waited in fearful silence for what had to come next. And for the last time the expressionless voice spoke:

Two weeks later, when a road-crew dug out the car, they found inside it the frozen corpse of a young woman, incredibly tranquil and serene. Between the blue and rigid lips was the pencil-thin column of ash from a hand-rolled cigarette, which had burned undisturbed until it had seared the lips and gone out. The crew-boss silenced his men, radioed a call to the State Police with remarkable calm . . .

And then went home and made savage love to his wife.

And that damned unnerving guitar fell to pieces on the E minor sixth, as resolved as it was ever going to be.

The silence persisted for a full minute before anyone so much as thought to look into his drink for any answers that might be skulking around in there. And when we did, we found none there, so we tried looking at each other. And when that failed, we turned as one to regard the stranger who had brought us this vision. His hand was back at his side, now, and the fireplace was back where it belonged, naively attempting to warm a room that had gone as cold as death . . .

"That, gentlemen," he said simply, "is Bobbi Joy."

No one said a word. I saw Doc Webster groping desperately for a wisecrack to break the spell, and it just wasn't there. The stranger had been right: now that it was over we could scarcely believe that it had happened, scarcely believe that we were still alive.

"Now that you know her," the stranger went on, "you're ready to hear her story, what made her what she is and what I hope to do about it."

Bobbi Joy (the Meddler continued) was born Isadora Brickhill in the back seat of a gypsy cab somewhere in Harlem, in the year 1952. I can see by your scowls, gentlemen, that I don't have to explain what *that* means. She didn't even have Billie Holiday's classic two choices—no one was hiring maids in those days. By the training and education she received, she was prepared only for the most basic trade there is: by 1966 little Isadora was an experienced and, if rumor is to be believed, accomplished whore.

Even in that most clichéd of professions she was an anomaly. She did not drink, touched no drugs save an occasional social reefer, and never seemed to project that desperate air of defeat and cynical surrender so characteristic of her colleagues. She had a fiery fighting spirit that demanded and elicited respect from all who knew her, and except for physically, no one ever touched her at all. Madams loved her for her utterly dependable honesty in the split, the girls loved her for her unflagging courage and willingness to be of help, and the johns loved her for the completely detached professionalism she brought to her work.

Then came the bust.

Some sort of political mix-up, as the story goes—a payoff missed, an official inadvertently offended, a particularly well-written expose that demanded token action. Whatever the reason, Hannah's House was raided in April of 1974 in the traditional manner, wagons and all. Bobbi, as she was by now known, was loaded into the wagons with the rest of the girls before she had a chance to grab a wrap. Consequently she attracted the attention of a patrolman named Duffy, who had come to appreciate that in such situations, a policeman hath rank privileges. He attempted to collect what he regarded as only his right, and was refused: Bobbi allowed as how she might be for sale but she was damned if she was for free. Duffy persisted, and bought a knee in the groin, whereupon he lost all discretion and laid open Bobbi's face with the barrel of his pistol. This so mightily embarrassed Duffy's sergeant, who was also Duffy's brother-in-law, that he was forced to ignore the wound, locking Bobbi in with the rest of the girls in the hope that her disfigurement could be passed off as the result of a razor fight in the cells. By the time she got medical attention, it was too late. She was scarred through and through, and forever unsuited for the only job she knew.

Almost a year later, a producer received an unsolicited tape in the mail. Such tapes are *never* played, but this one had the songs listed on the outside, and the producer's eye was caught by the first title: "The Suicide Song." It was a crude, home-taped version of the song you just heard, audio only. The producer played it once, and spent a frantic seventeen hours locating Bobbi Joy.

He didn't make her a star: he simply recorded her songs and made them available for sale. She *became* a star, a star like there had never been before. At least seven of her recordings, tape and holo, were proscribed from public broadcast—because areas in which they were played showed sudden jumps in the suicide rate. The seventies and eighties were not good years in which to live, and Bobbi Joy spoke for all too many of us all too well. She was a phenomenon, endlessly analyzed and never defined, and if some of us took a perverse kind of courage from her songs, maybe that was more reflection of us than of her. And maybe not.

In any event, the producer with remarkable ease became unspeakably rich. And it comforted him not. Poor devil, condemned to be the man who gave Bobbi Joy to the world, how could his heart be soothed with money? He gave most of it away to his mad brother, who thought he could build a time machine, just to be rid of it. He pickled himself in alcohol with the balance, and never, ever played her tapes for himself. Like all her fans, he ached to bring her peace and knew no man ever could; but there was more. He loved her with a ferocious and utterly hopeless desperation, and consequently avoided her company as much as possible. He dreamed futile dreams of fixing her hurt, and lost a great deal of weight, and when his mad brother told him one spring day that the time machine was a success, he knew what he had to do.

His brother, though mad, was not so mad as he was by now, and sought to reason with him. He spoke of possible disruption of the time-stream by the changing of the past, and other complicated things, and flatly forbade the producer to use the time machine.

Right now, years in the future, he's nursing a sore jaw and wondering whether I'm about to destroy the fabric of time. And so am I.

I've been wandering around in your time for two or three days. I gave myself some leeway to make plans, but I've been using it to cool off. And now I don't know what to do. Maybe my brother was right; he knows a lot more than I about it. *But I can't leave her in pain, can I?*

Oh yes, one more thing: the bust is tonight. About four hours from now.

What could we say? We had to believe him—the technology inherent in that holographic sphere was certainly well beyond the present state of the art. More important, if that voice truly existed in our time, we would have heard of it long since. It was impossible to disbelieve that voice.

Callahan summed it up for all of us.

"What do you figure to do about it, brother?"

The Meddler didn't answer, and suddenly I knew somehow, maybe from the set of his mouth, maybe a little from the glance he gave Tommy Janssen.

"I think I understand, Mike," I said softly. "I saw him talking to Tommy while I was up on the stand, and I saw Tommy cuss him out. Somewhere outside he ran into someone who told him where he could find a kid who used to be a heroin addict, a kid who would certainly know where to get him a gun. He's going to kill Patrolman Duffy. Aren't you, friend?"

The Meddler nodded.

"Then you've made your decision?" asked Callahan. "One murder'll fix everything?"

"It'll prevent that scar," said the Meddler. "And how can it be murder to kill a scum like that? The hell with a gun, I can get within knife distance easily—no one will be expecting anything, and I don't care what they do to me afterwards." He squared his shoulders, and looked Callahan in the eye. "You figure to stop me?"

"Well now, son," Callahan drawled, "I'm not certain I've got the right to meddle in something like this. Besides, I reckon it's no accident you're closer to the door than any of us. But it seems like I ought to point out—"

He broke off and stared at the doorway. So did the rest of us. A man stood there, where there had been no one a moment before. He looked like an older, wearier version of the Meddler, built much the same, but he wasn't wearing an overcoat so you could see that the pot-belly was actually an enormous belt strapped around his waist. Obviously, it was a time machine; just as obviously, he was its inventor, come to stop his brother from tampering with history.

But our attention was centered not on the machinery around his waist, but on the much smaller piece of it in his right hand. Made of glass and seemingly quite fragile, it could only have been the handgun of the 1990's, and the way he held it told us that we ought to respect it. I thought of lasers and backed away, fetching up against my amplifier.

"I can't let you do it, John," said the newcomer, ignoring the rest of us.

"You can't stop me," said the Meddler.

"I can kill you," his brother corrected.

"Look, Henry," the Meddler said desperately, "I'm not going into this blindly. I know what I'm doing."

"Do you?" His brother laughed. "You damned fool, you haven't the faintest notion what you could do by killing that fool policeman. Suppose a criminal he would have apprehended goes on to kill some innocent people instead? Suppose the simple removal of him from history suffices to disrupt this time-stream beyond repair? You may be killing every man, woman, and child in your time, John!''

"Don't you think I know that?'' cried the man in the overcoat. ''And do you suppose that's all there is to be afraid of? Suppose I'm entirely successful, and only bring about a world without Bobbi Joy. She brought us all a self-conscious awareness of collective guilt which had an enormous effect for good. *I don't know that I have the right to deprive the world of her music.*

"Suppose there's a Law of Conservation of Pain? Suppose pain can't be destroyed within a continuum? Then all I'll have done is redirected her pain: I suspect it will all be transferred to *me*—and I can't sing worth a damn. Henry, I admit I don't have any idea what the consequences of my action may be. But I do know what I have to do.''

"And I can't let you,'' his brother repeated.

He lifted the strange glass pistol and aimed it at the Meddler's heart, and I saw Callahan's big hands go under the bar for the sawed-off shotgun, and I saw Long-Drink and the Doc and Tommy Janssen start to close in on the gunman, and I knew that none of them would be in time, and without thinking I spun on my heel, twisted the volume knob savagely on my amp, clutched my E-string as high as I could and snapped the pick across it. A shrieking high-note lanced through the air, and I rammed the guitar in front of the monitor-speaker for maximum feedback.

A red-hot knife went through every ear in the room, freezing the action like a stop-motion camera. The guitar fed back and fed back, building from a noise like a gutshot pig to something that was felt rather than heard. Glasses began to shatter along the bar, then bottles on the long shelves behind it . . .

And all at once, so did that deadly little glass gun.

Quickly I muted the guitar, and our ears rang for a lingering minute. Blood ran from a couple of cuts on Callahan's face, and the gunman's hand was a mess. Doc Webster was at his side somehow, producing bandages and antiseptic from his everpresent black bag and steering the wounded man into a seat.

The Meddler sat down beside him. "How did you do it, Henry? I thought I had the only—''

"You do,'' Henry snapped. "You came back with it, you bloody maniac, and as soon as you reappeared I knew from the look on your face that you had succeeded. I didn't wait around to find out what change you'd made in the world I knew; I hit you with a chair and took the belt, determined to make one last desperate try to save my time. You laughed as you went down, and now I guess I know why. *Meddler!*"

The Meddler stood up, faced Callahan. "You've got a gun under that bar," he stated. "I want it."

Callahan stood his ground. "Not a chance," he said.

"Then I'll knife him, or bash in his skull with a rock, or drop a match in his gas tank." He headed for the door, and no one got in his way.

"Hold on a minute," I called out, and he stopped.

"Look," he told me, "I'm grateful for what you did, but—"

"Listen," I interrupted, "maybe we can't give you a gun . . . but we can sure pass the hat for you."

His jaw dropped as I whipped off the eleven-gallon hat and offered it to Noah Gonzalez. Noah dropped in a five-dollar bill without hesitating, and passed the hat to Slippery Joe. People began digging into their pockets, emptying their wallets, and dropping the swag in the hat as it came their way. It filled rapidly, and by the time it reached Fast Eddie I guess it had maybe a hundred dollars or better in it.

Eddie took it from Callahan and looked at the Meddler. "I ain't got no dough," he announced, "but I got a '65 Chevy outside dat'll do a hunnert'n'ten easy." He fished out a set of keys and dropped them into the hat. "Don't waste no time parkin' the bastard, you'll never find a parkin' space in Harlem dis time o' night. Double park it; I'll pick it up from de cops tomorra."

There were tears running down the Meddler's face; he seemed unable to speak.

"Okay," said Callahan briskly, "you've got three or four hours. That should be plenty of time. You drive to Hannah's as fast as you can, wave around that dough and tell Hannah you want to take one of the girls home for the night. She sees all that cabbage, she'll go for it. That'll get Bobbi clear of the bust, and what happens after that is up to you. Good luck."

He took the hat from Eddie and handed it to the Meddler, who took it with a trembling hand.

"Th-thank you," the Meddler said. "I . . . I hope I'm doing the right thing."

"You're doing what you have to do," said Callahan, "and you don't have to kill anyone. Now get out of here."

The Meddler got.

We sent his brother home eventually, and Eddie and I packed up our equipment for the night. We felt sort of inadequate after having heard Bobbi Joy, and anyway everyone in the joint was broke now. By closing time, we were all ready to leave.

The next night we were all there by seven, and although it was Punday Night nobody felt much like making jokes. A few of us had tried to get news of the previous night's raid from the police, but they weren't talking, and we were as filled with suspense as the fireplace was with glass.

Along about eight the sporadic conversation was silenced by the sudden appearance of the time-traveling belt on the bar, a soft green sphere and a single piece of paper encircled in it. The piece of paper proved to be a note, which read:

Didn't want to leave you hanging. Please destroy this belt.
    The next time we all might not be so lucky. Many thanks
    from both of us.

Callahan tossed the belt into the fireplace, and it landed with a crunching sound. Then he picked up the sphere, and held it in his big hand. For the second time in two days, the fireplace faded from sight, but this time it was replaced by a mountain stream, crisp clean pines in the background, an achingly beautiful sunset playing tag with ominous grey stormclouds.

Bobbi Joy sat by the stream, her guitar across her lap, and her unscarred face was more beautiful than all the sunsets that ever were. She gazed serenely at all of us, and fitted her fingers to the strings.

It began slowly, a simple statement of key woven out of two chords that rose and fell like cyclical hopes in a crazy time-signature. Gradually, the pauses between the ringing chords were filled in with rhythmic direction, picking up speed and becoming almost a calypso beat—save that calypso never used such chords. And Bobbi Joy sang:

I walk around with . . . doubt inside of me
I don't believe in . . . what I try to be
Words I whisper . . . seem like a lie to me

Strange thing
Wonder what's happening?

Her voice spoke of confusion and fear, of doubt and loneliness; and our hearts sank within us.

I'm scared that maybe . . . I'm what I seem to be
Today is only . . . another dream to me
Fading quickly . . . from my memory
Strange thing
Wonder what's happening?

All around the room I saw men respond to that plaintive question, saw them wince at the thought of failure, as Bobbi Joy went into the bridge of her song. Cradled in strings and an ironically mellow organ, she went on:

The sky is changing color
And the ground is far away
I wandered in my mind
And now I've lost the way . . .
Where are the places . . . that I used to go?
Who are the people . . . that I used to know?
Will things be any . . . better tomorrow?
Strange thing
Wonder what's happening?

And then, cutting through our despair as the sun cut through the holographic clouds, a full orchestra came out of nowhere, a warm carpet of sound that swelled in moments to an almost Wagnerian peak. Bobbi's face was transfused with a startling smile of pure joy, and fullthroated she sang:

And then I meet a Meddler
And the Meddler comes to me
He tells me of my future
And he comforts me . . .

And the final verse exploded in Callahan's Place like a hallelujah chorus of horns and violins, banishing all the fear and the uncertainty and the pain, turning them all to nothing more than paid dues, the admission price to happiness:

> *Now rain is falling . . . like a beatitude*
> *Trees are weeping . . . tears of gratitude*
> *There's been a change in . . . my whole attitude*
> *Strange thing*
> *Good things are happening*
> *Strange thing—*
> *Good things are happening*

And with a flurry of trumpets, the song died. Bobbi Joy smiled a deep, satisfied smile and disappeared, taking her mountain stream with her.

Callahan's arm came down fast, and the sphere exploded in the center of the fireplace. And in that moment we realized, all of us in Callahan's Place, that the Meddler's guess had been part right. Just as there are laws of Conservation of Matter and Energy, so there are in fact Laws of Conservation of Pain and Joy. Neither can ever be created or destroyed.

But one can be converted into the other.

JUST DESSERT

Sooner or later, just about every bar acquires that most obnoxious of nuisances: the practical joker. I'd have thought Callahan's Place would be immune to that particular kind of carbuncle—we don't seem to pick up the standard idiots that most saloons have to put up with, the weepy drunks and the belligerent loudmouths and the ones who drink to get stupider. It's almost as though some sort of protective spell ensures that the only people who find Callahan's are the ones who should—and the ones who must.

But very occasionally, some refugee from the Dew Drop Inn does accidentally wander in, usually for just long enough to make us appreciate his absence when he finally leaves. There was, for instance, the guy of an ethnic extraction I can't specify without getting a lot of Italians mad at me, who represented a jukebox concern. He made Callahan an offer he couldn't refuse—so Mike didn't bother refusing. The guy's broken arms eventually healed, I understand, but he never got over the amnesia. Then there was the gent who brought his young secretary in to get her drunk for carnal purposes. Callahan got a little sloppy that night: somehow all the ginger ale ended up in her glass and all the vodka in his. When he woke up he was a far piece from nowhere, minus a secretary and a rather sporty pair of pants.

When the Practical Joker arrived, however, it was not Callahan but Doc Webster who fixed his wagon.

It was a Friday night, and the place was more crowded than Dollar Day in a cathouse. Fast Eddie was sharing his piano bench with three other guys, Callahan and Tom Hauptman were behind the bar, busier than a midget mountain-climber, and we were plumb out of beer nuts. Me, I was sandwiched between Doc Webster and Noah Gonzalez at the bar, feeling the urgency of hydraulic pressure, wishing there wasn't a wall of folks between me and the jake.

I guess it was the huge number of cars scattered around out in the parking lot that made that sadistic jackass think he'd found the perfect place to pull off his little gag. Come to think on it, maybe Fate was leading him to Callahan's after all.

In any case, he came shouldering through the throng with his two buddies on either side of him at about eleven, and the three of them took up position at the bar just beside the Doc. I noticed them out of the corner of my eye and gaped like a fish with lockjaw. The guy in the middle was plainly and simply the ugliest man I had ever seen.

When they passed out necks he thought they said "sex" and asked for lots and lots. His chin and his Adam's apple looked like twin brothers in bunk beds, his nose appeared to be on sideways, and his eyes were different sizes. His ears were so prominent that from the front he looked like a taxicab coming down the street with the doors open, and his hair resembled a lawn with persistent crabgrass. The longest strands issued from his nostrils. As he reached the bar, the clock over the cashbox stopped, and I couldn't blame it a bit. I forgot about my bladder and gulped the drink I'd been nursing.

The Doc saw my face, swiveled his massive bulk around to look, and damn near dropped his Scotch; you have to understand that the Doc firmly believes in the Irish legend that on Judgment Day you will be suspended head-down in a barrel containing all the liquor you've ever spilled, and if you drown, to Hell with you. Even Callahan shuddered.

The guy glanced at the perfectly ordinary-looking accomplices on either side of him, pulled a fistful of singles from the pocket of his sportscoat, and said, "Boilermakers." The noise of the crowd had begun to abate as folks caught sight of the apparition, and the single word was plainly audible.

Callahan's cigar traveled from one side of his mouth to the other. He shrugged his broad shoulders and produced three shotglasses and three chasers, unable to take his eyes off the guy in the middle.

The three of them lifted their shots, upended them, then did the same with the beers.

"Again," said the ugly man, and Callahan refilled their glasses. The second round went down, if anything, faster than the first.

"Again."

Callahan blinked, shrugged again and made three more boilers. *Gulp-gulp-gulp.*

Now, even in Callahan's Place on a Friday night, amid some of the most dedicated drinkers that ever tried to outdo a sponge, this sort of thing is bound to attract some attention. The silence was nearly complete; some of the boys in the far corners began climbing up on tables and chairs to watch, and there were enough necks being craned to make a chiropractor dizzy with glee. Over at the piano Fast Eddie began a pool, taking bets on how many more rounds the three strangers could survive.

After the sixth set of boilers had been made and unmade, Callahan tried to call a halt. "Sorry, gents. If you want to commit suicide, you'll have to find another joint."

The two flankers nodded, but the ugly man reached into his sports coat pocket again, produced a chopstick, and balanced it on his index finger. "Peter Piper picked a peck of pickled peppers," he said clearly and distinctly. "British constitution. The Leith police dismisseth us. Sister Suzie's sewing shirts for soldiers . . ."

He kept it up until Callahan, exchanging looks with Doc Webster, put another shot in front of him. The guy shut up and gulped the sauce, sent a glass of beer after it, and waited expectantly.

Callahan sighed and opened a fresh bottle, and I could tell from the label that it was the colored water Tom Hauptman drinks when he's working (explaining to anyone who'll listen that "The wages of gin are breath"). I guess the big barkeep figured this mug was too far gone to notice the difference.

But as he reached out to pour, the unlovely customer put his hand over his glass. "Wait a bit," he said faintly, his voice suddenly wavering. "I . . . I don't know. Maybe I . . . oh Lord, I don't feel too good. I think I'm gonna be . . ." He clutched his middle and leaned over the bar, and a ghastly mess splattered on the counter-top.

A great disgusted groan went up, and those of the boys with weak stomachs began to make their way toward the door.

But the *real* stampede began when the hapless stranger's two companions, grinning wildly, produced a pair of spoons and dug in.

I would have bet my store teeth that nothing short of an earth-quake could empty Callahan's Place on a Friday night, but that about did it. Folks fled in all directions, out the front door, the back door, even the *windows,* horror on every face, hideous gargling cries fading into the night.

When the smoke had cleared and the commotion ceased, Calla-han, the Doc, and I were the only survivors, and even the indomi-table Callahan looked green about the gills. Tom was out cold on the floor behind the bar.

And that damned practical joker and his two cronies turned around, looked at the empty saloon, and began laughing hard enough to bust a gut, slapping their thighs and punching each other on the shoulder.

"What the *hell* . . ." I began, and the ugly man, looking fully recovered now, turned to face me, still laughing fit to kill. He pulled open his sports coat, disclosing a hot water bottle pinned over the inside pocket. "Beef stew," he gasped, and his pals began laughing even harder.

Callahan went from pale green to bright red, and his hand went under the bar, emerging with a softball bat.

"No, Mike!" I cried, "Don't! I know how you feel, but there's just a wild chance that some jury somewhere in the world might convict you."

Muscles bulged in his jaw, but he got a grip on himself and lowered the bat. The three waterheads kept on chortling, oblivious.

"All RIGHT, goddamn it," Callahan bellowed. "You've had yer fun. Now get the rest o' this crap off my bar and get outa here before I murder yez." I was startled to notice that Doc was grinning broadly. It didn't figure to be his kind of humor.

The three wits, sensing danger at last, nodded and began spooning up the remains of the stew. In no time the bartop was reasonably clean. The ugly joker offered Callahan a ten-spot for his trouble, and nearly had it for dessert. Still smiling idiotically, they headed for the door and disappeared into the night.

Callahan caught sight of the Doc's grin and glared at him, still furious. "What the hell are *you* laughin' at?" he growled, and the Doc's grin got even wider.

"I saw that gag pulled once before, Mike," he said, "and I recognized it right off."

"So that makes it funny?"

"Hell, no."

"Well then?"

"That guy's stomach must be pretty good to handle all that booze," the Doc said happily, "but I wonder how he and his buddies are gonna like the seasoning I put in the stew while their backs were turned."

The Doc opened his pudgy fist, and there was a little bottle in it, labeled, "serum of ipecac."

Callahan's eyes widened, and then he smiled.

"A VOICE IS HEARD IN RAMAH..."

How should I know?

It was a combination of things, I guess, and no one special reason. For one thing, the place doesn't look like much from the outside. Nor is the interior by any stretch of the imagination romantic—more like a cross between a Chinese firedrill and Tim Finnegan's last party, most nights. But then you can't tell that from the highway either. Whatever the reason, it just sort of turned out that women didn't come into Callahan's Place.

All right, maybe I'm ducking the issue. Maybe there was some kind of masculine aura about the place, a psychic emanation of chauvinist-piggery that kept it a male bastion for so long. Maybe we were extended adolescents, emotionally retarded, projecting a telepathic equivalent of the "No Girls Allowed" sign on Tubby's clubhouse. There's surely no doubt that Callahan's is culturally descended from the grand tradition of Irish bars, and they tend to be misogynistic. Long-Drink McGonnigle's father-in-law, Thirsty O'Toole, assures us that Irishmen go to pubs to get shut of the women.

But I can't really believe there was ever any prejudice intended. Callahan doesn't insist that his customers be *human*. Certainly no effort was ever made to bar women, as happened at McSorley's. But men didn't come to Callahan's Place to meet women, and that may be why the few that chanced to drop in generally left quickly.

Then one night a woman walked in and stayed, and I was real proud of the way the boys acted.

It was a Punday Night, as it happened, a little late in the evening. A perfectly good topic—"trees"—had been worked over for so long that the three surviving contestants, Doc Webster, Tom Flannery, and Long-Drink, were . . . pardon me . . . stumped. Callahan declared all three co-winners and, as custom demanded, refunded their night's tab. But as it was still a bit early we decided to hold a play-off for Grand Pundit, no holds barred, any topic, and the three champions agreed.

Long-Drink led off, his eyes filled with that terrible gleam that presages a true stinker. They call him Long-Drink because he is one long drink of water: when he sits he looks like he's standing, and when he stands he looks like three other guys. He doesn't mass much, and he is the only man I know who can talk and drink whiskey at the same time. He does a lot of both.

"Gentlemen," he drawled, demonstrating the trick, "the story I am about to relate takes place in the distant future. Interstellar travel is commonplace; contacts with alien races are familiar experiences. One day, however, a planet is discovered out Antares way whose sole inhabitant is an enormous humanoid, three miles high and made of granite. At first it is mistaken for an immense statue left by some vanished race of giants, for it squats motionless on a yellow plain, exhibiting no outward sign of life. It has legs, but it never rises to walk on them. It has a mouth, but never eats or speaks. It has what appears to be a perfectly functional brain, the size of a four-story condominium, but the organ lies dormant, electrochemical activity at a standstill. Yet it lives.

"This puzzles the hell out of the scientists, who try everything they can think of to get some sign of life from the behemoth—in vain. It just squats, motionless and seemingly thoughtless, until one day a xenobiologist, frustrated beyond endurance, screams, 'How could evolution give legs, mouth, and brain to a creature that doesn't use them?'

"It happens that he's the first one to ask a direct question in the thing's presence. It rises with a thunderous rumble to its full height, scattering the clouds, thinks for a second, booms, 'IT COULDN'T,' and squats down again.

" '*Migod*,' exclaims the xenobiologist, 'Of course! *It only stands to reason*!' "

There was an extended pause, in which the sound of Long-Drink blinking was plainly audible. Then a hailstorm of glasses, full and empty, burst in the fireplace, loud enough to drown out the great collective groan. Doc Webster's eyes rolled briefly, like loaded dice, and came up snake eyes. Callahan began passing out fresh drinks, a slightly stunned expression on his face.

The Doc contemplated a while, looking a lot like some of the merrier representations of the Buddha. "Bug-eyed punster sort of stuff, eh? Say, did you boys ever hear of the planet where the inhabitants were mobile flowers? Remarkably similar to Earthly blossoms, but they had feet and humanlike intelligence. The whole planet, from the biggest bouquet to the smallest corsage, was ruled over by a king named Richard the Artichoke Heart . . . anyhow, one day a pale-eyed perennial caught Richard's eye at a court orgy, and . . ."

I tuned the Doc out for a second. Fast Eddie, sensing some truly legendary horror in the offing, had stealthily left his piano stool and began edging casually toward the fire extinguisher in the corner, an expression of rapt attention on his monkey face. There's enough of the Doc to make two or three good targets, but I sidled out of the line of fire all the same.

". . . the smitten monarch engaged royal tutors of all sorts, to no avail," the Doc was saying. "Artists, musicians, philosophers, scientists, and mathematicians failed alike to engage the attention of the witless concubine, whose only apparent interest was in gathering pollen. At last the embarrassed Richard gave her up as hopeless and had some Rotenone slipped into her soup. As he exclaimed to this prime minister later that night, 'I can lead a horticulture but I can't make her think!' " The Doc's poker face was perfect.

And in the terrible pause that ensued, before Eddie could trigger the extinguisher, a clear, sweet, contralto voice asked, "What sort of flower was she?" and every head in the place swung toward the door like weathervanes in a windstorm.

And there she was.

*   *   *

She was a big woman, but none of it was extra, and she stood framed in the doorway with an easy grace that a ballerina might have envied. Her hair was long and straight, the color of polished obsidian. Her skin was fair without being pale, and she wore a long-sleeved, high-necked dress of royal purple that brushed sawdust from the floor. She was pretty enough to make a preacher kick a hole in a stained-glass window.

She fielded the combined stares of a couple dozen goggle-eyed males with no effort at all, a half-smile playing at the corners of her mouth, and I had the distinct feeling that we could all have turned into three-headed tree frogs without disturbing her composure in the least. Perhaps that was why our own composure was so manifestly smithereened and scattered to the four winds—but I'm more inclined to think it was the one-two sledgehammer punch of, *A woman in Callahan's?* followed by the equally startling, *Why the hell not?* What shocked us the most was that we had no idea why we should be so shocked. Like opening a ginger ale and finding Jamesons' inside: nothing wrong with it, but it sort of takes you by surprise.

Doc Webster tried unsuccessfully to clear his throat; his poker face was now royally flushed. "I . . . uh," he stammered, "don't know *what* kind of . . . uh . . . flower she was, young lady."

A grin struck red lips back from perfect teeth. "I just thought," she said clearly, "that the king might be suffering from fuchsia shock."

There was a pause, and the soft, subtle sound of eyeballs glazing: you can only absorb so much at once. But Callahan rose magnificently to the occasion.

"Sure and begonia," he breathed.

"Oh," she gasped, and blinked. "Perhaps I shouldn't be here. I didn't realize this was an Iris bar."

Long-Drink choked, spraying Bushmill's like a six-foot-seven aerosol. And suddenly we were all roaring, hooting, rocking with laughter, the kind that leaves your eyes wet and your sides sore. The timbers rang with merriment, a happy release of tension.

"Lord, Lord," the Doc gasped, wiping his eyes and clutching at his ample belly, "nobody's made a straight man out of me in twenty years. Whoooo-ee!" He shook his head ruefully, still chuckling.

"Lady," said Callahan, a world of meaning in the words, "you'll do." There was respect in his whiskey baritone, and a strange, deep satisfaction. She acknowledged the former with a nod and stepped into the room.

The bar had been crowded, but by the time she reached it she had enough room to park a truck, and a wide choice of seats. She picked one and sat gracefully, making a small noise of surprise and delight. "I never thought I'd see an armchair this tall," she said to Callahan, setting her purse on the bar.

"I don't believe in bar stools," Callahan explained. "A man should be comfortable when he drinks."

"A man?" she asked pointedly.

"Oh, a woman ought to be comfortable all the time," he agreed solemnly. "Hey, Eddie?"

"Yeah, boss?"

"You want to open a window? I think I smell bra smoke."

She reddened.

I looked at Eddie, was surprised to see a glare instead of a grin. *Migod*, I thought crazily. *Fast Eddie has been smit*. It didn't seem possible; ever since his wife divorced him a few years back, Eddie had been a confirmed loner.

"Touché," she conceded at last. "I had no call to criticize your speech patterns. I'm sorry."

"No problem," Callahan assured her. "My name's Mike." He stuck out a big calloused hand.

She shook it gravely. "I am Rachel."

"What'll it be, Rachel?"

"Bourbon, please."

Callahan nodded, turned around and began mixing I. W. Harper and ice cubes in the proper proportions. She opened her purse, removed a wallet from it and pulled out a five-dollar bill, and I found that I was talking.

"I'm afraid you can't use that fin in here, Rachel." It felt strange not to be paralyzed.

She turned to me, and I saw her eyes for the first time close up, and I felt my tongue being retied tighter than ever. I don't know how to describe those eyes except to say that they looked impossibly *old*, older than eyes could be. There was some pain in them, sure—most people that Fate leads to Callahan's Place have anguished eyes when they first arrive—but beyond the pain was a kind of unspeakable weariness, a terrible and ancient knowledge that had not brought satisfaction. My memory churned, and produced the only remotely similar pair of eyes I have ever seen: my grandmother, dead of cancer these twenty years.

"I beg your pardon?" she said politely, and I tried hard to climb back up out of her eyes. Tom Flannery sensed my distress and came to my aid.

"Jake's right, Rachel," he said. "Callahan doesn't believe in cash registers either. He only deals in singles."

"You mean everything in the house costs a dollar?" she asked in surprise.

"Oh no," Tom demurred. "Everything in the house costs fifty cents. There's a cigar box full of quarters down there—see?—and you pick up your change on the way out . . . *if* you've left your glass on the bar."

"What's the alternative?" she asked with a puzzled frown, as Callahan set her drink down before her.

"Smash your glass in the fireplace," Callahan said cheerfully. "Does you a world of good sometimes. It's worth fifty cents, easy."

Her whole face brightened. "A long time ago," she said thoughtfully, "I bought an entire house for the single purpose of smashing crockery in it. I think I like your place, Mike."

"That makes two of us," he said comfortably, and poured himself a beer mug of Bushmill's best.

"To Callahan's Place," she said, draining her glass in one easy motion and holding it high. Callahan didn't bat an eye. He inhaled his own whiskey as fast as it'd pour and raised his glass too. Two arms fell as one.

Glass shattered in the fireplace, and a spontaneous cheer went up from all around. Long-Drink McGonnigle began singing, "For She's a Jolly Good Fellow," and was stifled without ceremony.

She turned to face us. "Lots of bars make a woman feel welcome," she said. "This is the first one that ever made me feel *at home*. Thank you all."

Ever see a whole bar blush?

Fast Eddie came in the door—no one had seen him leave—with change of a five from the all-night deli across the street and gave it to her gravely, a solemn look on his wrinkled face. But Callahan refused the single she offered. One exquisite eyebrow rose quizzically.

"Rachel," he said, "this here is Punday Night at my Place, and the champeen punster doesn't have to pay his . . . or her . . . bar bill. From what I've heard already, I'd say you've got a shot at the title."

Her face lit with a merry smile. Callahan explained the format and the subject we were using and built her another drink.

She paused a moment in thought. "The Middle East," she began at last, "finally achieved a kind of uneasy stability in the late 1970's, Israel and the Pan-Arabian nations maintaining a fragile truce. Then one day the Arabian ambassador to Israel, Opinh Bom Bey, chanced to spy a carousel in the market place and, being intrigued by this Westernish recreation, decided to try it. Being a neophyte, he became extremely dizzy, dismounted from his wooden steed with great difficulty, and reeled out of the square. A Chinese shepherd called Ewe Hu was passing through Jerusalem at that time with three fine sheep, and Bom Bey staggered into their midst. The middle sheep promptly ate him.

"Horrific visions of the war that would inevitably ensue racing through his mind, Ewe Hu flung up his hands and cried, 'Middle lamb, you've had a dizzy Bey!' "

There was a ghastly silence, such as must exist on the airless wastes of the moon, and Callahan's ever-present cigar fell from his lips, landing with an absurdly loud splash in his glass. Oblivious, he lifted the glass and drank. When he set it down again, the cigar was back in his teeth, soggy and drooping.

Long-Drink made a face. "You didn't keep to the subject," he complained feebly, and Fast Eddie began to cloud up.

But she stood her ground, deadpan. "The story," she maintained, "was clearly about Zion's friction."

And the silence fell in a million shards, whoops of laughter, blending in with groans and the volley of breaking glass on the hearth.

Tom Flannery entered a forfeit about the same time Long-Drink and the Doc conceded defeat, and that was Rachel's first night at Callahan's Place. She returned on the following night, and then on the following Tuesday, and soon became something of a regular. She was there when Isham and Tanya Latimer got married right in front of the fireplace, and the night the Place caught fire, and that sad night when gentle, softly smiling Tom Flannery finally failed to show up (Tom's doctors had given him nine months to live, the day before he happened into Callahan's Place), and she just seemed to fit. Although she was never by any stretch of the imagination One Of The Boys, she fit in a way that reminded me very faintly of

Wendy in Never-Never Land. She was not disturbed by the hooliganry of her Lost Boys, nor dismayed by their occasional ribaldry—once when Doc Webster, slightly jealous of her superior puns, tried to embarrass her with an off-color joke, she responded with a gag so steamy and so hilarious that the Doc blushed clear down to his ankles and laughed himself silly. And she was incredibly gentle with Fast Eddie, who came to display the classic signs of a man goofy with love. Suddenly all he knew how to play was torch songs, and while she always praised them, she pointedly missed the point, yet somehow allowed him to keep his self-respect.

Curiously, Eddie was the only one of us to fall for her. Certainly, all of us at Callahan's were heir to the tradition of the B-movie—and the A-movie for that matter—that any female who enters your life in a dramatic manner must be your fated love. But somehow Rachel didn't elicit that reflex of imagined desire in us. She was never cold—you retained at all times an impression of vibrant femininity—but she never projected either the air of receptivity which provokes passes, or the studied indifference which is the same thing in disguise. We never even learned much about her, where she lived and that sort of thing. All we knew was that she was fun to be with: she was a note of nearly pure cheer even in a place where good cheer was commonplace.

But only nearly pure. There were those eyes. They reminded me in many ways of Mickey Finn's eyes when he first came around, and I knew it was only a matter of time before the right toast would unlock her heart and let out all that pain. Hell, we all knew it—but she had to do it herself. You don't pry in Callahan's Place.

It was nearly four months before she finally opened up, a Thursday I believe it was. She'd been abstracted lately, still taking part in convivial banter but strangely distant too, and I was half-expecting what happened.

Doc Webster had come bustling in about nine, later than usual for him on a Thursday since he has no hospital duties that night. So he bought a round for the house and explained. If asked, the Doc will assist at home birthings, a practice he's been at some pains to keep from the attention of both the AMA and the Suffolk County Police Department ever since the great Midwife Busts at the Santa Cruz Birth Center a few years back. Doc says that pregnant women aren't sick, that a lady ought to call the tune at her own birthing, all other things being equal—he has oxygen and other useful things in his car, and he hasn't lost one yet.

"She was a primipara," he said with satisfaction, "but her pelvic clearance was adequate, presentation was classic, she did a modified Lamaze, and damned well too. Fine healthy boy, eight pounds and some, sucking like a bilge pump the last I saw him. Lord, I'm thirsty myself."

Somehow news of new life makes you feel just plain good, and the Doc's own joy was contagious. When the last glass had been filled, we all stood up and faced the fireplace. "TO MOTHERHOOD!" we bellowed together, and it rained glasses for a while.

And when the racket had stopped, we heard a sound from inside the joint's single rest room, a literally unmistakable sound.

Rachel. Weeping.

Absurd situation. Over two dozen alarmed and anxious men, accustomed to dropping everything and running to anyone in pain. All of us clustered around the bathroom door (labeled "Folks") like winos outside a soup kitchen, and not one of us with the guts to open up the damned door because *there's a lady in there.* Fast Eddie's ferocious glare would have stopped us if scruples hadn't. Confused and mortally embarrassed, we shuffled our feet and looked for something tactful to say. Inside, the sobbing persisted, muted now.

Callahan coughed. "Rachel?"

She broke off crying. "Y . . . yes?"

"You gonna be long? My back teeth are floatin'."

Pause.

"Not long, Mike. I'll hurry."

"Take your time," he rumbled.

She did, but eventually the door opened and she came out, no tear tracks evident, obviously in control again. Callahan mumbled thanks, glared around at us furiously and went in.

We came to our senses and began bustling aimlessly around the room, looking at anything but Rachel, talking spiritedly. Callahan flushed it almost at once and came back out, looking as innocent as a face like that will let him. He went back behind the bar, dusting his meaty hands.

Rachel was sitting at the bar, staring at where a mirror would be if Callahan believed in encouraging narcissism: plain bare wall criss-crossed with all the epigrams, proverbs, and puns Callahan's found worth recording over the past I-don't-know-how many years of . . . ahem . . . flashing wit. The one she was looking at was attributed to a guy named Robinson. It said: ''A man should live forever or die trying.''

''Women too, I suppose?'' she asked it.

Callahan looked puzzled, and she pointed to the quote. He studied it a minute, then turned back to her.

''You got a better idea?''

She shrugged, held out her hand. The big barkeep filled it with a glass of I. W. Harper and poured one for himself. The sparkling conversation going on around the room seemed to sort of run down. She sipped daintily . . . then said a word I'd never heard her use before and gulped the rest.

Then she rose from her chair and walked to the chalky-line before the fire. The silence was total now.

''To Motherhood,'' she said distinctly, and deep-sixed the glass. It sounded like a shattering heart.

She turned then and looked at us speculatively, trying to decide whether to cut loose of it.

''I've been here over three months,'' she said, ''and in that time I've had a lot of laughs. But I've seen some real pain too, and I've seen you boys help the ones that hurt. That man with one leg; the one whose fiancée entered a nunnery, and was too devout to let himself be sad; the ski instructor who'd gone blind; poor Tom Flannery. I've heard much stranger stories too, and I think if anyone can help me, you can.''

I calculate that by now I must have heard at least a hundred people ask for help of one kind or another in Callahan's—it's that kind of a place. I only remember one getting turned down, and he was a special case. We indicated our willingness to help any way we could, and Fast Eddie fetched her a chair and a fresh drink. She had enough composure back to thank him gently; and then she began talking. During her entire narrative, her voice remained flat, impersonal. As though she were giving a history lesson. Her first words explained why.

''It's a long story,'' she said wearily, ''at least it has been for me. An uncommonly long story. It begins on the day of my birth, which is October 25, 1741.''

''*Huh?*'' said Doc and Long-Drink and I and—loudest of all— Fast Eddie. ''You mean 1941,'' Eddie corrected.

"Who's telling this story? I mean 1741. And if you boys aren't prepared to believe that, maybe I should stop right now."

We thought about it. Compared to some of the things I've heard—and believed—in Callahan's, this was nothing. Come to think, it explained a few things. Those eyes of hers, for instance.

"Sorry, Rachel," Callahan said for all of us. "So you're 232 years old. Go on."

Eddie looked like he'd been hit by a truck. "Sure t'ing," he said bravely. "Sorry I innarupted."

And in the six or seven hours that ensued, Rachel told us the most incredible tale I have ever heard, before or since. I couldn't repeat that tale if I tried; that uncharacteristically impersonal voice seemed to go on forever with its catalog of sorrows, outlining for us the happinesses and heartbreaks of more than two hundred years of active womanhood. You could probably drag it out of me word for word with deep hypnosis, for I never stopped listening, but the sheer length and weight of the narrative seemed to numb my forebrain for indeterminate periods of time; the aggregate memory is largely gone. But different bits and pieces stuck in the minds of each of us, and I compared notes later. Me, for instance, I recall how, when she was describing what it was like to be crammed in a root cellar while a roaring fire overhead ate her first husband—and her first six children—she kept saying over and over again how cramped it was and how frustrating not to be able to straighten up; it struck me that even after all the intervening years her mind continued to dwell on merely physical hurts. Tom Hauptman now, he remembered in detail the business of her second husband, the minister, going mad and killing her next five kids and himself because anyone who refused to age like God intended must be sent by Satan. Tom said what struck him was how little progress churches have made in two hundred years toward convincing people that the unknown is not by definition evil. Long-Drink is a war games nut—he retained the part about the Battle of Lake Champlain in 1814, which claimed her third husband and two more children. Fast Eddie remembers the story of her first days as a whaler's whore in Nantucket because she stopped in the middle and asked him solicitously if she was shocking him. ("Not *me*," he said defiantly, "I'll bet you wuz a *terrific* whore!" and she smiled and thanked him and continued, clinically, dispassionately.) Spud Montgomery recalls the three children that resulted from Rachel's whoring years, because Spud's from Alabama and never stopped fighting the Civil War and that's what they died in. Tommy Janssen remembers her last child, the imbecile, who never did learn to feed himself and took thirty-five long years to die, because Tommy grew up with a retarded sister. Doc Webster's strongest memory is of the final birthing, her first in a hospital, the still-born—after which the OB performed the hysterectomy. Doc identified strongly with the astonishment of a doctor faced with a patient in her late twenties whose uterus had delivered eighteen kids. Callahan characteristically recalls the man she was married to at the time, the first man since her psychotic minister to whom she felt she could tell the truth, with whom she did not have to cosmetically "age" herself, with whom she could share her lonely, terrible secret; the gentle and strangely understanding man who cured her of her self-loathing and self-fear and accepted her for what she inexplicably was; the good and loving man who had been killed, mugged for the dollar and a half in his pocket, a month or two before Rachel found Callahan's Place.

But not one of us retains anything like the complete text of Rachel's story. We wouldn't want to if we could, for condensing it into a comprehensibility would turn it into a soap opera. And, probably, we couldn't if we tried. If somebody gave me a guaranteed-accurate rundown of my own *future* in that kind of depth, I don't think I'd remember much more. It was one king hell mountain of a tale, and it displaced its own weight in alcohol as the hours of its telling dragged by.

Me, I'm thirty-five years old, and I have been there and back again, and when Rachel finished her virtually uninterrupted narration I felt like a five-year-old whose great-grandmother has just recited the Story of Her Life in horrific detail.

In the dead silence that grew from Rachel's last words there just didn't seem to be anything to say to her, no words in all my experience that wouldn't sound banal—like telling a leper that it's always darkest before the dawn. Not that there had been agony in her voice at any time during her recital, nor any on her face when she finished. That was the most ghastly thing about her tale; it was delivered with the impersonal detachment of an historian, recited like the biography of one long dead. You Are There At The Battle of Lake Champlain.

Oh, there was pain aplenty in her story, sure—but so buried, under two centuries of scars, that it could only be inferred. And yet the pain *had* been there earlier, had broken through to the surface for a moment at least, when Rachel had cried. How? Why?

I became peripherally aware of the men of Callahan's Place, arrayed around me with their mouths open. Even Callahan looked pole-axed—and that almost scared me. I glanced around, looking for even one face that held some kind of answer, some kind of consolation, some word for Rachel.

And found one. Fast Eddie's mouth was trembling, but there were words in it struggling to get out. He couldn't seem to bring himself to speak, but he looked like he sure and hell wanted to.

Callahan saw it too. "You look like you got something to say, Eddie," he said gently.

Eddie seemed to reach a decision all at once. Whirling to face Callahan, he jammed his hands in his hip pockets and snarled—snarled!—"Who ast you? I got *nuttin'* to say."

Callahan started, and if I'd had any capacity for shock left I'd have been shocked. *Eddie* barking at Callahan? It was like watching Lassie sink her fangs into Tommy's leg.

"Eddie," Doc Webster began reasonably, "if you have any words that might help Rachel here I think you ought to . . ."

"SHADDAP!" Eddie blared. "I tell ya I got nuttin' ta say, see?"

The silence returned, and stayed a while. We could only surmise that Rachel's tale of sorrow had unhinged the banty little piano player. Creeping Jesus, it had near unhinged me—and I wasn't in love with her. The central issue, then, was still Rachel. Well . . . if Eddie had nothing to say, who did?

Who else?

"So all you have left is immortality, eh Rachel?" Callahan rumbled. "Tough break."

That did seem to put a little perspective on it. Surely Rachel's run of bad luck was due to change soon. It was only logical. "Sure, Rachel," I said, beginning to cheer up. "You're bound to start getting the breaks anytime now."

But it was no good. There was a smile on her face, but not a happy one.

"It figures," Long-Drink said hurriedly. "You can have a run of bad cards that seems to last forever, but sooner or later you pick up your hand and find four aces. It's just the Law of Averages, Rachel. Things always even out in the end."

"Sorry, boys," Rachel said, still smiling sadly. "Nice try. I understand what you're saying—but there are a couple of holes in the logic. Two incorrect assumptions, one of them your mistake and one of them mine."

"What mistakes?" Callahan asked, his rugged face wrinkled in thought.

"Your mistake first, Mike. It's a natural one, I suppose, but it's a mistake just the same. What makes you think I'm immortal?"

"Eh?"

"I'm older than any four of you put together, yes. But longevity is not immortality. Mike, *nothing* is immortal: ask Dorian Gray. My clock runs as slow as his did—but it runs."

"But you . . ."

". . . look a lot younger than 232 years old," she finished. "Right. I look like I'm maybe crowding thirty. But Mike: *what's my natural lifespan?*"

He started to answer, than shut up, looking thoughtful. Who the hell knew?

"Someday I will die," Rachel went on, "just like you, like Tom Flannery. Like all humans; like all living things. I *know* that, I feel it in my bones. And there isn't a geriatrics expert in the world who can say when. There are no data to work with; as far as I know I am unique."

"I reckon you're right," Callahan conceded, "but so what? Anyone in this room could die tomorrow—we're all under sentence of death, like you said. But to stay sane a body just has to live as though they'll go on forever, assume there's a lot of years left. Hellfire, Tom Flannery lived that way, and he *knew* better. Maybe there ain't no way to figure the odds for you—but if I was an insurance salesman, I'd love to have your business. Jake and Long-Drink are right: there's good times around the corner, always, and I bet you live to see 'em.

"I may not be as old as you, Rachel, but there's one thing I've learned in the time I have been around: joy always equals pain in the long run."

She shook her head impatiently and sighed. "The second mistake, Mike. The one that's my fault, in a way. You see, the most spectacular points of the story I've told you all tonight are the bad times, and so it must seem like I've just always been a hard-luck kid. But that's not so at all. I've known happiness too, in full measure, with Jacob and Isaiah and even with Benjamin, and most of all with my second and most beloved Jacob. There were good times in Nantucket if it comes to that, and throughout the whoring years; the profession is vastly underrated. And my joys have been greater, I think, than any of you could know—because you are correct,

Mike: joy is the product of the pain that has gone before it, and vice versa. I know I could never have appreciated Jacob's quiet acceptance as much if I hadn't been looking for it for two centuries.

"Oh, the seesaw never stops, I learned that when Jacob was killed—but then again I was gladder to find this bar than any customer you've ever had."

"Then what . . . I mean, why uh . . . ?"

"Why am I hurting? Hear me, Mike: there is nothing like extended life to make you aware that you're going to die someday. I am more aware of my own mortality than any of you could possibly be. Damn it, I've been dying for two hundred years!

"And how do you, how do normal people come to terms with that awareness of mortality? How do *you* beat death?"

"Oh Lord," the Doc gasped. "I remember now. That toast . . ."

"Yes." Rachel nodded. "The one that gave me the weeps, for the first time in twenty years. 'To Motherhood.' I don't want to see or hear or say anything about motherhood ever again! A man or woman who's afraid of dying will either decide to believe in an afterlife . . . or have children, so that something of himself or herself will live on. I haven't believed in God since my years with Benjamin—and all my babies died childless and I can't have any more! I had nineteen chances at real immortality, and they all came up craps. I'm the last of my line.

"So what will I leave behind me? I haven't the gift to leave great books or paintings or music; I can't build anything; I have no eternal thoughts to leave the world. I've been alive longer than anyone on Earth—and when I'm gone I'll leave *nothing;* nothing more durable than your memories of me."

Her voice had begun to rise shrilly; her hands danced in her lap. "For awhile I had hope, for those of my children who shared my birthmark—an hourglass on its side, high on the left shoulderblade—seemed to have a genetic share in my longevity. But that damned birthmark is a curse, an unbeatable hex. Not one of the marked children had any interest at all in siring or bearing children of their own, and accident or illness cut them down, every one. If even one of them had left a child, I could die happy. But the curse is unbroken," she slammed her fist down on the bar. "When I go I'll be *gone*, solid gone without a trace. Centuries of living, and no heritage more durable than a footprint in the snow!"

*   *   *

She was crying again, her voice strident and anguished, contorted with pain. I could see Eddie, his own face twisting with strong emotion, trying to break in; but now that he wanted to talk she wouldn't let him.

"So what have you got to offer me, boys? What's your solution? Have you got anything more useful than four fingers of bourbon?" She got up and flung her empty glass at the fireplace, began grabbing glasses off the bar and throwing them too, grunting with effort, still speaking: "*What* kind of . . . *an*-swers have you . . . *got* for an . . . *old* old lady who's . . . *trapped* in a moving . . . *box* sliding . . . *downhill* to . . ." She had run out of glasses, and with the last words she gripped the long-legged armchair she'd been sitting on and heaved it high over her head to throw it too into the fire, and as she stood there with the heavy chair held high her face changed, a look of enormous puzzlement smoothing over the hysterical rage.

". . . death?" she finished softly, and crumpled like a rag doll, the chair bouncing and clattering into a corner.

The Doc was fast, and ten feet closer, but Fast Eddie beat him easily. He slid the last yard on his knees, lifted Rachel's head with great tenderness onto his lap, and hollered, "Rachel, *lissen* ta me!" The Doc tried to take her away from him, and Eddie backhanded him off his feet without looking up. "Lissen ta me Rachel, LISSEN goddamn it!" he thundered.

Her eyes fluttered open. "Yes, Eddie."

"Ya can't die, Rachel, not yet. You go and die on me an' I'll break both your arms, I swear to God. Lissen here, *if you want a daughter I can fix it.*"

She smiled, a faint and bitter smile. "Thanks, Eddie, but adoption just isn't the same."

"I ain't talkin' about adoption," he barked. "But I tell ya I can fix it. Ida spoke up sooner, but you said you didn't ever want to think about kids again. Now will ya lissen, or are you too busy dyin'?"

She was teetering on the edge, but I guess curiosity must be a powerful stimulant. "What . . . what do you mean?"

"I'm sterile too, damnit." Our eyes widened a little more at this revelation, and I was suddenly ashamed of how little I knew about Eddie. "But I kept my ears open an' I found out how to beat it, how ta leave somethin' behind, see? Did you ever hear of cloning?"

She looked startled. "You can't clone people, Eddie."

"Not today, you can't. Maybe you an' I won't live to see it

happen, either. But I can take ya inta Manhattan to a place where they'll freeze a slice o' yer skin, a lousy coupla million cells, an' keep 'em on ice till they *can* clone people. Tom Flannery's there now, frozen like a popsicle, waitin' for 'em to invent a cure for AIDS; he tol' me about it.''

I gasped in astonishment; saw Callahan beginning a broad grin.

"So how 'bout it, Rachel?" Eddie snapped. "You want cryonics? Or d'ya just wanna cry?''

She stared at Eddie for a long moment, focusing about five feet past him, and nobody dared exhale. And then two centuries of fighting spirit came through, and she smiled, a genuine smile of acceptance and peace.

"Thank you, Eddie," she breathed. Her eyes became for one timeless instant the eyes of a young girl, the eyes that belonged on that youthful face; and then they closed, and she began to snore softly. Rachel, who mourned for her lost children, and was comforted.

Doc Webster got up off the floor, checked her pulse, and slapped Eddie on the back. "Always a pleasure, *herr doktor*, to assist you in the technique which bears your name," he said jovially, spitting out a tooth. "Your medicine is stronger than mine."

Eddie met his gaze a little awkwardly, started to pick up Rachel's sleeping form, and then paused. "Gimme a hand, will ya, Doc?''

"Sure thing, buddy. We'll take her over to Smithtown General for observation, but I think she'll be OK." Together they lifted her gently and headed for the door.

But Eddie stopped when they reached it and turned toward Callahan, staring at the floor. "Mike," he began. "I . . . Uh . . . what I mean . . .'' The apology just wouldn't come.

Callahan laughed aloud for the sheer joy of it and pegged the stump of his cigar into the fireplace. "You guys," he said, shaking his head. "Always cloning around."

UNNATURAL CAUSES

There's been a lot of noise in the papers lately about the series of seismic shocks that have been recorded over the last few weeks in the unlikeliest places. Quake-predicting is a young art, from what I hear, and an occasional freak disturbance now and again should be no real cause for alarm—but an unpredicted miniquake every day for two or three weeks, spotted all around the globe, culminating in a blockbuster where a quake had no right to be, is bound to cause talk.

The seismologists confess themselves baffled. Some note that none of the quakes took place in a densely populated area, and are somewhat reassured. Some note the uniquely powerful though strictly local intensity of the blasts, and are perturbed. Some note the utter inability of their science to explain the quakes even after the fact, and fear that the end of the world is at hand.

But me—well, from here at the site of the first quake in the series, Suffolk County, Long Island, New York, U.S.A., I've got me a different idea.

*   *   *

If you've been paying attention so far, you probably know what a circus Callahan's Place can be on an ordinary night. Well I'm here to tell you that on holidays like Christmas and New Year's Eve, it becomes something to stagger the imagination. All the stops are pulled out, insanity reigns supreme, and the joint generally resembles a cross between a Shriner's convention and an asylum run by the Marx Brothers.

So perhaps it wasn't surprising that the first quake in the series struck damn near Callahan's Place on Halloween Eve. It certainly couldn't have happened the way it did on any other night.

The place was more packed than even I had ever seen it before, and I've been hanging out at Callahan's for quite a few years now. Added to the usual list of regulars and semi-regulars were a host of old-timers and ex-regulars, some of whom I knew only by reputation and some not at all. As I think I already told you, a lot of Callahan's customers stop needing to drink after they've been around long enough, and not many people in this crazy age enjoy judicious doses of ethanol for its own sake. So they stop showing up, or become more involved with their families, or simply move elsewhere—but holidays somehow draw them all back like chickens to the roost come sundown.

So by nine o'clock Callahan had already had to sweep the shattered glasses out of the fireplace to make way for incoming shipments, leaving Tom Hauptman to cover the bar, and more people were coming in all the time.

Nearly everyone had come in costume, lending a surreal air to a bar that's never been what you'd call mundane. There were four guys in gorilla suits playing poker in the corner, five or six sheeted ghosts doing a shuffle-off-to-Buffalo through the press of the crowd, and seventeen assorted bug-eyed monsters and little green men scattered here and there. I was profoundly glad to see that Eddie had finished his mourning and put away his grief; he had showed up in black-face and the most disheveled suit I'd ever seen, announcing, "I'm Scott Joplin—lookit my rags." Doc Webster had dressed up as Hippocrates and was instantly dubbed "Hippo-Crates" (having been forced to use a tarpaulin for a toga); Long-Drink McGonnigle appeared in an ancient frock-coat with a quill pen in the breast pocket, introducing himself as "Balzac—Balz to you;" Noah Gonzalez and Tommy Janssen had teamed up as a horse with a head at both ends because neither of them wanted to be the . . . aw, you get the idea. Callahan himself was dressed up as a grizzly bear, which suited his huge Irish bulk well, but he kept wincing when jostled, explaining to anyone foolish enough to listen that he was ''a b'ar tender.'' Me, I was dressed as a pirate with a black eye-patch and the name of a certain oil company painted across my chest.

I was watching the tumult and enjoying myself hugely, trying to guess the identity of friends through their masks, when I spotted one very familiar face unmasked.

It was Mickey Finn.

I hadn't seen Finn for quite a spell, since he moved up to the Gaspé Peninsula in Canada to do some farming, and I was delighted to see that he'd made the reunion.

''Finn!'' I hollered over the merry roar. ''This way.''

Another human might not have heard me, but Finn looked up right away, smiled across the room at me, and started working his way toward the bar.

There's some machine in Finn, the way he tells it, but I think there's a lot of human in him too. He could easily have put a hand through the wall, but he was extremely careful not to discommode anyone on his way to the bar. I looked him over as he approached, noted his workshirt, sturdy coveralls, and worn boots, and decided he was making a fair adjustment to his life of exile as a Terran. Wrinkles on either side of his smile said that it was no longer such an alien expression to him as it had once been.

He reached me at last, shook my hand gravely and accepted a glass of rye from Tom Hauptman. He offered Tom the traditional one-dollar bill.

''No thanks, Mr. Finn,'' Tom told him. ''Mike says your money's no good here.''

Finn smiled some more, kept the bill extended. ''Thank you, sir,'' he said in that funny accent of his, ''but I truly prefer to pay my own way.''

I shook my head. ''If you're gonna be human, Finn, you're gonna have to learn to accept gifts,'' I told him.

He sobered up and put away his money, nodding to himself as much as to me. ''Yes. This is a hard learning, my friend. I must not refuse a gift from Mr. Callahan, who gave me the greatest gift— my free will.''

''Hey, Finn, don't take it so hard,'' I said quickly. ''Accepting a gift graciously is something a lot of humans never learn. Why should you be more human than Spiro Agnew?'' I leaned back against the bar and took a sip of Bushmill's. "Come on, loosen up. You're among friends."

Finn looked around, his shoulders relaxing. "Some of these are unfamiliar to me," he said, gesturing toward the crowd.

"Lot's of 'em are strangers to me too," I said. "Let's amble around and get to know some of 'em. But first, tell me what you've been doing with yourself. How's life in Canada?"

"I am doing well," Finn said, "and I am also doing good, I think."

"How do you mean?"

"Jake my friend," Finn said earnestly, "the Gaspé is one of the biggest paradoxes on this continent: some of the richest farmland, and some of the poorest farmers. In addition to making my own living, I have been trying to help them."

"How do you do that?" I asked, interested.

"In small ways," Finn replied. "I see further into the infrared than their eyes can see; I can evaluate soil at a glance and compute yield, evaluate their growing crops much better than they, suggest what to plan for. That taught them to listen to my opinions, and of late I have been speaking of the necessity for alternate means of distributing their goods. It goes slowly—but one day those frozen acres will feed many hungry people, I hope."

"Why, that's just fine, Finn," I said, slapping him on the back. "I knew there was work for a man like you. Come on, let's meet some of the old-timers." Finn, being as tight with his words as some gents are with their money, nodded briefly and we plunged into the thick of the crowd.

I spotted four tables pushed together near the fireplace, at which were seated the Doc, Sam Thayer, and a whole bunch of apparent strangers in assorted odd costumes. Best of all, Callahan was standing nearby—it seemed like a great place to start. I steered Finn in that direction, collecting a couple of chairs on the way and signalling Callahan to join us. When he saw Finn his face lit with pleasure, and he nodded.

As we sat down, one of the unfamiliar gents, dressed as a shepherd, was just finishing a plaintive rendition of "I Know I'll Never Find Another Ewe," and was applauded by a chorus of groans and catcalls.

"Better take it on the lamb, Tony," Doc Webster suggested.

"Where there's a wool, Thayer's away," agreed Sam, rising as if to leave. One of the boys removed his chair with a thoughtful expression, and he sat back down rather farther than he had intended. Callahan lumbered up and appropriated the chair, the head of his bear-costume under his arm, and Sam promptly sat on Bill Gerrity's lap. This is funnier than it sounds, because Bill is a transvestite and was done up as Marilyn Monroe that particular night (while Callahan's is certainly not the only bar where Bill can indulge his peculiarity, it's the only one where he doesn't have to put up with the annoyance of being propositioned regularly—and Bill is *not* gay). As Sam was dressed as Mortimer Snerd, the effect was spectacular, and those around the room not otherwise occupied cheered and whistled. One of the gorillas in the corner looked up from his cards and scowled.

I glanced around the table, taking inventory: a fireman, a five-foot-seven duck, two bug-eyed monsters (one purple and tentacled, one green and furry) and one Conan the Barbarian. "Hey, Mike," I called to Callahan, "introduce me and Finn around and we'll swap stories." Callahan nodded and opened his mouth, but the Doc put a beer in front of it. "I bear beer, bear," he announced, and another groan arose.

"Okay," I said. "I'll start the ball rollin' myself. Howdy folks, I'm Jake. This here's Mickey Finn." Various hellos came from the group, and a pretzel landed in my drink.

"I've heard of you, Mr. Finn," said the shepherd, grinning. "They say you're hell to drink with."

Obviously the shepherd hadn't heard about *this* Mickey Finn, and I glanced at Finn to see how he'd take it. I needn't have worried—apparently he had been hanging around Callahan's Place long enough.

"You'll make me feel sheepish, sir," he said with a straight face, "if you take my name too litter-ally. Very baa-adly indeed, for I would fain have fun with a fine Finn fan."

Callahan and I guffawed, and Doc Webster's jaw dropped. "Lord God," the Doc expostulated, "I'm going to hang up my puns, I swear."

"A hypocritic oath," said the duck, and the Doc heaved a bag of beer nuts at him. "Duck, duck, the Doc," Callahan and I crowed together, and the table broke up.

"Look, Jake," said the shepherd when the commotion had died down, "what you said about swapping stories sounds good to me. As we introduce ourselves, let's explain what brought us here to Callahan's. I know some of you boys must have stories I'd like to hear—nobody seems to come here without a reason. What do you say?''

We all looked around. "Suits." "Okay by me." "Why not?" There was no apparent reluctance—Callahan's is the place you went to first because you needed to talk about your troubles—and the first time is always the hardest. "Fine," said the shepherd. "I guess I ought to start." He took a glass, filled it up and wetted his whistle. He was about my age, with odd streaks of white hair on either temple that combined with his classical shepherd's garb made him look like a young Homer. His features were handsome and his build excellent, but I noted with surprise that his left earlobe was missing. There was a scar on his right shoulder, nearly hidden by a deep tan, that looked like it had been put there with a crosscut saw.

"My name is Tony Telasco," he said when he had swallowed. "I give lectures and slide shows and make speeches, and sometimes I go to jail, but I used to do a lot of things before I came to Callahan's. I was a transcendental meditator for awhile, staring at my navel. Before that I was a junkie, and before that I was a drunk and before that I was a killer. That was right after I was a kid.

"See, the thing I *really* am is a Vietnam veteran."

There were low whistles and exclamations all around.

I was in my first year of college (Tony went on) when I got that magic piece of paper from my draft board. Business Ad majors just weren't getting deferments, and so I had the classic three choices: go to jail, Canada, or Vietnam.

Which wasn't a lot of choice. Make no mistake, I was scared spitless of Vietnam—I watched television. But I was scared and ashamed to go to jail, and scared and incompetent to emigrate. To be brought into a strange country to fight would be tough, but to move into one myself and make a living with no skills and no degree looked impossible to me.

So 'Nam seemed to be the lesser of three evils. I never made a moral decision about the war, never questioned whether going there was the right thing to do. *It was the easiest.* Oh, I knew a few guys who went to Canada, but I never really understood them—I liked America. And I knew one fellow in my English class who went to jail for refusing to step forward—but his third day there they found him on the end of his bedsheet, a few inches off the floor, his cellmate apparently asleep.

And so I found myself in the Army. Basic was tough, but tolerable; I'd always liked physical exercise, and I was in pretty good shape to start with. It was a lot rougher on my mind.

The best friend I made in Basic was a guy named Steve McConnell, from California. Steve was a good joe, the kind of guy really good to have with you in a rugged situation like Basic. He had a knack for pointing out the idiocies of military life, and a huge capacity for enjoying them. Kind of a dry sense of humor—he didn't laugh out loud, in fact he hardly ever laughed *aloud*, but he was perpetually amused by things that drove me crazy. Like me, he'd sort of drifted into the Army, but the more he thought about the idea, the less he liked it. Neither did I, but I didn't see anything I could do about it. We spent hours peeling potatoes together, discussing war and women and the Army and women and the Communist Menace in Southeast Asia and women and our D.I. Steve was an independent thinker—he didn't hang out with the other blacks in our outfit, who had cliqued up in self-protection. That can be tough for a black man in the U.S. Army, but Steve cut his own path, and chose his brothers by other criteria than the shade they were painted. I don't know why he and I were so tight—I don't know what his criteria were—but somehow we were so close I got the idea I really knew him, understood where he was at.

I was as surprised as anyone when he finally made his stand.

There comes a day, see, when they line you up on a god-awful cold February morning and truck up a couple of coffin-sized cartons. The D.I.'s are clearly more pretentious than usual, projecting the air that something sacred is about to happen. By Army standards they're right.

What happens is, you get to the head of the line and throw out your hands and one huge mother of a sergeant flings a rifle at you as hard as he can—you've been Issued Your Rifle, and mister, God have mercy on you if you drop it, or fumble your catch and let part of it touch the ground. Worse than calling it a "gun." A few guys do catch copper-plated hell for having fingers too frozen to clutch, and you spend your time on line furiously flexing your fingers and praying to God you won't blow it.

Steve was right in front of me in line, and curiously withdrawn; I couldn't get a rise out of him with even the sourest joke. I chalked it up to the cold and the solemnity of the occasion, and I guess I was part right.

All at once it was his turn and the big sergeant selected a rifle and pressed it to his chest and straightarmed it with a bit extra oomph because he was from Alabama and I prayed Steve would field it okay and he just simply side-stepped.

It was just like that: one rushing second and then time stopped. Steve pulled to his left and the rifle cartwheeled past him and struck earth barrel-first, *sank* a motherloving three inches into the mud, the stock brushing my knee. All around the parade ground people stopped cursing and joking and stared, stared at that damned M-1 quivering in the mud like a branch planted by an idiot, stared and waited for the sky to fall.

The big sergeant got redder than February wind could account for and swelled up like a toad, groping for an obscenity that could contain his fury. As he found it, Steve spoke up in the mildest voice I ever heard.

"I'm sorry, sergeant," he said, "but I can't take that rifle."

I thought the sergeant might actually have apoplexy. "That is the weapon I have issued you, *boy,* and you *will* take it! Get it out of the mud, now!"

Steve shook his head calmly. "Can't do it. That thing kills people, sergeant, and I do not accept delivery."

The sergeant suddenly became just as calm as Steve, a scary transition to witness. He pulled his sidearm and aimed it directly at Steve's navel. "This thing kills too, *private*. Pick up that rifle."

I looked at Steve, paralyzed by his crazy stunt. He was plainly scared to death, and I was as sure as he that he was about to die. *Pick it up, Steve*, I prayed. *You don't have to use it now, just pick the goddamned thing up.*

"Sergeant," he said finally, "you can make me pick it up, but you can't *ever* make me use it. Not even with that automatic. So what's the point?"

The sergeant glared at him a long moment, then holstered his .45 and waved over a couple of corporals. "Take this goddamn nigger to the guardhouse," he snarled, and bent over the carton again. Before I had time to think he heaved a rifle at me, and I made a perfect catch. "Next!" he bellowed, and the line moved forward. I found myself in barracks, looking at my new rifle and wondering why Steve had done such a crazy thing.

I went off to 'Nam soon after that—tried to get word to Steve in the stockade, but it couldn't be done. He got left behind with the rest of America, and I found myself in a jungle full of unfriendly strangers. It was bad—real bad—and I began to think a lot about

Steve and the choice he had made. I couldn't tell the people I was fighting from the people I was fighting for, and the official policy of "kill what moves" didn't satisfy me.

At first. Then one day a twelve-year-old boy as cute as Dondi took off my left earlobe with a machete while I got some K-rations out of my pack for him. The kid would have taken off my head instead of my ear, but a pretty tight buddy of mine, Sean Reilly, shot him in the belly while he was winding up.

"Christ, Tony," Sean said when he'd made sure the kid was dead, "you know the word: never turn your back on a gook."

I was too busy with my bleeding ear to reply, but I was coming to agree with him. Just as 'Nam had been easier than jail, catching the rifle easier than refusing to, killing gooks was easier than discussing political philosophy with them.

A week later it got to be more than easy.

Sean's squad had been sent upriver to reconnoiter, while the rest of us got our breath back for the big push. I was on sentry duty with a fellow whose name I misremember—not a bad guy, but he smoked marijuana, and I'd been raised to think that stuff was evil. Anyway this particular day he smoked a couple of joints while we sat there listening to jungle sounds and waiting for relief so we could eat. It made him thirsty, so I offered to spell him while he went to the river for a drink. He slipped into the jungle, walking a little unsteadily.

A minute later I heard him scream.

It was only fifty yards or so to the river, but I came circumspectly, expecting to find him dead and the enemy in strength. But when I poked my rifle through the foliage, there was nobody in sight but him. He was on his knees with his face buried in his hands. *Oh Jesus*, I thought, *what a time to freak out*. I started to swear at him, and then I saw what he had seen.

It was Sean, floating lazily against the bank with his fingers and toes dangling from a sort of necklace around his throat and his genitals sewed into his mouth.

A friend, a man who had saved my life, a guy who wanted to be an artist when he got home, carved up like a Christmas turkey by a bunch of slant-eye monkeys—it became much more than easy to kill gooks.

It became fun.

The rest of my tour passed in a red haze. I remember raping women, I remember clubbing a baby's skull with a rifle butt to encourage a VC sympathizer to talk, I remember torturing captured prisoners and enjoying it. I remember a dozen little My Lais, and I remember me in the middle with a smile like a wolf. Fury tasted better than confusion, and this time it was easier to *kill* than to think.

I don't know what would have happened to me if I'd come home kill-crazy like that. God knows what happened to the ones that did. But two weeks before I was due to go home I got a letter from a friend in the States, a supply corporal back at boot camp.

Steve McConnell had died in military prison. He "fell down the stairs" and broke nearly every bone in his body, but it was the ruptured spleen that killed him. There had been no inquiry; the official verdict was "accidental death." As accidental as Sean's—except our side did it.

In the time it took me to read that letter I went from kill-crazy all the way to the other kind, and the next morning I took my squad out and tried to die and loused it up and got my second Purple Heart and Silver Star. I never got another chance in 'Nam; they sent me home from the hospital with some neat embroidery on this seam on my shoulder and a piece of paper that said I was a normal human being again.

Killing myself just didn't seem as reasonable in the States as it had in 'Nam somehow, so I tried forgetting instead. For a while booze did the trick, but I couldn't keep it up; my stomach wouldn't tolerate the dosage required. Then for a while pot was a real help, but some ways made it worse: visions of spurting blood and Sean's fingers and Steve boneless like a Jell-o man. So I tried a hit of coke, and that was just fine, and one day a spade who looked a lot like Steve laid some smack on me. Heroin was just what I'd been looking for, and it wasn't any surprise when I got a jones, a habit I mean.

But it's funny . . . I guess I really *didn't* want to kill myself at all. I heard about this transcendental meditation stuff and started hanging around Ananda Marga Yoga Society meetings, and boy, I kicked clean. Instead of getting high on smack, I got high on big bites of bliss, which is cheaper, healthier, legal, and a much more satisfactory head all the way around.

It was over a year before I noticed I wasn't accomplishing anything.

But about that time I got lucky and took my Doctor Webster's advice and started coming to Callahan's Place. Things started getting clearer in my head, a lot clearer. Next thing I knew, I was on a stage giving a speech to the VVAW, and I learned that there are things worth fighting and fighting for—but fighting clean. I started giving talks and joining demonstrations and appearing on TV. I've been arrested four times, had my leg broken by a county cop, and they took my name off the Native Sons Honor Roll in my home town. My father won't talk to me—yet—and my phone is tapped.

I feel great.

". . . and it's all thanks to you, Mr. Callahan," Tony finished.

"Shucks, Tony," Callahan rumbled, "we didn't do anything for you that you couldn't have done yourself."

"You accepted me," Telasco said simply. "You made me understand that I was just a normal human being who'd been caught up in a nightmare, a nightmare that made him realize he had the makings of a killer ape in him. One night I told you and your customers this whole story and you didn't stare at me like a mad dog. You told me that I needed a bigger audience.

"You showed me that it wasn't my killer nature that was shameful, but the refusal to think things out that landed me in 'Nam in the first place. You showed me that just because it took me a while to make the sort of decision Steve made didn't mean that I didn't have Steve's kind of guts in me somewhere. I was sure I didn't have that kind of guts, and so I never looked for them. When I did . . . I found them. Because you had faith in me.

"Jail is no picnic," he told the rest of us, "but I want to do what I can to see that no one else gets caught in the meatgrinder like I did. But I don't do it from guilt. I do it for its own sake." He looked at Callahan. "I already got my absolution here."

Callahan topped off his glass and slapped him on the back. "Well spoke, Tony," he boomed, and we all raised our glasses and toasted him in unison. The fireplace exploded with glass when we were through.

"I knew it," said the Doc, "as soon as I saw him dressed as a shepherd I *knew* he had to be a vet." Groans arose, but the comic relief was timely.

"If you don't pipe down some, Doc, he won't be the only hoarse doctor around here," Callahan attempted.

"Now, now," said the Doc. "I'm a happily married man. I don't fool around with hoarse in either of our professional capacities."

I started to ask if the Doc's capacities were truly professional, but before I could, Mickey Finn grabbed Callahan's shoulder so hard he winced—something nobody else could have managed.

"My friend Mike," Finn said urgently, "That person there, in the green costume—it is not a costume. He is not human."

Callahan blinked, and such jaws as were visible dropped like gallows trapdoors. If anyone but Finn had said that—anywhere but Callahan's Place—we'd have thought he was crazy or drunk.

"I see further into the infrared range than you humans," Finn went on hurriedly. "I was watching the currents of heat from the fireplace make patterns in the air while I listened to your words, enjoying their lazy beauty . . . but I just caught the green one watching them too. Close examination shows me that his fur and features are genuine. Friends, this is an alien."

We all stared at the green fellow, waiting for him to take off his mask and say something. He *looked* human enough—the usual number of arms and legs, I mean. His mouth was a trifle too wide, now that I noticed, and the fur sure looked awful real. If those pointed, oversized ears were glued on, I couldn't see where.

He looked back at us, put down his glass and shrugged knobby, tufted shoulders. "There is no point in denying it, gentlemen. I am not human. In fact, I came here tonight specifically to tell you how unhuman I am. The words I have heard encouraged me to confess, but still I . . . hesitated. However, now that I have been identified by another non-human, I suppose I must speak. Will you listen?"

Callahan spoke for all of us. "Mister, if you've got troubles, you're in the right place. Go ahead."

The green alien nodded. His eyes were deeply troubled.

"My name, gentlemen," he said in a pleasing tenor, "is Brood-seven-Sub-Two Raksha, as well as it can be translated into your tongue. I am . . . well, the profession does not really exist as such here, but my function combines elements of sociologist, psychologist, soldier, and farmer. My people are the Krundai, and Krundar my home is located so far from here that your instruments have not yet detected its sun. There are several dozen Krundai on your planet, a team which has been here for over two thousand years . . . a team of which I am the least member." He paused, looked embarrassed.

"What are you fellers doin' here?" Callahan asked.

"That," said the alien hesitantly, "is what I have come here to tell you. It is . . . it is not an easy thing to tell. I have spent almost thirty of your years formulating my opinions in words and seeking someone to whom to speak them. Fifteen of those years sufficed to eliminate as confidantes all of my fellow Krundai; for another ten I debated whether I could conceivably unburden myself to a human. Unable to resolve the question, I spent the last five years picking those humans in whom I *might* confide. I found on your planet a total of only two or three thousand humans who I felt might be able to understand and help, and thirty-five of those are now present in this room.

"All of you at this table are such."

We looked around at each other, wondering whether we were all special or just crazy in the same way. I sure didn't feel special.

"Even now," Raksha went on, "I have not entirely resolved my debate. My decision is much like that of Mr. Telasco, but it is further complicated in that it could involve betraying my entire race. The presence of Mr. Finn, whom I find to be, as he says, as non-human as myself, complicates things considerably—although I suspect his origins may better enable him to empathize with me."

He faced Finn. "Space holds many viewpoints, Finn. You seem to be a traveler, of broader experience than these ephemerals. Will you try to understand me?"

Finn looked him square in the eye. "I will listen."

Raksha didn't seem to care much for that answer, but he nodded. He turned to us. "Will you . . . all of you . . . swear that no word of what I tell you will reach my fellow Krundai? I must warn you that confiding in other humans would accomplish this thing."

This time there was no more need for us to look around than there was for all of us to speak. "Every man at this table can keep his lip buttoned," Callahan said simply. "Speak your piece."

The green furry alien looked us all over one last time, one after the other, beginning and ending with Callahan. As his eyes met mine, I noticed for the first time that the surfaces of them rippled with faintly glistening semicircular lines, just like the one you look for when you're pouring coffee into a dark cup. They shifted position in a different way than the specks on a human eyeball do, independent of the motion of the eyes themselves. They scared the hell out of me somehow, more than the fur and the ears did.

He reached his decision.

"Yes, gentlemen, you are right. Come what may, I must speak. If I can be helped by any one, of any race, it is you. Brood help me if you cannot."

I grabbed a pitcher and got half of it down before Bill and Sam snatched it away.

"I must begin," the alien went on, "by explaining to you some central facts about my people.

"First, we live much, much longer than humans. An average Krundai sees his three-thousandth birthday before returning to the Great Pouch, and some have lived as much as five or six centuries longer. I myself am well over eight hundred years old, and I am the youngest Krundai on your world, having been born here."

"That explains how you know our language and idiom so well," I interrupted.

"My four immediate ancestors had a hand in its creation," Raksha said drily.

I shut up.

"Second, as you may well imagine, we are a very patient people, by your standards. Even allowing for the difference in our respective life spans, we move in much less haste than you, and plan projects in terms of how many of our generations they will require to complete. Our concern is for the continuing life of the race, rather than our individual lives, as the Broodmaster has decreed.

"Third, we have an ingrained loathing for killing or violence."

That cheered me quite a bit, although I don't think I was really scared with Finn around. That guy could maybe use this Earth to light a cigar with if he had a mind to. Besides, if the Krundai had intended us harm, it seemed to me they'd have done so centuries ago.

"We realize," Raksha went on, "that such things must be: the prime datum of the Universe is that life survives by eating life, and no other way. The expense of eating is, in great part, the resistance the second life offers to being eaten. For instance, the roast beef sandwiches you have provided for your friends, Mr. Callahan (and by the way they are easily the thickest I have ever seen in a tavern) are currently quite expensive, because of the size and unwieldiness of the system required to supply them to us.

"Suppose you could induce the cow to come here and drop obligingly dead next to your chopping block?

"Still, there are always some who prefer not to do their own butchering. No Krundai will do so voluntarily if it can be avoided. A surprising percentage of your own society, with all your heritage of murder, would like to believe that Life survives by going to the supermarket. So the ideal would be to train cattle to make butcher knives and take turns cutting each other up at a convenient location."

I didn't like the turn this story was taking.

"Which brings me to the fourth significant fact about my people. We have made an exact science of sociopsychology, both Krundai and animal, and refined it beyond your imagining. The closest things you have to it, I suppose, are what you call mob psychology and the actuarial tables your insurance companies use, and you do not even know why they work. The principles behind them, however, are universal, and part of a grand picture which your race will probably never perceive. One of your great writers invented something akin to it called 'psychohistory,' but even that unfulfilled daydream pales beside our knowledge—for psychohistory worked only for humans, and could not predict the appearance of genius or mutation. We can manipulate any sentient race that lives, produce geniuses to order by manipulating society's laboratory conditions; and the nature and causation of mutation are fundamentals of Krundai psychology.

"Of course, like psychohistory, our science works best in the mass, imperfectly with regard to individuals. You humans are at least aware of that supreme paradox—that free will exists to an extent for the individual, but disappears in the group—although you can't work with it. Brood!—you haven't even learned how to measure emotion yet. But we can predict the effects of even one man's *actions* on the society as a whole . . . and we know how to bring about the effects we desire, large scale or small, long run or short.

"Which leaves only one more basic attribute of my people: we are very, very hungry."

I had a ghastly feeling I knew what was coming next, and I didn't like it. The horrible suspicion that Raksha's words were building in my brain answered far too many questions I'd never been satisfactorily able to explain to myself before.

"So that's how that guy got elected," Callahan breathed, and I winced.

"Precisely," Raksha agreed. "You begin to understand why I am here."

"Lay it out, brother," Tony said grimly. "I think I get it, but I hope I'm wrong."

Raksha spread his hands. "Very simply, gentlemen, for nearly two thousand years your planet has been a Krundai game preserve."

"God bless my soul," said Doc Webster. I looked at Callahan: his face was expressionless, but his eyes were like coals. Tomorrow that table would have inch-deep fingerprints where Finn was holding it.

"For most of that time," Raksha continued, "the Krundai stationed here made no attempt to do more than control your population, inhibit your social evolution, and enforce your ignorance. A war here, a philosophical revolution there, discredit a few thinkers and discourage a line of inquiry or two: elementary maintenance. Rome, for instance, got entirely too civilized—even assassinating Caesar didn't help enough. Before long it began to look like they were developing a rudimentary medical science and cutting down the mortality rate.

"So we induced cultural decay, and added some hungry barbarians we found conveniently at hand. An earlier stroke of genius, supplying them with the notion of lead-based waterpipes and wine vats, paid off handsomely, and the threat was ended.

"We went on in this manner for hundreds of years, allowing just enough growth to preserve vigor and letting you graze freely. We had quite a bit of trouble with plagues—frankly, you're not very clean animals—and finally we decided to let you play with medicine as a simpler solution than running around stamping out an epidemic every few years. There was always war to use as a control and culling device, and anyway, there was plenty of pasture.

"About three hundred years ago, we were notified by Krundar to go into active status and step up production. A food shortage had been predicted, and we were told to expect at any time the order to begin harvesting the herd we had bred and tended so long. We began incubating North America.

"We tripled the usual propaganda to reproduce, filled the continent in an absurdly short time, and encouraged immigration with a massive word-of-mouth advertising campaign about the golden land across the sea, where freedom rang and the streets were paved with gold. It took a bit of finagling to keep Britain from flattening you at the start, but we were in—for us—a hurry. After the requisite wars, we lowered the death-rate considerably to compensate, and began to intensify our efforts.

"A hundred years ago, we received the last command. We have been preparing you to slaughter yourselves ever since."

"Holy Jesus, it figures," Bill Gerrity cried.

"You bet your sweet life it figures," I snarled. "After thousands of years of recorded history, in seventy-five years we go from the Model-T Ford to the cobalt bomb and the energy crisis. From corn liquor to Quaaludes. From young giant of a nation to tired old fraud. From . . .''

"Knock it off, Jake," Callahan rapped.

I shut my face. Callahan turned back to Raksha, put his huge meaty hands palm down on the table. "Go on," he said darkly.

The Krundai's fur bristled, and his eyes rolled in his head. Somehow through my rage I understood that this denoted extreme shame in one of his race, and began to cool off, remembering where I was. The air of calm he had worn was shattered now; he was clearly agitated.

"Humans, hear me!" he intoned. "Hear my sins, hear the full catalog of my infamy before you judge. *This is not easy to tell, and I must.*"

"Let him speak," Finn said dispassionately.

"We . . . I and others, I mean . . . instituted an explosive increase of knowledge in the physical sciences, smothered or subverted all the social and spiritual sciences. We cranked your technology to a fever pitch of frenzied production, led you to build yourselves a suicidal ethic and culture, gave you toys like the atom bomb and lysergic acid to play with: we gave a loaded gun to an infant. We manipulated elections and revolutions, staged assassinations, encouraged government to calcify beyond the ability of its people to endure, touched off riots, provided you with news media that would carry the news of growing cancer among you, and did all we could to bring into the minds of men a frustration and a terror that would lead inevitably to chaos. You, the steers, are nearly ready to butcher yourselves for our tables."

"I don't believe it," the man in the fireman costume burst out. "This is crazy, what you're saying is crazy, just plain nuts. What the hell is this anyway, some kind of a rib?"

"He's serious, Jerry," Callahan said calmly.

"The hell he's serious, Mike, did you hear what he said? You telling me you believe all this stuff?"

"Jerry's right," the duck said. "This guy's nuts."

"Oh, you fools!" Raksha burst out. "Are you too ignorant to see the pattern? Your whole history makes sense only by positing the four most far-fetched twistings and contradictions to human nature. Use Occam's Razor, by the Brood. Could any race be so suicidal and have lived for this long? Do you really think it accidental that your people went from outhouses to zero-gravity toilets in half a century? From the *Merrimac* to Skylab in one short century? By our own standards we have turned your planet upside down in a twinkling—are your lives so short that you have not perceived their acceleration? The pace of progress yanks you ahead faster than you can run. Do you not *notice?*''

Callahan looked across the crowded, oblivious room to Tom Hauptman behind the bar. ''Some of us notice,'' he said softly.

The fireman shook his head. ''I don't buy it. That sounds like some crazy sci-fi notion. Conspiracy of aliens my foot, I don't believe in little . . .''

''. . . green men?'' Raksha finished. ''The signs are everywhere around you, Jerry. But look beyond the physical evidence: do you believe it blind chance that physics has leaped vast spans while psychology muddled off into blind alleys? Do you really believe man is so incurious about himself that it has taken him thousands of years to even begin a science of sociology? Do you think it simply bad luck that the technology of your survival systems; of your food and water and power distribution networks, consistently fail to keep pace with population increase and are already strained to the failing point, even in the face of a technical revolution?

''Does it make sense that after living side by side with natural drugs and hallucinogens of all types for millennia, men have suddenly become dependent on them? Has the worldwide depression, economic and spiritual, escaped you? Does it not surprise you that no language spoken by any people on Earth corresponds with observable reality? Did you think the simultaneous collapse of an ages-old ethical system and a two-century-old value system to be mere unfortunate happenstance? You Broodless fool, *did you really think God died of natural causes?*

''No, my friend. Charles Fort was quite correct: you are property, and on the whole not very bright property. You follow your political and philosophical leaders blindly to the slaughter, grateful to be led, and one in a hundred of you is a Telasco or a McConnell, with the sense to pull out of the mad death-race. You *must* see it, man,'' he said to Telasco, ''you rejected the world we Krundai made for you.''

''Jerry,'' I said, ''one of my most precious possessions is a lapel button, white with black letters. It says 'Go Lemmings Go.' Raksha is telling the truth.''

The fireman shook his head like an enraged bull. ''This is crazy,'' he insisted. ''How can you be telling us all this? I mean, if you're right, what makes you think we won't tear you to pieces?''

"This is Callahan's Place," the alien said simply. "I am here for absolution."

That brought us all up short, even Jerry. He stiffened; his mouth opened but there were no words in it.

"Why?" cried Doc Webster in agony. "How could a race so old and wise be so savage and murderous?"

"We are *not*," Raksha returned, agony in his own voice. "You kill animals for food—we ourselves have never killed."

"People are not animals," Tony said with quiet force.

"To my people you *are*," insisted the green one. "You lack a ... an attribute for which there are naturally no words in your tongue. That attribute is central to the Krundai; without it, even if you went to the Great Pouch at the end of your days, you could not suck. To us you are less-than-Krundai. The Sign of the Brood is not upon you: you are food. My people feel no more guilt over engineering your destruction than you would if you could talk a cow into butchering itself."

"Why all this dancing around?" Callahan asked him. "Why not just wipe us out? Sounds to me like you've got the moxie."

"I have told you," Raksha cried. "We abhor violence. The fact that you can be induced to inflict it upon yourselves, is, to us, proof that you are food, less-than-Krundai. If you and other races did not spare us the necessity, we should be forced to kill our own food like beasts. But the Great Brood saw our needs and fashioned the lesser races to breed and feast upon, without the need to nurture violence in our own hearts. First the winged, heat-seeking *fleegh* of Krundar, which fell from the skies into our fires; then the blue-skinned ones of our neighbor planet, who destroyed their atmosphere just before they developed interplanetary travel; then the Krill from a nearby solar system, who warred to extinction among themselves. It has always been so; it is unforgivably bad form to slay one's own meat oneself. It indicates that one is not in the favor of the Brood."

"When did your people begin sort of ... *encouraging* the food into the pot?" Callahan asked.

"So long ago that it would be meaningless to you," Raksha told him. "We learned early that the gifts of the Brood are not free; we must labor for them, to earn a place in the Pouch."

"I still don't see how you could have done it," Jerry said, baffled but obviously believing now, convinced by the pain in the furry alien's voice and the aura of shame around him.

"In the same way that a statesman can be induced to do what he knows is insane," Raksha explained, "by appealing subtly to his own self-interest. We ran a continuous and subtle propaganda campaign, took away any valid reason for living other than personal enrichment and comfort, and then saw to it that the immediate personal interest of millions of people served our ends. One of the simplest methods was to install in an enormous number of people the compulsion to amass more money than they could possibly use: enough were successful to leech national economies into anemia. Another was to whip up an intense interest in sex, far beyond the demands of nature, to keep population-growth beyond your capacity to adapt. Much work was required to squelch interest in space-programs before they could provide an escape valve. You humans are so shortsighted, your lives themselves so short. It is easy to manipulate you."

"So what changed your mind?" Callahan asked. "You personally, I mean. If we ain't fit for this here Pouch, why are you spilling the beans?"

"I . . . I . . ." he stammered.

"We're nothing but dumb animals, right? Well, Colonel Sanders doesn't apologize to the chickens—*why are you here?*"

The green man groped for words, his pointed ears waving nervously.

"I . . . I don't know," he said at last. "I cannot satisfactorily explain it to myself. There is a climate of belief which runs all through your thought and literature, a conviction that you humans have a higher destiny. This idea has been of use to the Krundai many times, but we did not plant it; it was there when we came. It may be that it is contagious. I do not know; there is something about you humans, a . . . a curious dignity that upsets my heart and troubles my nights."

Finn spoke up, startling me. "I think I know what you mean, friend Raksha," he said in that flat voice of his. "Michael," he went on, turning to Callahan, "do not be so certain that Colonel Sanders does not apologize to his chickens, as you put it. I have myself brought about the extermination of several races, in the days when I served the Masters, and yet last week when I slaughtered my pigs, I grieved for them. They were stupid and dirty and mute—but even a pig may have dignity.

"They did not, could not, comprehend why they died—and yet in an irrational way I wished I could explain it to them." He turned, spoke again to the furry Krundai. "I believe I understand your motivation," he said. "I felt it too, once, and forebore to destroy this world. It seemed a planet of madmen—although much of that appears to be the doing of you and yours. But I knew that not, for you were well-hidden.

"Yet still I stayed the hands of my Masters, betrayed my purpose, because I learned here in this room that men have love."

"That is the quality I selected for in a human audience," Raksha admitted. "The thing you call love we Krundai had always found to be a symptom of the attribute I spoke of earlier. That humans possess the symptom without the attribute is one of the great anomalies that complicated my thought and delayed my confession until now."

"This propaganda stuff you talked about," Callahan persisted. "I still want to know how you put it across. Whisper in the Wright Brothers' ear? Write newspaper editorials? Spead rumors?"

"Sometimes," Raksha said, and hesitated. His features assumed a deeper green. "And sometimes," he went on with obvious reluctance, "by direct intervention."

"Disguised as humans, you mean? Fifth column and that?" The big Irishman seemed to be prompting, seeking something from Raksha that I couldn't figure out.

"All the Krundai on your world have, at one time or another, impersonated humans for varying reasons. One of us was Saul of Tarsus, another Torquemada, another Thomas Edison. Otto Hahn was yet another."

"And you," Callahan bored on implacably. "Who were *you*?"

I remembered suddenly how long ago Raksha had said he began to regret his job, and my blood went cold as ice.

"I . . ." he said, biting the words off with an effort, "I was known to men as Adolph Hitler."

The silence was a living thing that gnawed at our reason, paralyzed our thought. All around us a Halloween party continued insanely, heedless men laughing and dancing, the four gorillas in the corner playing poker. There was not a damn thing any of us could say, and after a time Raksha went on listlessly, "It was an easy role to play. It took no significant fraction of the training I had received in crowd control. It was so easy that I had time to think, to observe, to learn firsthand what I was doing.

"Perhaps it was because I was born here, and have seen Krundar only once. For whatever reason, I began to doubt; subconscious uncertainty spoiled my work. The major purpose of that campaign was to prolong hostilities long enough to force the development of atomic weapons, and I nearly succeeded in aborting the mission by folding too quickly. But my colleagues were able to redeem my error by drawing out the Pacific conflict just long enough. I told myself my depression was the stigma of personal failure, but I knew in my heart that it was in fact the repair of my mistakes that unsettled me. I have thought on it long and hard since, and now I am here and I have spoken."

Doc Webster produced a hip flask from somewhere on the south slope of his belly, upended it, and slapped it down empty. On all sides of us, people drank and chattered and laughed, oblivious to the drama in their midst.

The Doc found his voice someplace; it sounded rusty.

"What do you want from us?" he croaked.

"Absolution."

I looked at Tony and Jerry and Finn, winced as I thought for the first time in months of my dead wife and child, killed years ago in a crash when the brakes I installed myself to save a buck failed in traffic. This was the place for absolution, all right—it was Callahan's stock in trade. And this seemed like our greatest challenge.

The brawny Irishman's voice shocked me when he spoke: it was as cold and hard as an axe-handle in February. "That word has another word in it," he said. "Solution. First let's find a solution, and then absolution will take care of itself. How can you stop this pogrom?"

Raksha's fur bristled; he looked flustered. "I cannot," he wailed.

"Can't you talk your people out of this?" Sam Thayer asked. "Won't they listen to you?"

"Impossible," the alien said flatly. "They could not conceivably understand my words . . . I am not sure I do myself. Have vegetarians made any real impact on your planet?"

"They have wherever they could convince folks that a cow might have a soul," the Doc asserted.

"But you *do not have the attribute*," Raksha insisted.

"I don't know what the hell this 'attribute' is," Callahan growled, "but I get the idea we have the potential for it; the symptoms, I believe you said. Could it be we never developed it because our people have been under the . . . protection of yours since our infancy?''

''No Krundai would believe that,'' Raksha replied. ''If I voiced such an opinion, I would be judged insane and induced to suicide.''

''Can you sabotage the campaign?'' Telasco asked. ''Join our side and do the guerrilla? With you to help we might . . .''

''*No*,'' Raksha said violently. ''I cannot betray my people. It is unthinkable.''

''It was unthinkable for me once,'' Tony persisted. ''But when I saw what I had become, I repudiated what my people were doing, worked to stop it.''

''Me too,'' Jerry chimed in.

''You do not understand,'' Raksha hissed. ''You are *not-Krundai*—and this Finn may belong to a powerful, warlike race for all I know. I have committed an unthinkable crime by relying on your discretion and telling you all this—I can do no more.''

Tony had a soldier's tactical mind. ''Can you tell us where and how to locate your people? *We'll* stop them.''

Finn spoke up before Raksha could answer. ''That is not . . .''

''Possible,'' Callahan finished quickly, and I got the funny idea he'd kicked Finn's shin under the table. ''If these boys led us by the hand to the atom bomb, there ain't a lot we can do to stop 'em, Tony.''

''But . . . ouch,'' said Finn, and shut up.

''No,'' Callahan went on, ''if anyone can help us, Raksha, it's you. Or did you just fall by to make a headsman's apology?''

''I can do nothing for you,'' Raksha said miserably. ''I seek only absolution.''

''Brother,'' I said sympathetically, ''you're caught between a falling rock and a hard place.'' Sam and the Doc also began to make noises of commiseration, and Bill Gerrity started to ask Raksha what he was drinking. Just the men of Callahan's, offering understanding and help, as always.

But Callahan raised a hand. ''No,'' he said quietly.

We stared at him, stunned. *Callahan* withholding absolution?

''You can't drink in my bar, brother,'' he said, staring Raksha in the eye, ''and you can't have our forgiveness. There's a price for absolution on this planet, and it's called penance. Tony here gets arrested for joining demonstrations; Jerry has chucked away a potful of money he was making in real estate and started lobbying for greenbelts and cluster housing; Finn here exiled himself among a lot of obnoxious, smelly humans for the sake of the ones worth saving. Buddhist monks who couldn't influence their governments any other way set themselves on *fire*, by Christ, and for their souls I pray on Sunday. What do *you* figure to do for atonement?''

Raksha closed his eyes—they were double-nictitating—and knotted his brow. He was silent for a long time.

"There is nothing I can do," he said at last, his voice hollow and bleak.

"Then there is no absolution for you," Callahan said flatly, "here or anywhere. Get out o' my joint and don't come back."

Raksha's face fell, and for a timeless moment I thought he was going to cry, or whatever Krundai do that's like crying. But he got a hold of himself, nodded once, rose and left the bar, shouldering party-people aside as he went.

There was another silence when he had gone, and we all looked at Callahan. His jaw was set, and his eyes flashed, challenging us to criticize his judgment.

"Were . . . weren't you a little harsh on the guy, Mike?" Doc Webster asked after a while.

"Hell, Doc," Callahan exploded, "that clown was Adolph Hitler! You want me to pat him on the head and say *it's all right, you were only following orders?* Christ on a minibike, if it wasn't for him and his kind, I might not have to run this goddamned bar. And my bunions give me the dickens."

"I grieve for him," Finn said tonelessly. "I too was once in a similar position."

"Save your grief, Finn," Callahan spat. "You had the same choice, but you followed through. And you weren't gutless—you were *counterprogrammed*. If you could figure out a way around the sheer physical limitations of your machinery, why the hell couldn't he overcome his conditioning? Conditioning isn't an excuse, for Krundai any more than for humans—it's an explanation. Thanks to you and the work you're doing, the Gaspé Peninsula may be prosperous farmland some day. You're still paying your dues. But that guy didn't want to atone, just apologize. He and his kind made this sorry old world what it is today, and maybe I could forgive that. But I don't give absolution free. It costs, costs you right in the old will power, and he wasn't willing to ante up. Fuck him, and the horse he rode in on."

"I still think we should have jollied him along and tried to pump him, Mike,'' Tony said insistently. ''How are we going to find them to stop them now?''

Callahan looked tired. ''As Finn started to say before I tromped on his toes, that ain't necessary. Now Finn knows they're here, he can find 'em for us as easy as you could spot a wolf in a chicken coop. That wasn't the prob—''

There came a shattering roar from outside. The building rocked; glass sprayed inward from the windows and bottles danced behind the bar. Everyone began to shout at once, and most of the boys made a beeline for the door.

Only Callahan of all of us failed to jump. ''Like I said, no guts,'' he said softly.

He rose quietly, walked through the suddenly uncrowded bar to the chalk line before the fireplace, picking up someone's drink as he went. He looked surreally absurd in that damned bear suit he still had on, balding red head sticking out the top like a partially digested meal. He stood gazing into the flames for a moment, gulped the raw liquor and spoke in a clear, resonant baritone.

''To cowardice,'' he said, and flung the empty glass against the back wall of the fireplace with a savageness I had never seen in him before.

Fast Eddie stuck his head in the door. ''Jeezis Christ, boss, de whole unprintable parkin' lot blew up.''

''I know, Eddie,'' Callahan said gently. ''Thanks. Anybody hurt?''

Eddie scratched his head. ''I don't t'ink so,'' he allowed, ''but dere's a lotta dead cars.''

''Least of my worries,'' Callahan assured him. ''Call the cops, will you? Tell 'em whatever you like.'' Eddie got busy on the phone.

Callahan came back to our table, stood over Finn. ''Well, buddy, what do you say? Can you take 'em?''

Finn looked up at him for a while, figuring some things.

''That blast was powerful, Michael. They must have strong defenses.''

''That's why I stepped on your toes and let that joker go, Mickey. If you two tangled in here, we'd have lost a lot more'n a few cars we can't gas anyway. But you heard what he said about violence.''

''They abhor it,'' Finn agreed. ''Even if they will employ it in self-defense, they are unused to it. Michael, I can take them. I will.''

He rose and left the bar.

"Thanks, Mickey," Callahan called after him. "I reckon your dues are paid in full."

There's been a lot of noise in the papers lately about the series of seismic shocks that have been recorded over the past few weeks in the unlikeliest places. An unpredicted miniquake every day or two for three weeks, culminating in a blockbuster where no quake had a right to be, is bound to cause talk.

The seismologists confess themselves baffled. Some note that none of the quakes took place in a densely populated area, and are reassured. Some note the uniquely powerful though strictly local intensity of the shocks, and are perturbed. Some note the utter inability of their science to explain the quakes even after the fact, and fear the end of the world is at hand.

But me and some of the boys at Callahan's Place suspect it's more like the beginning.

THE WONDERFUL CONSPIRACY

I used to think that almost anything could happen at Callahan's Place. It wasn't long before I realized the truth: that anything can happen at Callahan's Place . . . and not long after that it was made clear to me that *anything* can happen at Callahan's.

But I confess I was still surprised the night I learned that A*N*Y*T*H*I*N*G can happen at Callahan's Place—and that, sooner or later, it probably will.

It was New Year's Eve, a natural time for introspection I guess. The Place was virtually empty, for the first time in a long while. Now that might strike you as downright implausible, but it's just another one of the inexplicable eccentricities of Callahan's that stop startling you after you've been hanging out there awhile. You see, the kind of folks that come in there regularly, if they've got families, tend to spend New Year's Eve with 'em at home.

It's that kind of crowd.

There are, of course, a handful who don't have families, and aren't willing to settle for the surrogate of a date, so Callahan stays open—but I'm sure he runs a net loss. This particular New Year's Eve, the entire congregation consisted of him, me, Fast Eddie, the Doc, and Long-Drink McGonnigle.

Funny. You take men who already consider themselves deep and true friends: they've been drinking together regularly for many years, have experienced some memorable moments in each other's company, have given each other an awful lot. And yet somehow, on a night when there's just a few of them, there because they have no better place to be, such men can find an even deeper level of sharing; can, perhaps, truly become brothers. At such times they relax the shoulders of their souls, and turn their collective attention to those profound questions that can overawe a man alone. They bring out their utterly true selves. We shared a rich plane of awareness that night, Callahan behind the bar and the rest of us sitting together in front of it, lost in the glow of that special kind of intimacy that drink and good company bring, looking back over the year gone by and talking of nothing in general and everything in particular. What we were doing, we were telling dumb puns.

It started when Callahan taped over the cash box a hand-lettered sign that read, "the buck stops *here*."

"Oh boy," rumbled the Doc, "I can see there'll be no quarter given tonight."—which is a pun because he chucked his glass into the fireplace as he said it, which meant the cigar box at the end of the bar held at least two quarters that *he* wouldn't be given tonight.

Long-Drink got up and walked to the chalk line, and I assumed he wanted to give Doc's stinker the honor of a formal throw. I should have known he was setting us up. He toed the mark, announced, "To the poor corpuscle," drained his glass, and waited.

The Doc had reflexively drained the fresh glass Callahan had already supplied unasked—Doc will drink to *any*thing, sight unseen—but he paused with his arm in midthrow. "Wait a minute," he said. "Why the hell should I drink to 'the poor corpuscle'?"

"He labors in vein," Long-Drink said simply.

"Ah yes," I said without missing a beat, "but he vessels vhile he vorks."

"Plasma soul," exclaimed Callahan.

The Doc's eyes got round and his jaw hung down. "By God," he said at last, "I've never been outpunned by you rummies yet, and I'm not about to go down on *medical* puns. As a doctor I happen to know for certain there's only one other blood pun—I got it straight from the Auricle of Delphi."

There was an extended pause, and I was saying to myself, yep, as usual, no one can top the Doc—when all of a sudden Fast Eddie spoke up. Now you have to understand that while he's a genius at the piano, lightning wit has never been Eddie's strong suit; I don't think I'd ever heard him attempt a pun in the presence of so many masters.

But he opened his mouth and said with the nearest thing to a straight face he owns, "Well I dunno about youse guys, but anemia drink."

And even *then* he was not done, because while the Doc spluttered and the rest of us roared, Callahan quietly went into the gag that— unknown to us—Eddie had worked out with him before the rest of us arrived. Instead of Eddie's usual shot, the barkeep *mixed* him a drink, and served it with a wooden *chopstick* jutting out of the glass.

"What the hell kind of a drink is that?" Doc Webster demanded grumpily. And Eddie delivered it magnificently.

"A hickory dacquiri, Doc."

And the laughter of a mere three of us nearly blew out the windows.

The Doc was a good sport about it. In fact, he laughed so hard at himself that he lost three shirt buttons. But you could tell he was severely shaken: he paid for the next round. I felt as though I'd just seen a bulldozer do a tapdance myself. *The world is full of surprises*, I told myself.

Callahan put it even more succinctly. "It's a miracle," he whooped, setting up fresh glasses. "A genuine damn miracle."

Long-Drink snorted. "Miracles are a dime a dozen in this joint."

"You know, Drink," I said suddenly, "you said a mouthful."

"Hah?"

"Miracles. That's Mike's stock-in-trade. This is the place where nothing is impossible."

"Horse feathers," Callahan said.

"No, I'm serious, Mike. I can think of half a dozen things that've happened in here in the past year that I wouldn't have believed for a minute if they'd happened anywhere else."

"*That's* sure true enough," the Doc said thoughtfully. "Little green men . . . *two* time-travelers . . . Adolph Hitler . . ."

"That's not exactly what I mean, Doc," I interrupted. "Those things're highly improbable, but if they could happen here, they could happen anywhere. What I mean is that, barring Raksha, every one of those jokers that walked in cryin' walked out smilin'—and even *he* could have, if he'd been willing to pay the freight. By me, that's a miracle."

"I don't getcha," said Eddie, wrinkling up his face. Even more, I mean.

"Take that business of Jim and Paul MacDonald. Near as I can see, they represent the basic miracle of Callahan's Place, the greatest lesson this joint has taught us."

"What's dat?"

"That there's nothing in the human heart or mind, no place no matter how twisted or secret, that can't be endured—if you have someone to share it with. That's what this place is all about: helping people to open up whatever cabinets in their heads hold their most dangerous secrets, and let 'em out. If you've got a hurt and I've got a hurt and we share 'em, some-crazy-how or other we each end up with less than half a hurt apiece." I took a sip of Bushmill's. "That's what Callahan's Place has to offer—and as far as I know, there's no place like it in all the world."

"I know one place kinda like it," Long-Drink said suddenly.

"What? Where?"

"Oh, I don't know that you'd spot the resemblance right off—*I* sure didn't. But did any o' you guys ever hear of The Farm?"

"I was raised on one," the Doc said.

"We know—in the barn," Long-Drink said drily. "I ain't talking' about *a* farm. I mean *The* Farm—place down in Tennessee. Better'n eight hundred people livin' on a couple o' thousand acres. One of 'em's my daughter Anne, an' I went down to visit her last month."

"One of them communes?" the Doc asked skeptically.

"Not like I ever heard of," Long-Drink told him. "They ain't got no house brand o' religion, for one thing—Anne still goes to Mass on Sundays. For another thing, them folks *work*. They feed themselves, an' they build their own houses, an' they take care of business. The heaviest drug I saw down there was pot, and they wasn't using that for recreation—said it was a sacrament."

"Tennessee," I said, and whistled. "They must get a hard time from the locals."

"Not on your tintype. The locals love 'em. I spoke with the Lewis County sheriff, and he said if everybody was as decent and truthful and hard-working as The Farm folk, he'd be out of a job. I tell you, I went down there loaded for bear, ready to argue Annie into givin' up her foolishness and comin' on home. Instead I almost forgot to leave."

"So what's all that got to do with this joint?" Callahan asked.

"Well, it's like Jake was sayin' about sharing, Mike. Them folks share everything they got, an' the only rule I noticed was that a body that was hurtin' some way was everybody's number one priority. They . . ." He paused, looked thoughtful. "They *care* about each other. Eight hundred people, and they care about each other—and the—whole damn world too. That kind of thing's been out of style since Flower Power wilted."

"Aw nuts," the Doc exclaimed. "Another one of them fool nut cults is what it sounds like to me. They never last."

"I dunno," Long Drink disagreed. "They been goin' for about five years now, and they just started setting up colonies, like. 'Satellite Farms' they call 'em, better'n half a dozen, all over the country." He paused, looking thoughtful. "What got me, though, was how little attention they paid to their physical growth. That just seemed to happen by itself, while they put their real attention on the Main Game: gettin' straight with each other, so's they could live together. Seems to me like the whole world oughta be doin' that. Seems like if you be a better person, you have you a better life. Seemed to me like The Farm was Callahan's Place for hippies."

"You're crazy," the Doc burst out. "Sure, there's a thousand ham-headed gurus creepin' out from under every burning bush these days. The old-time religion went into the drink, so they're scratching for a new one like hungry hens, goin' in for mysticism and the occult and astrology and the late God only knows what-all. But I'm *damned* if I see the resemblance between a Jesus-freak revival meeting and this here bar."

"Doc, Doc," I said softly, "Slow down a bit. Yes, they're mass-producing religions like popcorn these days, and some of them are as plain silly as the sixteen-year-old perfect goombah with his divine Maserati and his sacred ulcer. But that don't make 'em *all* crazy. The point is that all them conmen must be filling *some* kind of powerful need, or they'd be working some more profitable grift. And I think I agree with Long-Drink: the need they're filling is the same one that brings folks to Callahan's Place."

"Hmmph," the Doc snorted. "And what need is that, pray tell?"

"It's pretty easy to see. For the last century or two we turned our attention to the physical world, to mastering the material plane at the expense of anything else. A lot of that, I'm compelled to believe, had to do with Raksha and his kind, but the tendency was there to exploit. And so we've got a world in which physical miracles are commonplace—and nobody's happy. We got what it takes to feed the whole three billion of us—and half of us are starving. You can show a dozen guys murderin' each other on TV but you can't ever show two people making love. A naked blade is reckoned to be less obscene than a naked woman. Ain't it about time we started trying to get a handle on love, *from any and all directions?*

"I don't know how come this Farm doesn't collapse like all the other communes. I don't know how come a government with the best propaganda machine ever built failed to sell a war to a country, for the first time in history. I don't know how come three or four guys managed to pull down a corrupt thug of a president. I don't even understand how come all the things this here bar stands for haven't been drowned under a sea of the drunks and brawlers and hookers and hoodlums every other bar gets, why the only people that seem to come here are the ones that need to, that ought to, that have to. *That's* the real miracle of this joint, you know, not our telepaths and little green men!

"I can't explain any of this stuff, Doc, but couldn't it be that there's some kind of new force loose on the world, like a collective-unconscious response to Raksha and the Krundai, a new kind of energy that's trying to put us all back on the right track before it's too late? Couldn't it be that, now we've climbed out on a material-plane limb and started sawing at it, some mysterious force is trying to teach us how to fly? Whether it's our own stupidity or Krundai manipulation, we've stumbled across things that make a cobalt bomb look harmless: the human race is an idiot child in an arsenal. Couldn't it possibly be that under all these pressures, we're *beginning* to grow up?"

"Dat's what I loined from Rachel," Fast Eddie spoke up suddenly, startling me—I was so wrapped up in my own eloquence, I'd even forgotten my customary drawl and folksy speech-patterns.

"What do you mean, Eddie?" Callahan asked.

"Everybody's got roots in de past," Eddie explained. "But dey's got roots in de future too."

There was an awed silence. "I'll be damned," Callahan said after awhile. "That's twice in one night you've surprised me, Eddie. I never thought there was anything but music in that head o' yours. Guess even I can learn something in this joint." He shook his head and poured himself another shot.

Long-Drink tried to lighten the mood some. "I'll teach you something, Mike. What do you get when you put milk of magnesia in a glass of vodka?''

The Doc made a face. "Everybody knows that one: a Phillips screwdriver. The hell with that stuff: I want to hear more about this 'collective-unconscious' jazz.''

Long-Drink grinned. "Sounds like this place to a T.''

"Can it, I said. That 'mysterious force' stuff you were talkin' about, Jake—did you mean that literally?''

I thought about it. "You mean like a gang of sixth-column missionaries, Doc? A bunch of guys working undercover like Raksha an' his friends, only in reverse? No, I don't really think that's the way of it . . . *wups!*''

Reaching for my glass without looking, I knocked it skittering across the bar, and leaped to grab it before it could fall into Callahan's lap. I froze for a moment, leaning half-over the bar—but I've always rather prided myself in being quick on the uptake.

". . . on the other hand," I continued calmly, "maybe that's exactly right. Who knows?''

And Callahan—who was still sitting as I had seen him, his legs folded under him in the full lotus, suspended a good three feet off the floor—winked, poured my glass brimful of Bushmill's, and grinned.

"Not me,''. he lied, and puffed on his cigar.

"Hey youse guys," cried Eddie, eyes on the clock above us, "Happy New Year!''

PART II

From
TIME TRAVELERS STRICTLY CASH

This one's for Jim Baen, of course.

FIVESIGHT

I know what the exact date was, of course, but I can't see that it would matter to you. Say it was just another Saturday night at Callahan's Place.

Which is to say that the joint was merry as hell, as usual. Over in the corner Fast Eddie sat in joyous combat with Eubie Blake's old rag "Tricky Fingers," and a crowd had gathered around the piano to cheer him on. It is a demonically difficult rag, which Eubie wrote for the specific purpose of humiliating his competitors, and Eddie takes a crack at it maybe once or twice a year. He was playing it with his whole body, grinning like a murderer and spraying sweat in all directions. The onlookers fed him energy in the form of whoops and rebel yells, and one of the unlikely miracles about Callahan's Place is that no one claps along with Eddie's music who cannot keep time. All across the rest of the tavern people whirled and danced, laughing because they could not make their feet move one fourth as fast as Eddie's hands. Behind the bar Callahan danced with himself, and bottles danced with each other on the shelves behind him. I sat stock-still in front of the bar, clutched my third drink in fifteen minutes, and concentrated on not bursting into tears.

Doc Webster caught me at it. You would not think that a man

navigating that much mass around a crowded room could spare attention for anything else; furthermore, he was dancing with Josie Bauer, who is enough to hold anyone's attention. She is very pretty and limber enough to kick a man standing behind her in the eye. But the Doc has a built-in compass for pain; when his eyes fell on mine, they stayed there.

His *other* professional gift is for tact and delicacy. He did not glance at the calendar, he did not pause in his dance, he did not so much as frown. But I knew that he knew.

Then the dance whirled him away. I spun my chair around to the bar and gulped whiskey. Eddie brought "Tricky Fingers" to a triumphant conclusion, hammering that final chord home with both hands, and his howl of pure glee was audible even over the roar of applause that rose from the whole crew at once. Many glasses hit the fireplace together, and happy conversation began everywhere. I finished my drink. For the hundredth time I was grateful that Callahan keeps no mirror behind his bar: behind me, I knew, Doc Webster would be whispering in various ears, unobtrusively passing the word, and I didn't want to see it.

"Hit me again, Mike," I called out.

"Half a sec, Jake," Callahan boomed cheerily. He finished drawing a pitcher of beer, stuck a straw into it, and passed it across to Long-Drink McGonnigle, who ferried it to Eddie. The big barkeep ambled my way, running damp hands through his thinning red hair. "Beer?"

I produced a very authentic-looking grin. "Irish again."

Callahan looked ever so slightly pained and rubbed his big broken nose. "I'll have to have your keys, Jake."

The expression *one too many* has only a limited meaning at Callahan's Place. Mike operates on the assumption that his customers are grown-ups—he'll keep on serving you for as long as you can stand up and order 'em intelligibly. But no one drunk drives home from Callahan's. When he decides you've reached your limit, you have to surrender your car keys to keep on drinking, then let Pyotr—who drinks only ginger ale—drive you home when you fold.

"British constitution," I tried experimentally. "The lethal policeman dismisseth us. Peter Pepper packed his pipe with paraquat . . ."

Mike kept his big hand out for the keys. "I've heard you sing 'Shiny Stockings' blind drunk without a single syllabobble, Jake."

"Damn it," I began, and stopped. "Make it a beer, Mike."

He nodded and brought me a Löwenbräu dark. "How about a toast?"

I glanced at him sharply. There was a toast that I urgently wanted to make, to have behind me for another year. "Maybe later."

"Sure. Hey, *Drink!* How about a toast around here?"

Long-Drink looked up from across the room. "I'm your man." The conversation began to abate as he threaded his way through the crowd to the chalk line on the floor and stood facing the deep brick fireplace. He is considerably taller than somewhat, and he towered over everyone. He waited until he had our attention.

"Ladies and gentlemen and regular customers," he said then, "you may find this difficult to believe, but in my youth I was known far and wide as a jackass." This brought a spirited response, which he endured stoically. "My only passion in life, back in my college days, was grossing people out. I considered it a holy mission, and I had a whole crew of other jackasses to tell me I was just terrific. I would type long letters onto a roll of toilet paper, smear mustard on the last square, then roll it back up and mail it in a box. I kept a dead mouse in my pocket at all times. I streaked Town Hall in 1952. I loved to see eyes glaze. And I regret to confess that I concentrated mostly on ladies, because they were the easiest to gross out. Foul Phil, they called me in them days. I'll tell you what cured me." He wet his whistle, confident of our attention.

"The only trouble with a reputation for crudeness is that sooner or later you run short of unsuspecting victims. So you look for new faces. One day I'm at a party off campus, and I notice a young lady I've never seen before, a pretty little thing in an off-the-shoulder blouse. *Oboy,* I sez to myself, *fresh blood! What'll I do?* I've got the mouse in one pocket, the rectal-thermometer swizzle stick in the other, but she looks so virginal and innocent I decide the hell with subtlety, I'll try a direct approach. So I walk over to where she's sittin' talkin' to Petey LeFave on a little couch. I come up behind her, like, upzip me trousers, out with me instrument, and lay it across her shoulder."

There were some howls of outrage, from the men as much as from the women, and some giggles, from the women as much as from the men. "Well, I said I was a jackass," the Drink said, and we all applauded.

"No reaction whatsoever do I get from her," he went on, dropping into his fake brogue. "People grinnin' or growlin' all round the room just like here, Petey's eyes poppin', but this lady gives no sign that she's aware of me presence atall, atall. I kinda wiggle it a bit, and not a glance does she give me. Finally I can't stand it. 'Hey,' I sez, tappin' her other shoulder and pointing, 'what do you think *this* is?' And she takes a leisurely look. Then she looks me in the eye and says, 'It's something like a man's penis, only smaller.' ''

An explosion of laughter and applause filled the room.

"... wherefore," continued Long-Drink, "I propose a toast: to me youth, and may God save me from a relapse." And the cheers overcame the laughter as he gulped his drink and flung the glass into the fireplace. I nearly grinned myself.

"My turn," Tommy Janssen called out, and the Drink made way for him at the chalk line. Tommy's probably the youngest of the regulars; I'd put him at just about twenty-one. His hair is even longer than mine, but he keeps his face mowed.

"This happened to me just last week. I went into the city for a party, and I left it too late, and it was the *wrong* neighborhood of New York for a civilian to be in at that time of night, right? A dreadful error! Never been so scared in my life. I'm walking on tippy-toe, looking in every doorway I pass and trying to look insolvent, and the burning question in my mind is, 'Are the crosstown buses still running?' Because if they are, I can catch one a block away that'll take me to bright lights and safety—but I've forgotten how late the crosstown bus keeps running in this part of town. It's my only hope. I keep on walking, scared as hell. And when I get to the bus stop, there, leaning up against a mailbox, is the biggest, meanest-looking, ugliest, *blackest* man I have ever seen in my life. Head shaved, three days' worth of beard, big scar on his face, hands in his pockets.''

Not a sound in the joint.

"So the essential thing is not to let them know you're scared. I put a big grin on my face, and I walk right up to him, and I stammer, 'Uh . . . crosstown bus run all night long?' And the fella goes . . .'' Tommy mimed a ferocious-looking giant with his hands in his pockets. Then suddenly he yanked them out, clapped them rhythmically, and sang, ''*Doo*-dah, *doo*-dah!''

The whole bar dissolved in laughter.

"... fella whipped out a joint, and we both got high while we waited for the bus," he went on, and the laughter redoubled. Tommy finished his beer and cocked the empty. "So my toast is to prejudice,'' he finished, and pegged the glass square into the hearth, and the laughter became a standing ovation. Isham Latimer, who is the exact color of recording tape, came over and gave Tommy a beer, a grin, and some skin.

Suddenly I thought I understood something, and it filled me with shame.

Perhaps in my self-involvement I was wrong. I had not seen the Doc communicate in any way with Long-Drink or Tommy, nor had the toasters seemed to notice me at all. But all at once it seemed suspicious that both men, both proud men, had picked tonight to stand up and uncharacteristically tell egg-on-my-face anecdotes. Damn Doc Webster! I had been trying so hard to keep my pain off my face, so determined to get my toast made and get home without bringing my friends down.

Or was I, with the egotism of the wounded, reading too much into a couple of good anecdotes well told? I wanted to hear the next toast. I turned around to set my beer down so I could prop my face up on both fists, and was stunned out of my self-involvement, and was further ashamed.

It was inconceivable that I could have sat next to her for five minutes without noticing her—anywhere in the world, let alone at Callahan's Place.

I worked the night shift in a hospital once, pushing a broom. The only new faces you see are the ones they wheel into Emergency. There are two basic ways people react facially to mortal agony. The first kind smiles a lot, slightly apologetically, thanks everyone elaborately for small favors, extravagantly praises the hospital and its every employee. The face is animated, trying to ensure that the last impression it leaves before going under the knife is of a helluva nice person whom it would be a shame to lose. The second kind is absolutely blank-faced, so utterly wrapped up in wondering whether he's dying that he has no attention left for working the switches and levers of the face—or so *certain* of death that the perpetual dialogue people conduct with their faces has ceased to interest him. It's not the *total* deanimation of a corpse's face, but it's not far from it.

Her face was of the second type. I suppose it could have been cancer or some such, but somehow I knew her pain was not physical. I was just as sure that it might be fatal. I was so shocked I violated the prime rule of Callahan's Place without even thinking about it. "Good God, lady," I blurted, "What's the *matter?*"

Her head turned toward me with such elaborate care that I knew her car keys must be in the coffee can behind the bar. Her eyes took awhile focusing on me, but when they did, there was no one looking out of them. She enunciated her words.

"Is it to me to whom you are referring?"

She was not especially pretty, not particularly well dressed, her hair cut wrong for her face and in need of brushing. She was a normal person, in other words, save that her face was uninhabited, and somehow I could not take my eyes off her. It was not the pain— I *wanted* to take my eyes from that—it was something else.

It was necessary to get her attention. "Nothing, nothing, just wanted to tell you your hair's on fire."

She nodded. "Think nothing of it." She turned back to her screwdriver and started to take a sip and sprayed it all over the counter. She shrieked on the inhale, dropped the glass, and flung her hands at her hair.

Conversation stopped all over the house.

She whirled on me, ready to achieve total fury at the slightest sign of a smile, and I debated giving her that release but decided she could not afford the energy it would cost her. "I'm truly, truly sorry," I said at once, "but a minute ago you weren't here and now you are, and that's the way I wanted it."

Callahan was there, his big knuckly hand resting light as lint on my shoulder. His expression was mournful. "Prying, Jake? You?"

"That's up to her, Mike," I said, holding her eyes.

"What you *talkin'* about?" she asked.

"Lady," I said, "there's so much pain on your face I just have to ask you, How come? If you don't want to tell me, then I'm prying."

She blinked. "And if you are?"

"The little guy with a face like a foot who has by now tiptoed up behind me will brush his blackjack across my occiput, and I'll wake up tomorrow with the same kind of head you're gonna have. Right, Eddie?"

"Dat's right, Jake," the piano man's voice came from just behind me.

She shook her head dizzily, then looked around at friendly, attentive faces. "What the *hell* kind of place is this?"

Usually we prefer to let newcomers figure that out for themselves, but I couldn't wait that long. "This is Callahan's. Most joints the barkeep listens to your troubles, but we happen to love this one so much that we all share his load. This is the place you found because you needed to." I gave it everything I had.

She looked around again, searching faces. I saw her look for the prurience of the accident spectator and not find it; then I saw her look again for compassion and find it. She turned back to me and looked me over carefully. I tried to look gentle, trustworthy, understanding, wise, and strong. I wanted to be more than I was for her. "He's not prying, Eddie," she said at last. "Sure, I'll tell you people. You're not going to believe it anyway. Innkeeper, gimme coffee, light and sweet."

She picked somebody's empty from the bar, got down unsteadily from her chair, and walked with great care to the chalk line. "You people like toasts? I'll give you a toast. To fivesight," she said, and whipped her glass so hard she nearly fell. It smashed in the geometrical center of the fireplace, and residual alcohol made the flames ripple through the spectrum.

I made a small sound.

By the time she had regained her balance, young Tommy was straightening up from the chair he had placed behind her, brushing his hair back over his shoulders. She sat gratefully. We formed a ragged half-circle in front of her, and Shorty Steinitz brought her the coffee. I sat at her feet and studied her as she sipped it. Her face was still not pretty, but now that the lights were back on in it, you could see that she was beautiful, and I'll take that any day. Go chase a pretty one and see what it gets you. The coffee seemed to help steady her.

"It starts out prosaic," she began. "Three years ago my first husband, Freddie, took off with a sculptress named, God help us, Kitten, leaving me with empty savings and checking, a mortgage I couldn't cut, and a seven-year-old son. Freddie was the life of the party. Lily of the valley. So I got myself a job on a specialist newspaper. Little businessmen's daily, average subscriber's median income fifty K. The front-page story always happened to be about the firm that had bought the most ad space that week. Got the picture? I did a weekly Leisure Supplement, ten pages every Thursday, with a . . . you don't care about this crap. I don't care about this crap.

"So one day I'm sitting at my little steel desk. This place is a reconverted warehouse, one immense office, and the editorial department is six desks pushed together in the back, near the paste-up tables and the library and the wire. Everybody else is gone to lunch, and I'm just gonna leave myself when this guy from accounting comes over. I couldn't remember his name; he was one of those grim, stolid, fatalistic guys that accounting departments run to. He hands me two envelopes. 'This is for you,' he says, 'and this one's for Tom.' Tom was the hippie who put out the weekly Real Estate Supplement. So I start to open mine—it feels like there's candy in it—and he gives me this *look* and says, 'Oh *no*, not *now*.' I look at him like *huh?* and he says, 'Not until it's time. You'll know when,' and he leaves. *Okay*, I say to myself, and I put both envelopes in a drawer, and I go to lunch and forget it.

"About three o'clock I wrap up my work, and I get to thinking about how strange his face looked when he gave me those envelopes. So I take out mine and open it. Inside it are two very big downs—you know, powerful tranquilizers. I sit up straight. I open Tom's envelope, and if I hadn't worked in a drugstore once, I never would have recognized it. Demerol. Synthetic morphine, one of the most addictive drugs in the world.

"Now Tom is a hippie-looking guy, like I say, long hair and mustache, not long like yours, but long for a newspaper. So I figure this accounting guy is maybe his pusher and somehow he's got the idea I'm a potential customer. I was kind of fidgety and tense in those days. So I get mad as hell, and I'm just thinking about taking Tom into the darkroom and chewing him out good, and I look up, and the guy from accounting is staring at me from all the way across the room. No expression at all, he just looks. It gives me the heebie-jeebies.

"Now, overhead is this gigantic air-conditioning unit, from the old warehouse days, that's supposed to cool the whole building and never does. What it does is drip water on editorial and make so much goddamn noise you can't talk on the phone while it's on. And what it does, right at that moment, is rip loose and drop straight down, maybe eight hundred pounds. It crushes all the desks in editorial, and it kills Mabel and Art and Dolores and Phil and takes two toes off of Tom's right foot and misses me completely. A flying piece of wire snips off one of my ponytails.

"So I sit there with my mouth open, and in the silence I hear the publisher say, 'God *damn* it,' from the middle of the room, and I climb over the wreckage and get the Demerol into Tom, and then I make a tourniquet on his arch out of rubber bands and blue pencils, and then everybody's taking me away and saying stupid things. I took those two tranquilizers and went home.''

She took a sip of her coffee and sat up a little straighter. Her eyes were the color of sun-cured Hawaiian buds. ''They shut the paper down for a week. The next day, when I woke up, I got out my employee directory and looked this guy up. While Bobby was in school, I went over to his house. It took me hours to break him down, but I wouldn't take no answer for an answer. Finally he gave up.

'' 'I've got fivesight,' he told me. 'Something just a little bit better than foresight.' It was the only joke I ever heard him make, then or since.''

I made the gasping sound again. ''Precognition,'' Doc Webster breathed. Awkwardly, from my tailor's seat, I worked my keys out of my pocket and tossed them to Callahan. He caught them in the coffee can he had ready and started a shot of Bushmill's on its way to me without a word.

''You know the expression 'Bad news travels fast'?'' she asked. ''For him it travels so fast it gets there before the event. About three hours before, more or less. But only *bad* news. Disasters, accidents, traumas large and small are all he ever sees.''

''That sounds ideal,'' Doc Webster said thoughtfully. ''He doesn't have to lose the fun of *pleasant* surprises, but he doesn't have to worry about unpleasant ones. That sounds like the best way to . . .'' He shifted his immense bulk in his chair. ''Damn it, what *is* the verb for precognition? *Precognite?*''

''Ain't they the guys that sang that 'Jeremiah was a bullfrog' song?'' Long-Drink murmured to Tommy, who kicked him hard in the shins.

''That shows how much you know about it,'' she told the Doc. ''He has *three hours* to worry about each unpleasant surprise—and there's a strictly limited amount he can do about it.''

The Doc opened his mouth and then shut it tight and let her tell it. A good doctor hates forming opinions in ignorance.

''The first thing I asked him when he told me was why hadn't he warned Phil and Mabel and the others. And then I caught myself and said, 'What a dumb question! How're you going to keep six people away from their desks *without telling them why*? Forget I asked that.'

" 'It's worse than that,' he told me. 'It's not that I'm trying to preserve some kind of secret identity—it's that it wouldn't do the slightest bit of good anyway, I can ameliorate—to some extent. But I *cannot* prevent. No matter what. I'm not . . . not permitted.'

" 'Permitted by who?' I asked.

" 'By whoever or whatever sends me these damned premonitions in the first place,' he said. 'I haven't the faintest idea who.'

" 'What exactly are the limitations?'

" 'If a pot of water is going to boil over and scald me, I can't just not make tea that night. Sooner or later I *will* make tea and scald myself. The longer I put off the inevitable, the worse I get burned. But if I accept it and let it happen in its natural time, I'm allowed to, say, have a pot of ice water handy to stick my hand in. When I saw that my neighbor's steering box was going to fail, I couldn't keep him from driving that day, but I could remind him to wear his seatbelt, and so his injuries were minimized. But if I'd seen him dying in that wreck, I couldn't have done *anything*— except arrange to be near the wife when she got the news. It's . . . it's especially bad to try to prevent a death. The results are . . . ' I saw him start to say 'horrible' and reject it as not strong enough. He couldn't find anything strong enough.

" 'Okay, Cass,' I said real quick. 'So at least you can help some. That's more than some doctors can do. I think that was really terrific of you, to bring me that stuff like that, take a chance that I'd think you were—hey, how did you get hold of narcotics on three hours' notice?'

" 'I had three hours' warning for the last big blackout,' he told me. 'I took two suitcases of stuff out of Smithtown General while they were trying to get their emergency generator going. I . . . have uses for the stuff.' "

She looked down into her empty cup, then handed it to Eddie, who had it refilled. While he was gone, she stared at her lap, breathing with her whole torso, lungs cycling slowly from absolutely full to empty.

"I was grateful to him. I felt sorry for him. I figured he needed somebody to help him. I figured after a manic-oppressive like Freddie, a quiet, phlegmatic kind of guy might suit me better. His favorite expression was, 'What's done is done.' I started dating him. One day Bobby fell . . . fell out of a tree and broke his leg, and Uncle Cass just happened to be walking by with a hypo and splints." She looked up and around at us, and her eyes fastened on me. "Maybe I wanted my kid to be safe." She looked away again. "Make a long story short, I married him."

I spilled a little Bushmill's down my beard. No one seemed to notice.

"It's . . . funny," she said slowly, and getting out that second word cost her a lot. "It's really damned funny. At first . . . at first, there, he was really good for my nerves. He never got angry. Nothing rattled him. He never got emotional the way men do, never got the blues. It's not that he doesn't *feel* things. I thought so at first, but I was wrong. It's just that . . . living with a thing like that, either he could be irritable enough to bite people's heads off all the time, or he could learn how to hold it all in. That's what he did, probably back when he was a little kid. 'What's done is done,' he'd say, and keep on going. He *does* need to be held and cared for, have his shoulders rubbed out after a bad one, have one person he can tell about it. I *know* I've been good for him, and I guess at first it made me feel kind of special. As if it took some kind of genius person to share pain." She closed her eyes and grimaced. *"Oh, and Bobby came to love him so!"*

There was silence.

"Then the weirdness of it started to get to me. He'd put a Band-Aid in his pocket, and a couple of hours later he'd cut his finger chopping lettuce. I'd get diarrhea and run to the john, and there'd be my favorite magazine on the floor. I'd come downstairs at bedtime for vitamins and find every pot in the house full of water, and go back up to bed wondering what the hell, and wake up a little while later to find that a socket short had set the living room on fire before it tripped the breaker and he had it under control. I'd catch him concealing some little preparation from me, and know that it was for me or Bobby, and I'd carry on and beg him to tell me—and the *best* of those times were when all I could make him tell me was, 'What's done is done.'

"I started losing sleep and losing weight.

"And then one day the principal called just before dinner to tell me that a school bus had been hit by a tractor-trailer and fourteen students were critically injured and Bobby and another boy were . . . I threw the telephone across the room at him, I jumped on him like a wild animal and punched him with my fists, I screamed and screamed. 'YOU DIDN'T EVEN TRY!' " she screamed again now, and it rang and rang in the stillness of Callahan's Place. I wanted to leap up and take her in my arms, let her sob it out against my chest, but something held me back.

She pulled herself together and gulped cold coffee. You could hear the air conditioner sigh and the clock whir. You could not hear cloth rustle or a chair creak. When she spoke again, her voice was under rigid control. It made my heart sick to hear it.

"I left him for a week. He must have been hurting more than *I* was. So I left him and stayed in a crummy motel, curled up around my own pain. He made all the arrangements, and made them hold off burying Bobby until I came back, and when I did, all he said was . . . what I expected him to say, and we went on living.

"I started drinking. I mean, I started in that motel and kept it up when I went home. I never had before. I drank alone. I don't know if he ever found out. He must have. He never said anything. I . . . I started growing *away* from him. I knew it wasn't right or fair, but I just turned off to him completely. He never said anything. All this started happening about six months ago. I just got more and more self-destructive, more crazy, more . . . hungry for something."

She closed her eyes and straightened her shoulders.

"Tonight is Cass's bowling night. This afternoon I . . ." She opened her eyes. ". . . I made a date with a stockboy at the Path-mark supermarket. I told him to come by around ten, when my husband was gone. After supper he got his ball and shoes ready, like always, and left. I started to clean up in the kitchen so I'd have time to get juiced before Wally showed up. Out of the corner of my eye I saw Cass tiptoe back into the living room. He was carrying a big manila envelope and something else I couldn't see; the en-velope was in the way. I pretended not to see him, and in a few seconds I heard the door close behind him.

"I dried my hands. I went into the living room. On the mantel, by the bedroom door, was the envelope, tucked behind the flower-pot. Tucked behind it was his service revolver. I left it there and walked out the door and came here and started drinking, and now I've had enough of this fucking coffee. I want a screwdriver."

Fast Eddie deserves his name. He was the first of us to snap out of the trance, and it probably didn't take him more than thirty sec-onds. He walked over to the bar on his banty little legs and slapped down a dollar and said, "Screwdriver, Mike."

Callahan shook his head slightly. He drew on his cigar and frowned at it for having gone out. He flung it into the fireplace and built a screwdriver, and he never said a mumblin' word. Eddie brought her the drink. She drained half at once.

Shorty Steinitz spoke up, and his voice sounded rusty. "I service air-conditioning systems. The big ones. I was over at Century Lanes today. Their unit has an intermittent that I can't seem to trace. It keeps cuttin' in and out."

She shut her eyes and did something similar to smiling and nodded her head. "That's it, all right. He'll be home early."

Then she looked me square in the eye.

"Well, Jake, do you understand now? I'm scared as hell! Because I'm here instead of there, and so he's not going to kill me after all. And he tells me that if you try to prevent a death, something worse happens, and I'm going out of my mind wondering what could be worse than getting killed!"

Total horror flooded through me; I thought my heart would stop.

I *knew* what was worse than getting killed.

Dear Jesus, no, I thought, and I couldn't help it. I wanted very badly to keep my face absolutely straight and my eyes holding hers, and I couldn't help it. There was just that tiny hope, and so I glanced for the merest instant at the Counterclock and then back to her. And in that moment of moments, scared silly and three-quarters bagged, she was seeing me clearly enough to pick up on it and know from my face that something was wrong.

It was 10:15.

My heart was a stone. I knew the answers to the next questions, and again I couldn't help myself: I had to ask them.

"Mrs.—"

"Kathy Anders. What's the *matter?*" Just what I had asked her, a few centuries ago.

"Kathy, you . . . you didn't lock the house behind you when you left?"

Callahan went pale behind the bar, and his new cigar fell out of his mouth.

"No," she said. "What the *hell* has that—"

"And you were too upset to think of—"

"Oh *Christ*," she cried. "Oh no, I never thought! Oh Christ, *Wally*, that dumb cocky kid. He'll show up at ten and find the door wide open and figure I went to the corner for beer and decide it's cute to wait for me in bed, and—" She whirled and found the clock, and puzzled out the time somehow, and wailed, "*No!*" And I tore in half right down the middle. She sprang from her chair and lurched toward the bar. I could not get to my feet to follow her. Callahan was already holding out the telephone, and when she couldn't dial it, he got the number out of her and dialed it for her. His face was carven from marble. I was just getting up on my hind legs by then. No one else moved. My feet made no sound at all on the sawdust. I could clearly hear the phone ringing on the other end. Once. Twice. Three times. "Come on, Cass, damn you, answer me!" Four times. *Oh dear God*, I thought, *she still doesn't get it*. Five times. *Maybe she does get it—and won't have it*. Six times.

It was picked up on the seventh ring, and at once she was shrieking, "You *killed* him, you *bastard*. He was just a jerk kid, and you had to—"

She stopped and held the phone at arm's length and stared at it. It chittered at her, an agitated chipmunk. Her eyes went round.

"Wally?" she asked it weakly. Then even more weakly she said to it, "That's his *will* in that manila envelope," and she fainted.

"Mike!" I cried, and leaped forward. The big barkeep understood me somehow and lunged across the bar on his belly and caught the phone in both hands. That left me my whole attention to deal with her, and I needed that and all my strength to get her to the floor gently.

"Wally," Callahan was saying to the chipmunk, "Wally, *listen to me*. This is a friend. I know what happened, and—*listen* to me, Wally, I'm trying to keep your ass out of the slam. Are you listening to me, son? Here's what you've got to do—"

Someone crowded me on my left, and I almost belted him before I realized it was Doc Webster with smelling salts.

"—No, *screw* fingerprints, this ain't TV. Just make up the goddamn bed and put yer cigarette butts in yer pocket and *don't touch anything else*—"

She coughed and came around.

"—sure nobody sees you leave, and then you get your ass over to Callahan's bar, off 25A. We got thirty folks here'll swear you been here all night, but it'd be nice if we knew what you looked like."

She stared up at us vacantly, and as I was helping her get up and into a chair, I was talking. I wanted her to be involved in listening to me when full awareness returned. It would be very hard to hold her, and I was absolutely certain I could do it.

"Kathy, you've got to listen carefully to me, because if you don't, in just another minute now you're going to try and swallow one giant egg of guilt, and it will, believe me, stick in your throat and choke you. You're choking on a couple already, and this one might kill you—and it's not fair, it's not right, it's not just. You're gonna award yourself a guilt that you don't deserve, and the moment you accept it and pin it on it'll stay with you for the rest of your life. Believe me, I *know*. Damn it, *it's okay to be glad you're still alive!*''

''What the hell do you know about it?'' she cried out.

''I've been there,'' I said softly. ''As recently as an hour ago.'' Her eyes widened.

''I came in here tonight so egocentrically wrapped up in my own pain that I sat next to you for fifteen minutes and never noticed you, until some friends woke me up. This is a kind of anniversary for me, Kathy. Five years and one day ago I had a wife and a two-year-old daughter. And I had a *Big Book of Auto Repair*. I decided I could save thirty dollars easy by doing my own brake job. I tested it myself and drove maybe a whole block. Five years ago tonight all three of us went to the drive-in movie. I woke up without a scratch on me. Both dead. I smiled at the man who was trying to cut my door open, and I climbed out the window past him and tried to get my wrists on his chainsaw. He coldcocked me, and I woke up under restraint.'' I locked eyes with her. ''I was glad to be alive too. That's why I wanted to die so bad.''

She blinked and spoke very softly. ''How . . . how did you keep alive?''

''I got talking with a doctor the size of a hippo named Sam Webster, and he got me turned loose and brought me around here.''

She waited for me to finish. ''You—that's it? What is that?''

''Dis is Callahan's Place,'' Eddie said.

''This place is magic,'' I told her.

''Magic? *Bull*shit, magic, it's a *bar*. People come here to get blind.''

''No. Not this one. People come to this bar to see. That's why I'm ashamed at how long it took me to see you. This is a place where people care. For as long as I sat here in my pain, my friends were in pain with me and did what they could to help. They told stories of past blunders to make it a little easier for me to make my annual toast to my family. You know what gives me the courage to keep on living? The courage to love myself a little? It's having a whole bunch of friends who really give a goddamn. When you share pain, there's less of it, and when you share joy, there's more of it. That's a basic fact of the universe, and I learned it here. I've seen it work honest-to-God miracles.''

"Name me a miracle."

" 'Of all the gin joints in all the world, you come into this one.' Tonight, of all the nights in the year. And you look like her, and your name is Kathy.''

She gaped. "I—your wife?—I look—?''

"Oh, not a ringer—that only happens on *The Late Late Show*. But close enough to scare me silly. Don't you see, Kathy? For five years now I've been using that word, *fivesight*, not in conversation, just in my head, as a private label for precognition. I jumped when you said it. For five years now I've been wishing to God I'd been born with it. I was wishing it earlier tonight.

"Now I know better.''

Her jaw worked, but she made no sound.

"We'll help you, Kathy,'' Callahan said.

"Damn straight,'' Eddie croaked.

"We'll help you find your own miracle,'' Long-Drink assured her. "They come by here regular.''

There were murmurs of agreement, encouraging words. She stared around the place as though we had all turned into toads. "And what do you want from me?'' she snapped.

"That you hold up your end,'' I said. "That you not leave us holding the bag. Suicide isn't just a cop out; it's a rip-off.''

She shook her head, as violently as she dared. "People don't *do* that; people don't act this way.''

My voice softened, saddened. "Upright apes don't. People do.''

She finished her drink. "But—''

"Listen, we just contradicted something you said earlier. It seems like it *does* take some kind of genius person to share pain. And I think you did a better job than I could have done. Two, three *years* you stayed with that poor bastard? Kathy, that strength and compassion you gave to Cass for so long, the imagination and empathy you have so much of, those are things we badly need here. We get a lot of incoming wounded. You could be of use here, while you're waiting for your own miracle.''

She looked around at every face, looked long at Callahan and longest at me.

Then she shook her head and said, "Maybe I already got it,'' and she burst finally and explosively into tears, flinging herself into my arms. They were the right kind of tears. I smiled and smiled for some considerable time, and then I saw the clock and got very businesslike. Wally would be along soon, and there was much to be done. "Okay, Eddie, you get her address from her purse and ankle over there. Make sure that fool kid didn't screw up. Pyotr, you Litvak Samaritan, go on out and wake up your wheels. Here, Drink, you get her out to the parking lot; I can't hold her up much longer. Margie, you're the girlfriend she went to spend the weekend with yesterday, okay? You're gonna put her up until she's ready to face the cops. Doc, you figure out what she's contracted that she doesn't want to bother her husband by calling. Shorty, if nobody discovers the body by, say, tomorrow noon, you make a service call to the wrong address and find him. Mike—"

Callahan was already holding out one finger of Irish.

"Say, Jake," Callahan said softly, "didn't I hear your wife's name was Barbara? Kinda short and red-haired and jolly, grey eyes?"

We smiled at each other. "It was a plausible miracle that didn't take a whole lot of buildup and explanation. What if I'd told her we stopped an alien from blowing up the earth in here once?"

"You talk good on your feet, son."

I walked up to the chalk line. "Let me make the toast now," I said loudly. "The same one I've made annually for five years— with a little addition."

Folks hushed up and listened.

"To my family," I said formally, then drained the Irish and gently underhanded my glass onto the hearth.

And then I turned around and faced them all and added, "Each and every one of you."

DOG DAY EVENING

It absolutely *had* to happen. I mean, it was so cosmically preor-dained-destined-fated flat out *inevitable* that I can't imagine how we failed to be expecting it. Where else on God's earth could Ralph and Joe possibly have ended up but at Callahan's Place?

It was Tall Tales Night at Callahan's, the night on which the teller of the most outrageous shaggy-dog story gets his night's tab refunded. "Animals" had been selected as the night's generic topic, and we had suffered through *hours* of stinkers about pet rocks and talking dogs and The Horse That Was Painted Green and the Fastest Dog in the World and the Gay Rooster and a dozen others you probably know already. In fact, most of the Tale-Tellers had been disqualified when someone shouted the punchline before they got to it—often after only a sentence or two. The fireplace was filled to overflowing with broken glasses, and it was down to a tight contest between Doc Webster and me. I thought I had him on the run too.

A relative newcomer named B. D. Wyatt had just literally crapped out, by trying to fob off that old dumb gag about the South Sea island where "there lives a bird whose digestive system is so incredibly rank that, if its excrement should contact your skin, re-

exposure of the contaminated skin to air is invariably fatal." Named
for its characteristic squawk, it is of course the famous Foo Bird,
and the punchline—as I'm certain you know already—is, "If the
Foo shits, wear it." Unfortunately for B. D. ("Bird Doo"?), we
already knew it too. But it gave me an idea.

"You know," I drawled, signalling Callahan for a fresh Bushmill's, "like all of us, I've heard that story before. So many times,
in fact, that I decided there might be a grain of truth in it—hidden,
of course, by a large grain of salt. So my friend Thor Lowerdahl
and I decided to check it out. We investigated hundreds of South
Seas islands without success, until one day our raft, the *Liki Tiki*,
foundered on an uncharted atoll. No sooner did we stagger ashore
than we heard a distant raucous cry: 'Foo! Foo!'

"Instantly, of course, we dove back into the surf, and didn't stick
our heads up until we were far offshore. We treaded water for a
while, hoping for a glimpse of the fabulous bird, to no avail. Suddenly a seal passed us underwater, trailing a cloud of sticky brown
substance. Some of it got on Thor's leg, and with a snort of disgust,
he wiped it off. He expired at once. Realizing the truth in an instant,
I became so terrified that I *swam* back to the States."

I paused expectantly, and Fast Eddie (sensing his cue) obliged
me with a straight line.

"What truth, Jake?"

"That atoll," I replied blithely, "was far more dangerous than
anyone suspected—as any seal can plainly foo."

A general howl arose. Long-Drink chanced (by statistical inevitability) to have his glass to his mouth at the time; he bit a piece
off clean and spat it into the fireplace. I kept my face straight, of
course, but inwardly I exulted. *This* time I had Doc Webster beat
for sure, and with an *impromptu* pun at that. I ordered another.

But when the tumult died down, the Doc met my eyes with a
look of such mild, placid innocence that my confidence faltered.

"Fortunate indeed, Jacob," he rumbled, patting his ample belly,
"that you should have rendered so un*bear*able a pun. It reminds me
of a book about a bear I read the other day by Richard Adams—
Shardik, it's called. Any of you read it?"

There were a few nods. The Doc smiled and sipped scotch.

"For those of you who missed it," he went on, "it's about a
primitive empire that forms around an enormous, semimythical
bear. Well, it happens I know something about that empire that
Adams forgot to mention, and now's as good a time as any to pass

it along. You see, the only way to become a knight in Shardik's empire was to apply for a personal interview with the bear. This had its drawbacks. If he liked your audition, you were knighted on the spot—but if you failed, Lord Shardik was quite likely to club your head off your shoulders with one mighty paw. Even so, there were many applicants—for the peasantry were poor farmers, and if a candidate failed for knighthood his family received, by way of booby-prize, a valuable sheepdog from the Royal Kennels. This consoled them greatly, for truly it is written . . .''

And here he actually paused to sip his scotch again, daring us to guess the punchline:

''. . . 'For the mourning after a terrible knight, nothing beats the dog of the bear that hit you.' ''

A howl again began to arise—and then suddenly a howl arose.

I mean a *real* howl.

So of course we all swiveled around in our chairs, and damned if there wasn't a guy with a German shepherd sitting near the door. I hadn't seen them come in, and it took me a second to notice that the dog had a glass of gin on the floor in front of him, half-empty.

As we gaped, open-mouthed, the dog picked up the half-full glass in his teeth (without spilling a drop), carried it to the hearth, and with a flick of his powerful head, flung it into the fireplace hard enough to bust it. He turned and looked at us then, wagging his tail as if to make sure we understood that he was commenting on the *Doc's* tale. Then, to underline the point, he turned back to the fireplace, lifted his leg and put out a third of the fire.

We roared with laughter, a great simultaneous outburst of total glee, and the dog trotted proudly to his master. I looked the guy over: medium height, a little thin, nose like an avalanche about to happen and a great sprawling fungus of a mustache clinging to its underside. He wore Salvation Army rejects like Mr. Emmett Kelly used to wear, clothes that looked like what starts fires in old warehouses. But his eyes were alert and aware, and he was obviously quite proud of his dog.

Then he caught Callahan's eye, and winced. ''You got a house rule on dogs, Mister?'' he asked. You could hardly see his lips move under that ridiculous mustache.

Callahan considered the matter. ''We try not to be human-chauvinists around here,'' he allowed at last. ''But if he dumps on my floor, I'll clean it up with your shirt. Fair enough?''

"Are you kiddin'?" the guy mumbled. "*This* dog mess on the floor? Why, this is the Smartest Dog In The World."

He said it just like that, with capital letters.

"Uh-huh," said Long-Drink. "He talks, right?"

A strange gleam came into the shabby man's eyes.

"Yep."

"Oh for God's sake," Doc Webster groaned. "Don't tell me. A talking dog has walked into Callahan's Place on Tall Tales Night. If that hound tops my story, I'm going on the wagon—for the whole night."

That broke everyone up, and Long-Drink McGonnigle was particularly tickled (say that three times fast with whiskey in your mouth). "Patron saint of undershorts," he whooped, "it makes so much sense I almost believe it."

"You think I'm kidding?" the stranger asked.

"That or crazy," the Doc asserted. "A dog hasn't got the larynx to talk—let alone the mouth structure—even if he *is* as smart as you say."

"I've got two hundred dollars says you're wrong," the stranger announced. He displayed a fistful of bills. "Any takers?"

Well, now. We're a charitable bunch at Callahan's, not normally inclined to cheat the mentally disturbed. And yet there was a clarity to his speech that belied his derelict's clothes, a twinkle in his eye that looked entirely sane, and a challenging out-thrust to his chin that reminded us of a kid daring you to hit him. And there was that wildly improbable handful of cash in his hand. "I'll take ten of that," I said, digging for my wallet, and a dozen other guys chimed in. "Me too." "I'll take ten." "I'm in for five." Doc Webster took a double sawbuck's worth, and even Fast Eddie produced a tattered single. The guy collected the dough in a hat that looked like its former owner had been machine-gunned in the head, and the whole time that damn dog just sat there next to the table, watching the action.

When the guy had it all counted, there was a hundred and seventy bucks in the hat. "There's thirty unfaded," he said, and looked around expectantly.

Callahan came around the bar, a redheaded glacier descending on the shabby man. The barkeep picked him up by the one existing lapel and the opposite collar, held him at arm's length for a while, and sighed.

"I like a good gag as well as the next guy," he said conversationally. "But that's serious money in that hat. Now if you was to ask that dog his name, and he said 'Ralph! Ralph!' and then you was to ask him what's on top of a house and he said 'Roof! Roof!' and then you was to ask him who was the greatest baseball player of all time and he said 'Ruth! Ruth!', why, I'd just naturally have to sharpen your feet and drive you into the floor. You would become like a Gable roof: *Gone with the Wind.* What I mean, there are *very* few gags I've never heard, and if yours is of that calibre you are in dire peril. Do we have a meeting of the minds?" He was still holding the guy at arm's length, the muscles of his arms looking like hairy manila, absolutely serene.

"I'm telling you the truth," the guy yelped. "The dog can talk."

Callahan slowly lowered him to the floor. "In that case," he decided, "I will fade your thirty." He went back behind the bar and produced an apple. "Would you mind putting this in your mouth?"

The guy blinked at him.

"I believe you implicitly," Callahan explained, "but someone without my trusting nature might suspect you was a ventriloquist tryin' to pull a fast one."

"Okay," said the guy at once, and he stuffed the apple in his face. He beckoned to the dog, who came at once to the center of the room and sat on his haunches. He gazed up inquisitively at the shabby man, who nodded.

"I hope you will forgive me," said the dog with the faintest trace of a German accent, "but I'm afraid my name actually *is* Ralph."

There was silence, as profound as that which must exist on the Moon now that the tourist season is past. Then, slowly at first, glasses began to hit the fireplace. Soon there was a shower of glasses shattering on the hearth, and not a drop of liquid in any of 'em. Callahan passed fresh beers around the room, bucket-brigade fashion, his face impassive. Not a word was spoken.

At last everyone had been lubed, and the big Irishman wiped off his hands and came around the bar. He pulled up a chair in front of the dog, dropped heavily into it, and put a fresh light to his cigar.

"Sure is a relief," he sighed, "to take the weight offa my d . . . to sit down."

You must understand—we were all still so stunned that not one of us thought to ask him if he was bitching.

"So tell me, Ralph," he went on, "how do you like my bar?"

"Nice place," the dog said pleasantly. "You guys always tell shaggy- . . . uh, person stories?"

"Only on Wednesday nights," Callahan told him, and explained the game and current topic.

"That sounds very interesting," Ralph said, parodying Artie Johnson. His voice was slightly hoarse but quite intelligible, "Mind if I take a shot at it?"

"You just heard the Doc's stinker," Callahan said. "If you can beat that, you're top . . ."

"Please," Ralph interrupted with a pained look. "As you told me a moment ago, I've heard them all before. All right, then: I have an animal story. Did any of you know that until very recently, a tribe of killer monkeys lived undetected in Greenwich Village?"

The Doc had nearly found his own voice, but now he lost it again. Me, I'd already crapped out—but it was fun to see the champ sweat. I resolved to buy the dog a beer.

"To some extent," the German shepherd went on, "it was not surprising that they escaped notice for so long. They had extremely odd sleeping habits, hibernating for 364 days out of every year (365 in Leap Years) and emerging from the caverns of the Village sewers only on Christmas Day. Even so, one might have thought they could hardly help but cause talk, since they tended when awake to be enormous, ferocious, carnivorous, and *extremely* hungry. Yet in Greenwich Village of all places on earth they went unnoticed until last year, when they were finally destroyed."

The dog paused and looked expectant. Sighing, Callahan reached over the bar and got him a glass of gin. Ralph lapped it up in a twinkling, looked up at us, and delivered.

"Everyone *knows*," he said patiently, "that Yule gibbons ate only nuts and fruits."

Not, I am certain, since the days when Rin-Tin-Tin ran in neighborhood theaters has a German shepherd received such thunderous applause. We gave him a standing ovation, and I want to say Doc Webster was the first one to rise (despite the fact that, by virtue of his earlier rash promise, he was now on the wagon for the evening). Callahan nearly fell off his chair, and Fast Eddie tried to strike up

"At The Zoo," but he was laughing so hard his left hand was in G and his right in Eb. As the applause trickled off we toasted the dog and blitzed the fireplace as one.

And the man in shabby clothes, whose existence we had nearly forgotten, stepped up to the bar (minus his apple now) and claimed the hatful of money.

Callahan blinked, then his grin widened and he returned behind the bar. "Mister," he said, drawing another gin for Ralph, "that was worth every penny it cost us. Your friend is terrific, and I'm honored to have you both in my joint. Here's another gin for him, and what're you drinking?"

"Scotch," the shabby man said, and Callahan nodded and reached for the scotch—but I used to work in a boiler factory once, and so I choked on my drink.

Callahan looked around, puzzled. "What is it, Jake?"

"His lips, Mike," I croaked, wiping fine whiskey from my beard. "His *lips.*"

Callahan turned back to the guy, gently lifted the scrofulous mustache and examined the guy's lips. There were two. "So?" he said, peering at them.

"I read lips," I managed at last. "You know that. That guy's voice said 'scotch,' *but his lips said 'bourbon.'* "

"How the hell could you tell?" Callahan asked reasonably.

"I swear, Mike—he said 'bourbon.' Here: look." I wear a mustache myself, middlin' sanitary, but I covered most of it and all of my mouth with my hand. Then I said, "Scotch . . . Bourbon . . . See what I mean? It *ain't* the lips, entirely—the mustache, the cheek muscles—I'm telling you, Mike, the guy said 'bourbon'."

Callahan looked at the guy, then at me . . . and then at the dog.

"I'm sorry, Joe," the dog said miserably. "I thought sure you'd want to stick with scotch."

The shabby man shrugged eloquently.

"Well, I'll be a son of a . . ." Long-Drink began, then caught himself. "*You're* the ventriloquist!"

Doc Webster roared with laughter, and Callahan's eyes widened the barest trifle. "I surely will go to hell," he breathed. "I shoulda guessed."

But I was watching the look exchanged by Joe and Ralph, the way both of them ever so casually got ready to bolt for the door, and I spoke up quickly.

"It's okay, fellas. Don't go away—*tell* us about it."

They froze, undecided, and the rest of the boys jumped in. "Hell, yeah." "Give us the yarn, Ralph." "Let's hear it." "Get that dog another drink."

Ralph looked around at us, poised to flee, and then he met Callahan's eyes for a long moment. He looked *exactly* like a dog that's been kicked too often, and I thought he'd go. But he must have heard the sincerity in our voices, or else he read something on Callahan's face, because all at once he relaxed and curled up on the floor.

"It's all right, Joe," he said to the shabby man, who still stood undecided. "These people will not make trouble for us." The shabby man nodded philosophically and accepted a bourbon from Callahan.

"How come you can talk?" Fast Eddie asked Ralph. "I mean, if it ain't no poisonal question or nuttin'."

"Not at all," Ralph answered. "I was . . . created, I suppose you'd say, by a demented genius of a psychology major named Malion, who was desperate for a doctoral thesis. He had a defrocked veterinary surgeon modify my larnyx and mouth in my infancy, apparently in the mad hope that he could condition me to parrot human speech. But I'm afraid his experiment blew up in his face. You see," he said rather proudly, "I seem to be a mutant.

"This, naturally, was the one thing Malion had never planned for. How could he? Who could guess that a dog could actually have human intelligence? For all I know I am unique—in fact I fervently and desperately hope so. If there are other dogs of my intelligence, but without the capacity for speech, *who would ever know?*" Ralph shuddered. "At any rate, I destroyed all of Malion's hopes the first time I got tired of his damned yammering and told him what I thought of him *and* Pavlov *and* Skinner in no uncertain terms. At first, naturally, he was tremendously excited. But within a few hours, as I reminded him of highlights of our past life together, I could see dawning in him the fear that any lab-researcher—let alone a behaviorist—might feel upon realizing that one of his experimental animals is an aware attack dog.

"And eventually, of course, he realized the same thing that had kept my own mouth shut for so many months: that if he attempted to write *me* up for his doctorate, they'd laugh him off the campus. He abandoned me, simply kicked me out in the streets and locked my doggy-door. The next day he left town, and hasn't been heard from since."

"Cripes," said Eddie, "dat's awful. Abandoned by yer creator."

"Like Frankenstein," Doc Webster said.

"Damn right," Ralph agreed. "I'd like to get my paws on that pig Malion."

Then he realized what he'd just said and barked with laughter. The Doc drained his own glass with a gulp and tossed it over his shoulder, squarely into the fire.

"I beg your pardon," the shepherd continued. "Anyhow, I got by for quite a while. It's not too hard for a big dog to survive in Suffolk County, especially when the summer people go. But what drove me crazy was *having nobody to talk to*. After all those years of keeping my mouth shut, so as not to spoil my meal ticket with Malion, I was like a pent-up river ready to burst its dam. But every time I tried to strike up a conversation, the other party ran away rather abruptly. A few children would talk to me, but I soon stopped that too—their parents gave them endless grief for telling lies, and one day I found myself obliged to bite one. He took a shot at me—with a silver bullet.

"So I tried to sublimate. I found a serviceable typewriter in a junkyard, swiped paper and stamps and became a writer—of speculative fiction, of course. Since I lived mostly in the remaining farmland east of here, I selected pastoral pen names like Trout and Bird and Farmer—although occasionally I wrote under an old family name, Von Wau Wau."

"Holy smoke," Wyatt breathed. "So that's what that hoax was all about . . ."

"Eventually I acquired something of a following . . . but answering fan mail is not the same as *talking* with someone. Besides, I couldn't cash the checks.

"Then one day, outside a bar in Rocky Point, I happened to overhear some fools making fun of Joe here, because he was a mute. 'Dummy,' they called him, and his face was red and he was desperate for a voice with which to curse them. So *I* did. They fled the bar, screaming like chickens, and ten minutes later Joe and I left the empty bar with the beginnings of a partnership."

"I get it," I said, striking my forehead with my hand. "You teamed up."

"Precisely," Ralph agreed. "I could have the pleasure of conversing with people, at least by proxy—and so could Joe, simply by letting me put words in his mouth. He grew that mustache to help, and we worked out a fairly simple script and cues. To support ourselves, we hit upon the old talking-dog routine, which we have been working in taverns from Ronkonkoma to Montauk over the last six months. The beauty of it is that while people virtually always pay up, they *never* believe I can truly speak. Always they speak only to Joe, congratulating *him* on his fine trick even if they can't figure out how he does it. I suppose I should be annoyed by this, but truthfully, I find it hilarious. And at any rate, it's a living.''

Doc Webster shook his head like . . . well, like a dog shaking off water is the only simile I can think of. ''And to think it took you guys all this time to come to Callahan's Place,'' he said dizzily.

''I feel the same,'' Ralph said seriously. ''You are the first men who have ever accepted Joe and me as we are, who knew the truth about us and did not run away. Or worse, laugh at us.

''I thank you.''

And Joe pointed at his own chest and nodded vigorously. *Me too!*

Callahan's face split in a broad grin. ''Sure and hell welcome, fellas,'' he boomed, ''sure and hell welcome—*any* time. I can't think of any two guys I'd rather have in my joint.''

And another cheer went up. ''To Ralph and Joe,'' Long-Drink hollered, and two dozen voices chorused, *''To Ralph 'n' Joe.''* The toast was drunk, the glasses disposed of in unison, and the place started to get real merry. But an idea struck me.

''Hey, Ralph,'' I called out. ''You want a job? A real job?''

Ralph paused in midlap and looked up. ''Are you crazy? Who'd hire a talking dog?''

''I know the only place around that might,'' I told him confidently. ''Jim Friend over at WGAB has been talking about taking a year off, and he's a good friend of mine. How'd you like to run a radio talk show at 4 A.M. every morning?''

Ralph looked stunned.

''Yeah,'' Callahan agreed judiciously, ''WGAB would hire a talking dog. Hell, maybe they got one already. Whaddya say, Ralph?''

I could see Ralph was tempted—but German shepherds are notoriously loyal. ''What about Joe?''

''Hmmm.'' I thought hard, but I was stumped.

Joe was gesticulating furiously, but Ralph ignored him. ''No,'' he decided. ''I could not leave my friend.''

"I'll think of something," Callahan promised, but Ralph shook his head.

"Thank you," he said, "but there's no use in raising false hopes. I'm resigned to this life."

"Mister," Callahan said firmly, "that's what this Place is all about. We raise hopes, here—until they're old enough to fend for themselves. Wait—I *got* it! Joe!"

The shabby man looked up from his drink, shamefaced.

"Get that frown off yer phiz," Callahan demanded. "You can type, can't ya?"

Joe nodded, puzzled. "I taught him," Ralph said.

"Then I can help ya," the big Irishman told Joe. "How would you like a job over at Brookhaven National Lab?"

Joe looked dubious, and Ralph spoke up again. "I told you, Mr. Callahan—writing just isn't the same as talking to people."

"Hold on and listen," Callahan insisted. "Over at Brookhaven, they got a new computer they're real proud of—they claim it's almost alive. So they're reviving the old gag about having experts try to tell the computer from a guy on a teletype. They're lookin' for a guy right now, who don't mind carryin' on conversations through one-way glass on a teletype all day long. I bet we could get you the job. How 'bout it?" And he hauled out the blackboard he uses to keep score for dart games, and gave it and some chalk to Joe.

The shabby man took the chalk and carefully printed, THANK YOU. I'LL GIVE IT A TRY, in large letters.

"Well, Ralph," Callahan said to the dog, "it looks like you're a DJ."

And Ralph yelped happily, nuzzling Joe with his head, while we all started cheering once again.

And, hours later, as we all got ready to bottle it up and go, Ralph turned to Joe and said, almost sadly, "So, Joe my friend. After tomorrow, perhaps we go our separate ways. No longer will I dog your heels."

Joe winced and wrote, NO LONGER WILL I HEEL MY DOG, EITHER.

Doc Webster made a face at the plain Coca-Cola that sat before him on the bar. "I might have to heal the both of you if you keep it up," he growled, and I could see he was still a little miffed over his defeat by Ralph.

"Oh no," Ralph protested. "I want to get my new job right away. The only other work for a dog of my intelligence is as a seeing eye dog, *ja?* And radio work is better than replacing a cane, *nein?*"

"*Cane-nein?*" the Doc exploded. "*Canine?* Why you . . ."

But over what the portly sawbones said then, let us draw a censoring veil of silence. His bark always was worse than his bite.

Say—if Ralph really makes it on radio, and becomes a dog star: is that Sirius?

HAVE YOU HEARD THE ONE...?

There is clearly a kind of delirious logic to the way things happen at Callahan's Place, a kind of artistic symmetry—if by "artistic" you mean, like, Salvador Dali or Maurits Escher.

It just happened, for instance, that in 1979 the Fourth of July fell on a rainy Wednesday night—and Wednesday night is customarily Tall Tales Night at Callahan's. So naturally it was that night that the Traveling Salesman arrived.

And even with that much hint, the punchline surprised me.

Oh, would you like to hear about it?

The house custom on Wednesday nights is that the teller of the tallest tale gets his or her bar bill refunded, and I haven't missed a Wednesday in years. I have won a few times; I have lost quite a few times: there are some fearful liars at Callahan's bar. (Sometime customers include a paperback editor, a literary agent, and a former realtor.) Lately, however, the stakes had increased. A lady named Josie Bauer had begun coming regular to Callahan's the month previous, and she was pleasant and bright and buxom and remarkably easy to talk to. And she was something I'd never encountered before: a humor groupie. It was her charming and unvarying custom to go home with whoever won the Tall Tales contest on Wednesday nights and the Punday Night competition on Tuesdays. This caused the competition, as Doc Webster observed, to stiffen considerably.

But I had hopes that night, and I was sorry to see Gentleman John Kilian approach the chalk line with a gin-and-gin in his hand. John is a short dapper Englishman with a quick mind and a wicked talent for summatory puns. He's not on this side of the lake much, and a lot of folks dropped what they were doing to listen.

"I commanded a submarine in Her Majesty's Navy during the last World War," he began, tugging at his goatee, "and I propose to tell you of a secret mission I was ordered to undertake. The famous spy Harry Lime, the celebrated Third Man, had developed a sudden and severe case of astigmatism—and many of his espionage activities forbade dependence on spectacles. At that time only one visionary in all the world was working on the development of a practical contact lens: a specialist at Walter Reed Hospital. I was ordered to convey Lime there in utmost secrecy and despatch, then wait 'round and fetch him home again."

"Is this gonna be a Limey story?" Long-Drink McGonnigle asked, and Callahan took a seltzer bottle to him.

John ignored it magnificently. "He was an excellent actor, of course, but before long I began to suspect that there was nothing atall wrong with his vision. I searched his quarters, and found correspondence indicating that he had a girlfriend who lived some twenty miles from the hospital. So I called him into my cabin. 'I can't prove a thing against you,' I said, 'but I'm ordering you—' " For effect, he paused and elegantly sipped gin.

I hated to do it. I'm a liar: I loved doing it. In any case I had seen the punchline coming long since, and so I delivered it before he could. " '—to go directly from the sub, Lime, to the Reed oculist.' "

"Oh *damn*," he cried, and everyone broke up, Josie loudest of all. John glared at his gin, finished it in one gulp and pegged his glass into the fireplace.

"Sorry, John."

"Bullshit," he said, making an extra syllable out of the T. He grinned satanically and his eyes flashed. "Let's hear yours now, Jake."

"Aw, I haven't got any worth telling."

"None of that," he said sharply.

"And besides, you're so good at puns, John. You always smell 'em coming."

"Come out and fight like a man."

"Well . . ." I got up from the bar, took my Tullamore Dew to the chalk line before the fireplace. "I haven't got a tall tale, exactly." I wet my whistle. "What I've got is a true story that happened to me, that I've never been able to get anybody to believe."

"Better," said Gentleman John, mollified.

"No, *really*. I swear, this is true. Most of you know, I've been making a living with a guitar around the Island for some time now, and I've played a lot of *strange* places. I played the Village Pizza Restaurant Lounge, I played the Deer Park High School Senior Assembly, my old partner Dave and me played a joint once where the topless dancer had one arm, you had to show a razor and puke blood to get in. But the weirdest of all was a solo gig. I got a call from this big chain department store, Lincoln & Waltz; their PR lady heard me somewhere and wanted to know if I would come and sing in the Junior Miss Department. I thought she was drunk. Essentially they wanted something sufficiently odd to awaken the shoppers and attract a crowd, for which they would then have the local Girl Scouts model the new spring line. She figured I was hungry enough, and she figured right.

"Now, I'm not a superstitious man, but this is a pretty weird gig, even for me. So as I'm driving to the store I'm wondering if I've made a terrible mistake, and I kind of—there was a witness present—I look upward-like and I say out loud, 'Oh, Lord, give me a sign. Will my paycheck get cosigned, or is that going off on a tangent?'" Sustained groans. "All right, I'm embellishing. What I really said was, 'Should I go through with this? Lord, give me a sign.' At that moment I stop for a stop sign, and overhead a bird electrocutes itself on the high-tension lines and drops dead on the front hood of my car—"

Whoops of laughter.

"I swear to God, feet sticking up, I have a *witness*."

Doc Webster popped a vest button, and Josie was smiling dreamily.

"So I sit there at the stop sign awhile . . . shivering . . . tilt my head back and real soft I say, 'You didn't have to shout . . .'"

Roars. "Marvelous," Gentleman John cried. "You went home straightaway, of course?"

"Hell no, like a chump I showed up at the Junior Miss Department. To tell you the truth, I was curious. Nothing I played or sang or said attracted the attention of a single customer, and when they gave the Girl Scouts the go-ahead anyway, one of them stepped into my guitar case and broke a hinge, and I set fire to a fifty dollar dress with my cigar, and I didn't get paid. Worst single disaster of my career.''

John was shaking his head. ''Don't believe a word of it, old boy.''

''Of *course* not. Neither did I; that's why I was stupid enough to go through with it after a warning like that. I didn't believe. In retrospect it's obvious, but I just thought the damn bird was a sparrow or magpie or some such . . .'' I trailed off carefully.

''What was it then?'' John bit. ''Raven, I suppose?''

''I'm surprised at you, John,'' I said triumphantly. ''Obviously it was an Omen Pigeon.''

People grade a pun by their reaction to it. The very best, of course, as Bernard Shaw said, is when one's audience holds its collective nose and flees screaming from one's vicinity. Immediate laughter or groan is a *lesser* approbation. And in between these two is the *pause,* followed only after five or ten stunned seconds by cheers and jeers. It was this intermediate rating that I was accorded, and I savored the pause, and Josie's broad grin, and lifted my Irish whiskey to my lips to savor that too.

And sprayed a fine mist of Irish into the air.

Because before the pause could turn to applause, in that second or two of silence, we all heard—with a dreadful clarity—the unmistakable sound of hoofbeats on the roof.

Pretty near everyone had just drawn in a breath to cheer or groan; there was a vast *huff* as they all let it back out again. Cigar smoke swirled in tormented search for safe harbor, and the only sound now was the hoofbeats on the roof.

Mike Callahan is unflappable. He plucked his malodorous cigar from his mouth with immense aplomb, looked up at the ceiling and shouted, ''You're early, Fatso,'' and went back to polishing the bartop.

He received a scattered ovation, which died quickly.

I was as stunned as anyone else, but I think my strongest reaction was irritation at having my thunder stolen. There sure and hell were a lot of hooves up there. ''Eddie,'' I called out bitterly, ''someone has obviously gone to a lot of trouble to set up a gag. The least we can do is bite. Check it out, will you?''

Fast Eddie Costigan got up from his upright piano, eyes on the ceiling. "Sure t'ing," he said uncertainly.

There are two openings onto the roof. One is the access hatch near the fireplace, with a ladder up to it built into the wall. On warm nights Mike lets customers take their drinks up there and stargaze, which accounts for the second opening: a big dumbwaiter at the end of the bar. It carries dollar bills down and drinks and peanuts back up. Mike built it himself, and he made it big enough for parties. Both openings would have been in use that night, of course, if it hadn't been raining. Eddie went up the ladder with a hesitancy that belied his nickname, and poked the hatch door open most gingerly. A practical joke this elaborate might have teeth in it—and Eddie, being from Brooklyn, has a horror of livestock. Prepared for anything, he hooked his head up over the coaming for a quick look.

He froze there, half out of the room, for a long moment, rain dripping in around him. Then he just *slid* down the ladder, landing hard on his butt. His monkey face was snow white.

"Well?" Callahan asked.

"Sleigh," Eddie said. "Eight tiny reindeer. Heavyset guy with a white beard."

"Told ya," Callahan said.

Eddie nodded, dripping rainwater. "Ho ho ho."

The dumbwaiter came to life.

Callahan turned to face it and put his big hands on his hips. The room was absolutely still, absolutely quiet save for the sound of the little dumbwaiter motor being overworked. It stopped. The door opened.

Inside, a man was balanced on his head, juggling lit cherry bombs.

"*Zut alors*," he said. "Goddamn."

Callahan stepped back a pace.

The stranger fell forward, twisting as he fell so that he landed on his feet in front of the big barkeep, still juggling. As Mike opened his mouth, the hypnotic circle of burning fireworks opened out into a long arc whose terminus was the fireplace. All four cherry bombs exploded therein with a stupendous concussion. Broken glass sprayed outward, miraculously arranging itself on the floor to spell out the word AL.

The stranger vaulted the bar at once and cartwheeled into the middle of the room, people scattering frantically out of his way. He landed lightly on his feet and beamed.

"Phee is the name," he cried merrily, "Al Phee, and the first one who asks me what it's all about gets a boot in the plums. Phee's my name and commission's my game—gather round like cattle and you shall be herd. I bring you the bazaar of the bizarre, the genuine Universal Pantechnicon, at a cost of just pennies! *Sacre bleu! Baise mes fesses!* Everything must go! Me stony, you savvy? Plenty bankruptcy along me."

We all stared at him.

"Come *on,*" he shouted, "look alive, get with it. This is *opportunidad muy milagroso*—act now while this offer lasts. Step right up—who'll be the first? Oh *faddle*—" Suddenly he fell upon the room like a whirlwind, like a big mad mosquito or a horny hummingbird. He darted through the crowd, hugging people, kissing people, shaking hands, shaking feet, tugging on beards, introducing himself to the fire extinguisher and shaking its hose, grinning like Hell's PR man and talking a mile a minute. He took a scissor from his breast pocket, clipped the end off Long-Drink McGonnigle's tie and presented it to him with a bow. He produced a white mouse from a side pocket and gave it gravely to Josie, and when she only smiled he burst into delighted laughter himself, lifted her hand to his lips and kissed the mouse. He stuck his face an inch away from mine, tousled my beard and patted my ass and danced away.

Eddie had been misleading: he didn't look much like Santa. He was not that heavyset, for one thing. The beard *was* more salt than pepper, but the neat short hair was weighted the other way—and the beard itself was not a Santa-type but something in between a spade and a Van-dyke. I would say that he comported himself in a manner even more dapper and elegant than Gentleman John—certainly more flamboyant.

He wore a four-hundred-dollar blazer over a polka-dot pajama top. He wore no trousers, and fat beaming Buddhas were printed on his shorts. He wore phosphorescent lederhosen and jester's shoes with curled up toes and bells. A propellor beanie was rakishly canted over one eyebrow. The rain had not wet him. Behind wire-rim glasses, merry eyes sparkled.

About that time Long-Drink caught up with him, roaring something about his tie. Phee spun to meet him, smiled with the enormous delight of one encountering an old and dear friend, picked three glasses of whiskey from a nearby table and began to juggle them. Not a drop did he spill. Long-Drink stopped dead in his tracks and his long jaw hung down. Phee began to clap his hands rhythmically while he juggled, then slapped his thighs.

Without taking his eyes from the glasses, the Drink felt for his tie, yanked it from his neck and tramped it into the sawdust.

Phee backed away, still juggling and clapping, until he was back in the center of the room where he had started. Suddenly the glasses were all upside down in their stately circle, their contents in motion. Each cataract ended up in Phee's mouth, and his beard was dry when he finished.

His cyclone passage among us had shattered our group stasis—the room was filled with the *rooba-rooba* of many people talking all at once. When the last of the three empty glasses hit the hearth, and the fragments had spelled PHEE next to the AL, the murmur became a standing ovation.

"Mister," Long-Drink said, "that was the best goddamn juggling I ever saw in my life."

Phee smiled indulgently, shook his head. "You haven't lived until you've seen it done with chainsaws. Eek! Heavy, baby."

Eddie spoke for all of us. "What de fuck is goin' on?"

"Mutual introductions, of course. I am Al Phee, and you are, in order," he ticked us off, "Marshall Artz, Boyle Deggs, Tom Foolery, Rachel Prejudice, Dee Jenrette, Miss Fortune," (pointing at Josie) "Flemming Ayniss, Manny Peeples, and Euell P. Yorpanz. Now that we know *who* we are, we may consider *what* we are: *c'est simple, non?* Shitfire, and dog my cats. I am a yoofo."

"A which?"

"Not a foe of you, but a UFO. And you are all Hugos. Unidentified goggling objects. What's wrong with you imbeciles *ce soir*, don't you see? *Ding an sich*: I am from outer space."

"With reindeer?" Callahan asked.

"We used to make 'em look like dishware, but believe it or not, that wasn't silly enough—people who saw us kept *reporting* it. *Nobody* reports a sleigh and eight tiny reindeer."

I think Phee expected this latest announcement to be the most stunning so far. If so, he was disappointed. Long-Drink nodded and said, "Sure, that explains it," and there was a general air of *de*mystification everywhere. I wished that Mickey Finn were around that night. (Finn is an extraterrestrial himself, and I wondered what he would think of this guy. But of course it was summer, and Finn was way up north on the Gaspé Peninsula, tending his farm.)

"So what can we do for you?" Callahan asked imperturbably.

"What's a pantechnicon?" I added.

If he was disappointed at our collective sangfroid, Phee hid it well. "*Merde d'une puce,*" he exclaimed, eyes flashing, "don't you know your own language?" He had one of the loudest voices I'd ever heard.

"Furniture warehouse," Gentleman John put in.

"Correct," Phee admitted, "But not the meaning I meaning."

"Oh, you must mean the nineteenth-century bazaars in London," John said, light dawning.

"—where arts and crafts were sold, yes," Phee said, applauding silently. "B-plus. Pan plus technikos—*comme j'ai dit*, a bazaar of the bizarre."

Callahan's eyes widened. "Do you mean to tell me—?" he began, teeth clenched on his cigar.

Phee smiled like a flashbulb going off. "*Exactement*, my large. I am an Intergalactic Traveling Salesman."

People began to giggle, then laugh outright, then guffaw. Folks folded at the middle, slapped their thighs, pounded on tables with their fists, met each other's eyes and laughed anew. Even Callahan roared with gargantuan mirth, clapping his big knuckly hands together. Phee might have been excused for thinking we doubted his story—but I could see through my own tears of mirth that, after a moment's annoyance, he understood. Somehow he understood our laughter was not derision but delight.

It's like I said earlier—when you've been hanging out at Callahan's bar for a while, you begin to see a zany kind of symmetry to the way things happen there. "Hannibal's Holy Hairpiece, it's perfect!" Long-Drink crowed. "A traveling salesman has flown into Callahan's on Tall Tales Night. Sell my clothes, I'm gone to heaven!"

Phee bowed. "No fear? Marvelous; I impress. Hot damn. It is a business doing pleasure with you. I was told by blackguards that you did not civilize yet. Lies, by jiminy!"

"It just come on recent," Doc Webster said, and broke up again.

Phee waited politely until we were all finished. Then he produced a burning cigarette from out of thin air, flipped it into his face, and began chewing on the filter. "To business we then progress, *jawohl?*

Groovey. Innkeeper, *gib mir getrank*—a flagon of firewater. Darn the torpedoes. Gosh.''

Callahan poured whiskey and passed it across the bar. ''How come no sample cases, brother? What's your line?''

''Oh, but I have a sample case, sweetheart. *Mais oui.*'' He reached into the inside pocket of his blazer and removed a hole. It had no edges, no boundaries, and it was no color at all. It was just . . . a *hole*, about the size of the lid on a gallon of ice cream. He held it by the edge it didn't have, extended it to arm's length, and when he dropped his hand it stayed there, a circle of *nothing*.

There were whistles and much awed murmuring.

''Nonsense,'' Phee said airily, ''Is *nothing* sacred? *Voila le* sample case.''

''Say,'' Long-Drink began, ''how many of those would you think it'd take to fill the Alb—*ouch!*'' He glared at Doc Webster and began rubbing his shin.

''No, *compadres*,'' Phee said, ''it is not a hole-o-graph. It is a hyperpocket, a dimensional bridge to a . . . ahem . . . pocket universe. *Regardez!*''

He reached an elegantly manicured hand into the hole, and the hand failed to reappear on the other side. ''*Pardon,*'' he muttered, rummaging. ''Ah!'' His hand emerged. It was holding, by the throat, an extremely long-necked dragon, whose scaled head had barely fit through the hole. Reptilian eyes regarded us coldly, the fanged jaws opened, and a gout of flame set Phee's hair on fire.

''Damn,'' he said irritably, ''wrong drawer. One of these days I'm going to get this office organized.'' He thrust the dragon's head back into the hole with an air of embarassment. He ignored the fire on his head, and it seemed impolite to mention it, so it burned undisturbed as he rummaged, until his scalp was covered with black smoldering curls. The beanie was unaffected. ''*Boñiga de la mestizo enano* . . . aha! *Now* see.''

People edged discreetly away, and he pulled out a vaguely spherical object wrapped in soft cloth. He yanked on a corner of the cloth, and the object flew sparkling into the air; he caught it with his other hand. My first crazy thought was: ''burning ice.''

''My line,'' he said triumphantly. ''Jewels.''

It looked something like a cut diamond the size of a softball, at least in physical structure. It was symmetrically faceted, very nearly transparent, and contained within it, like flies trapped in amber, perhaps a dozen splashes and streaks of liquid color, unbearably pure and lambent. The colors and shapes harmonized. It was so beautiful it hurt to look at.

"Is there anyone here who is chronically worried?" Phee asked loudly.

Slippery Joe Maser stepped forward. "I got two wives."

"Splendid! *Kommen ze hier.*"

Joe hung back.

"*Umgawa,*" Phee rapped impatiently. "Don't be such a chick-enshit. Four centuries on the road this trip, and I haven't lost a customer yet. Come on, be a *mensch.*"

Joe approached uneasily.

"You *are* a worrier. Lucky I was passing by. Catch!"

He tossed the gleaming jewel to Joe, who caught it awkwardly in both hands. He stared down at the thing for a long moment.

"What do you worry about most?" Phee asked. "No, *mon vieil asperge*, don't tell me—just think about it."

Joe closed his eyes and thought about it.

From the places where his fingertips touched the jewel, streamers of a gray, milky substance began to infuse it, like milk being poured into a glass of weak tea from several points at once. Soon the entire interior of the gem was swirling gray, all the spatters of aching color hidden.

I tore my eyes from it to look at Joe. His face shone with the light that was obscured now in the jewel. Every feature was relaxed; for the first time since I've known him, his forehead was utterly smooth, no more wrinkles than a Gothic novel.

His eyes opened. "What the hell was I worryin' about?" he breathed contentedly. He worked his shoulders like a man who has just set down, at long last, a crushing burden.

"What's to worry?"

Callahan's voice was shockingly harsh. "Is that goddamn thing addictive?"

"*Nyet,*" Phee responded at once. "*Au contraire.* Watch."

Joe was looking at the gray-washed jewel in his hands, and his expression was mournful. "Geeze," he said sadly, "did *I* do that?"

"You see?" Phee said smugly. "To despoil such a loveliness is ashaming: the *sahib* feels like a jerk. The more he uses it, the more he is conditioned not to generate worry in the first place. *Bojemoi.* One's self-indulgence is less tolerable when it is made visible as dung on a diamond, *n'est-ce pas?*"

"What's de t'ing cost?" Fast Eddie asked.

"Just pennies, I told you," Phee said, rummaging in his hyper-pocket again. "Now this little sucker here is even more amazing, calculated to breed greed and fully warranteed." He produced and unwrapped a second jewel. It was similar to the first, but tinted rather than clear. The tint was the blue of a tropic lagoon before the white man came, restful to contemplate. Within it were not color impurities this time, but tiny angels. Miniature aleate females, the size of fireflies and correctly scaled. Somehow they flew slowly and gracefully to and fro within the jewel, as though it were filled with viscous fluid instead of being solid. It made my eyes sting.

"Is anyone here particularly angry?" Phee inquired.

Gentleman John looked long at Josie—who was watching Phee with rapt attention—and then at me. "Well," he said, "I'm not *generally* angry, but I suppose I am *particularly* angry. This bleeder here wrecked a perfectly good pun."

"I heard, from on high," Phee-agreed sympathetically. "Mon-strous. Insupportable. Tough shit. *Venez ici.*"

John took the jewel from him, glanced again at me, murmured, "rat bastard," and closed his eyes.

The jewel began to suffuse with red. The tiny angels tried un-successfully to avoid the red, and where it touched them it con-gealed like quick-setting Jell-O, imprisoning them. Soon they were invisible, and the jewel was an angry scarlet. People gasped.

John opened his eyes, blinked at the thing, and slumped. "What a vile thing anger is," he said bitterly. "I'm truly sorry, Jake." He smiled then. "Glad to be shut of it, though."

"Both jewels will clear again within an hour," Phee said brightly. "With real rage, this one becomes uncomfortably hot to the touch, in proportion to the strength of the fury. Both may be used repeatedly at hourly intervals, and will never wear out or mal-function. The Tsuris Trap and the Rage-Assuager, available only from your pal Al, *votre ami* Phee. *Sanitario e no addictivo—*"

"*Cuanto?*" Eddie said. "I mean, how *much?*"

"*C'est absurdité ou surdité.*" Phee frowned. "I already *told* you, ducks: just *pennies! Fritz du Leiber*, twenty-three skidoo! But you ain't seen *nothin'* yet." He looked at the hyperpocket. "Well, per-haps you have—but the best is yet to come, as the bishop said to the actress. Behold, deholed."

He produced a third jewel, and this one was untinted and con-tained hundreds of tiny beads of every color in the rainbow, writh-ing like kittens beneath the scintillant surface. It . . . wept music as he touched it, little plaintive chords and arpeggios.

"You," he said, pointing at me. "You say you play a guitar. Your face is furry, your hair abundant. You have experience of hallucinogens, *sí?*"

"So?"

"*Ca.*" He tossed me the jewel.

Phantasms flickered briefly around the room as I caught it, little not-quite-seen things. My fingers tingled where they touched it.

"Think of a piece of music," Phee commanded. "Any music that you love."

I picked the first thing that came into my head. Suddenly the room filled with lush strings. I jumped and they were gone.

"Again," Phee directed. "Roll 'em, baby."

The strings returned, and when they had finished their simple eight-chord prelude, Brother Ray sang, "*Georgia . . .*"

People sat back and smiled all over Callahan's bar.

At first it was precisely like the definitive recording that everybody knows—right down to the crackle-pop surface noise of the treasured copy I own. It skipped in the same place. That told me where it was coming from, so I experimented. I have never willingly missed an opportunity to record a Ray Charles TV performance, and I have eleven different versions of "Georgia on My Mind." I concentrated, and Ray suddenly slipped smoothly into the extended bridge he has been using the last few years, where the band and the drummer just go away and let him play with it awhile. The surface noise vanished; fidelity became perfect. When the bridge was over he segued back into the original without a seam, and murmurs of appreciation came from Fast Eddie and a few others.

I glanced down at the jewel, and it seemed that all the glowing beads vanished a quarter-second after my eyes touched it. There was a collective gasp, and I looked up and The Genius himself was sitting at Eddie's beat-up piano, big black glasses and the whitest teeth God ever made, rocking from side to side in that distinctive way and caressing the keys, singing "Georgia on My Mind" for the patrons of Callahan's Place.

His finish was fabulous. I'm proud to say it was not one he has ever, to my knowledge, recorded.

As the applause died down, he modulated from G down to E and began the opening bass riff of "What I Say?" The original Raeletts appeared next to the piano, Margie Hendrix and Darlene and Pat. I shivered like a dog and threw the jewel at Phee, and artists and music vanished.

"Don't get me started," I said. "But thank you from the bottom of my heart. All my life I've wanted to do that. What *is* that thing?"

Phee did not reply vocally, but suddenly there was a flourish of trumpets and the word VISUALIZER was spelled out in the air in letters of cool fire, like neon without tubes, rippling in random air currents. They flared and bisected, wedged apart by a new group of letters all in gold, so that the new construct read: VI-SUAL(SYNTHES)IZER. It flared again, and the parenthetical intruder departed once more.

" 'Synthes,' you've gone . . ." Phee sang, and Josie giggled. "It's a dream machine, dear boy. An hallucinator. Anything you can imagine, it gives auditory and visual substance to. *Je regrette* that at the present state of the art I cannot give you tactile—*but*, if you act *muy pronto* and because I like your face, I'm prepared to throw in olfactory for *not a dime extra*. Freebie, *kapish*?"

Make no mistake: I wanted that thing. But I reacted instinctively, with the reflex-response of a Long Islander to high-pressure sales tactics. "I don't know . . ."

"*Schlep*. Do you *know* what the olfactory mode can *do* for the porn fantasies alone?"

Eddie stared at his now-empty piano stool and shook his head. "How much?" he asked again.

Exasperated, Phee danced to the bar, grabbed up a funnel and took it back to Eddie. He stuck the business end in Eddie's left ear. "JUST PENNIES," he bellowed into it. "I'm telling you," he continued conversationally to the rest of us, "it's a steal. Good for fifteen minutes' use every four hours, an optional headphone effect for apartment use, and there's a failsafe that blows the breaker if you use it to scare people. Hoyoto! *Banzai!* Barkeep, more grog! "

"You ain't paid for the last one yet," Callahan said reasonably.

"Did I hear right through the roof earlier? On *ce soir* the teller of the tallest tale drinks *gratis?*"

"That's so," Callahan admitted.

Josie cleared her throat. "There's . . . another advantage."

Phee looked gallantly attentive.

She turned red. "Oh hell." She went up and whispered in his ear. His left eyebrow rose high, and the propellor beanie doubled its RPM.

"Hoo ha," he stated.

Josie looked around at us. "Well, it's just . . . I guess I'm grateful for a good laugh. Maybe it's an Oedipal thing: my dad is a brilliant jokester. And—and funny men are nicer lovers. They know about pain."

Phee bowed magnificently. "*Mademoiselle,*" he said reverently, "you are clearly the product of an advanced civilization. Furthermore you are spathic. Geologists' term: 'having good cleavage.' *Alors*, correct me now if I err: a truly great tall tale must, first, be a true story—or at least one which cannot be disproved. Second, it must be gonzo, *phweet!*, wacky, Jack. Third, it should conclude with a pun of surpassing atrocity, *nicht wahr?*"

There was murmured agreement all around. Folks ordered drinks and settled back in their chairs.

"Right. Dig it: a true story. I have witnessed this personally from my spacecraft and am prepared to document it. The toilet tanks on your commercial airliners often leak. This results in the formation of deposits of blue ice on the fuselage. The ice is composed of feces, urine, and blue liquid disinfectant. Now: occasionally, when a plane must descend very rapidly from a great height, especially near the Rocky Mountains, chunks of blue ice ranging up to two hundred pounds can—and *do*—break off and shell the countryside. *This is the truth,*" he cried, as we began giggling. "I have seen a UPI photo of an apartment in Denver which was pulped by a one hundred and fifty pound chunk of blue ice. The airline bought the tenants a house—and the landlord a judge."

People were laughing helplessly, and Gentleman John's face was so red I thought he'd burst. "My God," he howled, "can you imagine them *checking in at hospital?* 'Cause of injury, please?' " He caved in.

"Neither of them were hurt," Phee said. "And for a while— until it began to thaw—they were grateful for the coolness it provided. It was summer, you see, and the impact had destroyed their electric fan . . ."

Callahan was laughing so hard his apron ripped. Doc Webster lay on his back on the floor, kicking his feet. Long-Drink laughed his bridgework loose.

"So," Phee concluded, sitting down on thin air and crossing his legs, "even if you live where there are no strategic military targets, you can still be attacked by an icy BM."

Instant silence. A stunned, shuddering intake of breath, and then—the only group scream I have ever heard, a deafening howl of anguish insupportable. Somewhichway it turned, before it was done, into a standing ovation and a barrage of glasses hit the fireplace. Josie ran over and hopped on Phee's lap, renewing the applause. John and I beat our palms bloody.

Callahan came around the bar with a huge grin, a bottle of Bushmill's and three glasses. He held the glasses up, raised an eyebrow inquiringly at Phee, and let go. They stayed there. He poured them full, took one and held it out. "Fec-free for Phee," he boomed. "Keep the bottle." He gave one to Josie, pulled up a chair and sat down next to the third glass.

Phee inclined his head in thanks. "God bless your ass. *Caramba*—is all that you? *Comment vous appelez-vous?*"

"*Je m' appelle* Mike Callahan, *señor.*"

"Sure an' Gomorrah, the saints add preservatives to us, Michael, yer a foiner host than Jasus himself, and him with the free wine and all the fish you can eat. A toast, big cobber, a toast!"

"To Melba?" Callahan suggested.

"I hate Melba toasts. No. To interstellar commerce, *kemo sabe.*"

Callahan raised his glass, as did several others including myself. Oddly, Josie didn't. The toast was echoed and drunk, and the glasses disposed of.

"What else you got for sale?" the big barkeep asked then.

"One more item," Phee said. "Excuse me, Mama." Josie shifted on his lap so that he could reach the nearby hyperpocket. He took out a fourth gem. This one was pink-tinted, more translucent than transparent, and within it were a spiderweb of metallic filaments that made me think of printed circuits. He tossed it to Doc Webster.

"By the bag at your feet you are a medicine man, rotund person. Have you patients in this room?"

"All of them," the fat sawbones rumbled.

"Pick one sick one. That chap there, dear Hippo-crates. Brush him with the bauble." He pointed out Chuck Samms, who all too obviously had recently suffered a bad stroke: Chuck's left side was shot. The Doc frowned down at the pink jewel, and carried it to Chuck. A couple of tiny lights went on inside it as he approached.

"His thumb," Phee suggested.

The Doc looked at Chuck. "Okay?"

Half the mouth smiled. "Sure, Sam." Chuck held out his right thumb, the Doc lifted the jewel, contact was established.

The damned thing took a blood sample, flashed a few contemplative lights, and returned it. As his own blood flowed back into him, Chuck gasped, then yelped, and pushed the jewel violently away from him.

Using both hands.

He looked down at his left hand, and began to smile the first unlopsided smile he'd had in months. Doc Webster gaped at him.

"The price for all four items," Phee said, "FOB, shipping and handling plus applicable tax, is pennies. Literally. Every penny in this room, and nothing else."

"You mean you want all our dough?" Eddie asked.

"No, *cochon!* All your *pennies!*"

I happened to know that Mike keeps about a hundred bucks in pennies in a sack under the bar—we pitch 'em on Friday nights. Still, it sounded like a hell of a deal. Stranger bargains have been made at Callahan's Place, and our sales resistance was smithereened. I started to check my pants—

"*No!*" Josie cried, and leaped from Phee's lap, her face white with fury.

"Why, what is it, my pigeon?" Phee asked, still sitting on nothing. "What deranges you?"

She towered over him in her wrath. "Damn it, Phee, damn you. I was going to wait until I got you home—but this is the Fourth of July, and that was the fourth jewel lie, and the lie is even more abominable than the pun. Screw you, and the reindeer you rode in on."

He blinked. "Here? Now?"

"Damn straight." She took a tube of toothpaste from an inside pocket of her vest, and before the traveling salesman could move, she had circled his knees where they crossed with a loop of toothpaste. He scrabbled at it with his fingers, and she added another loop, pinioning his hands. He began swearing fluently in several tongues—for the "toothpaste" had hardened at once into something that seemed to have the tensile strength of steel cable. Though he tried mightily, Phee could not break free. His command of obscenity was striking, and it might just have melted ordinary steel cable.

"—and may you fall into the outhouse just as a platoon of Ukrainians has finished a prune stew and six barrels of beer," she finished, and she laughed merrily.

Callahan cleared his throat. If you engage the starter on an engine that's already running, it makes a sound like that. "Josie darlin'," he began, "if you don't mind my asking?"

"Aw, you damned fools," she burst out. "My father is right: people who don't read science fiction are the most gullible people there are. *Look at him*, for God's sake: *does he look like an extra-terrestrial to you?*"

Josie had no way of knowing that Noah Gonzalez and I both read SF. Of course Noah works on the Fourth—he's on the County Bomb Squad. "Well," I said, "I guess we just figured his real appearance was too horrible for us to look upon. He's obviously a master of illusions."

"Too right," she snapped, and snatched the propellor beanie from Phee's head. The propellor stopped, and Phee's invisible chair was yanked out from under him. Smiling Buddhas hit the floor hard, and he howled indignantly.

We all blinked and looked around. The change was too subtle to perceive at once. All four jewels had gone opaque, and there was nothing—or rather, there *wasn't* nothing—where the hyperpocket had been, but these things took time to notice. Even when Chuck Samms cried out, the reason was not immediately apparent, for *both* sides of his mouth were turned down . . .

"This is the illusion-maker," Josie said, waving the beanie. "All it is is a hypnotic amplifier. The illusions are gone, now—and he still looks human. Not," she snapped, "that I claim kinship with any pride!"

"Parallel evolution—?" I began.

"Don't be silly. No, *be* silly: assume he's really an alien who just happens to look human. Now explain to me why he came hundreds of light-years—past six other planets, a carload of moons and a million asteroids—to come in here and swindle you out of copper?"

There was only one other possible answer, then. I opened my mouth—and then closed it. I did not, for reasons I could not define, want Josie to know that I was a science fiction reader. You're more talkative if you think your audience doesn't understand you, sometimes.

"He's a time-traveler, you idiots!" she cried, confirming my guess. "Who else would need copper as desperately as your own descendants? With the couple of thousand pennies you morons were going to give him, he could have—well, quintupled his living space at the very least. And he would have left you *nothing*, except for four prop jewels and an admittedly great tall tale to tell.''

Isham Latimer is Callahan's only black regular, and he knows his cue when he hears it. ''Does dis mean dat de diamonds is worthless?''

Josie giggled, losing her anger all at once, and completed the quote. ''Put it dis way: he is de broker, and yo' is de brokee.''

All the tension in the room dissolved in laughter and cheers—leaving behind a large helping of confusion.

''So what's your angle, Josie?'' Callahan asked. ''Where do you come in?''

''Time travel is severely proscribed,'' she said. ''The possible consequences of tampering with the past are too horrible to contemplate.''

''Sure,'' Callahan said. He may not be an SF reader—but all of us at Callahan's know *that* much about time travel. We had another time-traveler in here once, who was worried considerable about that very issue—whether it was moral and/or safe to change the past of a lady he loved, to keep her from being hurt.

''And precisely because it's so tempting to 'mine the past' for all the precious things you wasted and used up on us, that is the most strictly prohibited crime on the books. Pennies are the best dodge for copper: you acquire a bunch in this era, bury them somewhere, then go back home and dig 'em up, properly aged and no way to prove it wasn't a lucky dig.''

''And you—''

''Temporal agents approached my father twenty years ago, and convinced him to sign up as a kind of local way station for authorized time-travelers, on a part-time basis. He's a science fiction writer—who *else* would they dare trust to understand the terrible dangers of time travel? He kept it from Mother and us kids—but about five years ago I found out. I blackmailed his employers into giving me a job on the Time Police.''

''Why?'' Callahan asked.

''Because it's the most *exciting* job I can think of, of course! You know my nature—I love jokes and paradoxes.'' She grinned. ''I'm not *sure*, but I have a hunch I'm going to grow up to be Mom.''

There was a stunned silence.

''So if I understand this,'' I said diffidently, ''Phee here came for the coppers, and you came here for the coppers?''

She whooped with glee, and tossed the beanie into the fireplace. ''Jake, are you busy tonight?''

I tingled from head to toe. "Aren't you?" I asked, indicating Phee.

I *knew* it was a silly question, but I didn't want her to know I knew. Aside from the most obvious benefits of her offer, as long as she didn't know I read SF there was a chance I could pump her for her father's name—and I was curious as hell.

"It won't take me any time at all to deal with him," she said. "Not yours, anyway." I made oh-of-course noises.

"What happens to *him?*" Chuck asked, and his voice was harsh.

"I'd like to cut him in half," Doc Webster said darkly. "Wouldn't be the first Phee I've split."

"He will be dealt with. Not punished—punishment accomplishes nothing. Nothing desirable, anyway. He is a brilliant man, a master hypnotist: he can be of service to his own era. He will simply be surgically implanted with a tiny device. If he ever again makes an unauthorized time-jump, he will acquire a massive and permanent case of BO."

Chuck broke up. "Fair enough."

Phee spoke for the first time since his torrent of profanity. "I apologize, sir, for what I did to you. That last lie *was* the cruelest— and perhaps unnecessary. I . . . I never *could* resist a good dazzle." He shook his head. "I'm sorry," he repeated.

Chuck was taken aback. The half of his face that could hold expression softened. "Well . . . it *was* kind of nice to be whole again there for a minute. I dunno; maybe the havin' of that minute was worth the losin' of it. I'm sorry I laughed at you, mister."

Sitting there in his shorts on the floor with his hands toothpasted to his knees, Phee managed to bow.

"I don't get it," Long-Drink complained. "If this guy wanted pennies, why not just time travel into a bank vault and take a *million* of 'em? Why go through all this rigamarole?"

Phee looked elegantly painted. "What would be the *fun* in that? That's the only thing about being busted that really bothers me: she was here waiting for me. I *hate* being predictable."

"Don't feel bad," Josie told him. "You couldn't have known. This place is a probability nexus. Why, this was the *priori* terminus for the first-ever time-jump."

Why, sure—when I thought about it, our previous time-traveler's brother had *invented* the first time machine. His had been a bulky belt—these people were more advanced.

Phee's eyes widened. He stared around at us. "By Crom, I'm impressed. What did you do?"

"We took up a collection for him," Eddie answered truthfully.

Phee shook his head. "And I took you for yokels. Take me away, officer."

In a way it was a little saddening to see the great Al Phee bestered.

Josie picked him up effortlessly and slung him over her shoulder. With her free hand, she reached into the purse that hung from her other shoulder.

"Uh," I said, and she paused. "You'll be right back?"

She grimaced. "Soon for you. Not for me. I'll be back as quick as I can, Jake—honest! But first I've got to take him in and make out the report and do all the paperwork, and then I promised Dad I'd drop in on him for a quick visit about twenty years from now. But I'll be back before you know it."

"Why twenty years from now?"

"I hate to bother him when he's working. By then he should be done with the Riverworld ser—" She broke off. "I'll be right back," she said shortly, and fumbled in the purse. She and Phee vanished.

And I fell down howling on the floor.

What made it twice as funny was that my ethics forbade me to share the joke with everybody else—I don't think I could have stopped laughing long enough, anyhow. Gentleman John almost killed me when he understood I wasn't going to explain it.

But hell, it was so obvious! I shouldn't have needed that last hint. I didn't even need to know enough German to know what "Bauer" means. I *know* that there's a kind of delirious logic to the way things happen at Callahan's Place, a kind of artistic symmetry.

So if a traveling salesman comes into Callahan's Bar on Tall Tales Night—whose daughter is going to turn out to be his downfall?

MIRROR/ЯОЯЯIM, OFF THE WALL

I have mixed feelings about him. He was, of course, a criminal in the technical sense, but I never cared much for such. And he did have some of the finest booze I ever tasted, and was quite generous with it, which counts for a lot even if it *didn't* taste as good to *him*. Furthermore, he was the only man I know who could have performed so unlikely a miracle as taking a hundred pounds off Doc Webster.

But on the other hand, he was the kind of man who was willing to betray himself to the feds, in order to save himself from the feds—and that strikes me as selfish. Struck him that way too, afterwards.

And so I don't feel too bad about having helped betray him to the feds myself. After all, it saved him from the feds, didn't it?

I'll tell you about it.

I generally don't get to Callahan's Place much before seven at night—but that morning my mailbox had saved my neighbor's life, so I decided noon wasn't too early for a drink or three.

Doris's Valiant had been slipping off the right shoulder, right across the street from my house, and was beginning to nose down off the twenty-foot drop to the marsh flats when it struck the mailbox. The box and the big six-by-six it stood on were of course punted some hundred yards at once, in flinders the smallest of which weighed five pounds, but they held for that millisecond necessary to lift her right front wheel and correct her angle of incidence. Instead of tumbling, the car went down like a cat, on all fours: from my point of view, across the street on my front stoop, she simply disappeared. She cleared the sloping bank by inches, hit the flats in a four-point Evel Knievel which only ruined the suspension system, and came to rest two hundred yards later in Stanley Butt's garden, the bumpers and crannies of the Valiant so crammed with marsh grass, hay, and lupines as to resemble a poor attempt at camouflage. We talked about it in my kitchen, Doris and I, and concluded that while a few inches lefterly would have made her miss the mailbox, fall kattycorner and explode on maybe the fourth bounce, a few feet to starboard would have put her into the telephone pole beside the mailbox and ended it right there. She needed a drink and a ride home, but I keep no liquor in the house (why would I drink *alone?*) and I'd had to leave my car keys and car at Callahan's Place the night before, so I walked her home and let her husband pour her a drink. I declined one, refused to let him take my ten-gallon hat, and left hastily, so that they could collapse in each others' arms and weep while the need was still sharp. I let my feet take me to Callahan's, while my mind ruminated on the fragility of these bags of meat we haul around.

Callahan and Fast Eddie were just pulling into the lot when I got there, and it wasn't until I saw the amp, mixer, and speakers in the bed of the truck that I remembered it was Fireside Fill-More Night, the night Eddie and I jam for Callahan's patrons. I've never tapped out on a gig before, but I didn't feel much like playing or singing, so I told them so, and how come. Callahan nodded and produced a flask from the glovebox, but Eddie began offloading the equipment anyhow—it looked like rain. While Callahan and I shared an afternoon swallow, Eddie staggered to the door with my big Fender Bassmaster, set it down, unlocked the door, hoisted the amp again, took two steps into the bar and dropped the Fender on his feet.

Curiously, I was more puzzled than dismayed—because I was certain that Eddie had screamed a split-second *before* the amp mashed his toes, rather than after.

He instinctively tried to cradle both wounded feet in his hands, but this left him none to hop on, so he sat suddenly down, raising dust from his jeans. But he wasted no time on getting up or even

on swearing—almost as he hit he was ... well ... *moving* backwards, without using hands or feet. Sort of levitating horizontally,
the way Harpo used to do when he wanted to break Groucho up in
the middle of a routine, propelling himself across the stage with his
hams alone. Eddie backed into the truck at high speed, his head
bouncing off the fuselage, and he sat there a moment, still cradling
his injured dogs, face pale.

Callahan and I exchanged a glance, and the big barkeep shrugged.
"That's Eddie for you," he said, and I nodded judicious agreement.

Fast Eddie stared vaguely up at us, and his eyes *clicked* into
focus. All things considered, his expression was remarkable: mild
indignation.

"Mechanical orangutan," he complained, and fell over sideways,
out cold.

Callahan sighed and nodded philosophically. "Probably shat rivets all over the floor," he grumbled, and picked Eddie up under one
beefy arm, heading for the door.

I got there first. I know in my bones that *anything* can happen at
Callahan's, and the Passing of the Mailbox had used up all the
adrenalin I had in stock—but I'd never seen a mechanical orangutan.

But I was not prepared for what I saw. As I cleared the doorway,
a tall demon with pronounced horns came at me fast out of the
gloom. Callahan and Eddie and I went down in a heap, with me on
top, and it knocked the breath back into Eddie. He said only one
word, but it killed three butterflies and a yellowjacket. We sorted
ourselves out and Eddie glared at me accusingly.

"Demon," I explained, and backed away from the open door.

Callahan nodded again. "Monkey demon. Probably lookin' for
Richard Fariña—he usta drink here." He dusted himself off and
lumbered into the bar, receding red hair disarrayed but otherwise
undisheveled. Somehow I knew he planned to buy the demon a
drink.

He cleared the doorway, slapped the lights on with his big left
hand, and stopped dead in his tracks. I was prepared for anything—I
thought—but the two things he did then astounded me.

The first thing he did was to burst into laughter, and a good-sized
whoop thereof: if the shutters hadn't been closed I'm certain dust
would've come boiling out the windows. *One way to drive off a
demon*, I decided dizzily, and then he did the second thing. He
reached into his back pocket, produced a comb and, still looking

straight ahead, put the part back into his hair. (Doc Webster once said of Mike's hair that the part is the whole.)

Then he turned back to me and Eddie, still laughing, and waved us to enter.

"It's okay, boys," he assured us. "It's only a mirror."

Only a mirror!?!

At any other bar in the world, the "only" might have been accurate—barroom mirrors are traditional. But Callahan follows his own eccentric traditions. Where most bars have a mirror, he has a blank wall on which are scribbled thirty years' worth of one-liners, twisted graffiti, and pithy thayingth. They range from allegedly humorous (*"Does a skinny ballerina wear a one-one?"*) to dead serious ("Shared pain is lessened; shared joy increased.") and include at least the punchline of every Punday Night-winning stinker ever perpetrated. Callahan says he'd rather encourage folk wisdom than narcissism. So I refused to be reassured.

I eased up to the door and peered past Callahan. Sure enough, with the lights on, it was evident that there was now an enormous mirror behind the bar, installed in the traditional manner behind the rows of firewater and the cashbox. Only if I squinted at the rolled ends of my ten-gallon hat could I make them look like horns, now, but my mind's eye could see much more clearly how Eddie might have mistaken a Fender with his face on top for a robot orangutan. A part of me wanted very much to laugh very hard, but most of me was too busy being flabbergasted.

I mean, *anything* can happen in Callahan's Place—granted. But the Place itself is supposed to be immutable, unchanging, at least in my mind. "What the hell is *that* doing there?" I yelped.

A man can live his whole life long without ever being granted a straightline like that. Callahan blinked and answered at once, "Oh, just reflecting on things, I guess."

Eddie and I, of course, briefly lost the power of speech, but the little piano man managed to express an opinion of sorts—and, behind the bar, his spitting image did likewise.

We examined the thing together. It was held in place by four clamps that resisted our every attempt to pry them loose—Callahan bent two pry bars all to hell in the attempt. The graffiti seemed unharmed beneath the mirror, as far as we could see, but we could not uncover them. There was no clue as to who might have installed the thing, or why.

"Must have been done overnight," Callahan said. "It sure wasn't here when I left."

We kicked it around for a while, but even a quart of Tullamore Dew failed to shed any light on the mystery. But it did kill most of the afternoon, and finally Callahan glanced up at the Counterclock over the door and tabled the subject. "Sooner or later some joker'll come 'round with a bill for it," he predicted, "and we'll use him to pry it off the wall with." And he busied himself opening up cases of glasses, barely in time. The regulars began showing up, and the glasses started hitting the fireplace. The more inventive the theory offered for the mirror's appearance, the more glasses hit the fireplace. Almost, I suspected Callahan of arranging the novelty himself in secret, for it tripled his average take and generated some fearsomely bad jokes. Nobody even missed my guitar or Eddie's piano.

Because of the commotion the mirror caused, I nearly failed to notice the newcomer. But on account of the mirror itself, I could hardly help it.

I became at least peripherally aware of any unfamiliar face in Callahan's Place. But when this guy appeared four seats down from me, next to Tommy Janssen, I heard him tell Callahan that "Dr. Webster said to say he sent me," so I knew he belonged *some* way or other. I glanced, saw no urgent need or pain in his face, and put him out of my mind. Things happen in their own good time at Callahan's.

And as I started to turn back to Long-Drink McGonnigle, I did the first and only triple-take of my life.

In the mirror, the chair next to Tommy was empty.

By this point in the day, my adrenals were not only out of stock, they were running out of room to file the back orders. So I can't claim any credit for the fact that I kept my composure. But I converted the triple-take into a headshake so smoothly that Long-Drink offered to connect me with a chiropractor and bought me a "neck-unstiffener" besides. When Callahan delivered it, I caught his eye and winked. One eyebrow rose a quizzical half-inch, and I nodded to the mirror, thanking Long-Drink effusively (and sincerely) the while. Poker-faced, Callahan turned back to the mirror, stood stock-still for a second, and then went back to his duties, no more chalant than ever. But as his reflection nodded imperceptibly at mine, I noticed him take a couple cloves of garlic out from under the bar and place them unobtrusively by the cashbox. *As long as the guy doesn't order a Bloody Mary*, I thought, and wondered if any of the firewood came to a point.

By unspoken mutual consent, Mike and I restricted ourselves to watching the stranger as the night wore on. He didn't look much like my notion of a vampire; I'd have taken him for a Democrat. He was of medium height and weight, with few distinguishing features: no long pointed canines, no pointed ears—just a small keloid scar on his left cheek. And yet somehow there was a . . . a *lopsidedness* to him, an indefinable feeling of wrongness that nothing appeared to justify. His hair was parted on the right, like a Jack Kirby character, but that wasn't it. When I saw where he kept his wallet I thought I had it: he was left-handed. One of the determined ones who even has his jacket cut so the inside pocket is on the right—for from that place he soon removed a quart-sized flask and offered it to Tommy Janssen, saying something I couldn't hear.

Callahan clouded up—does a hooker welcome amateur talent?—and began to descend on the stranger like the wolves upon the centerfold. But before he got there Tommy had thanked the guy and taken a hit, and as Callahan was opening his mouth Tommy suddenly let out a rebel yell that shattered all conversation.

"Waaaaaaa-A-A-A-A-*HOO!*"

Everybody turned to see, and the only sound was the lapping flames in the fireplace. Tommy's face was exalted. The stranger smiled a strangely lopsided smile and offered the flask to the nearest man, Fast Eddie. Eddie glanced from the flask to the stranger to the transfigured Tommy and took a suspicious snort from it.

Before my eyes, Eddie's forest of wrinkles began smoothing out one by one. The face revealed was undeniably human.

It smiled.

Long-Drink McGonnigle could contain himself no longer. Snagging an empty glass, he shouldered past me and held it out to the stranger, who smiled benevolently and poured an inch of amber fluid. Drink raised it dubiously to his nostrils, which flared; at once he flung the stuff into his mouth.

His eyes closed. Wax began to drip out of his ears. He screamed. Then he extended a tongue like the one on an old cork boot and began to lick the bottom and sides of the glass.

Callahan cleared his throat.

The stranger nodded, and held out the flask.

Callahan held it like a live grenade, and inspected Tommy, Eddie and Long-Drink. All three were still paralyzed, smiling oddly. He shrugged and drank.

"Say," he said. "That tastes like the Four-Eye Monongahela."

A gasp went up.

The stranger smiled again. "Exactly what I thought, the first time I had anything like it."

"Where'd you get it?" Callahan inquired eagerly.

"Liquor store."

"What *is* it?" the barkeep burst out incredulously.

"King Kong," the stranger said.

"King *Kong?*" Callahan exclaimed.

"What's that, Mike?" I asked. "I don't know it."

"I only had it once," Callahan said. "*Years* ago. It was gimme by some fellers who was camped out in a Long Island railroad yard. One swallow convinced me not to go on the bum after all." He looked down at the flask he still held. "It is the backwards of this stuff."

"I assure you," said the stranger, "that that is King Kong. I bought it in a standard liquor store, transferred it to a flask and brought it here straightaway, unadulterated, just as it came out of the bottle. Nothing has been added or removed."

"Impossible," Callahan said flatly.

"Truth."

"But this stuff tastes *good*. In fact, 'good' ain't even the word. I never had none o' the true Four-Eye, but a feller that had told me if I ever did, I'd know it. And this stuff fits that description."

"*De gustibus non es disputandum,*" the stranger observed. "The point is, I've got four quarts of this stuff out in the car, and I'm willing to trade 'em."

"*How much?*" Tommy, Fast Eddie and Long-Drink chorused, showing their first signs of life.

"Oh, not for money," the stranger demurred. "I'll swap even, for five quarts of your worst whiskey."

"Huh?" "Huh?" "Huh?"

"What's the catch?" Callahan asked.

"No catch. You line up five quarts of whiskey—and I demand

pure rotgut. I'll match them with five quarts of my King Kong . . . precisely like this one," he added hastily. "Sample them all you wish. When you're satisfied, we all go home happy. Think of me as a masochist."

"It helps," Callahan admitted. "All right, bring on your sauce."

The guy excused himself and headed for the parking lot, and an excited buzz went round the room. "Whaddya think, Mike?" "Think it's really the Four-Eye?" "What was it like, Eddie?"

The last-named groped for adequate words. "Dat incestuous child is de best oral-genital-contacting booze I ever drank," Eddie said approximately.

"I dunno from Four-Eye," said Long-Drink reverently, "but it's for *me*."

Tommy only eyed the flask. His face was wistful.

The stranger returned with the additional four quarts, and beheaded all four flasks. "Sample up," he urged, and a stampede nearly began. Callahan filled his great lungs and bellowed, and all motion ceased at once.

"I will sample the hooch," he said flatly.

Amid a growing hush, he bent to each flask and sniffed. Then he placed his tongue over the end of one, inverted it, and put it down again.

"Yep."

He repeated the procedure with the second.

"Yep."

The third.

"Yep."

The fourth.

His face split in a huge grin. "Yes, sir."

Pandemonium broke loose, a hubbub of chatter and speculation that sounded like a riot about to happen. The roar built like a cresting tsunami, and then was overridden by an enormous bellow from Callahan.

"If we can have some order in here," he roared, "there'll be drinks on the house for as long as this stuff holds out."

Sustained standing ovation.

When it had died down, the big Irishman turned to the stranger. "I don't believe I got your handle," he said.

"Bob Trevor," is what I thought he said.

"Bob," Callahan said, "I am Mike Callahan and I believe I owe you some nosepaint. What's your pleasure?"

"Oh," Trevor said judiciously, "I guess Tiger Breath'd do just fine."

Another gasp of shock ran round the room.

"*Tiger* Breath?" Callahan cried. "Why, the only use for that stuff is poison ivy of the stomach. Tiger Breath'll kill a cactus."

"Nonetheless," Trevor insisted, "it's Tiger Breath I'm bargaining for. Have you got any?"

Callahan frowned. "Hell yeah, I got a couple gallons in the back—I use it to unplug the cesspool. But that stuff's worse'n King . . . worse'n King Kong's *supposed* to be."

"Whip it out," the stranger said.

Shaking his head, Callahan lumbered out from behind the bar and fetched a half-keg from the back. Its only markings were four Xs (a nice classical touch, I thought) and a skull and crossbones. People made way for him, and he set it on the bar.

"You're welcome to all of it," the barkeep declared.

Trevor unstopped the bung. A clear ten feet away, a fly intersected an imaginary circle drawn round the bunghole. The fly went down like a shot-up Stuka, raising a small cloud of sawdust from the floor when it hit. The nondescript stranger tilted the barrel, and the slosh sounded like a dangerous animal trying to get out. He poured a sip's worth into an empty glass; the drops that spilled ate smoking holes in the mahogany bartop. Tiger Breath is industrial-strength whiskey, and it tastes like rotten celery smells. It is perceptibly worse than King Kong.

He sniffed the bouquet with obvious relish, and puckered up. As the first load went past his tonsils his face lit from within with a holy light, a warm soft glow like a gaslight jack-o'-lantern. His pupils opened to their widest aperture and I saw his pulse quicken in his throat. His smile was a beatitude.

"Done," he said.

He and Callahan shook hands on it, and the rest of us marched as one man to the bar and held out our glasses. Callahan returned to his post and began measuring out shots of Trevor's mystery mash, and not a word was spoken nor a muscle moved until two flasks were empty and the last glass full. Then Callahan's voice rang out.

"To Bob Trevor."

"*To Bob Trevor!*"

And we drank.

*   *   *

At once, my eyes clicked into true focus for the first time in my life, my IQ rose twenty points, and my cheeks buzzed. A thin sheen of sweat broke out over every inch of my body. My powers clarified and my perceptions sharpened; my pulse rate rose high and stabilized; the universe took on a crisp, brilliant presence; and none of these things was anything more than incidental to the *TASTE*, oh God the taste . . .

There are no words. "Rich" is pitifully inadequate. "Smoky" is hopelessly ambiguous. "Full" is self-descriptive, semantically meaningless, and "smooth" is actually misleading. It felt, to the tongue and to the taste buds, like I imagine a velvet pillow must feel to the cheek—and it kicked like a Rockette. It ennobled the mouth.

It was the Wonderbooze.

I gazed at my fellows—and knew them at once in a new and subtle and infinitely compassionate way, and knew that they now knew me too. We began to speak, within an empathy so profound as to be nearly telepathy, leaping a million parsecs and a hundred years of intellectual evolution with every fragmented sentence, happily explaining the alleged mysteries of life to each other and sorrowing cosmic sorrows. Men and women wept and laughed and embraced each other, and never a hail of more scrupulously empty glasses hit the fireplace. I found a new reason to admire Callahan's custom: it would have been sacrilegious to use those glasses again for a lesser fluid.

As the conversations gained depth and profundity, Long-Drink and I stepped up to Trevor and smiled from our earlobes. "Brother," said the Drink, "let us assist you."

"Why, thank you," he said, smiling back.

Drink and I picked up the half-keg between us and poured his glass full of Tiger Breath. Trevor drank deep, and since we already had the keg in the air it seemed foolish not to top off his glass, and then it seemed reasonable to line up some glasses for him and fill those so we wouldn't have to keep shouldering the keg, and in the end we poured six glasses full to be on the safe side, and sure enough he drank them all. So to be polite Drink and I had Callahan pour us some more of his King Kong, although it was the sort of booze that left no need for a second snort, and we sipped while Trevor gulped, and it got pretty drunk out. I remember walking over to where the fly lay dead on the sawdust, dipping my finger into my glass and letting a drop of Wonderbooze fall onto the fly. At once he rose from the floor in a series of angry spirals, spraying sawdust, and I swear he shouldered me aside on his way out the door. The conversation got a little hard to follow, then. I sort of remember the Drink insisting that a close analysis of Stephane Grappelli's later music clearly proved that infinity is translucent; I vaguely recollect Callahan challenging us to name one single person we had ever met or heard of that wasn't a jackass; I believe I recall Fast Eddie's reasoned argument for the existence of leprechauns. But the next stretch of dialogue I retain in its entirety.

Trevor: "Who's that stepping on my fingers?"

Me: "That's you."

"Oh. That's all right then. Beer for ev'body, on me. Gotta celebrate."

Callahan nodded and began setting 'em up.

"Fren'ly place," Trevor went on. "Helpful fellas. Hardly seem backwards atall."

"Naw," I agreed. "*Strange,* yes. Backwards, no."

"Strange?"

Callahan began passing beers around, and I snagged one. "Sure. Li'l green men. Time-travelers. *Anything* can happen in Callahan's joint. But not backwards. This guy here, now," I pointed at Long-Drink, "this long drink o' beer here, did you know sometimes at midnight he turns into a driveway?"

The punchline, of course, was that the Drink works as a night watchman two nights a week, and turns into the driveway of KDC Chemicals at midnight on the dot. But I never delivered.

"Mmmm," mused Trevor. "Like to see that. Wha' timesit?"

And Drink and I, not thinking a thing of it, gestured with our beers at the Counterclock.

The 'Clock has always seemed to suit Callahan's Place perfectly. I don't know where Mike got it, and I've only seen one other like it, in the New York apartment of a lovely lady named Michi Stasko, and I don't know where she got hers either. What it is, it runs in reverse. I mean, the numbers are reversed—I, ς, ε, ↳, etc.—and run *counter*clockwise from ςI, and the works are geared to run in reverse accordingly. It's a rather elaborate jape, but like I say it suits the Place, and if you hang out long enough at Callahan's you often have to stop and transpose in your head to make sense of a normal clock. Doc Webster has gone to the extent of having a mirror installed in the inside cover of his pocketwatch so he can tell the time at a glance. Apparently Trevor just hadn't noticed the Counterclock over the door until now, and I always enjoy observing people's first-time reactions to it. But I'd never witnessed so spectacular an effect before.

Trevor saw the clock; his eyes widened to the size of egg yolks and the blood drained out of his face. He let out a hell of a yell, backed off two paces, raced up to the bar and vaulted it, plunging headfirst into the mirror.

I mean *into* the mirror.

He had disappeared into it up to the hips and was still in headlong flight when Callahan's meaty hand trapped a flying ankle and yanked backwards, hard. Trevor came sailing back out of the mirror and into the real world like a dog jerked from a pond by its leash, and he dangled upside down from a fist the size of a catcher's mitt, swearing feebly. The big barkeep was expressionless, which is his scariest expression.

"You owe me ten bucks for them beers," he said quietly.

I don't care *how* drunk you are; if a chair bites you on the leg, you sober up at once. Your mind is perfectly capable of fighting off your own bloodstream if it must. It's an emergency system, beyond volitional control, and it doesn't *care* if it makes your head hurt. I found myself sober, at once.

But it probably didn't help Trevor any to be upside down. Clearly, his first action showed confused thought. He reached into his right hand pocket with his right hand, and pulled out and gave to Callahan a bill.

Callahan glanced at it and frowned. "Mister," he said, walking around from behind the bar, still holding Trevor by the ankle at arm's length, "up until a minute ago I liked you okay. But a man who'll try and stiff me twice running might try it a third time, and I can't be bothered." With no change in the tone or rhythm of his speech, he began during the last sentence to swing Trevor around by the ankle, in a wide circle paralleling the floor. Fast Eddie, divining the boss's intent with the supersonic uptake which has earned him his name, sprang forward and opened the front door.

Centrifugal force prevented Trevor from getting enough air into his lungs to shout, but I noticed something fluttering from his *left* hand, and read it the way you read the label on a spinning record.

"Hold it, Mike," I called out. "He's got the sawbuck he owes you."

"If it's like the last one, he'll only bounce the once," Callahan promised, but he slowed his swing, grabbed Trevor's collar with his other fist and set the hapless stranger down on the floor feet first. Trevor spun three times and collapsed into a chair.

"I don't understand at all," he said dizzily. "Which side am I on?"

"The flip side, apparently," I said, "if you really tried to cheat Callahan."

"But the mirror . . . that clock . . . I was halfway *through* the mirror, it *must* be a Bridge . . ." He shut up and looked confused.

I looked at Callahan. "The mirror must be a bridge. Because of the clock."

He nodded. "Mechanical orangutan."

Then I saw the first bill Trevor had offered Callahan, lying forgotten on the floor. It said it was a OI2 bill.

It actually began to make a twisted kind of sense. I turned back to Trevor and pointed a finger at him. "I only *thought* you said 'Trevor,' " I said wonderingly. "It was 'Trebor,' wasn't it? Robert Trebor?"

Trebor nodded.

"There's a mirror dimension," I went on, "one identical to our own, but mirror-reversed. And you invented a dimensional bridge . . ."

He looked at it from all sides and gave up in confusion. "Yes," he admitted. "It can only be *initiated* in my continuum, because the molecules of the activating substance, thiotimoline, have different properties when they're reversed. But if the first bill I gave you looks backwards to you, then I must be in the *other* dimension, where a Bridge can't be activated. But I *did* get halfway through that mirror instead of breaking it, and there's that clock—I just don't understand this at all."

"The clock?" Long-Drink spoke up. "Why that's just—ouch."

". . . just one of the many mysteries we have to consider," I finished smoothly, smiling at the Drink and rocking back off of his toes again. "So perhaps you'd better just tell us the whole thing."

Trebor looked around at us suspiciously "You'd blow the whis tle," he accused.

Callahan drew himself up to his full height (a considerable altitude). "If I understand this," he rumbled, "you ain't tried to cheat me after all, so I owe you an apology. But I'd as soon you didn't insult my friends.''

It's a traditional moment at Callahan's, familiar to all of us by now. The Newcomer Examines Us and Decides Whether to Trust Us or Not. Some take their time; some make a snap decision to open up. Nobody *ever* pressures them, one way or the other. Most of 'em cop. I had to admire Trebor at that moment. His mind must have been racing at a million miles an hour, just like mine, but he brought it under control for long enough to give his full attention to evaluating each of us one by one. Finally, as most do, he nodded. "I guess I've got to tell *some*body. And even if you wanted to cross me up, there isn't a sober witness in the lot of you. Okay.''

We all settled into listening attitudes, and Callahan passed around fresh beers to them as needed 'em.

"Yes, I am an inventor," he began, "and I did invent a dimensional Bridge—which my counterpart in *this* dimensional continuum could *not* do, since as I said thiotimoline doesn't work right here.''

"Then this *ain't* a perfect mirror of your world,'' Long-Drink interrupted.

"No, Trebor agreed. ''Not a perfect mirror. There are subtle, generally unimportant differences. In my continuum, for instance, all the rock groups are different and Shakespeare wrote Bacon. Disparities like that, that make no tangible difference to the world at large. But they're essentially similar—like 'identical' twins. It's only because of their vast congruencies that the two continua lie close enough together for a Bridge to be feasible at all.''

"Then you're like a time-traveler into the past,'' I pointed out, "at least in a sense. If you change *this* world in any significant way, you'll never be able to return to your own.''

"Precisely what I'm afraid of,'' Trebor agreed. ''Which is why this Bridge-mirror of yours disturbs me so much. Because I didn't build it, which means someone else did, which means the chances of some accident making the two continua diverge have just effectively doubled. At *least*. I ought to get home at once . . . but I *can't*.''

Because his Bridge couldn't be activated from this side? Surely he must have planned for such a contingency. I always buy a round-trip ticket.

Unless I'm rushed . . .

"What about your counterpart?" I asked, breaking his train of thought. "The Robert Trebor of *this* world, I mean?"

"Oh, I swapped places with him," Trebor said absently.

"Where's he now?"

"In jail, I should exp . . . uh, I don't know."

"I don't get this," Callahan growled, "but I don't think I like it."

I was still enough under the influence of the Wonderbooze to be capable of positively Sherlockean flights of deduction. "I think I get it, Mike. Trebor here invents a dimension-Bridge to our world, right? What does he do? Collect samples of our 'reversed' artifacts as proof of where he's been. Then when he gets home, he gets cagey and decides to keep his mouth shut. That makes sense: if too many people hear about the Bridge, it becomes useless.

"But he makes a fatal error. Through some mix-up, just like the one he pulled here tonight, he spends some of *our* money over *there*. This puts the feds onto him, and he finds it necessary to change neighborhoods in a hurry. So he steps through the Bridge to *our* world again, somehow suckers his mirror-twin into trading places with him, and burns his Bridge behind him. He probably has a second Bridge hidden somewhere, set to activate itself whenever the heat has died down—all he has to do is wait. His twin takes a fall on a bad-paper rap, and he walks away clean. Pretty slick."

There was a pistol in Trebor's hand. I noted absently that the safety was on the wrong side, and that it was off.

"Very astute," he said quietly.

"Listen, Trebor," I called, "don't be a jerk! Right now you're wanted by the cops in one dimension only—in *this* one your biggest problem is that a barfull of guys think you stink. Don't blow it." I spoke with great haste, but my mind was racing even faster.

"You have a point," he allowed. "As long as no one is foolish enough to get in my way, I believe I'll just take my Tiger Breath and toddle off." He picked up the half-keg in his right arm and started edging toward the door.

The deductions were coming like clusters of grapeshot now. I glanced up at the mirror, and what I saw there confirmed all speculation. Trebor *had* a reflection in the mirror, now, and the image looked straight at me with pleading eyes.

"Hold on, buddy," I barked. "The least you can do is tell us why you went through all this."

He stopped, about three feet out of position. I wanted him right on the chalk line from which one addresses the fireplace. "I don't expect you'll believe me, at this point, but I sincerely want to improve both worlds," he said.

"How? By swapping your booze for ours?"

"That's one small way," he agreed. "Alcohol has a symmetrical molecule, so either one gets you loaded. It's the congeners, the asymmetrical esters which produce the taste and the impact, that make one world's mead another world's poison." He paused, and giggled. To my annoyance, so did I. "But there are infinite possibilities. That's what I've been doing for the last week: walking around your world thinking of all the splendid possibilities. Once it's safe to use my auxiliary Bridge, I could . . . well, figure it out for yourself. Suppose I swapped our smog for yours, molecule by molecule, in bulk? The reversed ozone wouldn't be an irritant any more . . ."

"Brilliant," I said sarcastically. "It'd still block sunlight and foul our lungs, but it wouldn't be irritating enough to remind us to clean up the source any more. Remove the nuisance value and leave the menace intact, that's a *great* idea, Trebor." I was frantically trying to catch Callahan's eye without alerting Trebor, and at last I succeeded. I motioned imperceptibly toward the mirror, and Callahan casually turned to it. The mirror-image of Trebor gesticulated at him, and I prayed that Mike would dope it out in time. Just like Doris's Valiant and my mailbox: the only thing that could help Trebor now was an unexpected collision.

Trebor failed to notice. "Well," he said, plainly crestfallen, "then suppose I imported food from my dimension, and exported yours? Really fattening items, I mean. Tarts, creampuffs, banana splits. The stereisomer of a strawberry shortcake would taste as good as the real thing—I know, I've tested it—but your digestive system would ignore it entirely. All the fat people could get thin!"

Callahan answered this time, coming around the bar with an air of total innocence, plainly involved in the intellectual exercise of talking to this nice man with the pistol. Trebor moved to let him by, covering him carefully with the pistol, placing himself just where I wanted him to be. I hoped Mike understood his part.

"Nope, I'm afraid that's no good either, pal," he boomed. "Glandular cases aside, the only genuine cure for fat is to not be a hog. Your method would encourage fat people to keep on being hogs—so, they'll keep on being fat people, regardless of what they happen to weigh. You'd know one anywhere. That's the third time you've proposed to treat the symptoms instead of the disease.''

"*Third* time?" Trebor said, puzzled.

"Yeah. The first was when you decided you could get yourself out of a jam by throwing your mirror-twin to the wolves. They used to say when I was a kid that that kinda stuff'd grow hair on your palms. Self-abuse, I mean. And just like the last two 'cures' you proposed, it didn't cure a thing. *Look!*"

He pointed over Trebor's shoulder at the mirror, and Trebor smiled.

"That's an *old* old gag," he said reprovingly.

And then Fast Eddie caught sight of the mirror and yelped, and Trebor must have known the runty little piano man was no actor, for he whirled then, gun ready, and—

—froze. In the mirror, he saw himself, keg and all, but the "right" hand held no pistol, and it was upraised in a ritual gesture that loses nothing by mirror-reversal. Trebor's jaw dropped, he raised the pistol . . .

And Callahan kicked him square in the ass.

No other man among us could have pulled it off—but Callahan is built along the lines of Mount Washington, and I've seen him carry a full keg in each hand. His big size-twelve impacted behind Trebor's lap with the speed and power of a cannonball, lofting the inventor into the air, clean over the bar and into the mirror. As he struck it, he seemed to reverse direction and bounce back into the room, landing in a heap on the sawdust.

But when he landed, his hand was empty.

"Thanks," he gasped to Callahan. "I *needed* that."

And in the mirror, a man in a gray flannel suit stepped up to *that* Trebor, took away his pistol, and slapped handcuffs on him. The gray man turned to the mirror, aimed the pistol at it, and pulled the trigger. There was no bang, but the mirror exploded in a million shards, which fell to the floor of Callahan's Place with the multiple crashes you'd expect.

Fifteen minutes later, Bob Trebor—the one who *belonged* here—was sitting by the fireplace with his feet up, sipping at some Wonderbooze and rounding up the story of his exploits in Mirrorland.

"If the local police had apprehended me, it might have been a sadder story. But the IBꟻ has some people bright enough to add together my story plus the fact that my fingerprints were mirror-reversed plus the scar on the wrong cheek plus what the X rays showed and come up with the plain truth—and tough-minded enough to believe their own eyes. Pretty soon everybody I was talking to was named Smith, and they cooked up a plan to trap the other Trebor and send me home again. They put a top IBꟻ computer onto predicting Trebor's movements, using data I supplied them as well as their own dossiers. Then, with access to *his* lab and notes, I used my similar background and skills to build another Bridge. It took me a week. By that time computer analysis indicated that he was 89 percent liable to come in here, tonight, so we had the Bridge installed. I hope you didn't mind?''

"Not at all," Callahan assured him. "Livened up a dull night."

"I don't get it," Eddie complained. "Why din't the feds just come t'ru de Bridge an' bust 'im?"

"They couldn't, Eddie," Trebor said patiently. "Jurisdictional questions aside, the more changes they caused in *this* continuum, the greater the chance of separating the two forever. They were nervous about doing anything at all."

"So you worked it out with the folks at Callahan's Place—the *other* Callahan's—and they agreed to stage as perfect an exchange as possible," I said wonderingly. It was kinda nice to know that each world had a Callahan's—but I wondered if the other me still had his wife and kids. Probably not, or he wouldn't be there . . . but I wonder.

"Yes," Trebor agreed. "And fortunately for me, you were as quick on the uptake as your counterparts assured me you'd be. You followed my cues beautifully."

"The Wonderbooze helped," Callahan observed, sweeping the last of the mirror into the fireplace.

"That it did. Amazing what molecular reversal will do for liquor." He gazed meditatively at his glass.

"That's what *I* don't get," I admitted "Most of our food must have been wrong for his digestive system—and theirs must've been mostly useless to you. How come neither of you came down with malnutrition?"

"We were both starting to," Trebor said drily. "That's what brought *him* to Dr. Webster, which in turn brought him here. He must have planned to use his alternate Bridge to bring food across eventually, and he must have had a cache of food *with* him that he could ration out 'til then. If I find it at my house I'll bring it around.'' That, by the way, is how Doc Webster came to lose a hundred pounds. For a while, anyway—the hog. Don't tip him off, okay? ''I guess he simply expected me to starve—if he thought about it. He couldn't have been very imaginative, or he'd have realized that I had enough evidence to sell the truth to the ᴵᴮꟻ.''

''That kinda bothers me too,'' I said. ''The feds are not, for one reason and another, my favorite people—and I don't imagine a mirror-fed is any better. I have to admit I don't find it reassuring that men analagous to our FBI possess a secret bridge to our world.''

''True,'' said Callahan. ''But what do we do? Tell *our* feds? With no sober witnesses and no way to make a working Bridge in *this* world? If we *could* put it over, would it help—or make things worse?''

''Forget it,'' Trebor advised. ''Whatever their intentions, there isn't a lot they can do, for good *or* ill. If they take any action benefiting their continuum at the expense of ours, the two continua become too dissimilar and the Bridge is useless.''

Callahan burst into gargantuan laughter. ''I'll bet they're sittin' around a table right now, quiet as mice, wonderin' what the hell they can possibly *do* with the goddam thing,'' he whooped, and slapped the bar.

The picture of a dozen top government thinkers staring in silent frustration at a device more awesome than the atomic bomb—with no known use—was so lovely that we all broke up, and Eddie struck up Stevie Wonder's ''It Ain't No Use.''

''At least they got a half-keg o' Wonderbooze out of it,'' Long-Drink yelled, and we laughed louder; and then Eddie yelled, ''An' so did *we!*'' and a cheer went up that rattled the rafters.

But I noticed that Trebor wasn't smiling. ''What's wrong, Bob?''

He sighed moodily and sipped of the Wonderbooze. ''It's not fair,'' he said.

''How do you mean?'' Callahan asked. ''You're home free and your rotten twin is in ʜɈɹowꙅnɒvɘ⅃—what's your beef?''

''That's it precisely,'' Trebor said exasperatedly. ''My counterpart is, I agree with you, rotten. I knew him only for the half hour it took him to shanghai me into stepping through his damned Bridge, but in retrospect I don't believe I've ever met a more classic sociopath. I, on the other hand, like to think of myself as . . . well, as one of the good guys, and I believe I've conducted myself honorably throughout this affair. I even took a kick in the pants that

I'm not certain I deserved. That's why I think it's unfair."

He emptied his glass, tossed it into the fire, and sighed again.

"Why is it," he mourned, "that *I* will never again see my face in the shaving mirror without wincing?"

PART III

CALLAHAN'S SECRET

For Eleanor Wood, and Susan Allison

THE BLACKSMITH'S TALE

Once I bought a watch whose battery was rated for one year. The next time I gave it a thought was when it failed—four years later. Something familiar cannot be odd, until it stops.

Similarly, there is no set opening time at Callahan's Place. Once I came by at three in the afternoon, to talk to Callahan about something, and found that the place had been open for over an hour; another time I arrived at 7 P.M. and Mike was just opening the door. But somehow, for the better part of a decade, it never struck me that the Place was always open when I arrived—until the night it wasn't.

Nearly nine o'clock of a warm wet summer evening, and the door was shut tight. Only dim light came through the windows, nothing like the warm cheery glow the Place has when it's open, and the only thing in the parking lot besides my own car was a big beat-up van I didn't recognize.

The rain complicated things. I don't mind rain a lot, and I *like* it when it's warm—as it was that night—but it had been coming down hard for the last fifteen minutes, and so the note posted on the door was only partly legible. I could translate "***empor rily losed f r enovat ons***," and "***doo pens at***," but the *time* at which the doo' would 'pen was three blurs, all rounded at the top. Perhaps "9:00," perhaps "9:20" or "9:30." Or perhaps it read "8:30," and the job, whatever it was, was running overtime. Worst, there was a big long blur *after* the time. It might have said "9:00 sharp," but it could just as easily have been "3:00 Friday."

When that watch battery I mentioned earlier finally failed, I buried it in my backyard, respectful of its magnificent achievement. But that was after reflection. My first reaction was acute annoyance. I thought my watch had failed me.

So it was now. I could think of several ways to go kill some time—but how much time? Meanwhile I was getting soaked. So I did what I don't think I would have done under other circumstances.

I opened the door and walked in.

I knew it wouldn't be locked, because there is no lock on that door. In the dozen years I've been coming to Callahan's, there've been four attempted afterhours burglaries that I know of. None of them used the front door; none bothered to try. (Callahan dealt with them situationally. One is now a regular customer, and never mind which one; another, a hard-guy type, got two broken elbows.)

But I should have knocked first, and waited for Mike to open the door or holler "Come in," and gone away if he didn't.

Which he wouldn't have. When I had closed the door behind me there was no sign of him. But I failed to notice; once I'd wiped my glasses dry, I was too busy being thunderstruck.

Do you remember that time I told you about once, when I walked into Callahan's to find a mirror behind the bar, where no mirror had ever been before? And it disoriented me so much that I mistook my reflection for an approaching demon, with "horns" that were really the brim of my Stetson hat? This was like that. Something as familiar as Callahan's Place is not supposed to change. The watch battery is supposed to last forever. I may have actually twitched and squeaked, I don't know.

The light was as bad as it had been that other time, with the mirror, and so once again my brain, trying to resolve unexpected data into a pattern, made a first approximation that vaguely matched something in its files and served me up a trial hallucination. For a predator such as man, a wrong guess can be preferable to a slow one.

What I thought I saw, off to my left, a few yards away, was a *giant* ebony snake, scales shimmering in the semidarkness, maybe three feet in diameter, coiled around a tree. Tree and snake appeared to extend up through the ceiling without rupturing it.

I blinked and it wasn't a snake, it was an immense DNA double helix clinging to a barber pole, pulsing dully with life. So I blinked again.

(First the predator brain searches the file of Dangerous Things. If that doesn't work, it tries Nondangerous Living Things. Only then does it calm down and search all the other files. Two seconds, tops.)

It was a spiral staircase up to the roof.

"*Cushla machree*," I said softly.

What had made it seem to be a *double* helix was the heavy railing which paralleled the stairs. The "scales" were the spaces between the railing supports. The apparent shimmering and/or pulsing was because one of the very few lights in the room, a small flourescent behind the bar, was flickering rapidly.

I said (prophetically enough) that I would be dipped in shit, but I relaxed. I was beginning to understand.

Mike Callahan lets his customers take their drinks up on the roof if the weather's agreeable. There's a dumbwaiter to ferry cash down and drinks up. But until now the only access for humans and most other customers had been a vertical ladder and hatch. Some of the regulars had trouble getting up the ladder due to age or infirmity. Certain others could get *up* just fine—but found that the added ballast of four or five drinks seriously disrupted their balance on the way *down*. Something about the center of gravity shifting, Doc Webster said. Just a few days before, Shorty Steinitz had broken an ankle—and here was Callahan's response.

"Hey, Mike," I called out, and got no answer. The curtain behind the bar was closed. I had gall enough to enter Callahan's bar un-invited, but not his living space. I called his name once more and wandered over to inspect the new staircase.

It was a cast-iron joy to behold. I'm totally ignorant about such things, but I could tell that it was *old*, and *beautiful*, and very well designed. You could not fall down that staircase. You couldn't even bark your shin. It was so well installed that it looked like it'd been there for years—except for the odd bits of welding spatter in the sawdust on the floor—and indeed it fit right in with the atmosphere of Callahan's Place. Ornamented rather than starkly functional, sub-tly and ingeniously worked in ways I was not competent to appre-ciate even if the light had been adequate, it would not have looked out of place in a cellar jazz joint or a monastery, might have done time in both. It invited one to climb it.

So I did.

The footing was secure, the risers precisely the right height, the treads precisely the right depth. It had to be a modular assembly. A single giant staircase, even if it had happened to fit through the front door, would have required trucks, cranes, dollies, rollers, block and tackle, and much time—whereas an assembly job this size could conceivably have been installed in a single day by two or three big skilled men. But it was so *cunningly* assembled that it was hard to be sure. This had to have cost Callahan a bundle.

I wound my way around and up until I stood in a sort of hut with a door opening onto the roof. I thought about rainwater spilling down into the bar below, but when I experimentally opened the door a crack, there was no flood. I pushed it open and the everpresent sound of rain went from bass rumble to treble hiss. It seemed to be easing up.

The rain did not spill indoors because the floor of the hut was slightly higher than the roof. But you did not have to remember to step down; there was a short ramp. I know little more about carpentry than I do about iron work—but I know good design when I fail to trip over it. It figured that Mike Callahan would hire the best man available to do surgery on his Place.

The door closed quickly; some unseen damping mechanism kept it from slamming; in the rain it made no sound at all. I walked around the hut once, admiring it . . . then walked around it again, admiring the countryside.

I'm sure you know the strange, special magic of high places. Have you ever been on one at night? In the warm rain?

To be sure, Callahan's roof is a wonderful place from which to view the world in nearly any weather. The land falls sharply away to the north and east, and incredibly for Long Island (even for Suffolk County) it is largely undeveloped, raw trees as far as you can make out. To the south and west, beyond the parking lot, runs Route 25A, sparsely lined with garishly lit sucker traps. (Fairly heavy traffic, but Callahan doesn't get a lot of transient trade. The parking lot is hidden by tall hedges, the driveway is inconspicuous; the only sign is the one over the front door.) Beyond the highway you can just make out one of the more expensive subdivisions, well zoned, landscaped, and cared for; on Christmas Eve, with a couple of Irish coffees warming your belly and all the lights blazing in the distance, it looks . . . well, Christmasy.

Tonight the roof was a warm flat rock on which many large

somethings were peeing, from a great height. The highway looked glorious—people who wear glasses are lucky, we have stars on rainy nights—but my clothes were getting wet. Wetter. I considered ducking back inside . . . but as I said, I *like* warm rain. I particularly like to be naked in warm rain, and don't get a lot of opportunities. Mike wouldn't mind, and anyone else I would see drive up.

So I stripped and looked about for the driest place to stash my clothes.

The dumbwaiter seemed like the best bet; I could wedge its door open with something to keep it up here at roof level. I padded barefoot toward its tall housing—and discovered that it was already so wedged, with a chisel. Inside was a pile of clothing. Big man's clothes, faded jeans, denim shirt, boots, sized to fit only one man I knew. That solved the mystery of Callahan's whereabouts. He must be a secret naked-in-the-rain nut too. He was going to jump a foot in the air when I came around the dumbwaiter. This would be good for laughs—and it might cost him a couple of drinks to keep the story to myself . . .

It was just possible that my fellow nudist was not Callahan—in which case I was properly dressed to meet him. Onward.

I should have *lifted up* the jeans. The underwear might have warned me. I piled my clothes on top of the others, walked around the dumbwaiter, and became one myself. Waiting, dumb, one foot in the air. She was very beautiful, and in the instant I saw her I wanted urgently to *do this right*, to not make any mistakes. It was not going to be easy.

I am sorry to say that you would probably not have thought she was beautiful—unless you, too, are a pervert. I mean, going naked in the rain is one thing, but I'm talking major league perversion here. (From my point of view, I am the only sane man in a perverted culture. Perverts always feel that way.)

I will state the perversion: I like women who look like women. That is, my ideal of feminine beauty adheres closely to that which has been the generally accepted consensus from the dawn of time until quite recently and quite locally.

What you would probably have said if you'd seen her, naked or clothed, is, "Handsome woman; she could be beautiful if she lost the weight." You would probably have gallantly tried to avoid looking at, let alone commenting on her body—you almost certainly would not have drunk the sight of it the way I did.

She did not, in other words, look the way North America thinks women should look. She did not look like a thirteen-year-old boy with plums in his shirt pockets. Those were her clothes in the dumb-waiter. And I do not even mean that she was a Jayne Mansfield/ Loni Anderson type, with one of those big bodies that seem packed tight, compressed snugly by invisible plastic, firm as a weightlifter's shoulder. She had big glorious saggy tits, and what are sometimes affectionately called ''love handles,'' (that is, the people who use the term sometimes mean it affectionately) and a round belly and thighs that would jiggle when she walked.

She looked, in short, much like half the mature women in this sorry culture, and she would have opened the nose of most of the heterosexual males who ever lived. Praxiteles, Titian, Rubens, Ro-din, any of the great ones would have reached for their tools, if not their work utensils, at the sight of her.

You know: a whale. A hippo. I'm telling ya, Morty, this broad was two hunnert pounds if she was a friggin' ounce, no shit. One of America's millions of rejects, forever barred from The Good Life, too sunk in sloth or genetic degeneracy to torture herself into the semblance of an undernourished adolescent male. A pig. No char-acter, no willpower, no self-discipline, no self-respect, certainly no sex appeal. A lifelong figure of fun, doomed to be jolly, member of the only minority group that ''comedians'' can still get away with viciously assaulting.

I could tell I was beginning to get an erection.

So I used the second I had left to study her face. A socially difficult moment was imminent, and I wanted it to go well, so I needed to know as much about her as possible, immediately.

Big lush women and small slight men in our society go through life wrapped around a softball-sized chunk of pain; it breaks some of them and makes others magnificent. She was magnificent. Clearly visible on her face, written plain for any fool to see, were the char-acter, will power, self-discipline, self-respect, and warm sexiness which common wisdom said she could not possibly have without automatically becoming skinny. She had lots of laugher's wrinkles and a couple of thinker's wrinkles and no other kinds. She wore her hair in a big bush of curls that made no futile attempt to down-play her size; rain-sparkle made it a halo. The split-second glance

I got of her eyes, glistening in the light from the all-night deli across the road, focused on the far distance, made them seem serene, self-confident.

I went on computer time. And a very good computer it must have been, too, because I was able to run several very complex subprograms in the second or so allotted to me. One routine sorted through the several hundred thousand Opening Lines in storage for something suitable to Unexpected Encounter with Nude Stranger, but since it expected to come up empty, a more ambitious program attempted to create something new, something witty and engaging and reassuring, out of the materials of the situation. In hopes that one or the other would succeed, a simple and well-used program began selecting the tone and pitch of voice and the manner of delivery—soft enough not to startle, but not so soft as to seem wimpy; humorous but not clownish; urbane but not smug; admiring but not lecherous—prepared, in short, to begin lying through its/my teeth. Meanwhile, an almost unconscious algorithm had me keep my hands firmly at my sides and stand up a little straighter. And all of this together took up, at most, twenty percent of the available bytes—the rest was fully occupied in an urgent priority task.

Memorizing her . . .

Plenty of time! Computational capacity to spare! I knew that she was beginning to become aware of me several hundred nanoseconds before she did, integrated all the subprograms, picked a neutral Opening Line and pinned my hopes on delivery, ran a hundred full-dress rehearsals to derive best- and worst-case results, made the go decision, and had time to admire her lower left eyelash and myself before I heard my very own voice say, with all the warmth and tone and clarity I could reasonably have hoped for, "It certainly is a very nice tits."

My central processing unit melted down into slag.

It took her ten years to turn and look at me, and no thought of any kind took place inside my skull; horror fused every circuit. She looked me square in the eye, absolutely expressionlessly, for endless decades, while I marinated in failure and shame. Then her gaze left my eyes, panned slowly downward. It rested on my mouth for many years, moved on down again, did not pause until it reached my feet, then came back up again, paused where it was bound to eventually—but I was centuries dead by then, only a cinder of consciousness remained in my brain to be snuffed by the realization that my erection was now up to at least half mast, and so by the time her gaze got back up to my eyes, I don't see how she could possibly have seen glowing therefrom the slightest light of intelligence.

The animal who sleeps under my computer woke up and tried its best. It tried for a smile, doubtless produced a horrible grimace. It essayed a merry laugh, managed to generate a hideous gargling sound. It gestured vaguely, attempting a Gallic shrug and failing to bring it off. To all of this she displayed no visible reaction whatever. The old animal gave up.

The first plan I formed was to jump off the roof, but the problem with that was that it could only be done once and might not hurt enough long enough, so I stepped closer to the dumbwaiter housing and began battering my head against it to soften my skull up for the grand finale, and I liked the way it felt and began to get a rhythm going, and then and only then did she burst out into a magnificent bellow of laughter, a great trombone hoot of shocked merriment, and big as she was she was up and holding me away from the dumbwaiter before I could deliver it another blow, and then there was a great complicated rocking struggling hugging stumbling confusion of laughter and tears and rain that somehow left us sitting on our asses on that wet roof with our feet touching, both of us shuddering with mirth. We nearly got our breath back a few minutes later, but when she tried to speak all she got out was ''smooth'' before dissolving into hysterics again, and a little after that I managed to get out, ''My Freudian slip is—'' before I lost it, and when the earthquake had well and truly passed I was lying flat on my back with rain running up my nostrils and the soles of my feet pressed firmly against human warmth. My hands hurt a little from beating them on the roof.

I sat up.

So did she. I must have looked forlorn. My erection was gone. ''It's okay,'' she said, pressing her toes gently against mine. ''I've heard worse.''

''You don't understand,'' I moaned.

''Admittedly—but I think I got the message.''

''But—''

''It was, unquestionably, the most memorable meeting of my life, and nothing will ever top it.'' Oh, if only she'd been right.

I was beginning slowly to realize that this situation was salvageable—that the disaster was of such epic proportion as to be a kind of triumph. I had certainly made an impression on her. Was this not Callahan's Place—albeit empty—beneath my butt? Callahan's

Place, focus of strange and wonderful events, magical tavern in which nothing was impossible and few things even unlikely? Could there be any better, more fitting place for a miracle to happen than here on Callahan's roof?

But exactly where to go from here was hidden from me. "I'm Jake."

"I'm glad. I thought you might have really hurt yourself there."

"I meant that my name is Jake."

"Glad to hear it. What *is* your name?"

Better and better. I like them quick. "Damned if I know. What's yours? And *please* don't say, 'Thanks, I'll have a beer.' "

"I'm Mary, Jake."

With what feeble wits I had left, I attempted a cunning investigation. "You must know the guys who put in that splendid staircase, right?"

She went two degrees cooler. "I put in the staircase."

"Excuse me," I said faintly, and got to my feet. The dumbwaiter housing felt just as good as it had before; there was just enough give to it to cause an energetic rebound, but not so much as to soften the impact.

Unexpectedly my ears hurt, and the rhythm of my head was halted. *"Stop that,"* she said, twisting me by both ears to face her. "Damn it, I had no business getting chilly at you that way. I must be the first lady blacksmith you've ever run into, how the hell could you know? You did good: you didn't look disbelieving, just surprised."

I shook my head. It stayed on. "You're the *second* woman smith I've met. That's why I'm mad at myself—I should have guessed."

She stepped back a pace and put her hands on her hips. "Jake," she said softly, "you're trying too hard."

"I know. Is it flattering at least?"

Her laugh was a good hearty bray. "Yes, by damn. And not entirely ineffective: I can't wait to find out what you're like when you're normal."

I felt my breathing begin to slow and my shoulders begin to relax. "I've always wondered myself. But at my worst I should have known that you put in that staircase."

"Why?"

"Because you *look* like the person who did it. Everything it takes to do a job that good, you've got, I could see that before you knew I was here, so I should have figured it out."

She dimpled. "There, you see? You finally got a compliment out straight—you're getting better."

"Where did it come from?"

"It spent its early years in the library of a wealthy bishop. For the last thirty years it was in the best whorehouse in Brooklyn, but the place closed down a few months back—"

I was stricken. "Lady Sally's is *closed?*"

She nodded sadly. "Too much cut-rate competition. Changing fashions. Nowadays they all seem to want sleaze, and a place like Sally's is out of style."

"My God! I *know* that staircase! Do you mean to tell me that *Lady Sally McGee's staircase is here in Callahan's bar?*" I began to smile through my sorrow. "Ah, God, Sally," I said to the weeping heavens, "I'm sorry they closed you down, the world is a darker place—but at least all your treasures haven't fallen among heathens. Mary, where is the grand old lady, do you know?"

"Enjoying her retirement. This is a good home for the staircase, then?"

"Only the very best. This is *Callahan's Place*, do you see? No, how could you see?"

"The way you could see that I was a good smith, maybe. There *is* something about the place. But I—"

"Be sure. If the staircase had legs, it would have walked here. Miracles happen here—a little like the ones that happened at Lady Sally's, come to think. Is Mike planning to open tonight, do you know?"

"About half an hour from now, he said."

"Then you'll see. You'll like the gang—they're the best family I ever had. Did Mike tell you about the house rules?"

"House rules?"

"Every drink in the house costs half a buck. Mike accepts nothing but singles. On your way out you collect whatever change you have coming from the cigar box full of quarters on the end of the bar—unless you've been visiting the fireplace—"

"Hold it. The drinks are half a buck?"

"Yeah, why?"

"These days a *beer* in most bars costs more than a dollar."

"Really? I don't go to any other bars."

"And nobody rips off the quarters? He must watch the box like a hawk—"

"Nope. Nobody watches the box. That's some of what I mean about Callahan's Place."

She shook her head gently. "Go on. Something about 'visiting the fireplace'—"

"If you feel the urge to, or the need to, you step up to the chalk line and face the fireplace. You have to make a toast aloud, and everyone shuts up while you do. Then you deep-six your glass, into the fireplace. It costs you your change for that drink, but it can really take a load off your shoulders sometimes."

"My," she said softly.

"People tend to come here when they're in need of help, not always but pretty often. They get it, most times. We help each other. These days, it's getting hard to find a bar where the bartender'll even pretend to listen to your troubles anymore. At Callahan's Place *everybody* will listen to your problems. Respectfully. Carefully. You can't imagine the stories that get told here, sometimes."

"Sounds like a depressing place to get drunk."

I grinned. "You'll see. Everyone else must have come by earlier and seen that sign down on the front door before it got rained on, they'll be here soon. A merry crew, one and all. I give you fair warning: we are all paronomasiacs."

Her eyes widened in horror. "God, no! Not *punsters!*"

"But it's all right—tonight isn't Punday."

"Punday."

"The night on which the worst punster gets his or her tab refunded."

She staggered. "Christ, that was close. Too close."

"No, tonight is Tall Tales Night—and I'll tell you, it takes a lot to qualify as a tall tale in Callahan's. We've had a real talking dog, for instance. And a whole slew of time-travelers. Two aliens . . . Say, there's one of them now." I waved. *"Hi, Finn!"*

She turned and saw him, and stood very still.

Well, how *could* I have prepared her? Callahan's Place is like that, you have to sink or swim. It was her turn.

Mickey Finn had been decelerating sharply when I first caught sight of him; he came in the last hundred yards like a seagull and landed with much more grace. Rain declined to fall on him—one reason I'd spotted him in the darkness—and when he was standing beside us the rain ignored us too. "Hello, Jake my friend." He politely began to undress.

"Not necessary, Mickey. Real good to see you, man—it's been

too long! Allow me to present Mary. Mary, this is my friend Mickey Finn.''

Mary was transfixed. That surprised me. This woman had not been visibly fazed by encountering a naked stranger of the opposite sex, while herself naked, in a remote place; I had expected her to take Finn more or less in stride. I will admit that, considered dispassionately, a naked man *is* less startling than a flying man, particularly a flying man who stands six-eleven-and-a-half, has a magnificent craggy face and eyes like oxyacetylene blowtorches, and repels moisture. But *I* was the naked man in question. I found myself mildly irritated.

Still, if Mary was having difficulty rising to this social challenge, the gallant thing to do was to help. Finn was visibly wondering if he should offer his hand, so I offered him mine. After a genuinely warm handshake—I like the big cyborg—I gently tugged his hand in the direction of the new stairwell. "Mary put in the staircase over there. You ought to check it out, it's *special*." I winked with the eye Mary couldn't see. "Why don't you see if you can find Callahan while you're down there, see about getting this joint opened up for the night?"

Finn surprised me, too, a little—by taking his cue smoothly and without hesitation. He gets more sophisticated in human ways (excuse me, in Terran ways) every time I see him. "Certainly, Jake. We'll talk when you come down. It was very nice meeting you, Mary." He left quickly on those long legs, and even after the stairwell door had closed behind him, the rain kept failing to land on us. I would have loved to spend an hour trying to figure out how Finn did that—before asking him—but I was busy.

Mary was still standing exactly as she had been when Finn first landed, pivoted slightly to her left, looking even further left, smack through the spot where Finn had been. She hadn't moved a muscle.

I cleared my throat.

"Aliens, okay," she said in a clear, calm voice, still not moving, "but I don't believe you've had a talking dog."

I took it as a sign of recovery. "We didn't either, at first. Fella came in trying to cadge drinks with the old talking dog routine. Of course, we figured it was a ventriloquism scam—and so it was. The guy was a mute, and the dog was a mutant—*he was the ventriloquist*. They partnered up because they were lonely—nobody would talk to either of them, alone. They hang out here a lot, now."

She straightened from her pivot, worked her shoulders slightly, then relaxed. "He certainly is."

"Who certainly is what?"

"He certainly is a Mickey Finn."

She still wasn't entirely back in the world. But the part that was, was out of this world. Now that she was rainproof, droplets hung all over her body like facets on a precious stone, some standing still, some, like my gaze, trying to migrate downward. I wrestled my gaze up as high as I could manage, and thought of something that might reach her. "Those certainly are a very nice night."

It worked. It took her a second to get it, and then she laughed, about Force Six. "Jake," she said, "you've got a nice-looking evening yourself. I think I'm going to like this bar. Do you suppose this no-rain gimmick would work on our clothes if we took them out and put them on? Or is it necessary to dress before going downstairs?"

"Not necessary, no, but clothes *are* customarily worn. But don't ask me how Finn's technology works—the only way to find out is to try."

Sure enough, the rain avoided our clothing too. "Of course," I said, "they'll get wet when we put them—" and then stopped. I wasn't wet any more. Neither was she. Our *hair* was dry, and I hadn't felt a breeze. My own clothes, which had been damp when I left them, were dry, and stayed that way.

"Fascinating," she murmured, sounding for all the world like Mr. Spock.

I nodded. "Finn's great to have around in winter." I tossed her clothes to her, and she caught the stack. I began dressing myself. Do you think it silly that after having spent considerable time naked together, we averted our eyes as we dressed? I'm sure we both thought so—but we did it.

I liked her just as well, dressed. That is to say: dressed, she made me want to see her undressed again, as soon as possible. I wished the light was better. I could faintly hear sounds from below us, distant thuds and voices, one of them unmistakably Callahan's. Doc Webster's Studebaker pulled into the parking lot, followed by Long-Drink McGonnigle's truck, and way off down 25A I could hear Fast Eddie's Hideousmobile approaching. Callahan's Place was getting ready for a late opening.

She gestured vaguely at the weepy heavens above (and I couldn't help wondering how the raindrops knew enough not to fall in the path of her moving arm) and said, "Finn's from . . . well, out there, isn't he?"

"Yep. *Way* out."

"How long has he been here?"

"A little over ten years now, I make it."

"And he's spent the whole time hanging out in bars? What the hell was his mission?"

"The extermination of human life."

"Dammit, Jake, that's not funny."

"Don't panic—he defected. A long time ago, a couple of weeks after he arrived. His first night at Callahan's Place."

She visibly relaxed, but her face had a funny expression. "I see. Say no more, by all means. I think you've certainly covered all the high points of the story."

So I told her all about Finn, about the night he came to Callahan's and acquired his name—*just* in the nick of time. I told her about the night he took on Adolf Hitler out in the parking lot, and how big the resulting crater was, until he fixed it. I told her about his successive careers as a farmer, a fisherman, a forest fire-watcher, and a lighthousekeeper, and by then I got the idea that I was talking entirely too much about Finn and decided to try for a smooth segue to some more rewarding topic.

"But enough about Finn. Let's talk about me. I am, in no particular order, a singer, a songwriter, a guitar player, a nice person, and in no particular order. I play here some nights with Fast Eddie the piano player, and we're very good. I have many of my original teeth and no ex-wives or children living and I find you the most devastatingly attractive woman I've met in at least a decade. I would *very* much like to know you better."

"Are your intentions honorable?"

"Certainly. I want to sleep with you. Repeatedly if possible." My intentions went much further than that, actually—but some instinct told me to keep my mouth shut.

"Well, I'm not especially sleepy at the moment—but would you like to fuck?"

"Yes!" Sudden thought. "Uh, I'm fertile."

"I'm covered."

"You're certainly about to be."

*   *   *

When Mickey Finn reprograms reality, he does so with thoughtfulness and subtlety. The heap of clothes we made stayed dry, but now we could feel the warm rain on our bodies—except that nothing could make it run up our noses even when they were upturned. I didn't notice until after; I was preoccupied. She was warm and soft and limber and skilled and *very* enthusiastic; somewhere in there I started believing in God again just to have somebody to thank.

The distant sounds of my friends' voices came drifting up through the roof, and that seemed correct. One of the greatest pleasures in my life is turning people I like on to Callahan's Place; I get a big kick out of introducing a new friend to my old friends. I had never yet turned someone I *loved* on to Callahan's, simply because in the last dozen years I hadn't come to love anyone that I hadn't met in Callahan's, but I expected it to be at least twice as nice—and I already knew that I loved Mary. I was beginning to be *in* love *with* her (if you get the distinction), the first time I'd been in love since I killed my family, and the prospect of introducing a lover to Mike and the gang sounded heavenly. Just a sliver of a thought, this, that resonated every time the faint sound of a familiar laugh reached me, a warm certainty that there could have been no finer place to fall in love, and to make love for the first time, than where I was.

God, she was a sweet pillowy armful! I've had a few of the bony women everyone else claims to like: nothing to squeeze, nothing to admire, I had to be careful with my weight, I was afraid to let go for fear I might bruise something, and even so my pubic bone got sore. A woman like Mary, now: you can *roll around* on a woman like that. You can let yourself go, secure in the awareness that the system is roomy and cushioned, and you can explore forever without running out of things to see and appreciate, and you find, time after time, so often that I'm tempted to say always, that passion and compassion and sensuality each double for every pound above so-called "optimum weight." Take your skinny women and stick them up the same receptacle with hard beds and cold showers and red-line exercise and "natural" food and all the other things everyone earnestly pursues in the belief that pleasure and pain are nature's diabolical attempts to trick us, that the less you enjoy a thing the better it must be for you; take 'em and stick 'em, and give me something a man can enjoy!

Our lovemaking was about as good as a first time can be. It was not the telepathic experience it could become with practice and study, of course—perhaps even less so than a simple sporting event

might have been. I spent most of my time in my own head, startled
by the unexpected magnitude of my own need, and then bemused
by the discovery that hers was even greater. The urgency vs. tenderness ratio definitely tilted to the left, and there seemed to be
some question as to who was raping whom. It got pretty athletic in
spots. (Doubtless noisy as well, though I'm sure the rain blanketed
most of it.) Most of the information that we passed back and forth
came directly from the spinal column or just a little bit higher up.

But tenderness was in there too, and caring, and sharing, and
something oddly like nostalgia, and so all in all it was about as nice
a last time as you could have asked for, too. Our afterglow-durations
synched, which is always nice, and we picked little roofing-pebbles
from each other's backs, for all the world like monkeys hunting
lice. In the process we magically dried out again. It turned out that
we both smoked the same brand of cigarette, but when we took two
from the pack, Finn's magic selectively failed and they soaked
through. We wasted two more before giving up, then I cautiously
experimented and learned that a joint was immune. Opinionated
man, Finn—but maybe he knows something. We dressed while we
toked, and when we were dressed we started drifting over toward
the stairwell.

I stopped. "Mary, let's not go down yet. Once we do it'll be
wall-to-wall introductions and smiles and drinks and toasts. I want
you to meet my friends—but I haven't had a chance to get to know
you yet."

"As the old joke goes, it's been the equivalent of a formal intro-
duction."

"You know what I mean. I don't know where you live or where
you grew up or what you want to do with your life or how many
husbands you have—hell, I don't know your last name!"

"I don't know yours."

"My point exactly. The inmates downstairs, lovable and extraor-
dinary though they be, will keep—let's talk."

"Let's talk later: you know we will. Right now I want to go
where there are lights on."

"Yes, but—"

"I want to check the staircase over one more time too."

"—it's perfectly—"

"All right, I want to hear people admiring it."

"—you don't—"

"I want a drink."

"—I bow to superior intelligence."

Warm light and happy noise and the smell of good suds came flooding out the opened door; as we descended the stairs the sour, oddly pleasant aroma of Callahan's ever-present El Ropo cigars joined the mix. Under the laughter and talk, Fast Eddie Costigan was playing Mac Rebennac stuff, and occasionally one patron or another would scat along with him. Noah Gonzalez was working on a gag he'd picked up from Al Phee, juggling full shot glasses, and by God he finally had it down cold. A small cheering section had gathered; while they clapped, Noah started sipping from the shots as they passed his face. (Noah works for the Suffolk County Bomb Squad, which is why one leg is artificial, and a merrier man you'll never meet.) Mary and I joined the onlookers; true artistry is rare. Noah drained two tumblers, spilling no more than a teaspoon or so on himself, then swallowed, wiped his mouth without losing rhythm, and hollered out, "Open wide, Drink!"

Long-Drink McGonnigle never blows a cue. "Hit me," he cried, and opened his mouth wide.

This is what I think I saw: the shot glass still containing whiskey went up one last time, tilting this time in stately slow motion so that the contents *almost* spilled; then it came down, and Noah caught it, stopped it cold with three fingers, the contents departed on a high trajectory, Noah flung it back into the stream of traffic so that it made up the lost time, we held our collective breath—and the Drink whipped his head two inches to the left and the flying booze impacted squarely against the back of his throat. A roar went up, and Noah laughed so hard he lost all three glasses, and—perhaps most magnificent of all—Long-Drink did *not* lose so much as a drop of the load.

So rarely in life are we privileged to be present at such a moment. When I was ten, my family spent a summer vacation puptenting around New Hampshire, and inevitably we took the cog railway up Mount Washington, a journey itself worth remembering, but what I will never forget as long as I live is standing at the lookoff railing with the family, admiring the view while trying to keep from being blown over the edge by the fierce mountaintop wind, and the truly beautiful thing that happened then. Dad's hat blew off, before he could even try to save it, and sailed out over an indescribable gulf, bound for the state of Maine with every chance of making it. He'd been a little grumpy earlier that day, and had regained his good spirits by force of will only a short time earlier; the rest of us made small cries of dismay as we watched his hat recede. So did several bystanders. But Dad was heroically determined to keep his good mood: he forced a smile, and even essayed a joke. "Don't worry," he called above the wind, "there'll be another one along in a minute." He put up his hand as if to pluck a hat from the sky. And a hat flew into his hand.

This, you may say, and I will agree, is a wonderful thing, a marvelous thing. But the *beautiful* thing, the thing that came back to me again and again during my stormy adolescent battles with Dad and kept me from ever really hating him, is what he did then. He caught the hat, smoothly, and without the slightest hesitation placed it on his head, poker-faced. Even the fact that it was a perfect fit did not faze him. "You see?" he said, and held a deadpan all the way through the ensuing ovation. I've always loved and admired my dad, but in that two or three seconds he became immortal.

Some moments are golden, is what I'm saying, and what Noah had just pulled off was one of those, somebody playing above himself. It made me feel awed and happy and grateful. Callahan's Place had done me proud, serving up some magic for me just as I brought Mary in the door to meet it. After the inevitable storm of glasses had shattered in the fireplace, I joined the throng of people who wanted to buy Noah and Long-Drink a drink. We were all disappointed, as Callahan had caught the act and announced that the boys' tab was covered for the night—but I was mildly annoyed to notice that Mary too had offered the pair a drink . . . from a flask. She had insisted on coming down here, putting off our getting to know each other (*other* than in the biblical sense, I mean), because she wanted a drink—which she'd had with her. We could have sat up there on the roof and killed the flask, talked for hours before coming downstairs . . .

Hush, I told myself sensibly. Sexual intercourse vests no property rights. And how could I resent any combination of circumstances which had allowed me to witness the triumph of Noah and the McGonnigle? All around the room, people whose attention had been elsewhere were getting the tale secondhand and kicking themselves. Let it go, Jake—

"That was special," Mary told me, grinning and taking my hand.

"Yes, indeed. Noah claims he's working up a routine with live chainsaws, and now I think I believe him. What'll you have?''

She sniffed the air. ''Do I smell coffee?''

''Jamaican Blue Mountain. Mike has friends in Tokyo. And, anticipating your next question, he also has Old Bushmill's, distilled in Ireland, and fresh whipped cream, and he knows how. Come on.''

Callahan was working up a sweat behind the bar when we got there, but he stopped short as he came past us with twelve drafts in his big hands and said to Mary, gesturing in my direction, ''Mary, if your tastes are as simple as this, you might be interested in dating *me* sometime.''

''What can I do?'' she said. ''He's got the negatives. But thanks.''

Callahan wrinkled his big broken nose and grimaced. ''Damn. Jake, what'll you charge me for a print?''

''Sorry. The rights are tied up. Mike, you sure picked a good staircase-putter-inner. You *do* know where that thing came from?''

''Sure do,'' Callahan said. ''I made a point of asking Sally for it when I heard she was closing. Yeah, Mary does good work. What'll you folks have?''

''God's Blessing on us both, Mike,'' I told him. He nodded and went off with his dozen overdue beers.

Mary was smiling broadly. ''I *like* this place, Jake.''

''I already knew you had good taste. Pun intended.''

''Ouch. You did warn me.''

''Around here we don't even wait for straight lines.''

''Well,'' she said, absolutely poker-faced, ''the shortest distance between two puns is a straight line,'' and helped herself to some peanuts from the free lunch.

I felt like I had the time I was coming on just a little to a stranger about what a hot guitarist I was, and discovered too late that I was talking to Mr. Amos Garrett. (Remember the demonic guitar break in Maria Muldaur's ''Midnight at the Oasis''? *That* Amos Garrett . . .) ''And the success of any pun,'' I tried to riposte, ''is in—''

'' —the *oy* of the beholder,'' she finished for me.

Hmmm . . .

Mike returned with a pair of Irish coffees. ''Two God's Blessings,'' he announced. ''I could swear I still hear rain—but you two are bone-dry, and I don't see a brolly.''

''Finn's doing,'' I explained, and he nodded. ''Say, Mike, where do you know Mary from? And how come you never invited her around before?''

"Long story. Excuse me, will you? It's time to get the evening started.''

He emptied a glass that Shorty Steinitz had foolishly left unattended and banged it on the bartop. "All right, folks—Tall Tales Night is now in session. Who's first?''

Ralph Von Wau Wau was pushed forward by the crowd. "I do have a mildly interesting story for you all,'' he said, and I glanced at Mary to see how she would take it. I mean, I suppose it's a subjective thing, but I find a talking dog to be more intrinsically startling than a seven-foot flying cyborg. But she didn't blink. Well, I had warned her.

In that charming German accent of his (he *is* a shepherd), Ralph told a fairly complex story about a demonically possessed lady of his acquaintance whom he had exorcised after even a bishop had failed; the yarn built, inexorably, to the line, "Possession is nine points of the paw,'' and produced some very canine howls of agony from the innocent bystanders.

Which of course only inspired Doc Webster. "Damned if I'll be outpunned by a genuine son of a bitch,'' he boomed, and folks made way grinning for him as he stepped forward. Physically the Doc resembles a Sumo wrestler gone to fat. He is the All-Time Punday Night Champion and probably always will be; only Long-Drink and I still cherish a hope of supplanting him anymore.

"As many of you know,'' the Doc began, "I just got back from visiting Juan Ortiz, an obstetrician friend of mine in Los Angeles. He was nominally on vacation, but one day there was an emergency delivery he just had to attend, so he deputized his brother-in-law Obie Stihl—honest to God, that's his name, I'd never make up a name like that—deputized Obie to show me around town. We went to Disneyland. Obie turned out to be a dedicated Star Wars freak, with a sense of humor even more depraved than my own—we passed by three sailors on the way in, for instance, and when he noticed they were all chief petty officers, he made sure to point out the 'Three CPOs . . .' '' (sounds of gagging and dismay from the audience). "So he took me to Adventureland, where you go on a Jungle Boat Ride. Robot hippos come up out of the water and spit at you and so forth.'' ("Maybe they were relatives of yours,'' Long-Drink murmured, and Callahan shushed him.) "But the worst part was the damned boat captain. Through the whole voyage he kept up a running monologue that had shin splints: bad jokes, worse puns, mother-in-law jokes even. I was in severe pain; fella thought he was a real hot dog. But the wurst was yet to come.'' (Gasps.) ''As we got back to the wharf, just as I was stepping off the boat, Obie leaned over and whispered in my ear, 'Now you're getting to see the dock side of the farce . . .' ''

A roar of collective anguish went up, and glasses began to fly toward the hearth. ''Rest of us might as well fold up,'' Tommy Janssen said. ''That's a winner.''

''Strictly speaking,'' Callahan said with some reluctance, ''I'm afraid it ain't. That story'd probably take the honors if this was Punday Night—but I don't really see it as a Tall Tale.''

''He's right,'' Long-Drink said. ''It's nice if the Tall Tale ends with a crime like that, but the Tale itself has to have fantastic elements to it. Sorry, Doc: syntax error.''

The Doc frowned, but what could he say? They were right. And then divine fire touched me, as it had Noah a while earlier.

I wanted to impress my new love, and I wanted to help Doc Webster, and it just slipped out before I knew I was going to speak: ''I'm surprised at you boys. The fantastic element in that story is staring you all right in the face.''

Even the Doc looked puzzled. ''How's that, Jake?'' Callahan asked.

''Well, how many of you have ever toured Disneyland, or any-place else, with a fictional character?''

The Doc was the only one who saw it coming; his frown left.

''Doc *told* you who his guide was: O. B. Juan's kin, Obie.''

A frozen silence. Group catatonic shock. And then Ralph began to howl, and was joined by the rest. Every glass in the room, full or empty, began a journey whose terminus was the fireplace; Eddie tried to play the Star Wars theme but was laughing so hard he couldn't get his hands to agree on a key; Callahan reached threateningly for a seltzer bottle; Doc Webster shook my hand respectfully.

I glanced around for Mary to see if she was suitably impressed, and found her staring across the room. I followed her gaze, realized she was staring at Finn—and realized that Finn was in some kind of trouble.

He was sitting bolt upright in his chair, which he hardly ever does, being so tall, and he was paying no attention to the proceedings around him, and tears were running down his face. The last

time I'd seen tears on Finn's face, years before, the planet Earth
had been in serious jeopardy . . .

He got up and walked stiffly to the bar, and Mary and I moved
wordlessly to where we could see what Finn was doing.

He was offering Mike Callahan ten singles. He wanted ten of
something. Callahan was looking him over. "How much effect will
that have on him?" Mary asked in a whisper.

"About like you or I gulping a double."

"Oh." She relaxed slightly.

"But it is *extremely* out of character for Finn. The last time I saw
him order ten drinks was the first night he came here, years ago."

"*Oh.*"

Many others at or near the bar knew the story; an audience was
developing as Callahan reached his decision. "What'll it be,
Mickey?"

"Rye, Michael." Just like that night.

"You want to talk about it?" Callahan asked.

"First the toast."

Callahan nodded at that, and set to work. He builds drinks the
way Baryshnikov dances. Ten shots of rye soon sat before Finn.
One after another the tall alien downed them. That first night he
had thrown each individual empty into the fireplace and made the
same toast ten times; this time he didn't bother. When he was done,
some of the empties weren't even touching—but he picked the last
one up and the rest came with it. He walked to the chalk line, faced
the hearth. By now he had our attention.

"To my people," he said clearly and tonelessly, and flung the
cluster of glasses.

I hadn't known even Finn could throw that hard: there was a
violent explosion in the fireplace. It is designed like a parabolic
reflector, so that it is nearly impossible to make glass spray out of
it; nonetheless, that bursting should have littered the room with
shards. It did not for the same reason that my clothes were dry.

"Jesus, big fella," Long-Drink said. "What can we do?" There
was a vigorous rumble of agreement on all sides.

Mickey Finn came back to Earth—an expression perhaps
uniquely appropriate here—and looked around at us gravely. His

composed features were at odds with the droplets running down them; I had the crazy thought that these were the raindrops that had failed to fall on him, time-shifted somehow to now. But of course it was just that Finn's still not used to hanging human expressions on his pan, and tends to forget in times of crisis: he truly was hurting.

"My friends," he told us, "if I could think of anything you could do, I would surely tell you. Would surely have told you before now."

"Then tell us the problem," Tommy Janssen said. "Maybe we'll come up with something."

Finn tried a smile, a poor job. "I doubt it, Tommy. I have been thinking about this particular problem since I first came here, years ago, and I do not think there is a solution."

Callahan cleared his throat, a sound like a speeding truck being thrown suddenly into reverse. "Mickey, as you know, I don't hold with pryin' in my joint. If you don't feel like telling us your troubles, I'll coldcock the first guy that asks a leading question. But I strongly recommend that you unload. Little thing you might not know, having spent so many centuries alone out in deep space: sometimes, just naming your burden helps. But it's up to you, pal."

Finn thought it over. "You may be right, Michael. You always have been so far. In fact, you have stated my problem. *I am alone.* I have been alone for centuries. I shall always be alone, until my death comes."

"The hell you say," Long-Drink burst out. "Why, counting the regulars that ain't in tonight, I make it about a hundred and fifty close friends you've got. You can stay at my crib anytime, for as long as you like, and the same goes for the rest of us, ain't that right?"

There were universal shouts of agreement. Finn smiled a pained smile. "Thank you all," he said. "You are true friends. But your generous offer does not speak to my problem. I did not say I was lonely. I said I was *alone.*"

"Mickey," Josie Bauer began silkily, "I told you once already—"

"Again, thanks," he said, sketching a gallant bow. "But it would, forgive me, hurt more than it would help."

"Hurt how?" she asked, not in the least offended.

"Physically, for one thing, it would hurt *you.* You recall the Niven story you lent me once, about Superman's sex life?"

" 'Man of Steel, Woman of Kleenex,' sure," she said. "*Oh.*"

"Yes," Finn said sadly. "Orgasm involves involuntary muscle spasm—and while I am not as strong as Superman, I am much stronger than a Terran man. And you are slightly built."

"Oh."

There was something peculiar about Finn's face. The eyes, that was it. His eyes hadn't looked like that since the first night he'd come here. Hollow, burnt out, empty of all hope. Why hadn't they looked like that up on the roof? Or had I just failed to notice in the dark, distracted by lust? "It would hurt me too," he went on. "Not physically—spiritually. Human females often become angry when I try to explain this, Josie, *please* do not be offended, but would it not be fair to say that what you were just about to offer me was a transient sexual relationship?"

"Now, hold on a goddamn—"

"I *said*, 'Please,' Josie."

"—uh . . . dammit, Finn, I didn't mean a purely sexual—"

"Of course not; I do not believe myself that there is any such thing. No doubt it would have involved friendship and laughter and kindness and several other wonderful qualities for which you Terrans do not yet have words. But is not the key word 'transient'?"

"Well, for crying out—"

"I am wrong? You were proposing marriage?"

Josie shut very quickly up.

"Perhaps your subconscious intent was a liaison of days, or weeks, or even months. But I am sure that you were not offering to become my *mate*. No human ever would."

"Christ, Mickey, don't run yourself down. I don't happen to be the marrying kind, but I'm sure that some nice g—"

"*Look at me*," he roared suddenly, and everyone in the Place jumped a foot in the air. Deliberately, he pulled open his black sports coat, pulled open his shirt, pulled open his chest . . .

I tried to look away, could not. I tried to fit words around what I was seeing, could not. I tried not to be horrified, could not. A strange sound filled the room: many people sucking air through their teeth. I can't describe it, even now: take my word for it, whatever was inside Finn's chest, human beings aren't supposed to see things like that. Ever.

Finn closed up his chest.

A collective sigh went up.

"I have shown you my heart," Finn said softly. "Will you marry me?"

Josie began to whimper.

"Josie, I am sorry," he said at once, but it was too late—she was out the door and gone. He said a word then which I've never heard before and hope never to hear again, something in his native tongue that hurt him worse than it did us. Josie's a real nice lady, and Finn knew it.

Callahan cleared his throat.

"Mickey," he rumbled, "you're alone, we get it now. It's a hard thing to be alone. Everyone in here has been alone, some of us are now—"

"Not as I am," Finn stated. "Even the most unfortunate of you is less alone. No matter how remote the chance of your finding a mate . . . there is always the *chance*. Always you have hope, even as you despair. No human will ever pair-bond with me—and I dare not leave your planet. My Masters believe me dead; if they ever learned otherwise—"

"—they'd kill you," Long-Drink finished.

"Worse."

"They'd punish you."

"Worse."

"What's worse?" Shorty Steinitz asked.

"They would put me back to work, unpunished. They are not like humans, who sometimes kick a machine that is not working. They would simply restore the machine to service. And, as an afterthought, they would exterminate the organisms that caused the machine to malfunction."

"Us, you mean," Callahan said.

"Yes."

Mary and Callahan exchanged a look I didn't understand. "There's no chance you could sneak back to your home planet without these Master clowns catching on?" she asked Finn.

"None whatsoever," Finn said expressionlessly. "To begin with, my home planet no longer exists. It has not existed for several centuries, and I am the last of my people."

Mary winced. "What happened?"

"The Masters found us."

"Jesus—and killed everybody but you."

"They killed everybody *including* me. But the Masters are a prudent and tidy race; they always keep file copies of what they destroy, each etched on a molecule of its own. Like all of my people, I was slain, and reduced to a single encoded molecule. Some time after my death they felt need of a new scout, fashioned this body, and caused to be decanted into it a large fraction of my former awareness—withholding the parts that did not suit them, of course."

Mary gasped; she was horrified. "God, you must hate them."

Finn's voice was bleak. "I wish greatly that I had the ability. That is one of the parts that did not suit them."

I was as horrified as Mary. As a rule, Finn is disinclined to talk about his past, and of course none of us had ever tried to pry. I'd always wondered how he'd gotten into his former profession. Now I was sorry I knew.

(Still, I was tempted to ask him the other thing that had always puzzled me: why the body he wore looked human. Was human stock ubiquitous through the galaxy? Had his Masters designed him specifically to come *here?* Or did he somehow reform his body for each new planet, each new culture? I knew that at least half his body was organic—but did that half have anything in common with the body he had been born into?

Perhaps the answer was equally horrifying. In any case, my friend Finn was in pain: This was no time to be snoopy.)

"Mickey," Mary said softly, "if you are unable to hate your Masters . . . then you are unable to love them. Yes? That's why you were able to betray them."

"Yes. They do not wish to be loved. They would find the idea disgusting. Love baffles and repels them; they stamp it out wherever they find it in the galaxy. The Masters are motivated by self-interest."

"So are most humans," Mary said.

Finn actually laughed. "Excuse me, Mary my new friend, but what you said is funny. *All humans—without exception—want to love.* No organic or emotional or psychological damage can remove that need. Humans can survive, albeit in pain, without *being* loved—but lock a man in a dungeon and he will find an ant to love, or try. The sociopath, who feels no emotions, wishes he could, and is driven mad by his inability. Love is the condition in which the happiness and welfare of another are essential to your own. To any rational selfish mind, this is insanity. To a Master it would be obscenity: perhaps the corresponding horror for a human being would be ego-death.''

"Love *is* ego-death," Mary whispered.

"The Masters have run across love from time to time in their expansion through the galaxy. They're not at all afraid that it might infect *them,* nor do I believe that to be a possibility, but they always exterminate it with a special pleasure, a *frisson* of horror, a small thrill of disgust." Finn closed his eyes briefly. "It was the flaw for which my race died."

The Place was silent. Mary's fingers were digging painfully into my arm, and I couldn't protest because I was gripping her arm just as hard. Why was she glaring at Callahan?

"When first we encountered the Masters, we considered the problem they represented and evolved two possible solutions. One involved their complete annihilation, root, stock, and branch; the other was more risky. We loved Life, and especially Sentience, and they were sentient. We took the risk and were destroyed. Perhaps it was the wrong choice.

"In any case, I am nearly all that remains of my race, and so I am disinclined to die. I can neither love nor hate my Masters, but I can fear them and do."

"It must have been hard for you to quit them," Mary said.

"Yes, but not because of the fear. That came later. It was hard because I am only partly organic. I contain installations, which were programmed by the Masters. Betrayal was almost a physical impossibility for me: I was *counterprogrammed.* With an effort that burned out small components and may have taken a century off my life span, I was barely able to *hint* at how my programming might be circumvented—and these my friends were able to interpret my hints and act on them."

"Aren't your . . . Mick, I'm sorry, I just can't use that word. Aren't the Cockroaches likely to notice you're gone and come looking for you?"

"No, Mary. The galaxy is a big dark place, and the . . . Cockroaches, being rational, are cautious. If a scout fails to report in, the area he was exploring is left alone. My defensive systems are mighty; it would take a powerful enemy to destroy me without my consent."

Callahan set up another five shots. "Finn," he asked, "tell me if it's none o' my business, but is it possible for you to suicide?"

"No, Michael. Or I would have done so, before I ever came to your tavern that first night." He downed two of the shots. "But, as with my loyalty to the Cockroaches . . . thank you for that name, Mary . . . my will to live can be tampered with slightly. I could not suicide—but given the right conditions and a strong enough motivation, I could cooperate in my assassination." He finished the remaining shots. "You will recall that on that first night here, I begged you all to kill me."

"No, Mickey," Callahan said softly. "I don't recall that." He trod his cigar underfoot and lit a new one. "I don't ever plan to, either. One more personal question?"

"Of course, Michael."

It was a ten-cent cigar or worse, but Mike took his time getting it lit properly. "You said, 'strong enough motivation.' " Puff. "Tell me, buddy . . ." Puff. ". . . is loneliness a strong enough motivation?"

Not a chair creaked; not a sleeve rustled; not a glass clinked. The fire seemed to quiet in the hearth; the rain seemed to have stopped. Somewhere in there Mary and I had lost our grip on each other's arm; I wanted to get mine back, but something told me to stay still.

Finn sighed finally, and put ten more singles on the bartop. Callahan handed him a fresh fifth, and while he was drinking off the top quarter of it, Callahan said quickly and quietly, "Mickey, once upon a time you had a problem you couldn't solve, and dying looked like the only way out. But you kept on looking for another way out, and in the proverbial nick of time you found one."

Finn wiped his mouth with his long forearm. "Michael, I have been looking for a solution to this problem for a long time. All the time I have been on Earth. I think very quickly. In the same amount of time I could have deduced this solar system from one of your cigar stubs."

"Mickey," Mary began, and then caught herself. "Mickey Finn isn't your real name, is it?"

"Yes, it is, but in the sense you mean you are correct: it is not the birthname my father gave me."

"What is your birthname?"

Finn smiled sadly. "You couldn't pronounce it."

"Try me."

He started to argue but gave in and spoke his name. When I'd heard it I agreed with him. The closest I can render it is "Txffu Mpwfs." Whatever Finn's people had been like, I was sure their mouths were constructed differently than ours.

Mary got it dead-bang perfect the first time. "Txffu," she said, "weren't you just as lonely, or lonelier, when you worked for the Roaches? It must be a long time between star systems."

Finn blinked at hearing his name on another's lips for the first time in—how long?—but was distracted by her question. "For one thing, there was always the tiny but measurable possibility that the . . . the Roaches might have reactivated others of my race to become scouts, that I might, if I lived long enough, chance to meet such a one eventually, that we might—" He broke off and did more damage to his fifth. "There was hope. Microscopic hope, perhaps, but hope. But now I must stay here, and no other of my race will ever come, and there is no hope."

He looked at the bottle. It was almost empty. Perhaps he sympathized with it; he put it down unfinished. "And when I worked for the Mas—for the Cockroaches, I had a job. A function. A purpose. A less than desirable one, admittedly. But I was part of something greater than myself, and I had a role to play. What is my role here on Earth? I have tried to anchor myself to this planet, to 'put down roots'—I have pursued farming and fishing and hunting and several other most basic trades. I can imitate a terrestrial organism in general and a human in particular.

"But I am alien. I have no purpose here, no job which needs me to do it. This makes my loneliness all the sharper. Perhaps I could stand loneliness if I were not useless; perhaps I could stand uselessness if I were not lonely." His voice was eerily calm and flat as he finished, "The two together are more than I can bear."

The silence that ensued then was a familiar one. Someone names a problem—an act similar in many ways to giving birth—and then the rest of us sit around awhile in respectful, sympathetic, contemplative silence, admiring the newborn little monster and meditating ways to kill it. Although it's difficult to read a man who has facial and vocal expressions and body language only when he remembers to, I felt that Finn had completed his birthing, and I put my mind on solutions for his problems. This was going to be one of the longer silences.

I've tried my hand at matchmaking a few times, and learned that you should approach it like walking into a chemistry lab and mixing two unidentified beakers of chemicals: you might luck into a stable compound, or you might blow your hands off. I'm willing to take the risk for a good enough friend, and Finn qualified—but where do you find a mate for someone as uniquely alien as him? And in today's job market, how much demand was there for a fellow whose principal prior job experience involved locating and sterilizing planetary systems? I came up with a few dozen trial solutions, rejected them all, realized how little chance I had of finding one that Finn had not considered and rejected months or years ago.

But I was being premature. "Txffu," Mary said, "that isn't all of it, is it?"

He spun his head to look at her. Those eyes of his seemed to smolder.

"Mary," Callahan said reproachfully, "That's all he chose to tell us. We don't pry in here, you know that."

"He's asking us to fix two legs of a three-legged stool, Mike. I don't do work like that."

"Then sit this one out. But no pryin' questions in my joint. It's up to him whether to show you his legs or not."

She turned back to Finn. "As a card-carrying Sophist, I will now proceed to make some prying *statements*, and if you choose to react to any of them it won't be my place to stop you.

"The third leg of your stool, you stool, is called fear. I don't mean your fear of the Cockroaches, you've learned to live with that. Something else has you scared, and for some reason you don't want to talk about it. Not because you're afraid to admit you're afraid, like human males; it's something else. I for one would certainly like to hear about it."

Finn tilted his head slightly to one side. "I see farther into the infrared than humans, hear an extra octave on either side of human range. Do you see emotions others cannot perceive?"

She ignored the question. "You're stalling."

He closed his eyes briefly—I welcomed the momentary respite—and made his decision.

"Very well. I am afraid of the same thing that everyone in this room is afraid of."

Long-Drink McGonnigle nodded. "Death."

"No, Drink my friend. I do not fear death. Neither do some others in this room. I fear Apocalypse. Armageddon. Ragnarok and Fimbulwinter. I fear nuclear holocaust."

There was a murmur in Callahan's Place.

"Finn," Doc Webster said, "do you have reason to believe that it's coming?"

"No more reason than anyone else here, Sam," Finn assured him. "Is that not sufficient?"

"What's it to *you*, Mickey?" Mary asked suddenly.

"Mary!" I said, scandalized—no, shocked and dismayed.

It was her tone of voice, you see, the way she was coming on strong with Finn. If Callahan had said those words, in that tone, it would have been different. Lots of times I've seen him appear to bully someone into solving their own problem, adopt a gruff, belligerent manner as a way of getting through their self-involvement. The rest of us are a mite too sympathetic sometimes. But when he does it, we all know that it's just Callahan, that he's simply using rudeness as a way—an effective way—of loving.

But Mary was a stranger here. In a sense she had not yet earned the right to talk that way in here, to a friend of ours. Perhaps if she herself had already opened up to us in some way, aired some problem and been adopted by us, it would have been different. (But that sounded silly even as I was thinking it: what, did people have to show a scab at the door to get admitted to Callahan's Place?) All I knew was that it wasn't right for her to be using that harsh, challenging, almost cruel tone of voice with my friend Finn. And that dismayed me, because it was my first suggestion that maybe I did not know Mary as well as I thought I did.

"I just want to get it straight," Mary insisted. "Mick, Jake told me earlier you've studied a few stars—*from inside*. If you can survive in the heart of a fusion furnace, what do you care about a little thing like Armageddon?"

"It would destroy you and all your kind!" Finn said.

"So? You told us just a few minutes ago that the Cockroaches left you unable to hate or love."

"They left me unable to hate or love *them!*" he said forcefully. "I can love. I can love humankind. I do."

"Uh-huh," she said nastily, and Finn's face twisted and my heart turned over within me.

"Mary," I said quickly, "you don't know what you're talking about—"

"Shut up, please, Jake," she said. "Mick, why—"

"No, you shut up," I snapped. "He betrayed his Masters for us, he exiled himself here to save us, he *proved* his love—and again when the Krundai came, he fought for us! You don't know, you weren't here, you have no right, you don't know him—"

"Mick is your friend, and you told me about him for fifteen

minutes—if you forgot to tell me the important parts it's not my fault. Now I asked you to shut up, and I said 'please.' Look here, Finn, you noble spaceman—''

I shut up and let her browbeat my friend. I was busy trying to fall out of love.

(A rotten little voice in the back of my head was asking, are you sure you want to lose a body like that just to keep your self-respect? and I had to admit it was a good, if swinish, question.)

''—if you claim you quit your job out of love for humanity, and you claim to be scared of Apocalypse on our account, then why the hell is it that you haven't done one goddamn thing to prevent it?''

Finn opened his mouth.

''And if you give me the Star Trek Prime Directive,'' she cut him off, ''I'll spit right in your eye. Nobody who really cared about the ethics of interfering in the destinies of primitive cultures could ever have worked as an interstellar hit man—conditioning and counterprogramming be damned!''

''It is not that I would not prevent nuclear catastrophe,'' Finn said. ''I cannot.''

''Bullshit.''

''I can destroy nuclear weapons easily. But I cannot destroy *every* one, simultaneously, and anything less would only trigger the calamity.''

''Oh, for Christ's sake, Mick—you're not that dumb. You could think your way around the problem in about thirty seconds flat . . . if you weren't hamstrung by guilt.''

''Guilt?''

''That's right. Resolve the conflict in your conscience, and everything else will fall into place, you wait and see.''

''—'conflict'?—''

''For years now, ever since you first walked into this dump, you've been taking credit for saving the world out of love of humanity—and these chumps here bought it.'' She glared around at all of us, ignored the glares she got in return, and turned back to Finn. ''*Why don't you tell us the real reason?*''

And she got him! I was watching his face, and Finn may not have much human expression, but I know a direct hit when I see one. She knew something, she'd seen something we hadn't. I tried to do an emotional one-eighty, and got so disoriented I nearly missed Finn's reply.

At first it didn't look like there was going to be one. He froze up like a computer that's lost its cursor. People speak of someone "turning to stone"—but I don't think any human being could have come as close as Finn to doing that literally. Three or four seconds went by like zeppelins in a desultory breeze . . . and then suddenly he was shouting:

"All right, damn it: I am not immortal!"

The volume made the windows ring and people wince. Motorists may well have heard him out on 25A, rain and all. As the echo of his shout died away, Mary said, quite softly, "I figured it was something like that. You're going to be needing maintenance pretty soon, aren't you?"

Finn sighed and spoke in his normal voice. "If I do not receive fairly extensive maintenance within approximately two hundred and twenty years, I will experience critical systems failures. I will die. It is a trick of the Masters, another way to prevent their scouts deserting as I've done. When I arrived on this planet, I estimated that humanity could possess the necessary technological sophistication within a century or two . . . if it survived that long. If you had been less advanced, you would have been no use to me; more advanced, and you would have detected my approach and perhaps fired upon me. The 'window' was open. Your political immaturity made you a most dangerous gamble—but you were the best chance I had seen in countless millennia. I staked everything on you."

Callahan poured himself a shot of Bushmill's and tossed it back. "What kind of maintenance, Mickey? Organic or cybernetic?"

"Both, Michael. And one other kind for which your people do not yet have a name."

"Why'n'cha just teach it to us?"

Finn shook his head. "Could you have taught Leonardo da Vinci to build a railroad before it was railroading time?"

"So that first night you came in here, all of that was a charade?"

"No, Michael! Not at all. I meant it when I asked you to . . . well, you say you don't remember that. In any case, you refused to do it then. I was in agony. I realized that I had a chance to survive on this world—but I was programmed to transmit my observations of humanity to the Masters at a preset time, and I knew that when I had I would receive orders to sterilize your planet. I could not countermand that programming. The irony was crushing. It was only when you asked me my name that the idea came to me: if I could give you enough of a hint, you could drug me unconscious and prevent my transmission for me. And I managed to do so, and you took the hint.''

''But I mean, you didn't defect and save us for the reason you said, because you learned here that humans have love? You did it because we might get smart enough one day to keep your motor tuned for you? Is that the size of it?''

Finn didn't hang his head; his people must not have had that custom. ''My decision was predicated solely on self-interest, Michael. I *was* pleased to find that you had love—because it would make it easier to get you to help me, when one day you could.''

Shorty Steinitz was wearing the same look he'd had the day he broke Weasel Wetzel's face-bone—and Shorty *knows* that Finn could outpunch an F-111. ''Let me get this straight, Finn,'' he said darkly. ''You don't love the human race?''

''Oh hell, Shorty,'' Long-Drink said, ''*I* don't love the human race, comes to that. There's an ever-dwindlin' percentage I can *tolerate*.''

''All right,'' Shorty insisted, ''this *place,* then, these people . . . Finn, are you sayin' you got no love for Callahan's Place here? For us?''

Finn started to answer, and paused as Tommy Janssen shouldered his way forward. The kid's voice was low and soft and dangerous. ''You came in here the night these guys got me off smack,'' he said, ''and you watched them save me, watched while they sewed my balls back on, and then you got up and did your little dance *because you figured it was cheap medical insurance?* I'm the youngest guy here, twenty-five, if I quit smoking I might live another fifty, sixty years—*if* the goddamn bomb doesn't go off tomorrow. Some of the other people here . . . hell, Tom Flannery's *died* since the night you came in here. And you're worried about Apocalypse because it might cut you back to another two or three centuries of sunrises? Now, where did I put my violin?''

God help me, I spoke up. ''Finn—all these years we've been knockin' our brains out trying to make you feel at home in a strange land, helping you get papers and teaching you about baseball and trying to teach you how to sing and all that . . . all that time you were just *using* us?''

I shut up then, because Finn's feelings had become so violent as to reach the surface of his face. One thing apparently all humanoid life forms have in common: the grimace of extreme anguish.

"This is not fair," he roared, and flung his bottle of rye into the fireplace.

SMASH! Cracks appeared in some of the bricks.

There was a general murmur rising in the room now, but Mary's soft laughter cut right through it, deflating it. I turned, to look at her with new eyes. I resented her for being privy to this intimate matter, for having provoked this hassle, for being cruel to my friend the rotten son of a bitch . . . Pushy, and nasty, and castrating, and *fat* . . .

I transferred to her all my conflict; as I had on the roof, I poured my need into her.

And this time she didn't accept it. I opened my mouth to say something or other that would end our affair, and she ignored me, spoke directly and only to Finn.

"Now you're getting it," she said, smiling. "It *isn't* fair. Enjoying it, Mick? Have I given you enough, now? Have you got a way to store it digitally and play it back later? Can you put it on a loop and run it continuously or something?"

He blinked at her.

"You marinate in guilt soup for enough years, you suck all the juice right out of it, have to go get some new vegetables to throw into the pot, that's understandable. But eventually you'll use up this bag. What'll we do next—spread the news around, put you on the Phil Donahue Show? Sooner or later, somebody'd figure out a way to kill you, and you know it too, you big dumb jerk. Can't you make this last you for a while?"

These were hammer blows she was landing, from a distance of about a foot and a half. I opened my mouth to say something, and suddenly she whirled around to face us. Finn's got a more efficient speaker than any human, but she certainly had an impressive bellow onto her—we jumped farther than we had when he let go.

"Will you clowns stop indulging him now?"

The dust settled, Callahan picked his cigar butt up off the floor and blew sawdust off it, and she cut back to about Force Eight and went on:

"What is the *matter* with you morons? A mutt comes in here, a guy you claim is your friend, with a sign on his forehead says, 'Masochist,' and you people get out the whips and chains, is that it? Txffu's committed the cardinal sin, eh? He doesn't love humanity: hang him. And Handsome over there too, and half the people in this bar, probably . . . what the hell is so special about humanity that not loving it is a sin? Finn said his people loved sentient life: I respect that a lot more, and I'm not at all sure that humanity qualifies, on average—''

(By ''Handsome,'' she referred to Long-Drink, whose name she didn't know, and I found time to wonder if Mary was a pervert too, queer for scrawny men. Long-Drink is even taller and skinnier than me—put him and me and Finn side by side and we look like a pine mountainside . . .)

''—How about an analogy: will that strain your brains too much? Say you work for a South American real estate developer; he has you go out into the bush and exterminate tribes of monkeys where he wants to build new condominiums. You don't like the work, you'd rather quit and jungle up, but the boss has thoughtfully planted a booby-trapped transceiver on you. To make matters worse, you're a diabetic, and he only gives you a limited supply of insulin for each trip.

''One day you run across a tribe of monkeys clever enough to disable the transceiver. It may even be possible to train them to manufacture insulin. *Is it necessary that you love them before you can accept their aid?* I could maybe, given time, learn to get attached to three or four individual monkeys, maybe as many as a dozen or so—be amused by them, grow fond of them, even respect them in certain ways. I could see being concerned if I learned that their tribe was locked into some kind of suicidal behavior pattern—really concerned, not just on my own account. But *love* them? Or their kind in general?

''And should I be ashamed for wanting insulin so that I can live another forty or fifty years—when the monks can only hope for ten or twenty? Oh, you jackasses, I can understand *HIM* being that dumb, he's smarter than any of us—but how could you *morons* be so stupid?''

Many feet were shuffled. She had opened up our friend's hidden wound . . . and we had all picked at it. I was belatedly beginning to realize her technique. Sometimes a mocking voice whispers vile things in a man's ear, things he can't shut out because he half believes they're true. But if you can *personify* that voice, and get him to fight it, to reject it . . .

''He comes from a race so fatheaded noble and ethical that they couldn't bring themselves to destroy their assassins—*perhaps,* he says, they made the wrong choice. Naturally he'd feel guilty about exploiting us by trying to keep us alive, about his inability to love monkeys. All the years he's been on this planet, none of you noticed any pattern in the kind of professions he's followed?''

I found that I was speaking. ''I figured he picked basic, earthy trades as a way of rooting himself to this planet. Our primal cultural basics: farming, fishing, watching the forest, contemplating the sea—''

''Solitary, lonely jobs, every one, the way he went about them. Hermit jobs.'' She turned to Finn. ''You probably find most of us actually repellent, don't you, Txffu?''

His face was expressionless again. ''Candidly, yes.''

''Physically disgusting?''

''Well . . . deformed, on the average. Your males are all so *short* . . . and your females are all so undernourished . . .''

Her ears grew points. ''Really?''

''Yes. Among my people, you yourself would be considered— well, not emaciated, but almost unfashionably slender. As it happens, I have an unconventional taste for slender women . . . but most human females your size hate themselves so much it is unpleasant to be near them—''

''Txffu?'' she interrupted.

''Yes, Mary?''

''Will you marry me?''

I screwed my eyes so tight I saw neon paisley. Somewhere behind their lids was the switch that would turn my breathing back on, and I had to find it pretty quickly.

Finn was utterly still for five long seconds. ''You are not serious.''

''No, thank God, and that's going to be a break for you in the years to come—but my proposal is dead serious. What's your answer?''

''But you—''

''Finn, you've been unable to love because you haven't loved yourself because you haven't loved us—it's time somebody got you off the loop. You ninny, of course you didn't save us out of love! You did it out of *compassion*. That's something that's underrated, but I think it's just as good as love—who knows, maybe better. You can love only your equals—with your superiors or inferiors, compassion is the best you can do, and it's pretty damned good, at least as high up on the ethical scale. With time, it can lead to love. I speculate that it could even be the basis of a pretty fair marriage. Do you think?''

"You saw what is in my chest—"

"Yeah, I'm fascinated. Is there an owner's manual for it?"

"You cannot be serious. You do not even know if we are sexually compatible—"

"The hell I don't. I can see fingers and a tongue from here; anything else is gravy. And I've got *some*thing or other that appeals to you; I knew that back up on the roof when I met you."

That breathing switch had to be around here someplace; just a question of finding it . . .

"—we are not cross-fertile—" Finn tried.

"What of it? Maybe we'll adopt. Hell, we'll adopt this whole goddamn bar—they need *someone* to bring 'em up. Quit stalling: yes or no?"

I think maybe I'd known it all along, sensed it up there on the roof when Finn first flew out of the rainy night. I suppose there are worse ways to say good-bye . . .

"Yes," Finn said finally. "Yes, Mary, I would be honored to marry you. On one condition." He turned to the rest of us. "*All* of you, male and female, must agree to be my Best Man."

A roomful of people looked guiltily to Mary.

She nodded serenely. "Deal."

A cheer went up that rung the rafters. I even got my lungs going in time to join it. Sure it hurt.

But it felt good too.

Finn's face remained blank for another few seconds—and then he remembered to share his joy with us, and hung that expression on himself; I was pleased and proud that he took the trouble.

"Would you two," Callahan boomed, "do me the honor of gettin' married here in my joint? Say, over there on the staircase?"

"Where else?" Mick and Mary said together, and another cheer went up, even louder.

It came to me that I might find some use for a bucket of alcohol, so when Callahan began the bucket brigade of free drinks for the house I hogged three or four. It's amazing how fast you can throw down booze if you work at it, and so before long I found myself bellying up to the bar.

"Innkeeper," I said when he reached me, "give me drink."

He understood my situation—had probably understood from the moment Mary popped the question. Not much gets past Mike Callahan, and nothing that pertains to the human heart. "Healthy re-action," he said, nodding judiciously. "I think you'll live, Jake."

"Have you ever hated your best friend's guts, Mike?"

"Careful, pal: don't get into the same guilt-loop Finn did. Mel-odrama is for TV. Finn's not your best friend, just a garden variety pal. And if you feel like hating him for a while, go to it: it'll pass."

"You haven't said much tonight, Mike. How do *you* feel about all this?"

"Well, the way I look at it, I'm not so much losing a daughter as I am gaining an alien."

I stared at him, and by the time all the tumblers had finished clicking into place, he was handing me an oversized mug of Irish coffee.

"Mary is your—"

"Lady Sally and I have always been real proud of her," he said contentedly, puffing on that miserable stogie.

"Why the hell didn't she ever come around here before?" I asked. "All these years—"

"Well, she couldn't, Jake. She lived too far away, and she used to work nights. Until Sal retired . . ."

You burn your tongue when you drink Irish coffee too fast, so I burned my tongue. So I had another to keep my tongue numb, and then another, and I started having so much fun that the idea sort of caught on generally, and that's more or less how Mike and I and about a dozen of our friends eventually ended up naked in the rain on Callahan's roof, me for the second time that night.

Do you know, from that day to this, rain won't land on me—or any of us that were there—unless we ask it to?

PYOTR'S STORY

Two total drunks in a single week is much higher than average for anyone who goes to Callahan's Place—no pun intended.

Surely there is nothing odd about a man going to a bar in search of oblivion. Understatement of the decade. But Callahan's Place is what cured me of being a lush, and it's done the same for others. Hell, it's helped keep Tommy Janssen off *heroin* for years now. I've gotten high there, and once or twice I've gotten tight, but it's been a good many years since I've been flat-out, helpless drunk—or yearned to be. A true drunk is a rare sight at Callahan's. Mike Callahan doesn't just pour his liquor, he serves it; to get pissed in his Place you must convince him you have a need to, persuade him to take responsibility for you. Most bars, people go to in order to get blind. Mike's customers go there to see better.

But that night I had a need to completely dismantle my higher faculties, and he knew that as I crossed the threshold. Because I was carrying in my arms the ruined body of Lady Macbeth. Her head dangled crazily, her proud neck broken clean through, and a hush fell upon Callahan's Place as the door closed behind me.

Mike recovered quickly; he always does. He nodded, a nod which meant both hello and something else, and glanced up and down the bar until he found an untenanted stretch. He pointed to it, I nodded back, and by the time I reached it he had the free lunch and the beer nuts moved out of the way. Not a word was said in the bar—everyone there understood my feelings as well as Callahan did. Do you begin to see how one could stop being an alcoholic there? Someone, I think it was Fast Eddie, made a subvocal sound of empathy as I laid the Lady on the bartop.

I don't know just how old she is. I could find out by writing the Gibson people and asking when serial number 427248 was sent out into the world, but somehow I don't want to. Somewhere in the twenty-to-thirty range, I'd guess, and she can't be less than fifteen, for I met her in 1966. But she was a treasure even then, and the man I bought her from cheated himself horribly. He was getting married *much* too quickly and needed folding money in a hurry. All I can say is, I hope he got one hell of a wife—because I sure got one hell of a guitar.

She's a J-45, red sunburst with a custom neck, and she clearly predates the Great Guitar Boom of the Sixties. She is *handmade*, not machine-stamped, and she is some forgotten artisan's masterpiece. The very best, top-of-the-line Gibson made today could not touch her; there are very few guitars you can buy that would. She has been my other voice and the basic tool of my trade for a decade and a half. Now her neck, and my heart, were broken clean through.

Long-Drink McGonnigle was at my side, looking mournfully down past me at the pitiful thing on the bar. He touched one of the sprawled strings. It rattled. Death rattle. "Aw," he murmured.

Callahan put a triple Bushmill's in my hand, closed my fingers around it. I made it a double, and then I turned and walked to the chalk line on the floor, faced the merrily crackling fireplace from a distance of twenty feet. People waited respectfully. I drank again while I considered my toast. Then I raised my glass, and everybody followed suit.

"To the Lady," I said, and drained my glass and threw it at the back of the fireplace, and then I said, "Sorry, folks," because it's very difficult to make Mike's fireplace emit shards of glass—it's designed like a parabolic reflector with a shallow focus—but I had thrown hard enough to spatter four tables just the same. I know better than to throw that hard.

Nobody paid the least mind; as one they chorused, "To the Lady" and drank, and when the barrage was finished, *eight* tables were littered with shards.

Then there was a pause, while everybody waited to see if I could talk about it yet. The certain knowledge that they were prepared to swallow their curiosity, go back to their drinking and ignore me if that were what I needed, made it possible to speak.

"I was coming offstage. The Purple Cat, over in East Hampton. Tripped over a cable in the dark. Knew I was going down, tried to get her out from under me. The stage there is waist-high, her head just cleared it and wedged in under the monitor speaker. Then my weight came down on her . . ." I was sobbing. ". . . and she *screamed*, and I . . ."

Long-Drink wrapped me in his great long arms and hugged tight. I buried my face in his shirt and wept. Someone else hugged us both from behind me. When I was back under control, both let go and I found a drink in my hand. I gulped it gratefully.

"I hate to ask, Jake," Callahan rumbled. "I'm afraid I already know. Is there any chance she could be fixed?"

"Tell him, Eddie." But Eddie wasn't there; his piano stool was empty. "All right, look, Mike: There are probably ten shops right here on Long Island that'd accept the commission and my money, and maybe an equal number who'd be honest enough to turn me away. There are maybe five real guitar-makers in the whole New York area, and they'd all tell me to forget it. There might be four Master-class artisans still alive in all of North America, and their bill would run to four figures, maybe five, assuming they thought they could save her at all." Noah Gonzalez had removed his hat, with a view toward passing it; he put it back on. "*Look at her.* You can't *get* wood like that anymore. She's got a custom neck and fingerboard, skinnier'n usual, puts the strings closer together—when I play a normal guitar it's like my fingers shrunk. So a rebuilt neck would have less strength, and the fingerboard'd have to be hand-made . . ." I stopped myself. I finished my drink. "Mike, she's dead."

Long-Drink burst into tears. Callahan nodded and looked sad, and passed me another big drink. He poured one for himself, and *he* toasted the Lady, and when that barrage was over he set 'em up for the house.

The folks treated me right; we had a proper Irish wake for the Lady, and it got pretty drunk out. We laughed and danced and reminisced and swapped lies, created grand toasts; everyone did it up nice. The only thing it lacked was Eddie on the piano; he had disappeared and none knew where. But a wake for Lady Macbeth *must* include the voice of her long-time colleague—so Callahan surprised us all by sitting down and turning out some creditable barrelhouse. I hadn't known he could play a note, and I'd have sworn his fingers were too big to hit only one key at a time, but he did okay.

Anyhow, when the smoke cleared, Pyotr ended up driving better than half of us home, in groups of three—a task I wouldn't wish on my senator.

I guess I should explain about Pyotr. . . .

The thing about a joint like Callahan's Place is that it could not possibly function without the cooperation of all its patrons. It takes a lot of volunteer effort to make the Place work the way it does.

Some of this is obvious. Clearly, if a barkeep is going to allow his patrons to smash their empties in the fireplace, they must all be responsible enough to exercise prudence in this pursuit—and furthermore they must have better than average aim. But perhaps it is not obvious, and so I should mention, that there is a broom-and-scoop set on either side of the hearth, and whenever an occasional wild shard ricochets across the room, one of those broom-and-scoops just naturally finds its way into the hands of whoever happens to be nearest, without anything being said.

Similarly, if you like a parking lot in which anarchy reigns, with cars parked every which way like goats in a pen, you must all be prepared to pile outside together six or ten times a night, and back-and-fill in series until whoever is trying to leave can get his car out. This recurring scene looks rather like a grand-scale Chinese Fire Drill, or perhaps like Bumper Cars for Grownups; Doc points out that to a Martian it would probably look like some vast robot orgy, and insists on referring to it as Auto-Eroticism.

Then there's closing ritual. Along about fifteen minutes before closing, somebody, usually Fast Eddie Costigan the piano player, comes around to all the tables with a big plastic-lined trash barrel. Each table has one of those funnel-and-tin-can ashtrays; someone at each table unscrews it and dumps the butts into the barrel. Then Eddie inserts two corners of the plastic tablecloth into the barrel, the customer lifts the other two corners into the air, and Eddie sluices off the cloth with a seltzer bottle. Other cleanup jobs, mopping and straightening and the like, just seem to get done by somebody or other every night; all Mike Callahan ever had to do is polish the bartop, turn out the lights, and go home. Consequently, although he is scrupulous about ceasing to sell booze at legal curfew, Mike is in no hurry to chase his friends out, and indeed I know of several occasions on which he kept the Place open round the clock, giving away nosepaint until the hour arrived at which it became legal to sell it again.

And finally, of course, there's old Pyotr. You see, no one tight drives home from Callahan's bar. When Mike decides that you've had enough—and they'll never make a Breathalyzer as accurate as his professional judgment—the only way in the world you will get another drink from him is to surrender your car keys and then let Pyotr, who drinks only distilled water, drive you home when you fold. The next morning you drive Pyotr back to his cottage, which is just up the street from Callahan's, and if this seems like too much trouble, you can always go drink somewhere else and see what that gets you.

For the first couple of years after Pyotr started coming around, some of us used to wonder what he got out of the arrangement. None of us ever managed to get him to accept so much as a free breakfast the morning after, and how do you buy a drink for a man who drinks distilled water? Oh, Mike gave him the water for free, but a gallon or so of water a night is pretty poor wages for all the hours of driving Pyotr put in, in the company of at least occasionally troublesome drunks, not to mention the inconvenience of spending many nights sleeping on a strange bed or couch or floor. (Some of the boys, and especially the ones who want to get pie-eyed once in a while, are married. Almost to a woman, their wives worship Pyotr; are happy to put him up now and then.)

For that matter, none of us could ever figure out what old Pyotr did for a living. He never had to be anywhere at any particular time next morning, and he was never late arriving at Callahan's. If asked what he did he would say, "Oh, a little bit of everything, whenever I can get it," and drop the subject. Yet he never seemed to be in need of money, and in all the time I knew him I never once saw him take so much as a peanut from the Free Lunch.

(In Callahan's Place there *is* a free lunch—supported by donations. The value of the change in the jar is almost always greater than the value of the Free Lunch next to it, but nobody watches to make sure it stays that way. I mind me of a bad two weeks when that Free Lunch was the only protein I had, and nobody so much as frowned at me.)

But while he is a bit on the pale side for a man of Middle European stock, Pyotr certainly never looks undernourished, and so there was never any need for us to pry into his personal affairs. Me, I figured him for some kind of a pensioner with a streak of pure altruism, and let it go.

He certainly looks old enough to be a pensioner. Oh, he's in very good shape for his age, and not overly afflicted with wrinkles, but his complexion has that old-leather look. And when you notice his habit of speaking into his cupped hand, and hear the slight lisp in his speech, and you realize that his smiles never seem to pry his lips apart, you get the idea that he's missing some bridgework. And there's something old about his eyes. . . .

Anyway, Pyotr was busier than usual that night, ferrying home all the casualties of Lady Macbeth's wake. It took quite awhile. He took three at a time, using the vehicle of whoever lived farthest away, and taxied back for the next load. Two out of every three drunks would have to taxi back to Callahan's the next day for their cars. I was proud of the honor being paid my dead Lady. Pyotr and Callahan decided to save me for last. Perhaps on the principle that the worst should come last—I was *pissed*, and at the stage of being offensively cheerful and hearty. At last all the other wounded had been choppered out, and Pyotr tapped me on one weaving shoulder.

"So they weld—well hell, hi, Pyotr, wait a half while I finish telling Mike this story—they weld manacles on this giant alien, and they haul him into court for trial, and the first thing he does, they go to swear him in and he swallows the bailiff whole."

Mike had told *me* this gag, but he is a very compassionate man. He relit his cheroot and gave me the straight line, "What'd the bailiff do?"

"His job, o'course—he swore in the witness. Haw haw!" Pyotr joined in the polite laughter and took my arm. "Time to bottle it up, Pyotr you old lovable Litvak? Time to scamper, is it? Why should you have to haul my old ashes, huh? Gimme my keys, Mike, I'm not nearly so drunk as you think—I mean, so thunk as you drink. Shit, I said it right, I *must* be drink. All right, just let me find my pants—"

It took both of them to get me to the car. I noticed that every time one of my feet came unstuck from the ground, it seemed to take enormous effort to force it back down again. A car seat leaped up and hit me in the ass, and a door slammed. "Make sure he takes two aspirins before he passes out for good," Callahan's voice said from a mile away.

"Right," Pyotr said from only a few blocks distant, and my old Pontiac woke up grumbling. The world lurched suddenly, and we fell off a cliff, landing a million years later in white water. I felt nausea coming on, chattered merrily to stave it off.

"Splendid business, Pyotr old sock, absolutionally magnelephant. You drive well, and this car handles well on ice, but if you keep spinning like this we're going to dend up in the itch—I mean, we'll rote off the ride, right? Let's go to the Brooklyn Navy Yard and try to buy a drink for every sailor on the USS *Missouri*—as a song-writer I'm always hoping to find the Moe juiced. Left her right there on the bartop, by all the gods! Jus' left her and—turn around, God damn it, I left my Lady back there!"

"It is all right, Jake. Mr. Callahan will leave her locked up. We will wake her for several days, correct Irish custom, yes? Even those not present tonight should have opportunity to pay their respects."

"Hell, yeah, sure. Hey! *Funeral.* How? Bury or cremate?"

"Cremation would seem appropriate."

"*Strings?* Gearboxes? Heavy metal air pollution? Fuggoff. Bury her, dissolve in acid, heave her into the ocean off Montauk Point and let the fish lay eggs in her sounding box. Know why I called her Lady Macbeth?"

"No, I never knew."

"Used to sneak up and stab me inna back when didn't expect it. Bust a string, go out of tune, start to buzz on the high frets for no reason at all. Treacherous bitch. Oh, *Lady!*"

"You used each other well, Jake. Be glad. Not many have ever touched so fine an instrument."

"Goddamn right. Stop the car, please. I want to review inputs."

"Open the window."

"I'll get it all over the—"

"It's raining. Go ahead."

"Oh. Not sure I like Finn's magic. Have to pay attention to notice it's raining. Right ho. *Oh.*"

Eventually the car stopped complaining and rain sprinkled everything but Pyotr and me and then my house opened up and swallowed me. "Forget aspirins," I mumbled as my bed rushed at me. "Don' need 'em."

"You'll be sorry tomorrow."

"I'm sorry now."

The bed and I went inertialess together, spun end over end across the macrocosmic universe.

I was awakened by the deafening thunder of my pulse.

I knew that I was awake long before I had the power to raise my eyelids. I knew it because I knew I lacked the imagination to dream a taste like that in my mouth. But I was quite prepared to believe that the sleep had lasted at least a century; I felt *old*. That made me wonder if I had snored right through the wake—*the wake!* Everything came back in a rush; I flung open my eyes, and two large icicles were rammed into the apertures as far as they would go, the points inches deep in my forebrain. I screamed. That is, I tried to scream, and it sounded like a scream—but my pulse sounded like an empty oil tank being hit with a maul, so more likely what I did was bleat or whimper.

Something heavy and bristly lay across me; it felt like horsehair, with the horse still attached. I strained at it, could not budge it. I wept.

The voice spoke in an earsplitting whisper. "Good morning, Jake."

"Fuck you too," I croaked savagely, wincing as the smell of my breath went past my nose.

"I warned you," Pyotr said sadly.

"Fuck you twice. Jesus, my eyelashes hurt. What is *lying* on me?"

"A cotton sheet."

"Gaah."

"You should have accepted the aspirins."

"You don't understand. I don't get hangovers."

Pyotr made no reply.

"Damn it, I don't! Not even when I was a lush, not the first time I ever got smashed, not *ever*. Trick metabolism. Worst that ever happens is I wake up not hungry—but no head, no nausea, no weakness, never."

Pyotr was silent a long time. Then, "You drank a good deal more than usual last night."

"Hell, I been drunker'n *that*. Too many times, man."

"Never since I have known you."

"Well, that's true. Maybe that's . . . no, I've fallen off the wagon before. I just don't get hangovers."

He left the room, was gone awhile. I passed the time working on a comprehensive catalog of all the places that hurt, beginning with my thumbnails. I got quite a lot of work done before Pyotr returned; I had gotten halfway through the hairs on my forearms when he came in the door with a heavily laden tray in his hands. I opened my mouth to scream, "Get that *food* out of here!"—and the smell reached me. I sat up and began to salivate. He set the tray down on my lap and I ignored the pain and annihilated bacon, sausage, eggs, cheese, onions, green peppers, hot peppers, bread, butter, English muffins, jam, orange juice, coffee, and assorted condiments so fast I think I frightened him a little. When I sank back against the pillows the tray contained a plate licked clean, an empty cup and glass, and a fork. I was exhausted, and still hurt in all the same places—that is, in all places—but I was beginning to believe that I wanted to live. "This is crazy," I said. "If I *am* hung over, the concept of food ought to be obscene. I never ate that much breakfast in my life, not even the morning after my wedding night."

I could *see* Pyotr now, and he looked embarrassed, as though my appetite were his fault.

"What time is it?"

"Seven P.M."

"God's teeth."

"It was four in the morning when we arrived here. You have slept for thirteen hours. I fell asleep at noon and have just awakened. Do you feel better now that you have eaten?"

"No, but I concede the trick is possible. What's good for total bodily agony?"

"Well, there is no cure. But certain medications are said to alleviate the symptoms."

"And Callahan's has opened by now. Well, how do we get me to the car?"

In due course we got to Callahan's where Lady Macbeth lay in state on top of the bar. The wake was already in full swing when we arrived and were greeted with tipsy cheers. I saw that it was Riddle Night: The big blackboard stood near the door, tonight's game scrawled on it in the handwriting of Doc Webster. On Riddle Night the previous week's winner is Riddle Master; each solved riddle is good for a drink on the Riddle Master's tab. The Doc looked fairly happy—every *un*solved riddle is a free drink for him, on the house.

The board was headed PUBLIC PERSONALITIES. Beneath that were inscribed the following runes:

I.
a)   Hindu ascetic; masculine profession
b)   tramp; crane
c)   profligate; cheat
d)   span; tavern, money
e)   fish; Jamaican or Scottish male, caviar
f)   certainly; Irish street
g)   handtruck; forgiveness

II.
a)   pry; manager
b)   smart guy; Stout
c)   chicken coop; more loving
d)   bandit; crimson car
e)   coffin; baby boy
f)   tote; subsidy
g)   moaning; achieve

III.
a)   irrigated; laser pistol
b)   Nazi; cook lightly
c)   British punk; knowledge, current
d)   chicken coop; foreplay
e)   wealthier; nuts to

IV.
a)   Italian beauty; stead, depart, witness
b)   toilet; auto, senior member
c)   be dull; Carmina Burana
d)   grass; apprentice, younger
e)   valley; odd
f)   burns; leer at

Example: penis; truck = peter; lorry = Peter Lorre. Extra drinks for identifying Categories I-IV.

People were staring at the board, seemed to have *been* staring at it for some time, but none of the riddles were checked off yet. I paid my respects to the Lady, said hello to Mike, accepted a large glass of dog-hair. Then, deliberately, I turned away from the Lady and toward the board. (Why don't you take a crack at it before reading further?)

"Got one," I said at once, and allowed Long-Drink to help me to the board. "First one in line," I said, marking with chalk. "Hindu ascetic; masculine profession. That's Jain; Man's Field, and Category One is Actresses."

Doc Webster looked pained. "Say Film Women," he suggested. "More accurate. Mike, one for Jake on me."

Given the category Section I was fairly simple. I got b) 'Bo; Derrick. Long-Drink McGonnigle got c) Rakehell; Welsh. Tommy Janssen figured out that d) and e) were Bridge It; Bar Dough and Marlin; Mon Roe. Josie Bauer took f) Surely; Mick Lane and g) Dolly; Pardon. We collected our drinks gleefully.

I suspected that the second category would be Male Actors (or Film Men), but kept my mouth shut, hoping I could figure them all out and do a sweep before anyone else twigged. This turned out to be poor tactics; I got a), b), d) and f), but while I was puzzling over the rest, Shorty Steinitz spoke up. "The category is Male Film Stars, and the first one is Jimmy; Steward!" I tried to jump in at once, but Long-Drink drowned me out. "Got b): Alec; Guinness! Hey, and f) has to be Carry; Grant."

"And d)," I said irritably, "is Robber; Red Ford. But what about the others?" We stared at them in silence for a while.

"A hint," Doc Webster said at last. "With reference to g), the first name is what I'll be doing if you do the second."

"Got it!" Long-Drink cried. "Keenin'; Win." The Doc grimaced. Callahan was busy keeping score and distributing the prizes, but he had attention left to spare. "That third one there, c): That has to be Hennery; Fonder."

There was a pause, then. Nobody could figure out "coffin; baby boy." (Can you?) After a while we turned our attention to the remaining two categories, but the silence remained unbroken. The Doc looked smug. "No hurry, gents and ladies," he said. "Closing time isn't for several hours yet." We all glared at him and thought hard.

Surprisingly, it was Pyotr who spoke up. "I have a sweep," he stated. "Category IV in its entirety."

Folks regarded him with respectful interest. He was committed now: if he missed *one*, he would owe the Doc all six drinks. The Doc looked startled but game—he seemed to think he had an ace up his sleeve. "Go ahead, Pyotr."

"The category is Famous Monsters." The Doc winced. "The first is Bella; Lieu Go See." Applause. "Then John; Car a Dean." More applause.

"Not bad," the Doc admitted. "Keep going."

"The next two, of course, are among the most famous of all. Be dull; Carmina Burana *has* to be Bore Us; Carl Orff. . . ." He paused to sip one of the three drinks Callahan had passed him.

"Brilliant, Pyotr," I said, slapping him on the back. "But I'm still stumped for the last three."

"That is because they are tricky. The first is tortured, and the last two are obscure."

"Go ahead," Doc Webster said grimly.

"The first is the famous Wolfman: Lawn; Trainee Junior." Delighted laughter and applause came from all sides. "The others are both Frankenstein's Creature, but it would require an historian of horror films to guess both. Glenn Strange played the Monster in at least three movies . . ." The Doc swore. ". . . and the last shall be first; the man who played the Monster in the very first film version of *Frankenstein*."

"But we already had Karloff," I protested.

"No, Jake," Pyotr said patiently. "That was the first *talkie* version. The very first was released in 1910, and the Monster was played by a man with the unusual name of Charles Ogle. Read 'chars' for 'burns' and you come close enough."

We gave him a standing ovation—in which the Doc joined.

All of this had admirably occupied my attention, from almost the moment of my arrival. But before I turned to a study of Category III, I turned to the bar to begin the third of the four drinks I had won—and my gaze fell on the ruined Lady. She lay there in tragic splendor, mutely reproaching me for enjoying myself so much while she was broken. All at once I lost all interest in the game, in everything but the pressing business of locating and obtaining oblivion. I gulped the drink in my hand and reached for the next one, and a very elderly man came in the door of Callahan's Place with his hands high in the air, an expression of infinite weariness on his face. He was closely followed by Fast Eddie Costigan, whose head just about came up to the level of the elderly man's shoulder blades. Conversations began to peter out.

I just had time to recall that Eddie had vanished mysteriously the night before, and then the two of them moved closer and I saw why everybody was getting quiet. And why the old gent had his hands in the air. I didn't get a real good look, but what Eddie had in his right hand, nestled up against the other man's fourth lumbar vertebra, looked an awful lot like a Charter Arms .38. The gun that got Johnny Lennon and George Wallace.

I decided which way I would jump and put on my blandest expression. "Hi, Eddie."

"Hi, Jake," he said shortly, all his attention on his prisoner.

"I tell you for the last time, Edward—" the old gent began in a Spanish accent.

"Shaddap! Nobody ast you nuttin'. Get over here by de bar an' get to it, see?"

"Eddie," Callahan began gently.

"Shaddap, I said."

I was shocked. Eddie *worships* Callahan. The runty little piano man prodded with his picce, and the old Spaniard sighed in resignation and came toward me.

But as he came past me, his expression changed suddenly and utterly. If aged Odysseus had come round one last weary corner and found Penelope in a bower, legs spread and a sweet smile on her lips, his face might have gone through such a change. The old gent was staring past me in joyous disbelief at the Holy Grail, at the Golden Fleece, at the Promised Land, at—

—at the ruined Lady Macbeth.

"Santa Maria," he breathed. *"Madre de Dios."*

Years lifted from his shoulders, bitter years, and years smoothed away from his face. His hands came down slowly to his sides, and I saw those hands, really *saw* them for the first time. All at once I knew who he was. My eyes widened.

"Montoya," I said. "Domingo Montoya."

He nodded absently.

"But you're dead."

He nodded again, and moved forward. His eyes were dreamy, but his step was firm. Eddie stood his ground. Montoya stopped before the Lady, and he actually bowed to her. And then he looked at her.

First he let his eyes travel up her length the way a man takes in a woman, from the toes up. I watched his face. He almost smiled when he reached the bridge. He almost frowned when he got to the scars around the sounding hole that said I had once been foolish enough to clamp a pickup onto her. He did smile as his gaze reached the fingerboard and frets, and he marveled at the lines of the neck. Then his eyes reached the awful fracture, and they shut for an instant. His face became totally expressionless; his eyes opened again, studied the wreck with dispassionate thoroughness, and went on to study the head.

That first look took him perhaps eight seconds. He straightened up, closed his eyes again, clearly fixing the memory forever in his brain. Then he turned to me. "Thank you, sir," he said with great formality. "You are a very fortunate man."

I thought about it. "Yes, I believe I am."

He turned back and looked at her again, and now he *looked*. From several angles, from up close and far away. The joining of neck to body. The joining of head to neck-stub. "Light," he said, and held out his hand. Callahan put a flashlight into it, and Montoya inspected what he could of Lady Macbeth's interior bracings through her open mouth. I had the damndest feeling that he was going to tell her to stick out her tongue and say "Ah!" He tossed the flashlight over his shoulder—Eddie caught it with his free hand—and stooped to sight along the neck. "Towel," he said, straightening. Callahan produced a clean one. He wiped his hands very carefully, finger by finger, and then with the tenderness of a mother bathing her child he began to touch the Lady here and there.

"Jake," Long-Drink said in hushed tones. "What the hell is going on? Who *is* this guy?"

Montoya gave no sign of hearing; he was absorbed.

"Remember what I said last night? That there are only maybe four Master-class guitar makers left in the country?"

"Yeah. This guy's a Master?"

"*No*," I cried, scandalized.

"Well then?"

"There is one rank higher than Master. Wizard. There have been a dozen or so in all the history of the world. Domingo Montoya is the only one now living." I gulped Irish whiskey. "Except that he died five years ago."

"The hell you say."

Fast Eddie stuffed the gun into his belt and sat down on his piano stool. "He didn't die," he said, signalling Callahan for a rum. "He went underground."

I nodded. "I think I understand."

Long-Drink shook his head. "I don't."

"Okay, Drink, think about it a second. Put yourself in his shoes. You're Domingo Montoya, the last living guitar Wizard. *And all they bring you to work on is shit.* There are maybe fifty or a hundred guitars left on the planet worthy of your skill, most of which you made yourself, and they're all being *well* cared for by careful and wealthy owners. Meanwhile, fools keep coming in the door with their broken toys, their machine-stamped trash, asking Paul Dirac to do their physics homework for them. Damn-fool marquises who want a guitar with the name of their mistress spelled out in jewels on the neck; idiot rock stars who want a guitar shaped like a Swiss Army knife; stupid rich kids who want their stupid Martins and stupid Goyas outfitted with Day-Glo pick-guards by the man everyone knows is the last living Wizard. Nobody wants to pay what honest materials cost nowadays, nobody wants to wait as long as true Quality requires, everybody wants their goddamn lily gilded, and *still* you can't beat them off with a club, because you're Domingo Montoya. You triple your fee, and then triple it again, and then square the result, and still they keep coming with their stupid broken trash—or worse, they purchase one of your own handmade masterworks, and use it ignobly, fail to respect it properly, treat it like some sort of common utensil." I glanced at Montoya. "No wonder he retired."

Montoya looked up. "I have not retired. If God is kind I never will. But I no longer sell my skill or its fruits, and I use another name. I did not believe it was possible to locate me."

"Then how—"

"Two years ago I accepted an apprentice." My brows went up; I would not have thought there was anyone worthy to be the pupil of Domingo Montoya. "He is impatient and lacks serenity, but both of these are curable with age. He is not clumsy, and his attitude is good." He glowered at Eddie. "*Was* good. He swore secrecy to me."

"I went ta school wit' 'im," Eddie said. "P.S. Eighty-t'ree. He hadda tell *some*body."

"Yes," Montoya said, nodding slowly. "I suppose I can see how that would be so."

"He come back ta de old neighborhood ta see his ma. I run into 'im on de street an' we go to a gin mill an' pretty soon he's tellin' me de whole story, how he's never been so happy in his life. He tells me ta come out to Ohio an' meetcha sometime, an' he gimme yer address." Eddie glanced down at the gun in his belt and looked sheepish. "I guess he sh'unta done dat."

Montoya looked at him, and then at Lady Macbeth, and then at me. He looked me over very carefully, and to my great relief I passed muster. "No harm done," he said to Eddie, and for the first time I noticed that Montoya was wearing a sweater, pajamas, and bedroom slippers.

I was bursting with the need to ask, and I *could not ask*, I was afraid to ask, and it must have showed in my face, at least to a gaze as piercing as his, because all of a sudden his own face got all remorseful and compassionate. My heart sank. It was beyond even his skill—

"Forgive me, sir," he said mournfully. "I have kept you waiting for my prognosis. I am old, my mind is full of fur. I will take you, how is it said, off the tender hooks."

I finished my drink in a swallow, lobbed the empty into the fireplace for luck, and gripped both arms of my chair. "Shoot."

"You do not want to know, can this guitar be mended. This is not at issue. You know that any imbecile can butt the two ends together and brace and glue and tinker and give you back something which looks just like a guitar. What you want to know is, can this guitar ever be what she was two days ago, and I tell you the answer is never in this world."

I closed my eyes and inhaled sharply; all the tiny various outposts of hangover throughout my body rose up and *throbbed* all at once.

Montoya was still speaking. "—trauma so great as this must have subtle effects all throughout the instrument, microscopic ruptures, tiny weakenings. No man could trace them all, nor heal them if he did. But if you ask me can I, Domingo Montoya, make this guitar so *close* to what it was that you yourself cannot detect any difference, then I tell you that I believe I can; also I can fix that buzz I see in the twelfth fret and replace your pegs."

My ears roared.

"I cannot guarantee success! But I believe I can do it. At worst I will have to redesign the head. It will take me two months. For that period I will loan you one of my guitars. You must keep your hands in shape for her, while she is healing for you. You have treated her with kindness, I can see; she will not malinger.''

I could not speak. It was Callahan who said, ''What is your fee, Don Domingo?''

He shook his head. ''There is no charge. My eyes and hands tell me that this guitar was made by an old pupil of mine, Goldman. He went to work for Gibson, and then he saw the way the industry was going and got into another line. I always thought that if he had kept working, kept learning, he might have taught me one day.'' He caressed the guitar. ''It is good to see his handiwork. I *want* to mend her. How daring the neck! She must be a pleasure to play once you are used to her, eh?''

''She is. Thank you, Don Domingo.''

''Nobody here will reveal your secret,'' Callahan added. ''Oh, and say, I've got a jug of fine old Spanish wine in the back I been saving for a gentleman such as yourself—could I pour you a glass on the house? Maybe a sandwich to go with it?''

Montoya smiled.

I swiveled my chair away from him. *''Eddie!''* I cried.

The little piano man read my expression, and his eyes widened in shock and horror. ''Aw Jeez,'' he said, shaking his head, ''aw, *naw*,'' and I left my chair like a stone leaving a slingshot. Eddie bolted for cover, but strong volunteers grabbed him and prevented his escape. I was on him like a stooping falcon, wrapping him up in my arms and kissing him on the mouth before he could turn his face away. An explosion of laughter and cheers shook the room, and he turned bright red. ''Aw *Jeez!*'' he said again.

''Eddie,'' I cried, ''there is no way I will *ever* be able to repay you.''

''Sure dere is,'' he yelled. ''Leggo o' me.''

More laughter and cheers. Then Doc Webster spoke up.

''Eddie, that was a good thing you did, and I love you for it. And I know you tend to use direct methods, and I can't argue with results. But frankly I'm a little disappointed to learn that you own a handgun.''

''I bought it on de way to Ohio,'' Eddie said, struggling free of my embrace. ''I figger maybe de Wizard don' wanna get up at seven inna mornin' an' drive five hunnert miles to look at no busted axe. Sure enough, he don't.''

''But dammit, Eddie, those things are dangerous. Over the course of a five-hundred-mile drive . . . suppose he tried to get that gun away from you, and it went off?''

Eddie pulled the gun, aimed it at the ceiling, and pulled the trigger. There was no explosion. Only a small clacking sound as the hammer fell and then an inexplicable loud hiss. Eddie rotated the cylinder slightly. In a loud voice with too much treble, the gun offered to clear up my pimples overnight without messy creams or oily pads.

It actually had time to finish its pitch, give the time and call-letters, and begin Number Three on the Hot Line of Hits before the tidal wave of laughter and applause drowned it out. Montoya left off soothing the wounded Lady to join in, and when he could make himself heard, he called, ''You could have threatened me with nothing more fearsome, my friend, than forced exposure to AM radio,'' at which Eddie broke up and flung the ''gun'' into the fireplace.

Eventually it got worked out that Eddie and Montoya would bring Lady Macbeth back to Eddie's place together, get some sleep, and set out the next morning for Montoya's home, where he could begin work. Eddie would bring me back the promised loaner, would be back with it by the night after next, and on his return we would jam together. Montoya made me promise to tape that jam and send him a dupe.

What with one thing and another, I finished up that evening just about as pickled as I'd been the night before. But it was happy drunk rather than sad drunk, an altogether different experience, in kind if not in degree. Popular myth to the contrary, drink is not really a good drug for pain. That is, it can numb physical pain, but will not blunt the edge of sorrow; it can help that latter only by making it easier for a man to curse or weep. But alcohol is great for happiness: it can actually intensify joy. It was perfect for the occasion, then; it anesthetized me against the unaccustomed aches of my first hangover, and enhanced my euphoria. My Lady was saved; she would sing again. My friends, who had shared my loss, shared my joy. I danced with Josie and Eddie and Rachel and Leslie; I solved Category III of Doc's riddle and swept it without a mistake; I jollied Tommy out of being worried about some old friend of his, and made him laugh; with Eddie on piano and everybody else in the joint as the Raelettes I sang ''What'd I Say'' for seventeen choruses; for at least half an hour I studied the grain on the bartop and learned therefrom a great deal about the structure and purpose of the Universe; I leaped up on the same bartop and performed a hornpipe—on my hands. After that it all got a bit vague and hallucinatory—at least, I don't *think* there were any real horses present.

A short while later it seemed to be unusually quiet. The only sound was the steady cursing of my Pontiac and the hissing of the air that it sliced through. I opened my eyes and watched white lines come at me.

"Pyotr. Stout fellow. No—water fellow, won't drink stout. Why don't you drink, Pyotr? S' *nice*."

"Weak stomach. Rest, Jake. Soon we are home."

"Hope I'm not hung over again tomorrow. That was awful. Cripes, my neck still hurts. . . ." I started to rub it; Pyotr took my hand away.

"Leave it alone, Jake. Rest. Tonight I will make sure you take two aspirins."

"Yeah. You're the lily of the valley, man."

A short while later wetness occurred within my mouth in alarming proportions, and when I swallowed I felt the aspirins going down. "Good old Pyotr." Then the ship's engines shut down and we went into free fall.

Next morning I decided that hangovers are like sex—the second time isn't *quite* as painful. If the analogy held, by tomorrow I'd be enjoying it.

Oh, I hurt, all right. No mistake about that. But I hurt like a man with a medium bad case of the flu, whereas the day before I had hurt like a man systematically tortured for information over a period of weeks. This time sensory stimuli were only about twice the intensity I could handle, and a considerably younger and smaller mouse had died in my mouth, and my skull was no more than a half size too small. The only thing that hurt as much as it had the previous morning was my neck, as I learned when I made an ill-advised attempt to consult the clock beside me on the night table. For a horrified moment I actually *believed* that I had unscrewed my skull and now it was falling off. I put it back on with my hands, and it felt like I nearly stripped the threads until I got it right.

I must have emitted sound. The door opened and Pyotr looked in. "Are you all right, Jake?"

"Of course not—half of me is left. Saved me for last again, eh?"

"You insisted. In fact you could not be persuaded to leave at all, until you lost consciousness altogether."

"Well, I—OH! *My guitar.* Oh, Pyotr, I think I'm going to do something that will hurt me very much."

"What?"

"I am going to smile."

It did hurt. If you don't happen to be hung over, relax your face and put a finger just behind and beneath each ear, and concentrate. Now smile. The back of my neck was a knot of pain, and those two muscles you just felt move were the ends of the knot. Smiling tightened it. But I had to smile, and didn't mind the pain. Lady Macbeth was alive! Life was good.

That didn't last; my metabolism just wasn't up to supporting good cheer. The Lady was *not* alive. Back from the dead, perhaps—but still in deep coma in Intensive Care. Attended, to be sure, by the world's best surgeon. But she did not have youth going for her— and neither did the surgeon.

Pyotr must have seen the smile fade and guessed why, because he said exactly the right thing.

"There is hope, my friend."

I took my first real good look at him.

"Thanks, Pyotr. Gawd, you look worse than I do. I must have woken you up, what time is it, I don't dare turn my head and look."

"Much like yesterday. You have slept the clock 'round, and I have just finished my customary six hours. I admit I do not feel very rested."

"You must be coming down with something. Truly, man, you look like I feel."

"How *do* you feel?"

"Uh—oddly enough, not as bad as I expected to. Those aspirins must have helped. Thanks, brother."

He ducked his head in what I took to be modesty or shyness.

"You should take a couple yourself."

He shook his head. "I am one of those people who can't take asp—"

"No problem, I've got the other kind, good for all stomachs."

"Thank you, no."

"You sure? What time did you say it was?"

"Normal people are eating their dinners."

"Their—*dinner!*" I sat up, ignoring all agony, got to my feet and staggered headlong out of the room, down the hall to the kitchen. I wept with joy at the sight of so much food in one place. That same eerie, voracious hunger of the morning before, except that today I was not going to make Pyotr do the cooking. I was ashamed enough to note that he had cleaned up the previous night's breakner (a compound word formed along the same lines as "brunch"), apparently before he had gone to sleep.

I designed a megaomelet and began amassing construction materials. I designed for twin occupants. "Pyotr, you old Slovak Samaritan, I know you have this thing about not letting people stand you to a meal the next day, and I can dig that, makes the generosity more pure, but I've been with you now close to forty hours and you've had bugger all to eat, so what you're gonna do is sit down and shut up and eat this omelet or I'm gonna shove it up your nose, right?"

He stared in horror at the growing pile on the cutting board. "Jake, no, thank you! No."

"Well, God damn it, Pyotr, I ain't asking for a structural analysis of your digestion! Just tell me what ingredients to leave out and I'll double up on the rest."

"No, truly—"

"Damn it, anybody can eat *eggs*."

"Jake, thank you, I truly am not at all hungry."

I gave up. By that time all eight eggs had already been cracked, so I cut enough other things to fill an eight-egg omelet anyhow, figuring I'd give the other half to the cats. But to my surprise, when I paused to wipe my mouth, there was nothing left before me that I could legitimately eat except for a piece of ham gristle I had rejected once already. So I ate it, and finished the pot of coffee, and looked up.

"Cripes, maybe you really are sick. I'm gonna call Doc Webster—"

"Thank you, no, Jake, I would appreciate only a ride home, if you please, and to lie down and rest. If you are up to it. . . ."

"Hell, I feel practically vertebrate. Only thing still sore is the back of my neck. Just let me shower and change and we'll hit the road."

I pulled up in front of Pyotr's place, a small dark cottage all by itself about a half a block from Callahan's Place. I got out with him. "I'll just come in with you for a second, Pyotr, get you squared away."

"You are kind to offer, but I am fine now. I will sleep tonight, and see you tomorrow. Good-bye, Jake—I am glad your guitar is not lost."

So I got back into the car and drove the half block to Callahan's.

*   *   *

"Evenin', Jake. What'll it be?"

"Coffee, please, light and sweet."

Callahan nodded approvingly. "Coming up."

Long-Drink snorted next to me. "Can't take the gaff, huh, young-
ster?"

"I guess not, Drink. These last two mornings I've had the first
two hangovers of my life. I guess I'm getting old."

"Hah!" The Drink looked suddenly puzzled. "You know, now
I come to think of it . . . huh. I never thought."

"And no one ever accused you of it, either."

"No, I mean I just now come to realize what a blessed long time
it's been since I been hung over myself."

"Really? You?" The Drink is one of Pyotr's steadiest (or un-
steadiest) customers. "You must have the same funny metabolism
I have—ouch!" I rubbed the back of my neck. "Used to have."

"No," he said thoughtfully. "No, I've *had* hangovers. Lots of
'em. Only I just realized I can't remember when was the last *time*
I had one."

Slippery Joe Maser had overheard. "I can. Remember *my* last
hangover, I mean. About four years ago. Just before I started comin'
here. Boy, it was a honey—"

"Ain't that funny?" Noah Gonzalez put in. "Damned if I can
remember a hangover since I started drinking here myself. Used to
get 'em all the time. I sort of figured it had something to do with
the vibes in this joint."

Joe nodded. "That's what I thought. This Place is kinda magic,
everybody knows that. Boy, I always wake up hungry after a toot,
though. Hell of a stiff neck too."

"Magic, hell," Long-Drink said. "Callahan, you thievin' spal-
peen, we've got you red-handed! Waterin' your drinks, by God, not
an honest hangover in a hogshead. Admit it."

"I'll admit you got a hog's head, all right," Callahan growled
back, returning with my coffee. He stuck his seven o'clock shadow
an inch from Long-Drink's and exhaled rancorous cigar smoke. "If
my booze is watered down, how the hell come it gets you so damn
pie-faced?"

"Power of suggestion," the Drink roared. "Placebo effect. Contact high from these other rummies. Tell him, Doc."

Doc Webster, who had been sitting quietly hunched over his

drink, chose this moment to throw back his head and shout, "*Woe is me!*"

"Hey, Doc, what's wrong?" two or three of us asked at once.

"I'm ruined."

"How so?"

He turned his immense bulk to face us. "I've been moonlighting on the side, as a theatrical agent."

"No foolin'?"

"Yeah, and my most promising client, Dum-Dum the Human Cannonball, just decided to retire."

Long-Drink looked puzzled. "Hey, what the hell, unemployment and everything, you shouldn't have any trouble lining up a replacement. Hell, if the money's right, *I'll* do it."

The Doc shook his head. "Dum-Dum is a midget. They cast the cannon special for him." He sipped bourbon and sighed. "I'm afraid we'll never see an artist of his caliber again."

Callahan howled, and the rest of us accorded the Doc the penultimate compliment: we held our noses and wept. He sat there in his special-built oversize chair and he looked grave, but you could see he was laughing, because he shook like Jell-O. "Now I've got my own back for last night," he said. "Guess my riddles, will you?" He finished his bourbon. "Well, I'm off. Filling in tonight over at Smithtown General." His glass hit the exact center of the fireplace, and he strode out amid a thunderous silence.

We all crept back to our original seats and placed fresh orders. Callahan had barely finished medicating the wounded when the door banged open again. We turned, figuring that the Doc had thought of a topper, and were surprised.

Because young Tommy Janssen stood in the doorway, and tears were running down his face, and he was *stinking* drunk.

I got to him first. "Jesus, pal, what is it? Here, let me help you."

" 'Ricky's been kicking the gong—' " he sang, quoting that old James Taylor song, "Junkie's Lament," and my blood ran cold. Could Tommy possibly have been stupid enough to . . . but no, that was booze on his breath, all right, and his sleeves were rolled up. I got him to a chair, and Callahan drew him a beer. He inhaled half of it, and cried some more. "Ricky," he sobbed. "Oh, Ricky, you stupid shit. He taught me how to smoke cigarettes, you know that?"

"Ricky who?"

"Ricky Maresca. We grew up together. We . . . we were junkies together once." He giggled though tears. "I turned him on, can you dig it? He turned me on to tobacco, I gave him his first taste of smack." His face broke. "Oh *Christ!*"

"What's the matter with Ricky?" Callahan asked him.

"Nothing," he cried. "Nothing on Earth, baby. Ricky's got no problems at all."

"Jesus," I breathed.

"Oh man. I *tried* to get him to come down here, do you know how hard I tried? I figured you guys could do it for him the way you did for me. Shit, I did everything but drag him here. I shoulda dragged him!" He broke down, and Josie hugged him.

After a while Callahan said, "Overdose?"

Tommy reached for his beer and knocked it spinning. "Shit, no. He tried to take off a gas station last night, for the money, and the pump jock had a piece in the desk. Ricky's down, man, he's down. All gone. Callahan, gimme a fucking whiskey!"

"Tommy," Callahan said gently, "let's talk awhile first, have a little java, then we'll drink, OK?"

Tommy lurched to his feet and grabbed the bar for support. "Don't goddammit ever try to con a junkie! You think I've had enough, and you are seriously mistaken. Gimme a fuckin' whiskey or I'll come over there an' get it."

"Take it easy, son."

I tried to put my arm around Tommy.

"Hey, pal—"

He shoved me away. "Don't patronize me, Jake! *You* got wasted two nights running, why can't I?"

"I'll keep serving 'em as long as you can order 'em," Callahan said. "But son, you're close to the line now. Why don't you talk it out first? Whole idea of getting drunk is to talk it out before you pass out."

"Screw this," Tommy cried. "What the hell did I come here for, anyway? I can drink at home." He lurched in the general direction of the door.

"Tommy," I called, "wait up—"

"No," he roared. "Damn it, leave me alone, all of you! You hear me? I wanna be by myself, I—I'm not ready to talk about it yet. Just leave me the hell alone!" And he was gone, slamming the door behind him.

"Mike?" I asked.

"Hmmm." Callahan seemed of two minds. "Well, I guess you can't help a man who don't want to be helped. Let him go; he'll be in tomorrow.'' He mopped the bartop and looked troubled.

"You don't think he'll—''

"Go back to smack himself? I don't think so. Tommy hates that shit now. I'm just a little worried he might go look up Ricky's connection and try to kill him.''

"Sounds like a good plan to me,'' Long-Drink muttered.

"But he's too drunk to function. More likely *he'll* go down. Or do a clumsy job and get busted for it.''

"Be his second fall,'' I said.

"Damn it,'' the Drink burst out, "I'm goin' after him.''

But when he was halfway to the door we all heard the sound of a vehicle door slamming out in the parking lot, and he pulled up short. "It's okay,'' he said. "That's my pickup, I'd know that noise anywhere. Tommy knows I keep a couple bottles under the seat in case of snake bite. He'll be okay—after a while I'll go find him and put him in the truckbed and take him home.''

"Good man, Drink,'' I said. "Pyotr's out with the bug; we've got to cover for him.''

Callahan nodded slowly. "Yeah, I guess that'll do it.'' The Place began to buzz again. I wanted a drink, and ordered more coffee instead, my seventh cup of the day so far. As it arrived, one of those accidental lulls in the conversation occurred, and we all plainly heard the sound of glass breaking out in the parking lot. Callahan winced, but spilled no coffee.

"How do you figure a thing like heroin, Mike? It seems to weed out the very stupid and the very talented. Bird, Lady Day, Tim Hardin, Janis, a dozen others we both know—and a half a million anonymous losers, dead in alleys and pay toilets and gas stations and other people's bedrooms. Once in every few thousand of 'em comes a Ray Charles or a James Taylor, able to put it down and keep on working.''

"Tells you something about the world we're making. The very stupid and the very sensitive can't seem to live in it. Both kinds need dangerous doses of anesthetic just to get through a day. Be a lot less bother for all concerned if they could get it legal, I figure. If that Ricky wanted to die, okay—but he shouldn't have had to make some poor gas jockey have to shoot him.''

Another sound of shattering glass from outside, as loud as the first.

"Hey, Drink,'' Callahan said suddenly, "*how* much juice you say you keep in that truck?''

Long-Drink broke off a conversation with Margie Shorter. "Well, how I figure is, I got two hands—and besides, I might end up sharing the cab with somebody fastidious."

"Two *full* bottles?"

All of us got it at once, but the Drink was the first to move, and those long legs of his can really eat distance when they start swinging. He was out the door before the rest of us were in gear, and by the time we got outside he was just visible in the darkness, kneeling up on the tailgate of his pickup, shaking his head. Everybody started for the truck, but I waved them back and they heeded me. When I got to the truck there was just enough light to locate the two heaps of glass that had been full quarts of Jack Daniels once. The question was, how recently? I got down on my hands and knees, swept my fingers gingerly through the shards, accepting a few small cuts in exchange for the answer to the question, is the ground at all damp here abouts?

It was not.

"Jesus, Drink, he's sucked down two quarts of high test! Get him inside!"

"Can a man die from that?"

"*Get him inside.*" Tommy has one of those funny stomachs, that won't puke even when it ought to; I was already running.

"Where are you—oh, right." I could hear him hauling Tommy off the truck. Callahan's phone was out of service that week, so the Drink knew where I had to be headed. He was only half right. I left the parking lot in a spray of gravel, slipped in dogshit just off the curb, nearly got creamed by a Friday-night cowboy in a Camaro, went up over the hood of a parked Caddy and burst in the door of the all-night deli across the street from Callahan's. The counterman spun around, startled.

"Bernie," I roared, "call the Doc at Smithtown. Alcohol overdose across the street, *stat*," and then I was out the door again and sprinting up the dark street, heading for my second and most important destination.

Because I knew. Don't ask me how, I just knew. They say a hunch is an integration of data you did not know you possessed. Maybe I'd subconsciously begun to suspect just before the Doc had distracted me with his rotten pun—I'd had a lot of coffee, and they say coffee increases the IQ some. Maybe not—maybe I'd never have figured it out if I hadn't *needed* to just then, if figuring it all out hadn't been the only thing that could save my silly-ass friend

Tommy. I had no evidence that would stand up in any kind of court—only hints and guesswork. All I can tell you is that when I first cleared the doorway of Callahan's Place, I knew where I would end up going—hipping Bernie was only for backup, and because it took so little time and was on the way.

Half a block is a short distance. Practically no distance at all. But to a man dreadfully hung over, afraid that his friend is dying, and above all absolutely, preternaturally *certain* of something that he cannot believe, a half block can take forever to run. By the time I got there, I believed. And then for the second time that day I was looking at a small, dark cottage with carven-Swiss drolleries around the windows and doors. This time I didn't care if I was welcome.

I didn't waste time on the doorbell or the door. There was a big wooden lawn chair, maybe sixty or seventy pounds I learned later, but right then it felt like balsa as I heaved it up over my head and flung it through the big living room window. It took out the bulk of the window and the drapes behind; I followed it like Dum-Dum the Human Cannonball, at a slight angle, and God was kind: I landed on nothing but rug. I heard a distant shout in a language I did not know but was prepared to bet was Rumanian, and followed it through unfamiliar darkness, banging myself several times on hard objects, destroying an end table. Total dark, no moon or starlight, no time for matches, a door was before me and I kicked it open and there he was, just turning on a bedside lamp.

"I know," I said. "There's no more time for lying."

Pyotr tried to look uncomprehending, and failed, and there just wasn't any time for it.

"You don't drink blood. You *filter* it." He went white with shock. "I can even see how it must have happened, your trip at Callahan's, I mean. When you first got over here to the States, you must have landed in New York and got a job as a technician in a blood bank, right? Leach a *little* bit of nourishment out of a lot of whole blood you can feed without giving serious anemia to the transfusion patients. An ethical vampire—with a digestion that has trouble with beef broth. I'll bet you've even got big canines like the movie vampires—not because size makes them any more efficient at *letting* blood, but because there're some damned unusual glands in 'em. You interface with foreign blood and filter out the nourishment it carries in solution. Only you couldn't have known how they got blood in New York City, who the typical donor is, and before you knew it it was too late, you were a stone alcoholic."

I was talking a mile a minute, but I could see every single shot strike home. I had no time to spare for his anguish; I grabbed him and hauled him off the bed, threw clothes at him. "Well, I don't give a shit about that now! You know young Tommy Janssen, well he's down the block with about three quarts of hooch in him, and the last two went down in a gulp apiece, so you move your skinny Transylvanian ass or I'll kick it off your spine, you got me? *Jump*, goddammit!"

He caught on at once, and without a word he pulled his clothes on, fast enough to suit me. An instant later we were sprinting out the door together.

The half-block run gave me enough time to work out how I could do this without blowing Pyotr's cover. It was the total blackness of the night that gave me the idea. When we reached Callahan's I kept on running around to the back, yelling at him to follow. As we burst in the door to the back room I located the main breaker and killed it, yanking a few fuses for insurance. The lights went out and the icebox stopped sighing. Fortunately I don't need light to find my way around Callahan's Place, and good night sight must have been a favorable adaptation for anyone with Pyotr's basic mutation; we were out in the main room in seconds and in silence.

At least compared with the hubbub there; everybody was shouting at once. I cannoned into Callahan in the darkness—I saw the glowing cheroot-tip go past my cheek—and I hugged him close and said in his ear, "Mike, trust me. Do *not* find the candles you've got behind the bar. And open the windows."

"Okay, Jake," he said calmly at once, and moved away in the blackness. With the windows open, matches blew out as fast as they could be lit. The shouting intensified. In the glow of one attempted match-lighting, I saw Tommy laid out on the bar in the same place Lady Macbeth had lain the night before, and I saw Pyotr reach him. I sprang across the room to the fireplace—thank God it was a warm night; no fire—and cupped my hands around my mouth.

"ALL RIGHT, PEOPLE," I roared as loud as I could, and silence fell.

Damned if I can remember what I said. I guess I told them that the Doc was on the way, and made up some story about the power failure, and told a few lies about guys I'd known who drank twice as much booze and survived, and stuff like that. All I know is that I *held* them, by sheer force of vocal personality, kept their attention focused on me there in the dark for perhaps four or five minutes of impassioned monologue. While behind them, Pyotr worked at the bar.

When I heard him clear his throat I began winding it down. I heard the distant sound of a door closing, the door that leads from the back room to the world outside. "So the important thing," I finished, locating one of those artificial logs in the dark and laying it on the hearth, "is not to panic and to wait for the ambulance," and I lit the giant crayon and stacked real maple and birch on top of it. The fire got going at once, and that sorted out most of the confusion. Callahan was bending over Tommy, rubbing at the base of his neck with a bar rag, and he looked up and nodded. "I think he's okay, Jake. His breathing is a lot better."

A ragged cheer went up.

By the time we had the lights back on, the wagon arrived, Doc Webster bursting in the door like a crazed hippo with three attendants following him. I stuck around just long enough to hear him confirm that Tommy would pull through, promised Callahan I'd give him the yarn later, and slipped out the back.

Walking the half block was much more enjoyable than running it. I found Pyotr in his bedroom. Roaring drunk, of course, reeling around the room and swearing in Rumanian.

"Hi, Pyotr. Sorry I bust your window."

"Sodomize the window. Jake, is he—"

"Fine. You saved his life."

He frowned ferociously and sat down on the floor. "It is no good, Jake. I thank you for trying to keep my secret, but it will not work."

"No, it won't."

"I cannot continue. My conscience forbids. I have helped young Janssen. But it must end. I am ripping you all up."

"Off, Pyotr. Ripping us off. But don't kick yourself too hard. What choice did you have? And you saved a lot of the boys a lot of hangovers, laundering their blood the way you did. Just happens I've got a trick metabolism, so instead of skimming off my hangover, you gave me one. And doubled your own: the blood I gave you the last two nights must have been no prize."

"I stole it."

"Well, maybe. You didn't rob me of the booze—we *both* got drunk on it. You *did* rob me of a little nourishment—but I gather you also 'robbed' me of a considerable amount of poisonous by-products of fatigue, poor diet, and prolonged despair. So maybe we come out even.''

He winced and rolled his eyes. ''These glands in my teeth—that was a very perceptive guess, Jake—are unfortunately not very selective. Alcoholism was not the only unpleasant thing I picked up working at the blood bank—another splendid guess—although it is the only one that has persisted. But it must end. Tomorrow night when I am capable I will go to Mr. Callahan's Place and confess what I have been doing—and then I will move somewhere else to dry out, somewhere where they do not buy blood from winos. Perhaps back to the Old Country.'' He began to sob softly. ''In many ways it will be a relief. It has been *hard,* has made me ashamed to see all of you thinking I was some kind of *altruist,* when all the time I was—'' He wept.

''Pyotr, listen to me.'' I sat on the floor with him. ''Do you know what the folks are going to do tomorrow night when you tell them?''

Headshake.

''Well, *I* do, sure as God made little green thingies to seal plastic bags with, and so do you if you think about it. I'm so certain, I'm prepared to bet you a hundred bucks in gold right now.''

Puzzled stare; leaking tears.

''They'll take up a collection for you, asshole!''

Gape.

''You've been hanging out there for years, now, you *know* I'm right. Every eligible man and woman there is a blood donor already, the Doc sees to that—do you mean to tell me they'd begrudge another half liter or so for a man who'd leave a warm bed in the middle of the night to risk his cover and save a boy's life?''

He began to giggle drunkenly. ''You know—hee, hee—I believe you are right.'' The giggle showed his fangs. Suddenly it vanished. ''Oh,'' he cried, ''I do not deserve such friends. Do you know what first attracted me about Callahan's Place? There is no mirror. No, no, not that silly superstition—mirrors reflect people like me as well as anyone. That's just it. *I was ashamed to look at my reflection in a mirror.*''

I made him look at me. ''Pyotr, listen to me. You worked *hard* for your cakes and ale, these last few years. You kept a lot of silly bastards from turning into highway statistics. Okay, you may have had *another* motive that we didn't know—but underneath it all, you're just like everybody else at Callahan's Place.''

''Eh?''

"A sucker for your friends."

And it broke him up, thank God, and everything worked out just fine.

And a couple of weeks later, Pyotr played us all a couple of fabulous Rumanian folk songs—on Lady Macbeth.

AUTHOR'S NOTE

I should have known better.

When, in the first appearance of "Pyotr's Story" (*Analog* October 12, 1981), I left six riddles unsolved, and published my address at the end of the story, offering a chit good for a free drink at Callahan's to any reader who correctly deduced the answer and the category—well, let's face it, I did anticipate that I might notice a slight bulge in my mail for a while. I mean, I *was* asking for it, there's no argument there.

Be careful what you ask for; you might receive it.

I used to publish my mailing address regularly in book-review columns for *Galaxy* magazine, and each appearance was good for from five to twenty letters a week over the ensuing month. I knew that *Analog* had a significantly larger readership than *Galaxy*, and adjusted my expectations accordingly—I thought. I projected perhaps a hundred responses, a hundred and fifty tops.

I did not keep a fully accurate accounting, but I would estimate that as of February 9, 1982, I had received somewhere between 800 and 1,000 pieces of mail as a result of that fool riddle contest.

As soon as the first sack arrived (that's not hyperbole: I mean a full sack of mail, the first of several), I took in the situation, grasped the full extent of my folly (don't let on; grasping your folly in public is illegal in Nova Scotia), and, with the cool aplomb and courage-under-fire which has made my name a sellword on Wall Street, instantly formed a dynamic plan: I kicked the sack into a corner and fled the country. My wife, Jeanne (founder and Artistic Director of **Nova Dance Theatre**, the finest Modern dance company in Canada), had received a providential invitation to perform with Beverly Brown Dancensemble: Theatre for Bodies and Voices, at the Riverside Dance Festival in what David Letterman refers to as "one of the more interesting cities in the tri-state area," New York—so I threw my suitcase, my typewriter, my child and my Ray Charles tapes into the trunk of the car and went with her. And sacks of mail grew in her dance studio behind us in Halifax (for it was that address I put in *Analog,* in a feeble attempt to divert process-servers) . . .

And then some helpful soul at DancExchange forwarded all those sacks to us in New York.

Since I had expected to be answering those letters from Canada, where U.S. stamps are worthless, I had carefully requested that respondents enclose an International Reply Coupon (supposed, by law, to be obtainable at any post office in the U.S. or Canada). Some 25 percent of respondents failed to follow this injunction, enclosed U.S. stamps or nothing at all, but forget that a moment: here I am on Manhattan Island in August with about 400 to 500 IRCs in my hands, and I wait in line for an hour and a quarter in the post office (a structure to which the Black Hole of Calcutta is frequently favorably compared for summertime comfort), and when finally I stagger up to the window, a surly homunculus with a genuinely incredible goiter informs me, with immense satisfaction, that regulations forbid him to accept more than 10 IRCs at a time. I whip out my calculator: 500 IRCs at 10 per transaction at 1.25 hours per transaction = 62.5 hours on line, or roughly eight days . . .

So I burned petrol and wasted cargo space to haul those sacks back home to Halifax. Where I united them with their less-traveled cousins, which had arrived in our absence, and settled down to answering the goddammed things . . .

Tabulations:

Oddly, the ratio of right to wrong answers remained rock-constant: every time I stopped and ran subtotals, it ran almost precisely two right answers for every wrong. Call it a 67 percent success rate for the *Analog* audience as a group. (Some of the wrong answers were absolutely brilliant!)

The only correlation I noted of any significance was that responses which came on university departmental letterhead were usually wrong—and several of the exceptions turned out to be grad students or TAs using their professor's stationery. In other words, holders of tenure at institutes of higher education averaged dumber than the general populace or any other discernible group in the sample.

Another thing I found instructive about all this was the performance of *Analog* readers (certainly not an undereducated group) in following the simplest of explicit written instructions. I had asked that each respondent enclose a self-addressed envelope or SAE along with the above-mentioned IRC. Now, some few readers claimed ignorance of IRCs, or said that their local postmaster claimed ignorance, and the expedients they tried instead were many and various. Three or four sent *cash,* and of those only one was bright enough to send *Canadian* cash. (In those palmy days of yesteryear, the Canadian/American exchange rate hovered around par, which meant I took a conversion-fee bath on the money.) But at least 10 percent of the responses I received contained *no* return postage—and the rate-to-States *doubled* the month I got home to Halifax. (The royalty I will eventually receive for this particular book you hold in your hands comes to less than the present cost of a Canadian stamp—considerably less if you live in the States. And they're talking about raising the rates again.) Postageless letters that were not particularly amusing or endearing were used to insulate the attic. And 25 percent of respondents enclosed no return-address envelope: same doctrine applied.

It wasn't a total loss, even when you figure in the cost of Xeroxing form letters (one for right answers, one for wrong) and the postage and envelopes I got burned for, and the hours of work-time lost, and the wear and tear on my tongue (did you ever lick a thousand envelopes and several hundred stamps?). For one thing, I took the opportunity to make up a *third* form letter—a press release listing all the books I had in print and where to get them and such— and folded one into every envelope. For another, I was able to insulate my entire attic and make a start on the root cellar.

For another, the vast majority of the letters I got were *delightful!* Some were hilarious. Some were heartwarming. Some were ingenious. Some were touching. Some were enlightening. Remarkably few "faded into the woodwork," became just one-more-goddamn-letter-to-be-processed—in any event, I didn't get any complaints from Mike Callahan regarding the people who came to cash in their chits. (Of course, I just provided the chit—*finding* the Place was their problem.) Taken all together, the response pleased me, cheered and encouraged me in my work.

On the other hand, a substantial number of respondents enclosed riddles of their own—enough to make a life-size fully detailed papier-mâché replica of the space shuttle. I'm sure they were all disappointed that I didn't try to answer their no-doubt ingenious riddles, but honest to God, there are thousands!

And that's not the worst. The worst is that *the damned responses are still coming in to this day!*

Analog is published all around the planet, with a translation lag that apparently ranges up to a couple of years. Furthermore, people keep coming across back issues in libraries and secondhand bookstores, stumbling over the riddle-contest, and uttering small cries of delight.

I arbitrarily established a cut-off date, and stopped sending chits some time in mid-1982. (For one thing, my tab at Callahan's started reaching the proportions of the American National Debt.) I have kept to that—indeed, as you will shortly learn, it is no longer possible for me to supply any chits—but I still feel a faint twinge of guilt every time I get another letter that begins, "Dear Mr. Robinson, I think I've solved Doc Webster's riddles—"

And the last thing I want is to compound the problem here.

So no, I'm not going to publish my mailing address here, and no, I will not issue any more drink-chits, and yes, I am going to put the answers to the unsolved riddles below. If you want to solve them for yourself first, skip them. If you solve them successfully, don't tell me about it. And no, frankly, I'm not overwhelmingly interested in trying to decipher your riddles, however clever and funny they may be. In the immortal words of disc jockey Don Imus, "Keep those cards and letters!"

No, that's not true. I love getting mail, and I need audience feedback to continue growing in my work. By all means drop me a line in care of Tor Books—especially if you can find it in your head to enclose SAE and IRC.

Just don't mention riddles.

The Answers to Doc Webster's Riddles:

The category is "Male American Politicians," or any variant thereof. The individual answers are:

a) irrigated; laser pistol = runneled; ray gun = *Ronald Reagan*

b) Nazi; cook lightly = Jerry; Brown = *Jerry Brown*

c) British punk; knowledge, current = Teddy; ken, eddy = *Teddy Kennedy*

d) chicken coop; foreplay = hennery; kissing her = *Henry Kissinger*

e) wealthier, nuts to = richer; nix on = *Richard Nixon*

An embarrassing thing happened. Astute readers will have noted that I also left riddle IIe) unsolved. When the responses started coming in, I discovered that this riddle had proved the hardest: everybody wanted to know who "coffin; baby boy" was. The problem was that I had, by this point, mislaid my first draft of "Pyotr's Story"—and I had forgotten the solution. To my horror, I found that I could not figure it out myself!

After months of shame, I sat bolt upright in bed one morning and realized I had the solution again—so I incorporated it into the story you are about to read, "Involuntary Man's Laughter."

One last word about "Pyotr's Story," though. If by any chance you missed its several respectful salutes to William Goldman, I hope you will seize the next opportunity to run out and purchase his immortal classic, *The Princess Bride*.

INVOLUNTARY MAN'S LAUGHTER

Some of the people who hang out at Callahan's Place aren't all there—this is widely known. But a few of them aren't there at all.

Well, obviously they *are* there, at least in a sense. Otherwise I'd be offering you a paradox, and Sam Webster is the only Doc we have here at Callahan's bar. But if a customer cannot be seen, heard, felt, smelt, or dealt a hand of cards, if he casts no shadow, empties no glass, and never visits the men's room—can he really be said to be there? Even if you're having a conversation with him at the time?

We have two or three regulars at Callahan's who fit that nondescription: old and dear friends of ours who have never set foot in the place. One of them, for instance, is a ghost, and I'll tell you about him another time, when we've both had a couple more drinks. But the one I'd like to tell you about right now is a human being— and while I have seen him once, I don't think I ever will again.

It was a Punday Night last year when the Cheerful Charlies showed up looking glum. This was quite unusual, enough so to engage my attention when I caught sight of them both—for the Cheerful Charlies have, quite literally, earned their name.

Doc Webster had already won the Punday competition—something he does with about the same consistency with which Mr. T wins arguments. The only way the Doc can possibly lose is if all possible puns on a given topic have been exhausted before it's his turn—and far more often, when everyone else has come up empty, the Doc still has four or five up his sleeve. You might say that our chronic asteismus is iatrogenic . . . but of course you probably wouldn't.

Like now, for instance: the evening's topic had been one of those so broad as to seem inexhaustible—"animals"—and owl give ewe the gnus: most of us cats and chicks were falcon hoarse as we toad the lion and shrew our glasses into the fire in sheepish cabitchulation. But Dog Websteer was still game, cheerfoal as venison the springtime, a weaselly grin on his puss that got my goat.

"—always puzzled me," he was saying, "that females of all species except the human seem, at best, utterly disinterested in mating. Most will actively resist it until compelled by glandular pressure, and even then seem to derive little enjoyment from the business. Why, I wondered, should human females alone be blessed with the capacity to enjoy the inevitable?"

A good question. I'd always wondered that myself.

"The answer turns out to be simple. Man is a *bald* ape."

"Oh God," Shorty Steinitz groaned. "Even for you, Doc, that's an *awful* pun."

The Doc blinked and then grinned. "You misunderstand me, sir—for once the pun was unintentional. No, I mean that man is relatively hairless—whereas, through some sadistic quirk of nature, most other male animals are endowed with hairy penises. A cat's penis, for instance, is covered with short, spiky hairs—*which face in the wrong direction.*"

Murmurs of surprise and sympathy ran around the tavern; a few ladies winced.

"Small wonder, then," the Doc went on, folding his hands across his expansive belly, "that a female cat doesn't much feel like putting out—for any tom dickin' hairy."

The horrified silence stretched out for nearly five seconds . . . and then we awarded him the Supreme Accolade: as one we left our drinks where they stood, held our noses, and fled screaming into the night.

It was a nice night out there (not that that matters to any friend of Mickey Finn these days); I found that I was in no hurry to follow the rest of the gang back inside. My drink was perfectly safe where it was, and I wanted a few minutes alone with myself. I was feeling . . . well, "troubled" would be too strong a word, but I don't know a word for the shading between there and "content." Just one of those mild itches of the soul that a man doesn't particularly feel like sharing with all his friends, a passing impulse to toot for a few bars on the old self-pity horn.

It was, perhaps inevitably, just as I was finishing a contemplative cigarette and saying "Sometime again," to the full moon that the Cheerful Charlies drove up in their '57 Thunderbird and wedged it into the confusion. (By honored custom, the parking lot at Callahan's always looks as though a platoon of psychopaths had turned a game of Bumper Cars into an unresolvable snarl and wandered off. A half-dozen times a night we all have to pile outside to let somebody out, and it doesn't inconvenience us in the least.) Just the sight of their splendid old heap cheered me up some.

Neither of them is named Charlie; that's their professional designation and job description. They cheer people up for a living. You may have seen their ad in the paper:

> *DEPRESSED? Gamble a little time on The Cheerful Charlies. $25 if we cheer you up, nothing at all if we don't: you decide! 24-hr. emergency service available (rates double from 10 P.M. to 8 A.M. Call CHE-ERUP for an appointment: What have you got to lose?*

And, of course, their business card sums it up even more succinctly: HAVE FUN, WILL TRAVEL.

They did not found the business. That was done by Tom Flannery a few years back. Tom was one of the most infectiously cheerful men I ever met, and he had a certain natural advantage in cheering people up: at the time he founded his enterprise, Tom had about eight months to go on the nine-month sentence his doctors had given him (and did in fact eventually die on schedule almost to the day). He didn't talk about it much, but it made a terrific hole-card for dealing with cases of intractable self-pity. How many people have the gall to be depressed around a smiling fellow who says he'll be dead before your tax return comes back? Tom hadn't expected to make money at his job—but to his surprise he left a sizable estate.

The present Cheerful Charlies began as clients of Tom's. Each was depressed by the same two things: both were chronically unemployed, and both bore names of the sort that parents ought to be prevented by law or by vigilante violence from giving to their children. The Moore family pronounced their name "More," and saw fit to name their son Les; while the Gluehams, with a malignant case of the cutes, named their daughter Merry.

The coincidence of names was just too much for Tom Flannery to resist, I guess. He convinced them both that one of the best ways to cheer yourself up is to try and cheer other people up (it worked for him, after all), and took them both on as apprentices, thus solving their unemployment problem. As he must have hoped, they fell in love—and when they married, they solved the question of does-she-take-his-last-name by swapping even-steven. With irresistible appropriateness, she became Merry Moore and he became Les Glueham. They carried on Tom's business after he died, and the story of their names itself is sometimes sufficient to get a client smiling.

Les and Merry have no set routine, but rather a whole spectrum of techniques which they tailor to fit the individual case. They are wise and warm people, with professionally tuned empathic faculties, and they seem to have made a remarkably comfortable marriage. One of their early cases, for instance, was a lonely old widower who had lost all his joy in living: after all their best efforts had failed, Merry and Les talked it over, decided that it might help and that in this specific case it probably couldn't hurt—and then Merry took the old gentleman to bed. It did the trick, and since then they have (very infrequently) had occasions to use lovemaking as cheer-up therapy, singly or together. It has always worked so far, and they always refuse their fee in such cases. This is both to avoid breaking laws, and to motivate themselves to exhaust all other possibilities before resorting to Old Reliable-but-Risky; it inhibits the human tendency to rationalize oneself into the sack. But some cases of depression will yield to no other medicine.

And if even *that* doesn't work, Merry and Les bring 'em to Callahan's Place.

*   *   *

But they didn't appear to have a client with them tonight. They got out of the T-Bird, a little slowly I thought, and came my way. Merry was carrying something that looked like a big piece of stereo gear, and Les seemed to have a hardcover book with him. "Hey, Jake— what's the matter?" Merry called to me.

"God's teeth," I said under my breath. Then aloud: "From twenty feet across a parking lot by moonlight you can tell I've got something on my mind. From what? The echo of an expression I was wearing before you pulled up? You people are incorrigibly good at what you do, you know that?"

"Ouch," Les said softly.

They had almost reached me by now, and the third thing I saw was that Les's hardcover was a boxed videotape, and the second thing I saw was that Merry's stereo was a VCR, and the first thing I saw was that Les and Merry were—astonishingly, most uncharacteristically—miserably depressed. Their expressions, their stride, their body language, all said that they were so far down that up was for astronomers; they had, to quote a song of mine, the Industrial Strength Blues.

"Jesus Christ on a moped, what's the matter with you two?" An unpleasant thought began to form. "Oh hell, you didn't lose one, did you?" That happened a year ago, a sleeping-pill job, and it took us all about a week to put the Cheerful Charlies back together again. It is the occupational risk, and a failure rate as low as one a year means that the Cheerfuls are supernaturally good at what they do. (They have to be; there is no malpractice insurance for their racket.)

"No," Merry answered, "not yet anyway."

"Well, *tell* me about it."

"You tell us yours first."

"Mine? Hey, on a scale of ten I'm a point two five and you guys are up in the eights—and I think it's a log scale, like the Richter."

"Come on, give. If it's a simple one, great: we could use the confidence right now."

I shrugged. "Okay. I was just going a few rounds with envy."

"Of whom?" Merry asked, setting the VCR down on the Datsun I was using for a bench.

"The Doc."

"Ah."

"I like to make people laugh. So I troll for the best jokes I can find, make up the best ones I can devise, work on my timing, try to work the audience into it and use their feedback—and it works pretty well, most times they laugh, or groan, or whatever I was looking for. The Doc could recite his Social Security Number, dead-pan, and lay 'em on the floor. Dammit, I tell better jokes than he does, I even think I tell 'em better—and he gets more laughs. With his incredibly tortuous set-ups and his corny voice and his Paleozoic punchlines, we all fall down laughing. Even me! He's just an in-trinsically funny man—and I'm just a guy who tries to be funny."

"And the worst of it," Les said, "is that he's such a totally nice guy, you can't even dislike him for it."

"Bull's-eye."

Merry grinned, a ghost of her usual grin. "This is ironic." She and Les shared a glance.

I shook my head ruefully. "For you guys, no doubt. So okay: in the words of Mr. Ribadhee to the Hip Ghand, 'Straighten me, 'cause I'm ready.' "

"Jake," Les said, "a few years ago you lent us a novel called *Lord of Light,* by Roger Zelazny. Remember it?"

"Sure. An SF novel about a world patterned after Hindu my-thology."

"Right—and then along came Buddha to kick over the applecart. Now, remember how the people who had become 'gods' were each able, at will, to take on an Aspect and raise up an Attribute?"

"Yama could become Death, and drink your life with his eyes, Mara's Aspect was Illusion, and his Attribute was to cloud your mind with a gesture. And so forth."

"You've got it. Well, it's like that with the Doc. His Aspect is Humor. In a figurative, but very real sense, Doc Webster *is* Hu-mor—at least when he chooses to take on his Aspect. And his Attribute is the ability to make you piss yourself laughing. Envying him is like envying a flower because it never needs deodorant."

"Huh," I said. "I think I get you. It's silly to envy the gods."

"Especially when you are one."

"*Eh?*"

"Jake," Merry said, "when was the last time someone inter-rupted you while you were singing?"

"Well . . ." I couldn't bring such an instance to mind. People do tend to quiet down when I take my guitar out of her case.

Les did his uncanny Martin Mull imitation. " 'Remember the Great Folk Music Scare of the Fifties?' " he quoted. " 'That shit almost caught on.' Jake, haven't you noticed that you're about the only folksinger left on Long Island who can still find regular work?

Don't you know why you don't need electronics and a thousand watts and a rhythm section to get gigs? Man, when you pick up Lady Macbeth and put her across your lap and open your mouth, you take on your Aspect—and when you wring her neck and coax sound out of her sounding-box and sing along with her, you're raising up your Attribute. You take people out of themselves, for as long as you choose to go on singing. Doc Webster is Humor, Jake, and you are Music. Don't you know that?''

I thought it over—and suddenly grinned. "How did you guys ever get the name Cheerful Charlies?''

"Maybe because we own the complete works of Walt Kelly,'' Les hazarded. "Come on, let's go inside.''

"Wait—what about *your* problem? Cheering-up ought to be like breastfeeding, you know, mutually satisfactory.''

"Tit for tot?'' Merry asked innocently.

Les mock-glared at her. "I think our problem should be taken inside,'' he said. "We need a group head on this one.''

So we went in and took chairs at the bar.

Mike Callahan came ambling over, wiping his big hands on his apron, smiling broadly when he saw the Cheerfuls. He took out one of the *non*-safety stick matches he imports from Canada, struck it on his stubbly chin, and put a fresh light on one of the stunted malodorous cigars he imports from Hell. "Well, if it ain't the Beerful Barleys! What'll it be, folks?''

I finished the beer I had left on the counter and answered for all three of us. "Bless us, Father, for we have thirst.''

Callahan nodded and made up three portions of God's Blessing. It is called Irish Coffee by the vulgar, and I'm told there are actually places where they don't sugar the rim of the glass before making it—but we who drink at Callahan's Place have a proper respect for the finer things in life. "Here you go, folks.'' I could tell from his expression that Mike had picked up on the Cheerfuls' state of mind, and wanted to know what they were down about. But . . . look, I've been hanging out at Callahan's for a good many years now. But if I walked in tomorrow night with a toilet bowl tattooed on my forehead, Mike Callahan would fail to notice it unless and until I brought the matter up. Mike likes that people should open up and talk about their troubles in his bar—and so he has given standing orders to Fast Eddie the piano player that anyone caught asking snoopy questions is to be discouraged with a blackjack.

Occasionally, though, he will allow himself to lead a witness. "So how's life been treating you?" he asked as he Blessed us.

Merry answered obliquely. "Mike, is that babble box in the back room still operational?"

The big Irishman blinked. "Well, yeah. I use it for a monitor on my microprocessor."

Callahan's Place has been fully wired for cable television—but the only times in my memory that the tube has ever been hooked up for viewing and switched on were coronations, assassinations, space shots, and the final episode of *M*A*S*H*. Its operation requires either the unanimous vote of all customers present, or—even more rarely—whim of Mike Callahan.

Merry lifted the VCR from her lap and set it on the bar. "Would you whip it out, Mike? We want to call a meeting."

The redheaded barkeep was as mystified and curious as I was—I could tell—but he just nodded.

Well, of course, by the time the boob tube was hot and the VCR connected, the Cheerfuls had the undivided attention of everyone in the room. Callahan passed around fresh drinks for those who needed them, and we sat back to see what the Cheerfuls had for us.

"Folks," Merry said, popping the tape into the deck and laying her finger on the PLAY button, "we've got a client we don't know what to do with, and we'd like to ask your help."

There was a ragged chorus of reply. "Sure," "Of course," "You got it," and, from Long-Drink McGonnigle in the corner, "Whyn't you just bring him or her around?"

Merry looked pained. "Ordinarily we would. But this case is a little unique, and we thought it might be advisable if we prepared you first. You may not be able to help us, and if you can't it'll hurt worse than not trying."

"I am offended," the Drink said, only half-kidding. "This here is *Callahan's Place*. Did you need to prepare us before you brought around that guy with no jaw?"

"No," Merry conceded, "and you were all splendid. But this is different."

"We just have to be sure," Les said. "This guy is right on the edge. So here's the deal: the tape Merry is about to run lasts about two minutes. If you can all watch it all the way through in dead silence—without a single sound—we'll bring him around tomorrow night. Deal?"

"This tape is of your client?" Callahan asked.

"That's right."

"Piece of cake," Long-Drink stated. "Fire it up."

Merry nodded, and pushed down the PLAY button—

—and we all fell down laughing.

She stopped the tape, and the laughter chopped off raggedly, leaving a stunned silence.

She reached to start it again, and we redoubled our determination not to laugh . . . and within five seconds the last of us had collapsed again in helpless, horrified laughter.

She stopped and started it once more, and this time I bit my tongue hard enough to draw blood, and again I could *not* prevent myself from whooping with laughter. Nor could any of us—Callahan included.

"You see why your problem outside seemed so ironic to us, Jake," Merry murmured, stopping the tape for the last time and popping it up out of the machine. I nodded, thunderstruck.

Did you ever find yourself in a situation where it is hideously inappropriate to laugh—and you just can't help yourself? It is a horrid sensation, much like shitting your pants. Now I began to understand why the Cheerfuls weren't. Imagine if Doc Webster literally *couldn't* help being funny . . .

"What de fuck was dat?" Fast Eddie breathed.

"That," Doc Webster said grimly, "was the worst case of Tourette's syndrome I ever saw in my life."

"Doc," Long-Drink said indignantly, "are you trying to tell me that that was some kind of *disease*? What kind of guy do you think God is, anyway?"

So the Doc told us all about Tourette's syndrome. Nobody knows what causes it. You may have seen Dick Cavett doing a public-service commercial about it, late at night when the network has run out of paying customers. I had—and recognized the symptoms almost as quickly as the Doc had—but it was hard to imagine that there could be an unhappier victim anywhere in the world than the Cheerfuls' client; he was afflicted with an extremely exaggerated version of the syndrome.

The symptoms of Tourette's include involuntary twitching, grunting, and barking. No sufferer is happy with it—but this young fellow just happened to have a recurring twitch that looked *exactly* like what might be produced by the greatest comedian in the world going flat out for a laugh, and his grunts sounded *precisely* like a gorilla making love, and his constant barking was not only *uncannily* canine, but issued from a face which looked more like a cocker spaniel's than even early-period Ringo Starr did. The overall effect was devastatingly—diabolically—hilarious; the three symptoms, funny enough separately, heterodyned together.

"His name is Billy Walker, and he's eighteen years old," Les said. "The disease came on at age fifteen—it usually hits the young—and the usual palliatives, Haldol and so forth, don't help him in the slightest. Unlike most sufferers, he can't suppress or control his symptoms, even for a short time. This tape was made by a couple of specialists from Johns Hopkins, and they had to leave the room while the camera was rolling or they would have spoiled the audio track. For the last two years Billy has lived shut up in a little cottage in Rocky Point, supported by his parents. The only friend he's had since the onset was a blind and deaf guy he met at Hopkins. They lived together for a year. The guy died two weeks ago, and Billy saw our ad and got in touch with us."

"And now I don't know what we're going to do for him," Merry finished sadly.

"How'd he get in touch with you?" I asked.

Merry looked even sadder. "I hate to admit this. He called us three times on the phone, and each time we just assumed that it was a gag call. The third time, Les got mad and told him off—so he sent us a letter."

"How could he hold a pen steady enough with a twitch like that?"

"He couldn't. He typed the letter, timing the twitches."

"Jesus."

"As if things weren't bad enough, of course, he happens to be extremely intelligent and sensitive, with the remnants of what was once a terrific sense of humor."

"You've spent time with him?" Callahan asked.

"With great difficulty, about half an hour," Merry said. "The longest I could go without giggling was about ten or twenty seconds, and eventually I gave up, assured them that I had something terrific up my sleeve, and got out of there. My ribs still hurt. There's something about that bark that you just can't get used to. Look, does anyone here have any idea what we could do for this poor son of a bitch? He's so damned lonely that the tears pour down your face while you're laughing, honest to God.''

There was a general rumble of sad negation. ''Beats the hell out of me.'' ''Help the poor guy do himself in as painlessly as possible.'' ''Maybe it'll go away . . . in time.'' ''Find a whole lot of blind and deaf guys . . . nah, that's no good.'' Les and Merry looked more and more downcast.

''I think I got it,'' Callahan said, and they both looked around sharply, hope beginning to form. ''Hey, Drink! Lend me your copper-topper a minute, will you?''

The McGonnigle, puzzled but willing, tossed Mike the night-watchman's cap that he wears off-duty (because it looks so much like a policeman's hat that he is never ever passed, cut off, or tailgated on the highway). Mike caught it, opened the cash register and took out a fistful of bills, dropped them into the hat.

''Ladies and gentlemen,'' he boomed, ''I'm looking for about three hundred bucks.'' And he passed the hat to me.

I looked around, saw there were about fifty or sixty of us present, and tossed in a fin. Then I remember how many of the regulars had lost jobs lately, and added another five, and passed the hat on.

When it got back to Callahan it was overflowing with cash. He totaled it up, and it came to four and a quarter. He beamed around at us all. ''Thanks, folks. The cash register just closed for the night.'' And he began a bucket-brigade of fresh drinks for everyone present.

''Whaddya gonna do wit de cabbage, Boss?'' Fast Eddie asked.

''You'll see tomorrow night, Eddie. Or maybe the night after; it might take a while to set up.''

''Set up *what?*'' Les and Merry chorused.

''Meet me here tomorrow at noon and I'll show you,'' Callahan promised.

The next evening was Fireside Fill-More Night, on which Fast Eddie and I traditionally join together. There were four people missing that I had expected to see: the Cheerfuls, Eddie and Callahan himself. Tom Hauptmann, the second-string bartender, could tell us nothing except that Mike had called him late in the day and asked him to fill in. So I did a solo, and it went well enough . . . but halfway through I got an idea, and invited Doc Webster up to do a bunch of comedy songs—and we brought the house down together.

I pulled in the next night at about a quarter to eight. Callahan was there in his usual place behind the bar, and Tom Hauptmann was with him. That was a little odd: Mike usually only needs help on weekends, when the crowd is thickest, and there weren't enough customers tonight to justify two barkeeps. The TV (no, not Bill Gerrity; I mean the television) was back on the bartop, but the station it was tuned to didn't seem to be on the air, horizontal stripes chased each other up its face. Callahan saw me come in, sized me up with a glance and had a shot of Bushmill's and a beer ready by the time I reached him. As usual, it was just what I'd have ordered if he'd given me a chance. "Evening, Jake."

"Hi, Mike. How'd you make out on that Billy Walker thing?"

He drew on his cheroot. "We'll find out together at nine o'clock."

"Okay, be mysterious." I sipped and chased a few times, enjoying the contrast of tastes and textures. "Hey, where's the blackboard? This *is* Riddle Night, isn't it?"

On Riddle Night, one of us makes up riddles and the rest of us try and unscramble them. Each solved riddle costs the Riddle Master/Riddle Mistress a drink; each unresolved riddle is a free drink for him/her. Most often we use the classic "Invisible Idiot" or mangled-translation format. You must have heard the old dodge about the translator who rendered "out of sight, out of mind" literally as "invisible idiot." Like that. For example, "festive, meathooks; finish second" would be correctly deciphered as "gala, hands; place" or "Callahan's Place." Semicolons mark the end of a word, commas separate parts of a single word. They can get quite tricky—it once took me months to translate "coffin; baby boy" as Paul Newman. Ordinarily the Riddle Master (last week's champ) would have had at least half a dozen riddles already chalked up on a big blackboard by the door for study—but last week's champ was Callahan himself, and he hadn't even trotted out the board yet. "We'll get to them later too," he said, and wandered off to replenish the free lunch.

So I washed down my curiosity with the world's oldest whiskey (they got their charter to distill in 1608) and listened to Fast Eddie stitch his way through a medley of Eubie Blake, Willie the Lion, Pinetop Smith, and Memphis Slim. Eddie had to get special hammers for his piano; the thumbtacks used to keep falling out. I was mildly sorry I'd left my guitar at home; I'd missed my weekly jam with him. The joint filled up while he played, and our spirits danced to his merry tune. When Eddie's on a roll like that, people tend to shut up and dig it. Once a loud newcomer distracted the runty little piano man in the middle of "Tricky Fingers." Eddie got the sap from his boot and pegged it across the room, laid the fellow out, and damned if the sap didn't bounce back right to his hand—and not a note did he fluff during the procedure. They raise 'em tough in Red Hook.

About the time my hands were getting sore from clapping time with him, Eddie went into a classic barroom walkout and nailed it shut behind him, to thunderous applause. A storm of empty glasses converged on the fireplace and shattered together in tribute, and the two bartenders were busy for a time. And then Callahan called for order. I glanced at my watch; it was nearly nine.

"Ladies and gentlemen and regular customers," he announced, "tonight is Riddle Night. By our customs, I am Riddle Master, on account of I wiped the floor with you mugs last week. But I'm yielding the floor—or at least part of the counter—to a guest Riddle Master." He reached under the bar, and took out a flat object patch-corded to the back of the television. His microprocessor keyboard. He did something to it, and the stripes stopped chasing each other up the screen.

Okay, I'm slow. "The computer is going to make riddles?" I asked.

"Not exactly."

"What's that thing wired to the back of the terminal?" Long-Drink asked.

"A modem," Callahan said, and just then there were two sounds. My digital watch chirped, and the phone rang.

The big redheaded barkeep picked up the handset and put it down on the modem cradle. At once letters began to appear on the screen.

HI, FOLKS. I'M YOUR RIDDLE MASTER FOR THE NIGHT. MY NAME IS BILLY WALKER.

I could feel a big grin growing on the front of my face. "Mike, you Hibernian ham, you're a genius. Lemme at that keyboard."

He showed me how to use it, and I typed in HI, BILLY. MY NAME'S JAKE.

IT'S JAKE WITH ME IF IT'S JAKE WITH YOU, came the reply. I

noticed that there was a pause about every tenth character, and realized that each pause represented a twitch.

OKAY, LET'S HAVE SOME RIDDLES. The whole gang was clustered around the monitor now, chattering and laughing; those who hadn't been around the night before last were being filled in.

YOU FOLKS READ SCIENCE FICTION, I UNDERSTAND?

Noah Gonzalez and I always did; as for the rest of the crowd, well, somewhere between the second time-traveler and the third alien we got in Callahan's, most of them picked up on it too. YEAH.

HERE YOU GO, THEN, he replied, and the next lines appeared so rapidly he must have had them stored and ready.

SCOTTISH MT.; FIDDLESTICK, ASSERT
HYDROPHOBIC; Y'KNOW? (CAN.); DRUNK AND MENDACIOUS
ORBS, FEH!; S. AMER. PALM, (COLOR OF ITS FRUIT)
MARVEL COMICS; (QUIET!), GLOVE
WASHROOM; CLONE YOURSELF; ECCENTRIC WHEEL, NON-SENSE.

WHAT'S THE TOPIC? I asked him.
YOU TELL ME.
NOW I KNOW WHY THEY CALL IT A CURSOR.

Well, we all took turns chatting with Billy while we worked on his riddles, and it took us several hours to work out that the topic was "SF Writers" and that the answers were, in order:

"Ben; bow, aver" = Ben Bova
"Rabid; eh?; high 'n' lyin' " = Robert A. Heinlein
"Eyes, ech!; asa (mauve)" = Isaac Asimov
"Stan Lee; (shh!), mitt" = Stanley Schmidt
"John; double you; cam, bull" = John W. Campbell, and by that time Doc Webster had come up with the idea of Billy applying for a grant to start up a computer network for shut-ins, and we were all on the way to becoming good friends. Oh, once in a while I'd get a mental picture of the man on the other end of the hookup and giggle in spite of myself. But he never knew it. I've always hated that hairy old nonsense about high technology being inherently de-humanizing.

And as Doc Webster said, Billy's barks were much worse than his bytes.

THE MICK OF TIME

New Year's Eve at Callahan's Place, and I was feeling about as much contentment as an unmarried man can know, thinking of how many New Year's Eves I'd spent in this warm, well-lit, cozy room with the best friends I'd ever known, thinking happily of how many more there would be to come. You'd think that would have warned me.

Somehow or other the conversation had turned to conundra—the kind of questions that are good for keeping you entertained on an insomniac night, and not a whole lot else. They're sort of like test programs for the mind, and I guess New Year's Eve is a natural time for such things.

It was early on, not gone eight o'clock and only a handful of the regulars in attendance yet. Tommy Janssen had asked Long-Drink McGonnigle something, I forget what, and the Drink replied something along the lines of, "Son, that's one of those great Questions That Will Never Be Answered."

Doc Webster snorted. "Flapdoodle. Any meaningful question can be answered—and will be, sooner or later. Questions just never go away until they are."

Callahan finished reloading the coffeepot and came over to join us. "Doc," he rumbled, "if any question can be answered, maybe you can help me with one that's been occupyin' my mind for a long time now. How many angels can dance on the head of a beer?" There was a general giggle.

"I said, 'meaningful questions,' " the Doc replied. "Your question has no meaning because one of its crucial terms is undefined. Tell me—specifically—what you mean by an 'angel,' and I'll answer your question. Or rather, you'll have answered it yourself."

"Aw hell, Doc," Long-Drink said, "you know what an angel is."

"If I did, I wouldn't be paying alimony. My point is, it's easy to make up questions that don't have answers because they don't really ask anything. Can God make a rock so big he can't lift it? Where was Moses when the lights went out?"

"We're certainly into a theological vein here," said Tom Hauptmann, the former minister. "There's one that's always puzzled me, Doc, and I think it has meaning. Water is a clear, colorless fluid. So how come when you splash it on a towel, the towel gets darker?"

The Doc was silent for a moment, chewing on that, and Tommy and Long-Drink began to chuckle. "There's an answer," the Doc insisted. "I never said I knew all the answers—but if the question has meaning, the answer is knowable."

I thought of one that's kept my own mind harmlessly occupied for hours at a time. "Hey, Doc, I've got one. A thought experiment, and a humdinger: It's one of those that causes a system crash in the brain. The beauty of it is that one day soon it will be possible to try it out in the real world and *see* what the answer is—but right now, even though all the components of the question are meaningful and known, I'll bet a case of Anchor Steam Beer nobody here can come up with an answer and prove it."

"Hey," Susie Maser (Slippery Joe's senior wife) said, "for a case of all-barley beer, I'll take on Zeno's Paradox with one hand tied halfway behind my back. Whip it out, Jake." Several others leaned forward attentively.

"I've put this question to about thirty scientists in ten different disciplines," I said, "and to educators, and science fiction writers and editors I met at conventions, and the funny thing is that they all reacted the exact same way. I'd lay out the question, and they'd all start to answer right away . . . and then they'd catch themselves, and fall silent, and get a far look . . . and a minute or so later, they'd change the subject.''

"Come on, come on," the Drink said. "Lay it on us."

"You're right," I said mournfully. "I'm taking too long to get to it. A man'll do that sometimes, when he's dehydrated—"

Long-Drink sighed and reached into his pants pocket. "Give the bastard a beer, Mike."

"Okay," I said when I'd blown the foam off and taken a sip, "this experiment could actually be done in sloppy form right now— but it purifies it a great deal if we imagine it taking place in space, in a microgravity environment. Let's say that somewhere up in orbit, there's a perfectly spherical object whose inner surface is mirrored: a spherical mirror, all right? Naturally, it's dark in there. Floating with his eyes at dead center is an astronaut—never mind how he got there," I said hastily as Susie began to object. "Maybe the mirror was blown around him; anyway, he's there. He's scared of the dark, so he takes a flashlight out of his pocket and turns it on. *What does he see?*''

Everyone in the room started to answer at once—

"Well, he—"

"The back of—"

"All of him at—"

"Nothing but pure white—"

—and then they all caught themselves. And fell silent. And got a far look.

After about ten seconds, Susie started to open her mouth. "Does it make any difference," I asked, "which way he points the flashlight? How would what he see change if he pointed the thing at himself? Or if he put it in his mouth and made Monster-Cheeks?" and Susie closed her mouth again.

When the silence had lasted for nearly a minute, Doc Webster said, "Another classic question I've always wanted to know the answer to is how and why evolution designed the human taste buds to love a poison like sugar."

I looked questioningly at Callahan, and he nodded. "Subject change," he agreed. "Appears to me that these birds owe you a case of Anchor Steam, Jake." He counted heads. "I make it a beer apiece; ante up, folks."

Grumbling, everybody did reach into their pockets, but they brightened considerably when Mike handed across my case and I started passing out the beers.

About that time Mick and Mary Finn came in, by the wrought-iron staircase from the roof. (Finn could just have easily landed on the ground, of course; the parking lot was still empty enough to make an excellent LZ—but he's had a sentimental attachment to that roof ever since the night he met his wife up there, and to the staircase since he married her on it, and he always comes in that way now.) There was a time when if Mickey came in, in the middle of a conversation, it had to sort of pause for a few minutes while we all helped him work his way into it. But marriage has, among the many other ways it's been good for the big alien, tended to humanize him a little, to make it easier for him to plug into things smoothly.

"Well, what do you know, it's a sawbuck!" I called out, and did not have to patiently explain to Finn that a sawbuck is two fins; he either got it or let it go. "Howdy, folks. Welcome to the feast of reason. The topic is Ponderable Questions—and the fine line between them and the imponderables. You two got any good ones?" I gave him a beer, and then I gave his wife a beer, and I don't even know why I bother mentioning that Mary smiled when I gave it to her, because the smile didn't do anything more than flay the skin off my body, sandblast every nerve and ligament, Osterize a few major organs and fry my eyeballs in their own grease; I made no visible sign that could possibly have been detected by anyone except the people present in the room. I'm over her completely.

"Certainly," Mickey said. "The more I live with humans, the more questions I have, and the more imponderable they become. Mary is better than any human I have ever known at explaining them—even better than you, Michael," he said to Callahan, "—but even she has no more than a sixty percent success rate."

"Ah, now we've hit pay dirt," Doc Webster said. "What does an intelligent nonhuman think of the human race? We're such vain creatures it's one of the most fascinating questions we can imagine—spawned thousands of myths and books and movies."

"Well, naturally," Long-Drink agreed. "Man alone cannot know himself. The container can't contain itself."

Mickey Finn looked politely puzzled. "I do not understand what you mean. Do not all containers contain themselves? If not, what does contain them?"

The Drink got another far look. Finally the Doc said, "What puzzles you the most about humans, Mick? Politics? Sexual customs? Art? Philosophy?"

"Bathrooms," the big alien said at once.

"Jump *back*," Long-Drink said incredulously.

"I am serious, Drink, my friend," Finn told him. "I don't understand why *humans* are not puzzled by their bathrooms. I have wondered about this since before I quit working for my former Masters. I understand the concept of a blind spot, but it is hard to comprehend one of this size."

"There's usually something substantial kinda blocking the view in that direction, Mickey," Callahan said dryly. "What exactly is it that puzzles you about bathrooms?"

"Everything, Michael. The first item one finds in a typical bathroom is the sink. I have made tests: half of the time and energy spent at a sink are used in adjusting water temperature. Your technology makes cheaply available thermocouples which will reliably deliver water of any specified temperature—yet in every single bathroom in the world the job is done by hand, with every use. Unbelievable waste of time and water and heated water.

"Next the medicine cabinet: I have never seen one designed with the intelligence of the average spice rack. You *have* to spill everything into the sink to access the aspirins.

"The human bathtub could only have been invented to help weed out the elderly, careless, and unlucky; it could be argued that this is laudable, but why must even the survivors be made so *uncomfortable* during what ought to be a delightful chore? Why are comfortable head supports not standard; why must tubs always be too short, too narrow, too *hard* and too difficult to keep clean; why build them of such preposterous materials; and above all, why is the single showerhead almost invariably located where it cannot be brought to bear on the specific areas where it would be most useful and most pleasant?

"As for the commode . . . it would take a volume to simply list its gross deficiencies. Forget the insanity of throwing precious fecal matter into the ocean, along with gallons-per-bolus of drinking water—how could humans possibly have designed for daily use and accepted as a universal standard an artifact which is acutely physically painful to use, enforces an unnatural and inefficient posture, and has no facilities whatsoever for cleansing either its user or itself? And why do you persist in using them for male urinals though they are manifestly unsuitable for that purpose?

"To be fair, I must admit that given your level of technology there is not much to criticize in the towel rack—but my friends, from an engineering point of view it is the only pardonable object in a human bathroom.''

Well, a few of us said a few things, but there's no sense kidding; Finn had us cold. It seemed strange that these things had never occurred to any of us before. Of course, we took bathrooms for granted, we'd grown up with them, but still . . .

About that time the door opened and a crisp breeze blew two men into the room; there was a glad shout as we recognized them.

"By all the Saints in Leslie Charteris's bookshelf," boomed Callahan, "if it ain't the MacDonald Brothers! About time you two bums showed up here. It's been too damn many years.''

After a short merry interval of backslaps and handshakes and let-me-get-your-coats we got Jim and Paul seated at the bar with God's Blessings in front of them. "God, it's good to be back here," they chorused, and then Jim took over the vocalizing for both of them. "I make it three years," he said to Callahan, and, "Yes, Jake, two years ago, and yes, it is," to me, and "Upstate in Plattsburgh—and it's getting pretty sane there," to Long-Drink, and "Perfect, thanks; we're learning some things about repairing ourselves," to Doc Webster, and, "No, Eddie—we don't need one," to Fast Eddie, and, "No, Reverend, and don't think we haven't tried," to Tom Hauptman, and then, to all of us: "We're sorry, we ought to let you vocalize the questions so you can all share the answers—but there were so many in the first round that we wanted to save a little time.''

Jim and Paul are telepaths, you see. What I'd been wondering was if they'd finished getting certified as psychiatrists yet, and if so whether it was working out the way they'd hoped. Some of the others' questions I could puzzle out. Callahan had been wondering how long it's been since their last visit; the Drink was going to ask where they were practicing; the Doc was going to ask after their health. Eddie's and Tom's questions eluded me.

"Hello, Mary," Jim went on, "it's good to meet you too. God, what a lovely marriage you two have! No, really? But that's *wonderful!* Don't worry, we wouldn't dream of it. Thanks. Finn, that's really fascinating stuff about the human bathroom. Do you see a pattern? Do the rest of you?" I'd been thinking of filling Jim and Paul in on the conversation that'd been in progress when they arrived, but of course they were a step ahead of me. "Consider: the same inherent stupidity Finn points out can be found in the typical kitchen. Fridges that spill money on the floor when you access them; stoves and ovens that spill money on the ceiling; a heat-maker and a heat-waster side by side, unconnected; sinks with the same problems he mentioned and others; waste-management techniques that belong in the Stone Age.

"In the typical bedroom you'll find just as much inexplicable thoughtlessness. It's only in the last year or two that anyone even thought of adapting hospital-bed technology to home beds. The three rooms all people *must* spend time in every day, none of them rationally designed. Yet in the den you'll probably find a computer that's a masterpiece of skullsweat and micromachining, and overhead there are satellites beeping in high orbit and footprints on the moon. Right now Paul and I are planning to spend over a thousand dollars on a hard-disk drive for our Macintosh, because it drives us crazy having to wait more than seven seconds to boot in, and it never occurred to either of us to spend fifty dollars on a thermocouple to save us hours a week of adjusting hot and cold water taps. Humans seem to have the idea that it's okay to devote thought and money and energy to our jobs, but not to our selves."

He paused courteously to let Doc Webster say aloud, "I don't know; we indulge ourselves pretty good in some ways. They make some pretty fancy entertainment gear, stereo and video and computer games and so forth."

"Nothing near as fancy as the stuff people use for work. In our *Mac Buyer's Guide*, business applications programs outnumber software games ten or twenty to one. All the stuff you mention was used for work for years before they made home consumer versions. And you can't sit in anything *near* as comfortable as a dentist's chair to enjoy them all. Holdover of the Puritan ethic: work can be noble, but the self is not worth attention. Considering that useful work is getting harder to come by, it's an attitude we're going to have to change eventually."

"I dunno," Doc Webster said. "I think we put in plenty of time on enjoyin' ourselves; maybe too much."

"Maybe. But I think we enjoy ourselves in inappropriate ways, at inappropriate times, to inappropriate degrees, just *because* we're so unused to doing it, so uncomfortable with wanting to, so reluctant to put thought into it. Paul and I find that most of our patients don't love themselves enough, so they treat themselves so badly it's hard for them to love themselves enough—it can be a literally vicious circle.''

Finn glanced at Mary on that one, and she smiled fondly. ''See, kid? It's not just a human problem, is it?'' He smiled sheepishly back. ''Don't worry, you're making progress.'' She turned back to the MacDonald brothers. ''I'm glad to meet you fellows, and you've got a mighty insight going there, which come to think of it is no surprise, but . . . *can we tell it now?* You know I'm dying to.''

Jim and Paul both smiled, and this time it was Paul who did their talking. ''Of course, dear. I don't know how you've held it in this long. Go ahead.''

She turned to the rest of us. ''You folks know what's been keeping Mick awake nights since he got to this planet, right?''

''Sure,'' Tommy Janssen said. ''Same thing that keeps a lot of us human type beings awake nights too.''

''And I don't know about the rest of you,'' the Doc insisted on saying, ''but Armageddon awful tired of it.''

Mary ignored him magnificently. ''That's right: nuclear holocaust. It wouldn't bother him any, physically, of course—and by the way, it wouldn't bother me or any of you physically either. You know how raindrops ignore friends of Mick's? Well, ionizing radiation and blast forces behave the same way, now.'' She reached over the bar, took out Callahan's riot baton, and brought it down on my head as hard as she could. A microinstant after it struck, the top of my head turned hard as titanium alloy.

''That's fantastic,'' I said as soon as I could get my breath. ''I felt a little sting, as though you slapped me with your open palm.''

''That's the most pain you'd feel even if I shot you with Pop's twelve-gauge,'' she said, grinning broadly. ''However you die, Jake, it won't be by violence. But that's beside the point. Nuclear devastation would be a sad thing even for us who survived. We'd miss the rest of the human race—''

''Speak for yourself,'' the Doc interjected.

''—and as for Mick, without a high-tech civilization, he'd die in a few hundred years for lack of maintenance. So he and I have been working on the problem ever since we got married, kind of putting our heads together, and the reason we came here tonight is—''

''To kick around some ideas, sure,'' Tommy said. ''Great. As long as we're all brainstorming the Unanswerable Questions, we might as well tackle the Big One.''

''Well, no, actually,'' Mary said. ''I mean, we'd be glad to kick around ideas on some other topics with you later, if you like. But this one we've sort of . . . uh . . . solved.''

''*WHAT?*''

I let go of my drink; Long-Drink started so sharply his watchman's cap flew from his head; Tommy spit a cigarette across the room; Fast Eddie the piano player had what musicians call a "train wreck''; the Doc was caught without a wisecrack of any kind; and Callahan—imperturbable Callahan— poured coffee on his hand and let out a bellow. It is worth mentioning that my drink didn't go anywhere, the Drink's cap returned to its perch, Tommy's cigarette landed in wet sawdust and extinguished itself, the Doc's flabby old heart did not stop, and the coffee failed to burn Callahan's wrist. The MacDonald Brothers were grinning a mile a minute, and even Finn had a happy expression pasted on his long gaunt face. Mary looked more embarrassed than anything else, like someone who's solved the whole crossword in two minutes and spoiled everyone's fun. *Jake*, I thought to myself, taking hold of my glass again, *you sure can pick 'em*. It seemed astonishing that I had ever thought myself this woman's equal, imagined us living together . . . (It's stupid to be jealous of someone with Mickey Finn's unique advantages, especially when he's such a good friend. But I had learned lately that I'm easily that stupid.)

None of us doubted her for a moment, of course. In the first place this was Callahan's Place, where *anything* can happen—and frequently does; in the second place, she was Mike Callahan's daughter, and therefore capable of anything she put her mind to; in the last place, she was Finn's wife. Me, I gave up using the word "impossible'' after the time I watched Fast Eddie win a large bet by successfully skiing through a revolving door. If Mary Callahan Finn said nuclear war wasn't a problem anymore, then it was time to start converting my fallout shelter back into a root cellar again, that was all . . .

The tone of Callahan's voice, now there was something genuinely startling. "Darlin','' he said darkly, "I would like to know, if you wouldn't mind telling me, exactly *how* you and Mick solved this little problem.''

"No, Mike, no,'' Jim or Paul hastened to assure him. "Nothing like that.''

Mary apparently knew her old man well enough to read him as well as two professional telepaths. "You ought to know me better than that, Pop. No—to answer your question out loud for everyone else's benefit—we did *not* solve the problem of nuclear war by making any changes in human nature. I'm not saying Mick couldn't pull it off if he tried, with enough lead time, but he wouldn't. Besides, I wouldn't let him. The very aggressiveness that makes the human race dangerous to itself is what's going to take us to the stars one of these days—you couldn't filter it out without changing humanity for the worse, maybe destroying it.''

"My own race lacked that sort of aggressiveness," Finn put in. "I am its last living member, and it has not escaped me that there may be a connection. I am more advanced, more knowledgeable than any of you—and even I am not competent to alter a psyche, individual or collective, Michael.''

Callahan relaxed. "Well, that's okay then. I misgive my misgivings. Irish Coffee, anybody?''

Long-Drink exploded. *"How did you fucking do it?"*

"Well," Mary said, "you all have to promise not to tell a soul— anybody that isn't a regular, I mean . . .''

She was cut off by the sound of the blender as Callahan whipped cream for the Irish coffee. The big redheaded son of a bitch made us wait on eleventerhooks until he was done, had Mary hold off until he had Blessed everyone in the room, then waved her to go ahead. Jim and Paul were smiling their faces off. I took a deep gulp of my own black magic healing potion, and decided that Callahan had good instincts and a nice judgment.

"You all know," she said, "that Mick and I have been spending our honeymoon traveling. I'd always wanted to see the world, and what with one thing and another I'd never managed to find the time to visit more than a dozen countries or so. So Mick indulged me. You know, it's funny how fast you can use up the tourist attractions of this planet when none of your time is wasted in the fiddle-faddle of getting there, and hauling and storing your stuff, and eating and drinking, and all of that chaff. On top of that, I hardly ever sleep since I took up with Mick—I don't *need* to anymore, and it makes me feel a little silly and selfish to go off and leave him for eight hours at a time like that. So in an astonishingly short time I discovered I was bored and there was nothing left to see.

"Well, you all know how polite this big cyborg is, but eventually he broke down and managed to diffidently suggest that Terra is *not* the only or even the most beautiful tourist attraction in this solar system.

"You want to know the truth, people? It's not even in the Top Ten . . .

"So lately we've been doing some *real* traveling, having a wonderful time. One day we were hanging out in The Rings—"

"Saturn?" I burst out.

"I *said* it with a capital T, Jake. Hanging out in The Rings, just sort of digging, you know, and chewing the fat now and then. We talked about the Cockroaches" (the name Mary came up with for Finn's former employers when she could not bring herself to call them The Masters) "and some of the other planets and civilizations he's seen, and so forth. And of course Topic A kept coming up— you just can't look at a sterile planet for long without thinking about it—and all of a sudden Finn asked me a question."

Just like a human husband, Finn interpreted her pause and took up the tale. She's had a considerable effect on him. "The news had been full of the Disarmament Talks when we left; you will recall that the Russians refused to even discuss the subject unless Reagan promised to abort his plans for a defensive satellite network—"

"Oh," said Long-Drink, "you mean the Star W—" Callahan hefted the big fifteen-cup coffee pot in one hand like a set of brass knuckles. "—the Strategic Defense Initiative, sure," the Drink finished.

"Yes," Finn agreed. "I asked Mary: why does not Reagan say to Gorbachev, 'Let us mutually agree to found together, in a neutral country such as Switzerland or New Zealand, *a single factory* which manufactures defensive satellites; divide the inventory at random; and launch them two by two until each side feels safe. Until that time is reached, each of us shall have a button which will destroy the factory if he suspects the other is cheating in any way. In that way—"

"If the Russians could build them things on their own, they'd be doing it," Long-Drink said argumentatively. "The U.S.'d contribute a lot more to the party than the Russians."

"So what?" Finn said simply.

The Drink opened his mouth. After a moment he reached up and closed it with his fingers.

"So what'd you answer, darlin'?" Callahan asked his daughter.

"I told him that it wouldn't work, but I couldn't explain why not. He said that was his thinking too; just checking. But it gave me a honey of an idea—''

"I am ashamed that I never thought of it myself," Finn said. "It is so obvious—''

"My love," she told him, "from a human's perspective there are only two deficiencies in your character: aggressiveness, as we discussed before, and audacity." *And a sense of humor*, I thought jealously, and suppressed the thought. Funny how you start censoring yourself when there's a couple of telepaths in the room. "But not imagination. Once I laid it down, you picked it up and ran with it." She turned back to the rest of us. "Mick's thoughts had been along the lines of figuring out some way to destroy nuclear warheads, and of course the problem was that even he couldn't get all of them simultaneously—and anything less would probably *trigger* a nuclear exchange. Even if he managed it, he might have just kicked off a conventional war that'd be damn near as bad. Well, it occurred to me that a satellite umbrella system would make the nut just fine, except that neither side wants the other to have one *first*, and they're too damn paranoid to coordinate or synchronize with each other.

"So Mick and I decided to do it for them."

After a frozen second or two, people began to grin along with Jim and Paul.

"We ducked over to the Asteroid Belt for raw materials, Finn drew up the blueprints and I set up a smithy, and we started turning out defensive satellites, freelance. A little more sophisticated than the ones Reagan's advisors have in mind. They're in place now; we just hung the last one an hour or two ago."

Callahan frowned. "You sure nobody caught you at it?"

"Relax, Mike," she told him. "Nobody sees Mick, on any wavelength whatsoever, unless he wants them to. As for the hardware, the largest components, the four system brains, are the size of ghetto blasters—and as transparent as glass. You could *tell* NASA roughly where they are, and give them twenty years, and they'd never find 'em.

"But for gosh sakes, don't tell anybody," Mary went on. "A general tends to freak out when he finds out his dick won't shoot. Of course, if they're dumb enough to let the situation, uh, come up, then the hell with their feelings—but for now, let's leave them with the comforting illusion that they hold the fate of mammalian life in their hands—it'll keep 'em out of serious mischief."

A rebel yell went up from someone, and like the first firecracker in a string it kicked off the loudest, and happiest, and most sincere cheer I had ever participated in or heard of in my life. It started loud, and built to a crescendo, and then squared itself, and then sustained, and eventually, there being a limit to the capacity of human lungs, dwindled, Dopplered down, attenuated, and finally was reduced to a single voice. And, astonishingly, the voice was very soft, very quiet, very flat, almost totally devoid of any emotion at all. It was an oddly chilling effect. *Oh, for heaven's sake*, I told myself, *it's just that it's Finn, and he forgets to put expression into his voice sometimes*, and as my blood started to unchill it froze solid because I heard what he was murmuring so gently, over and over:

"I have made a terrible mistake."

What made it even more horrible was that Jim and Paul Mac-Donald, dumbstruck, were nodding along with him.

Mary's face paled; I think if both her parents had been Caucasian she would have been white as a sheet. "What *is* it, Mick? What's wrong, for Christ's sake? I thought about it for weeks, you thought about it for hours, *what did we miss?*"

If anyone could have reached Finn it was Mary, but he didn't seem to hear her. She shook him, kicked him in the shin, and beat a tattoo on his face with her fists, without attracting his attention; he was a tall thin jukebox with a stuck record, repeating over and over again, "I have made a terrible mistake."

"Jim," Callahan said sharply, "what's wrong with him?"

But it was older brother Paul who answered. "The same thing that was wrong with me the first night my brother came in here, Mike. He's mindblown."

"Damn straight," Tommy Janssen said. "But what by?"

"We'll get to that," Callahan said. "First of all, how do we get him out of it before he wears a groove into his brain?"

"It won't be easy," Paul said. "When something scares you shitless, you just go back up inside your head and hide. But when the thing that scares you *comes* from inside your head, you . . . well, you go to a place that isn't a place, erasing your footsteps behind you. It'll be hard to find him: even he doesn't know where he is right now."

"I can get him back," Mary said positively.

I halfway expected her to borrow Callahan's scattergun and shoot Mick in the head—it seemed like a reasonable idea; it couldn't hurt him or anything—but what she did was, if you think about it, even more dramatic.

She leaned close to him and said, quietly but clearly over the sound of his litany, "Mick, I need you."

"Yes, Mary." His eyeballs powered up, tracked her, and locked on.

"Standby mode, sweetheart. I'll reboot you when it's time."

"Yes, dear." His face smoothed over and he turned to stone.

"Nice job, Mary," Paul said.

"Oh shit," she said, "the *job* hasn't started yet. Before I start him up again, I've got to have his universe rebuilt for him, or he'll just split again. So start talking: what's his problem?"

"Oh, it's ours too," he assured her, "and it's a beaut. Finn's Masters just entered the fringes of the cometary zone. They're headed this way."

"The fucking Cockroaches," Mary whispered, and literally pissed her pants. She glanced down at the widening stain on her jeans, smiled, and Paul and Jim caught her as she started to fall. She's so big it's a good thing there were two of them, but they got her down gently. She was out cold. Neither Mike nor I had even started to move to help her.

"Oh, spiffing!" Jim said. "Two down, one dozen to go."

He was paraphrasing a mordantly funny *Fawlty Towers* episode known to every one of us in the room, in a very good imitation of John Cleese's voice, and it may sound horrible but it was the most perfect way I can imagine to reach all of us, keep *us* from going bugfuck too. Nobody cracked up, but nobody cracked up either, if you follow.

"But it's impossible!" I burst out. "He said they wouldn't—they're cowards—he said they'd write him off when he failed to report—"

"Wishful thinking, maybe," Callahan said softly.

Paul and Jim shook their heads. "No, Mike," Jim said. "To the best of Finn's knowledge, what's happening is unlikely to the point of impossibility. He can't account for it. There's got to be something he doesn't know about the situation. My own suspicion is that he's not as expendable as the Cockroaches told him he was, for some reason, but that's just a hunch. In any case, they're on the way.''

"Do they know that Mickey's here?" Callahan asked.

Jesus—if they did, they were on their way to *this room*.

"Not yet," Jim replied. "But they will, soon. Finn's expecting to hear the call any minute: *'Report!'* When it comes, he'll answer it. Nothing in the world he can do about it."

"Not even in that condition?" Callahan asked, gesturing toward the catatonic Finn.

"He's not capable of ignoring a direct command from a Master: he's counterprogrammed. That's why he needed you folks to help him that first night he walked in here."

"No sweat, then," Callahan said, and reached under the bar for the chloral hydrate. "We'll just slip him another shot of his name-sake." It happens that chloral hydrate is one of the very few things that affect Finn exactly the same way they do a human: it is about the only thing that can render him truly unconscious.

"It's not that simple. Mary put him on standby—"

"So we pry his mouth open and pour the stuff down his throat—"

"Mike, in this mode, his stomach won't uptake."

"Oh. Well, can you power him back up again?"

"We'll have to wake Mary up: she's the only Authorized User inside the orbit of Neptune. Give us some silence, people. She's had a shock; it's going to be hard to do this without damaging her . . ."

We shut up and let them work. After maybe five long silent seconds, Mary opened her eyes and sat up. "We'll have to hurry," she said, "the Roaches could jerk his chain any second now." She got to her feet quickly enough to surprise even me, who have reason to know how limber she is. Obviously Jim and Paul had brought her up to date in the process of waking her. "It's time to get up, darling."

The statue of Finn came to life. The eyes started to smolder.

"Don't worry, now," she said quickly. "Open your mouth and drink what I give you."

"Yes, Mary."

Without taking her eyes from him she held up her hand, and the little bottle of chloral hydrate that Callahan tossed landed squarely in it. (I thought of my own father, and Mount Washington, and a hat.) "About thirty cc's," he called, and she beheaded the bottle and poured the dosage past her husband's teeth. Fast Eddie and

Long-Drink and I were alert; we reached Finn in time to help Mary and the MacDonalds break his fall. Finn's more than six-eleven, but thinner than me; he looks and moves like he weighs less than his wife. But this was the second time I'd helped carry him, and I'd guess him at six hundred pounds or better. Lead in the alloy? A grain of neutronium? I'd always meant to ask. We laid him out near where Mary had been a moment ago, straightened up, and rubbed our kidneys.

"Well," Long-Drink rumbled, "everything's fine, now. Finn's the most powerful critter that ever walked the earth, and the people who scare the crap out of *him* are on the way to exterminate us, and we've successfully put out the lights of the only guy who might have any ideas. Anybody feel like playing darts?"

"We've still got Finn, in a sense," I said. "Jim-Paul, you took a reading on him."

"All we've got is data," Paul answered for them. "Not the meta-programmer part, the part that generates ideas and thinks ten times faster than a human." He looked helpless. "And not much of the data, either. We've never been able to read more than about fifty percent of Finn's mind, and we only got maybe the surface five percent of that—a human brain just doesn't have the storage capacity, Jake. Not even two human brains."

"Mike," Long-Drink McGonnigle said hollowly, "drinks for the house, on me."

Do you know, I had room left in my brain to be startled by that? Of course, I realized at once, he was going to put it on his tab ...

"Did you get a reading on how soon the Cockroaches will get here?" Mary asked as Callahan began passing out fresh booze. "And what'll happen when they do?"

"They'll check Mars first, then come here; they should reach high orbit in an hour or so. Not having heard any response from Finn, the first thing they'll do is to scan the planet for clues to his fate. If they don't find any, they'll sterilize Earth and go on to check out Venus—then when they don't find him there either, I guess they'll—"

Fast Eddie spoke up from his place on the piano bench. "I don't t'ink I give a shit what dey do after dey sterilize de Oyth, Paulie."

He sighed. "I don't suppose I do either, Ed."

"What happens if they *do* find Finn?" Callahan asked.

"If he wakes up between now and then, you mean? Why, I guess they'd come here and look him over, find out what caused him to malfunction and see if he could be restored to service. *Then* they'd sterilize Earth—probably have Mickey do it for them, to make sure he was working properly again.''

"How many of 'em do you figure there are?''

Both MacDonalds shrugged. ''Impossible to say, Mike. Finn couldn't come up with a reason why *any* of them would come here.''

''Are they vulnerable to anything?''

''Oh, yes. If they were as strong as Finn, they wouldn't need scouts like Finn. That's why he can't imagine what would bring them here; he's certain there are no other scouts along with them. Anyway, all you'd have to do is detonate a small tactical nuke in their immediate vicinity and you'd have Cockroach Soup.''

''Well, hell,'' Doc Webster said, ''NORAD can handle that! With Finn to spot for 'em, maybe . . .'' He trailed off as it dawned on him. ''Aw, shit.''

''NORAD doesn't have any H-bombs anymore,'' Callahan rumbled. ''Mick *said* he made a terrible mistake.''

Mary buried her face in her hands. ''Oh, Pop! *I made it too!*'' She began to sob.

I wanted to rush to her and comfort her, take her in my arms and tell her everything was going to be all right. I never moved a muscle and I never said a mumbling word.

Her father came around the bar and put an arm around her. ''So did I, darlin', so did I. Not your fault. We guessed wrong, that's all.''

''Pop, what'll we do now?''

''I'm not exactly certain, hon, but the first step is to blow our cover.''

Her head came up fast. ''Are you *sure?*''

The big barkeep grinned at her, waggled his cigar. ''Hell, no! Got a better idea?''

She frowned. ''I guess not. Your privilege; they're your family.''

Callahan turned to the rest of us. ''Folks, I'm afraid it's time for Mary and I to face the music, and tell you people who we really are . . .''

And having said that much, the big redheaded son of a bitch stood there and looked at us for a while. He's always had a pretty expressive face, but I'd never seen so many expressions chase themselves around it before. And while I've always known that Michael Callahan was a subtle and thoughtful man, I'd known it by his actions more than his face; his expressions had always been sort of carved out in broad strokes before. This was a change so sharp as to be perceptible. Somehow I knew that I was looking at a different man. No: at a different side of a man I knew. It was something like watching a brilliant actor step out of character after the lights have gone out.

It was exactly like that. I began to add up a number of things that I have always known but somehow had never felt inclined to think about for very long. Not, say, for long enough to reach the inevitable conclusions.

I glanced toward the MacDonalds. Jim's eyes were waiting for mine, and he was nodding. I opened my mouth . . . then shut up and let Callahan say it.

"Friends," he said slowly, "this isn't going to be easy. A lot of words I need, I don't have. Not that they don't exist, but none of you know 'em—and I don't have time for a language lesson. Uh . . . Mary and I aren't from around here—"

"We know that, Mike," Long-Drink said. "Brooklyn, right?"

"Dat's where me and Mike hooked up," agreed Eddie, the oldest denizen of Callahan's Place. "At Sally's joint."

Callahan shook his head. "That ain't where I'm from, boys."

Eddie shrugged. "Well, you never said it was."

"Thanks, Eddie." Callahan smiled at the monkey-faced little piano man. "I'm pleased you noticed that."

"All right," Doc Webster said. "I'll play. Where *are* you from?"

"A place that calls itself Harmony."

"Isn't that in New Zealand?" somebody asked.

"Nope. It's about twenty trillion miles farther away, and quite a few years from now."

There was silence for a time. Mary sat down at the nearest table and commandeered someone's neglected drink. She watched Finn snore while she sipped it.

"Well," Doc Webster said finally in a conversational tone, "that explains a lot. Always said there was something weird about you, Callahan. Anyone who would permit puns like mine in his establishment is just not normal."

"Time-traveler, huh?" Tommy Janssen mused. "You must be from farther up the line than The Meddler or Al Phee."

"Or Josie Bauer and her Time-Police," Callahan agreed. "To

my time, yours and theirs are pretty much indistinguishable.''

"How far is that, Mike?" I asked.

"Well," he said, "where I come from, the human race has got it together. Nobody's hungry; nobody's angry.''

That far!

"And we're startin' to learn a few things. Oh, we'll be a *long* time learning—but at least we're finally on the case.''

"Jesus Christ," I said faintly, "I wish I had time to ask you about five hundred questions.''

"Me too, Jake," he said. "But I'll tell you right now, better'n half of them I'd never be able to answer, in any words that'd have meaning for you. Like, right now, most of you are probably wondering about time paradoxes and so forth, and the answers simply won't mean much to you.''

"Let's try anyway," Doc Webster said. "Did you know this showdown with Finn's Masters was gonna happen? Is that why you've been running this bar all these years?''

"Yes and no," Callahan said promptly. "See what I mean?''

"Dammit," the Doc growled, "I started out this night saying that all questions have answers.''

"If they're meaningful," Callahan agreed. "Doc, you just plain can't frame a meaningful question about time-travel in English. The language itself hasn't got the room: it's based on the assumption that time travel is not possible.''

The Doc frowned. "So it is. Can you do any better than 'yes and no'?''

"It is known in my time that *some* event takes place at this locus in space/time. Something so major, so crucial to the history that produced my time, that it makes Pearl Harbor seem no more important than yesterday's hockey scores. What that event is, is hidden from us. So is the certainty of its outcome. Some things in our past we can't affect. Some things we *have* to affect. We don't always know the difference. And no, that's not the only reason I set up this bar, although it would have been enough. I know all that doesn't make sense, in English, but if you want me to do even a little better than that, we'll still be talking when the Cockroaches get here.''

Good point. "All right," I said, "let's cut to the chase. You've got to have some kind of futuristic wonder-gizmo you can zap the Cockroaches with, right?''

I don't know when I've ever been sorrier to see a man shake his head. "It doesn't work that way, Jake. You have to work with available materials. Whatever's already in place in that space/time.''

"Mike . . ." I hesitated. "If it was anybody but you, I'd say that was preposterous. How do you get your own time machine through?"

"We don't use machines for time travel."

"Oh." I would think about this another time. If there ever was one. "But in any case we can relax, no? At least a little? The fact that you're here, from our future, means that the human race is *not* going to be exterminated in the next hour, *nicht wahr?* But we could suffer heavy casualties or something?"

That was when I've been sorrier to see a man shake his head. "Again, Jake, what you're saying sounds logical—because you're saying it in English. Take my word for it: my home space/time is just as likely as yours to stop existing in the next hour or so. Worse, to stop ever *having existed* in this continuum. If the Cockroaches steam-clean this planet, there'll be no way for my home to ever come to pass." He frowned. "This whole era is a tinderbox; we've got agents spotted all through here/now, doing what we can to cool things out. But we always knew that there was going to be at least one really major something around about now. What we *thought* was that the crucial event in question would be a nuclear firestorm. The shape of history seemed to point that way. We thought we had it covered, thanks to Finn." He looked sadly at his catatonic friend. "But it was us made the awful mistake, not him."

Long-Drink McGonnigle summed it up very succinctly, I thought: "Aw, shit."

"Don't feel bad, Mike," I said. "You bet with the odds—nobody can fault you for using Occam's razor."

He shook his head ruefully. "Thanks, Jake—but you'd be surprised how many chins William can't shave. With the stakes this high, we should never have bet the farm."

"William who?" Fast Eddie wanted to know. "And what's dis about razors?"

That almost made me smile. Eddie must use an electric razor with an offset shim: at all times, he has exactly three days' growth of beard. "William of Occam, Eddie. Stated the principle of Least Hypothesis—"

"Is dat, like, cheaper than a rented hypot'esis?"

Bless the runty little piano man, that *did* make me smile, and simplify my explanation even further than I had planned.

"Occam's razor is a principle that says, if there's more than one explanation for something, the simplest one is most likely to be true.''

''Not 'certain,' '' Callahan amplified. '' 'Most likely.' ''

Eddie looked thoughtful—not an easy trick with that face— and shook his head. ''I dunno. Most o' my life, de complicated explanation was de one to bet on. I don't buy dis William o' What- ever—''

''Occam,'' I said.

''—an' de horse he rode in on,'' Eddie agreed. ''He sure got it wrong dis time.'' He frowned slightly at our grins. ''Well, what's our next move, boss?''

The grins went away.

''Mike!'' I said as an urgent thought struck me. ''It's New Year's Eve! The rest of the gang are going to start showing up any sec- ond—all of 'em, not just the regulars. Shouldn't we try to head 'em off? Go set up roadblocks? *Some*thing?''

He took one of those foul cigars of his from a shirt pocket and sniffed it meditatively. What more proof did I need that he wasn't a normal human being? ''I don't think so, Jake. In the immortal words of Percy Mayfield—''

''—'The Danger Zone is *everywhere*,' yeah, I understand that. They're no safer at home than they would be here. But do we want 'em all around underfoot, complicating the fight?'' I felt my voice get hoarser. ''There's going to be a fight here, isn't there?''

He lit his cigar. ''Damn straight there is,'' he rumbled. He dropped the dead match on the floor, trod it underfoot, and took Mary's hand. ''Damn straight.'' Suddenly he grinned. ''But who ever said a fight was complicated by reinforcements? Let 'em come, by Christ. Let 'em all come! If we have to, we can all go to Hell together—maybe there's a group rate.''

''Callahan's right, Jake,'' Long-Drink said. ''There ain't a one of the gang wouldn't rather be *here* on Judgment Day, and you know it.''

Doc Webster nodded vigorous agreement, jowls flapping. ''Damn well told. If the world is about to end, we can at least have a drink on it together before we go!''

There was a general chorus of agreement.

''All right,'' Callahan boomed, ''let's get to it. There's two phone lines in this joint, and the one for the computer is miked. I'll boot the directory disk and get a printout by last name—I'll take A through M; Doc, you take N through Z—''

"Mike," Jim and Paul MacDonald said simultaneously.

He broke off and tried to look at both at once. "Yeah?"

"It's not necessary to use the phone," they chorused.

He looked startled—then broke into a big grin. "Why, no, it ain't at that. What's your range these days?"

"With *family?* Callahan's People? We could find one of you on the moon if we had to."

"Go to it then, sons."

Jim and Paul found a vacant table, sat down on opposite sides. They took each other's hands and smiled at one another. Then their eyes rolled up and their mouths went slack and they seemed to slump slightly.

Can you remember the very first time you used stereo headphones, and heard a voice speaking or singing *inside* your head? Or were you too young at the time to find that remarkable? This was a little like that: perceiving "sound" where sound had never been before.

(Further: You know that with stereo headphones an aural image can seem to move, from left to right or the other way around. In the Decca, Georg Solti recording of Wagner's *Der Ring des Nie-belungen* there's a passage in which Fafnir roars—and on headphones the sound seems to move *up* from your throat to the crown of your head. An illusion, of course, and I've always wondered how Decca's engineers managed it. Similarly—and just as impossibly—the combined "voice" of Jim and Paul MacDonald, which I heard now in my head, seemed to move *from back to front,* as though two tiny Paul Reveres entered the back of my skull, transited my brain at high speed, and left through my forehead.)

The double-tracked voice was quiet, calm—but so emphatically urgent that I was certain it would have waked me out of the soundest sleep.

"*Mike Callahan needs you,*" it said. "*Hurry!*"

The cold winter wind was choppy at this height, and the ledge was slippery; Walter clutched at the brick façade with slowly numbing fingers and at the pretty brunette's gaze with tearing eyes. She was nice to look at, leaning out the window, the last pretty girl he ever expected to see—but he knew all the things she was likely to say, and knew that none of them would work. "You're wasting your time," he told her and her husband, whose head was visible beside hers. "I know all the clichés, and I just don't want to talk about it."

"You've got to come in soon, Walter," she called from the window. "If you stay there much longer you'll get Window-Washer's VD."

"What?" To be surprised astonished him.

"It's a terrible thing," her husband said earnestly. "You get a watery blue discharge, with a funny smell."

"What the *hell* are you talking about?"

"Herpes windex," she said.

He laughed long and hard, to a point just short of hysteria. "You two really are good at what you do, you know that? I was in a lousy mood. This is a better mood to die in."

"That's something, at least," the husband called over the sound of the wind. "But—"

"I still don't want to talk about it," Walter yelled. "Why I'm doing this is none of your business."

"Nobody asked you," the wife said. "What Les and I want to know is why you're doing it so badly."

He blinked at them.

"Merry's right. Some janitor has to mop up you and his breakfast; a bunch of cops and ambulance attendants get brought down; a whole streetful of passersby have a great dark demoralizing omen literally drop into their lives—see that little girl across the street down there? Her mother is the one who's going to need to explain this, not us."

"And what *about* us?" Merry asked. "We're professionals, with a reputation to protect. You hired us to come over here and try to cheer you up. You say we succeeded, and now you want to skip out without paying. Are we supposed to—" She broke off short.

"*You don't understand!*" Walter shouted to the night sky. He closed his eyes, and sighed deeply. If he told them how it was, they would see that he really had no choice. "All right: I'll explain it to you. You deserve that much." He turned his face back to them, to see the empathy he knew he would find in Merry's eyes, and she and Les were both gone from the window. "Hey! Do you want to hear this or not?" There was no reply. "*Hey!*"

The Cheerful Charlies were gone.

Walter stood there on the ledge, confused, unready to jump, too stiff and cold to risk climbing back in the window unassisted, his scenario thrown completely off the rails. Anger came to him, bring-

ing warmth to his fingers and strength to his limbs. He made it
safely inside, and reached the street in time to see the Charlies
driving away; furious, he flagged a cab and followed them.

Patrolman Jimmy Wyzniak trailed the sergeant through the empty
corridors of Suffolk County Police Headquarters; the only sounds
were their footsteps and the occasional ringing of phones that no
one was going to answer. Jimmy was young, and just barely experienced enough at his job to have some appreciation of the magnitude of his ignorance, but he had no fear: his sergeant was with
him, and the Sarge was the best there was. It had been bravery and
not bad judgment that lost him a leg.

"People are sure funny, you know?" Jimmy said plaintively. "I
mean, Captain Whitfield is taking this like it was personal—like
they put it here just for him. Never seen him so mad."

The Sarge spoke over his shoulder. "You notice he didn't try to
do the damned thing himself first. He called for the experts." His
limp was barely perceptible.

Jimmy shifted his trunk-shield like an umpire looking for a fresh
plug of tobacco and grinned. "Well, that just proves he's smarter
than we are."

His mentor snorted. "Son, *everyone* is smarter than we are. Here
we go: Storage Closet 5. The phone tip said it was in here."

"Who claimed credit for this one?"

"Who cares?"

"Boobies on the door, you figure?"

"Never can tell—so we assume there are." Jimmy set down the
heavy backpack of equipment, and they spent a few minutes assur-
ing themselves that the door was *not* booby-trapped. "I hope they're
professionals," the Sarge grunted. "Pros are tricky sometimes—but
at least they use good equipment. An amateur job, who knows *what*
the hell it's gonna do?" Then, rank having its "privileges," the
Sarge sent Jimmy thirty feet down the hall and around a corner.
The young patrolman waited anxiously, heard the sound of the
Sarge trying the knob.

"Zoroaster in lingerie," he heard the Sarge say.

He ran back and looked through the door of Closet 5. "What the
hell is it?" he asked. "That doesn't look like anything we covered
in training."

"*I* saw one once," the Sarge said very softly. "When I was in the Army. I'd guess it's not especially powerful—nothing like the one that did that slum clearance on downtown Nagasaki. By today's military standards it's not even a cherry bomb.''

Jimmy regarded the object. ''You're saying that's a nuke,'' he said in a calm, conversational tone, as though confirming the time—then, big: ''*It looks like a fucking miniature vacuum cleaner!*''

''Sure does—probably doesn't weigh more than thirty pounds all told. Now, the military could make one that size with some real bang onto it—but looky there at the airline bag they carried it in. Amateur job.''

It was not machismo that kept Jimmy's cool for him—this was beyond even the machismo of a demolitions man. But if the Sarge wasn't worried, Jimmy wasn't worried. Hell, the Sarge could probably disarm an ICBM in flight if he had to! ''So it won't do more than annihilate Riverhead if it goes off, huh?''

The Sarge shook his head. ''Not even that bad, is my guess. This building, for sure. The block, possibly. This thing is just a pony nuke.''

A guess for Sarge was Gospel for Jimmy. ''So what's our first move?''

''Well, that time fuse says it's got almost two hours left. That should be plenty of time. I suppose we—'' The Sarge broke off, stood as though listening to something. Jimmy smiled: The Sarge had done this several times before, with conventional but difficult bombs—explaining afterward that he was ''trying to outthink the guy that built it''—so everything really was okay after all. Any minute now, the Sarge would—

—start running like a bastard, back the way they had come—

''*Sarge!*'' Jimmy cried, but his instincts were good: he was already in motion. His legs were good too, and he had two of them: he was neck and neck with the Sarge within ten strides. Suddenly the Sarge put on the brakes and doubled back; Jimmy did not. As he cleared the door to the outside Jimmy could hear the Sarge's uneven footsteps coming up fast behind him again. Captain Whitfield and the other cops waiting outside scattered in all directions when they saw both running men.

The Sarge made a beeline for the Bomb Squad truck, leaped behind the wheel. He was carrying an airline bag.

''Sarge! Goddamn it—hey, *Sarge!*''

Sergeant Noah Gonzalez ignored him, started the truck and sped off.

*   *   *

Ralph spotted a likely looking bitch, got close enough to smell her and growled deep in his throat. He had little difficulty in cutting her out of the pack she was with. He knew, as they did not, that in a matter of hours she would be panting for it. Confusing and mesmerizing her with his deep, softly accented voice, he led her away from her friends and into the darkness.

Sound Beach is a seasonally schizophrenic area of Long Island. For Ralph it was a walk on the wild side—literally. In the summer the vacation cottages are filled with the nearly wealthy. In winter the region is sparsely populated by half-frozen college students from the nearby State University—and by packs of feral dogs. They are the watchdogs routinely abandoned by the nearly wealthy at season's end. Dobermans, Shepherds. They pack up, and raid garbage cans, and kill and eat the pets of the college students, and it is usually February or March before the county cops have shot the last of them. As a general rule, by the time they are hungry enough to attack a human, they are too weak to pull it off—though there are occasional exceptions.

Ralph Von Wau Wau neither smelled nor behaved domesticated, and he sounded like Arnold Schwarzenegger in pitch, tone, accent, and confidence; he could move among his savage cousins in relative safety. He had only been forced to fight twice in the five years he had been wintering on Long Island, and had won both fights handily. The feral dogs were cunning, but Ralph was intelligent, and it made all the difference.

Though he was a mutant, Ralph had all the normal urges of any red-blooded son of a bitch, and house pets just didn't do it for him. Too tame, too boring. His true preference was for women, and he was currently on intimate terms with half a dozen—but three were vacationing to the south with their husbands, two were preparing final exams for their students, and one was preparing to run for reelection. Ralph had not gotten laid in several weeks, and his opinion was that the next best thing to an adventurous and sophisticated lady was a wild outlaw bitch. They were less inventive, but more instinctively satisfying—and cross-fertile besides.

He had certain moral rules of his own devising, which might seem exotic to a human. He always fed a bitch, before and after. If necessary, he protected her to the best of his ability. If she got pregnant, he behaved as honorably as any other dog would—and scrutinized the offspring for indications that his mutation might have bred true—which so far it had not. If a hyperintelligent pup *had* resulted, he would have bent every effort to get it the same larynx-modification surgery he himself had once had, then taught it to talk. But by now he had almost given up hope.

He'd tried moving a few mates in with him, but it never worked out: they never really had enough in common to relate to one another, and it always upset them when he typed for hours at a time.

This particular bitch excited him a great deal, for reasons too subtle and subconscious for him to analyze. (Regrettably, the Freud of canine psychology has not yet emerged.) Something about the fur at the back of her neck, something about her walk, something about her smell . . . there was no defining it. She was new to him, puzzled by the contradiction between what her eyes and nose told her, and what her ears told her, and he found her innocence charming. She was cooperative but not slavishly obedient. Her eyes flashed. Her scent was . . . piquant.

So they gave the rest of the pack the slip, and he took her to a warm and sheltered place he knew. There he opened a can of deviled ham—a rather extravagant wooing-gift, but one of the annoyingly few meats available in pop-top can format—and waited politely while she wolfed it down. Then they romped a bit, and nuzzled a bit, and presently he taught her some things about foreplay that astonished her. (The Masters & Johnson of canine physiology have yet to emerge as well—but when they do, Ralph Von Wau Wau will be massively represented in their footnotes.) Shortly after that, she taught him some things about hindplay. As mentioned, Ralph was a love 'em and leave 'em sort of fellow, but the summons from Jim and Paul MacDonald came at an extremely unfortunate, uh, juncture, and he was compelled to bring her halfway to Callahan's with him . . .

Joe and Susan Maser had sent their wife Suzie on ahead to Callahan's because they wanted to put the finishing touches on the chili they intended to bring for the New Year's celebration; the summons came as Joe was stirring up the coals in the firebox of his woodstove. He dropped the poker and sprinted with Susan for the car, leaving the fire door open on the stove. Pulling out of the driveway, he realized what would probably happen, but he didn't have time to do anything about it. Behind him, the draft whipped the fire to its hottest and sucked all the heat up the chimney . . . which had not been cleaned recently enough. Since Joe and Susan had also left the front door of the house open, much the same thing eventually happened to the building; by dawn all the Masers would own was the clothes on their backs and the contents of their pockets.

Similarly, Shorty Steinitz left his own lovingly restored '57 Thunderbird jacked up with one wheel off by the side of Route 25A and ran the last quarter-mile; he never saw it again. Lady Sally McGee was entertaining a very old and dear friend when the call came; he had never been intended to remain in that position for more than fifteen minutes, but the silken cords were strong, and he could not reach the slipknots. Pyotr left his bottle of breakfast sitting on his kitchen table, and few foods go bad faster or uglier than blood. And Bill Gerrity was caught in the middle of getting dressed: this would have been embarrassing for anyone, but for Bill "half-dressed" for a party meant dark nylons, purple garter belt, black panties, and an hour's worth of makeup (high heels too, but he ditched them within the first half block); in the three and a half miles he had to jog to Callahan's, he was forced to hospitalize four young toughs who mistook him for a homosexual, two policemen who correctly identified him as an attractive nuisance, and a persistent politician who simply would not get out of the way.

It was not, in short, without cost that the men and women of Callahan's Place answered the Call, even though nearly all of them were getting ready to go there at the time. But it is a matter of proud record that every single one of them paid the cost, unhesitatingly. Within an hour, the Place was packed to capacity with all the regulars past and present, with all the people to whom this tavern had ever been *home* for a time, and nobody had any complaints to make. The MacDonald Brothers had followed up their initial Call with a synopsis of the situation; everyone arrived with a fair grasp of what was going on.

Josie Bauer was the first to arrive, of course, since it took her literally no time at all; she materialized before the bar, took the shot glass of Irish whiskey that Callahan was holding out for her and set it down on the bartop, plucked the cigar from his lips and kissed him firmly. "You sneaky bastard," she murmured. "I never guessed. I should have guessed. You must be from *much* farther up the line than my outfit."

"Not as much as you might think, hon'," he told her.

She turned to Mary and kissed her too. "Hang in there, sugar. He'll be okay."

The next arrival was Shorty, and he did just what Josie had done. I'd be willing to bet Shorty had never kissed another male in his life before, but he did so with no hesitation or sign of embarrassment. That set the pattern. Every new arrival, and those already present, collected a shot and a kiss from Callahan and his daughter. No one drank; we waited for Mike to propose the toast. All of us were smiling, and all of us were crying, and all of us were touching, and none of us said a word, save for occasional briefly murmured greetings to old friends too seldom seen. No one had anything pertinent to say, and no one felt the need to mouth off without saying anything; it was enough to be together, to share whatever would come. I saw friends I hadn't seen in years—Ben, Stan, Don, Mary and Stephen, both Jims, Big Tom, Susan, Betsy, Mark, Chris, Robert and Ginny, Herb and Ricia, Diana, Joe and Gay, Jack, Vinny, Railroad George, Ted, Gordy, Dee for Chrissakes, Tony and Susan, Wendy, Bob, Kirby, Eleanor, Charlie and Evelyn, and of course David—and it came to me as the crowd grew and the Place filled up that I could not have asked for a better time or place to die. There was no place on Earth or off it that I loved as much, nor any people I had ever loved better—no, not even the wife and daughter I'd killed a decade ago by doing my own brake job with a self-help book—and New Year's Eve seemed an appropriately backassward date for Judgment Day.

After a little more than a half hour of murmured greetings, multiple embraces and general warm happiness, Paul MacDonald spoke to Callahan. "Okay, Mike. Everybody who's going to arrive in time is here now."

The room became totally quiet, filled with a mood of exuberant desperation. The locker room before the big game. Backstage waiting for the house lights to go down. The hold of the Huey as the LZ appears in the distance.

We were as ready as we were going to be.

Callahan nodded slowly. "It's about time," he rumbled. He trod his cigar underfoot and lit a new one. "It's all about time." He poured a shot of Bushmill's for himself, walked slowly around the bar. "Isn't it?" The sawdust squealed under his boots. Fast Eddie left the piano and tossed a couple of sticks of dry birch onto the fire; there was a crackle as the bark began to catch, and that fine sharp-sweet smell of burning birch joined the symphony of pleasant smells in the room. Callahan toed the chalk line, faced the rattling hearth. I didn't mind the tears; they fell too quickly to obscure my vision. He raised his glass, and we all raised ours. The bright lights shattered on all that glass and the room sparkled like a vast crystal.

"To the human race," Mike Callahan said clearly in that gravelly baritone. "God help us, every one." He drank off the Bushmill's in one long, slow draught, smacked his lips and whipped the glass underhand into the fireplace.

"To the human race," we chorused, and the largest barrage of glasses in the history of Callahan's Place began.

And when the great shout and cheer had subsided and the last shard of glass skittered to its final resting place, we began to build something.

I perceived it in musical terms, of course: to me what we built was something like a vast symphony orchestra, save that in addition to the usual ordnance of a full orchestra it incorporated saxophones, electric guitars, tin flutes, tablas, trap drums, Yamaha synthesizers, steel drums, vocoders, kazoos, baby rattles, Zal Yanovsky's Electric Gorgle and the Big Jukebox in *Close Encounters*, included every means the race has ever devised for making music and some that haven't been invented yet, the whole thing integrated into a vast tapestry of sonic and tonal textures that was indescribable and probably unimaginable—certainly I had never imagined anything like it before that night—and primevally satisfying to what a Buddhist might call my "third ear."

Imagine that you assembled such a superorchestra in a room. First there is cacophony, as each musician sounds his or her instrument and limbers it up, no individual or group predominating for more than a few seconds. Then one loud true voice takes up and holds a 440 cps A, and gradually everyone tunes to it; for several seconds everyone is playing the same note and it's like a giant "OM" chant. Then it diverges again, as each player goes into scales or warmup exercises. Imagine then that, seemingly by pure random chance, the vast assemblage of instruments happens to stumble onto a single, stupendous chord, an accidental aural architecture of terrifying beauty, a chord so complex that the most knowledgable musician there cannot name it, yet so *elemental* that each feels he has always

known it in his heart. It holds, swells, falters momentarily as per-
cussive notes fade and lungs empty of breath and bows reach the
limit of their traverse, then returns and steadies and fills the room
to bursting, each musician thinking, *keep playing—yes, try to notice
and remember what note you're playing, but for God's sake* keep
playing, *if we lose this thing we may never find it again and if that
happens I believe I may need to die—*

The thing we built was like that. There was no sound to it, any
more than there was substance to it, but it hung invisibly in the air
around us, annihilating the space between us, and to me that's music. The 440 A that we all tuned to was the voice, the essence, the
nature of Mike Callahan, echoed and amplified by the MacDonalds.
But neither he nor they led us to that "chord"—we found that
ourselves. Shortly it changed from something as static as the word
"chord" implies to something dynamic, as though individual musicians, confident now that the chord would not be lost, began to
jam around it, to dress it with trills and arpeggios and scraps of
melody and rhythmic accents; it changed from a pretty sound to
true music, although no human ear could have resolved music like
that. It was timeless, like raga, and frantic, like bebop; it swung like
Carl Perkins, and it purred like Betty Carter; it was simple like Bach
and complex like Ray Charles; it was hot and cool and hip and
square and lush and spare—I know no music can be all those things
together, but this was. In the back of my mind I could hear Lord
Buckley, rest his ticker, talkin' 'bout, "My lords and my ladies,
I'm gon' hip you: you may have heard a lot of jam sessions blowin'
off, you may o' heard o' New Orleans flips, you may have heard
it Chicago style, you may have heard all kinds o' jazz jumpin' the
wildest an' the most insane, you may have heard o' many musical
insane flips, but you studs an' stallions an' cats an' kitties *never
dug any session like these cats BLEW . . . !*"

To others present it did not suggest music at all. Shorty Steinitz
was a sculptor; to him it was as though all of us struck together
simultaneously at a magnificent block of Carrera marble, reducing
it in an instant to a perfect and complete statue, which began in that
moment of its creation to walk and talk. Susie Maser was a Modern
dance choreographer; she felt that we were inventing zero-gravity
dance together. Indeed, Long-Drink McGonnigle, who had cher-
ished a perverse interest in entomology ever since February 7, 1964,
felt that whatever it was resembled pictures he'd seen of webs woven by spiders in free fall, in Skylab. Doc Webster saw us all as

neurons learning to work together, to form ". . . well, not a brain, not even a small one—but a ganglion, by God!" Tom Hauptman, the former minister, perceived what we built as a perfect prayer, pleasing to God, who is a tough critic of prayers.

I do not know all this from having compared notes afterward. I knew it then, and everyone there knew and understood the analogy mode that worked for me just as well as I knew theirs. Just because I perceived it as music didn't make it music for Fast Eddie: the little piano man felt that we were setting up and executing a hundred-cushion billiard shot in ultraslow motion and cascading instant replay. Of course, he appreciated my appreciation of it as music—but no more than did Tom Hauptman, who is totally tone deaf (or rather, had been until then). Perhaps the most insightful analogy we conceived was that of Joe and Susan and Susie Maser, who saw us all as building a group marriage akin to their own triad.

Or perhaps it came from Noah Gonzalez, who pictured us constructing, entirely by intuition, a cobalt bomb.

All this happened at the top of our minds, in the forefront of our combined consciousness. Along with that, we were simultaneously, but not separately, growing closer to one another, getting to know each other in even greater depth than we already did, sharing and cherishing. Tom, for instance, was discovering music for the first time in his life, and finding it both more and less than he had imagined it must be. Long-Drink and the Doc and I were discerning some interesting things at the root of our long-standing rivalry at punning. Tommy Janssen was understanding for the first time why heterosexual Bill Gerrity enjoyed wearing drag. Tom Hauptman was learning things about eroticism from Josie Bauer that would have shocked him cockeyed an hour before, and she was learning equally unsettling things about chastity from him. All of us were learning things from the Callahans, husband, wife, and daughter, that I can't put down here. It's not that you don't have the words. You don't have the concepts to put words on.

At Callahan's Place we were used to sharing, to letting down barriers, to opening up to and for one another. Callahan's frequently proclaimed policy of violently discouraging snoopy questions had always been a sham, a custom honored more in the breach than in the observance, a prohibition that we now perceived was designed to teach us to learn how to circumvent it—hell, the Cheerful Charlies had it down pat. Not to mention the MacDonalds. Or Callahan himself, who sucked secrets out of you with his twinkling eyes. We thought that we already knew what it meant to *be one* together; we had been students of sharing here for many years together.

This was more, deeper, stronger, better. A sizable fraction of the people there were folks I didn't know well or at all, ex-regulars from before my time who had still been alive and around to hear The Call, and Walter the failed suicide: while devoting the bulk of our individual and collective attention to the thing that we were building, we became blood brothers and sisters without wasting time or words.

Words. It is interesting that none of us perceived the thing we built in terms of a structure of words. It was sheer pattern-recognition—images, gestalts, sensory impressions and emotional rhythms, a nonstop cascade of data that reached even the subvocalized level only in scattered, fragmentary form, like verbal buckshot:

*(warm!/and so when she died I/Heavenly Father . . . /merry, by God!/roll 'em baby/you're beautiful/thank you/you're beautiful too/ thank you/*It's *beautiful/always wanted to tell you that I/do that again/ain't it?/never thought it could be like/pulsing/steady now/ere do I remember this fr/fast!/would have done the same thing my/take it/strong!/remember re-member reMember ream ember/more treble, we're losing the highs/hi!/hie/hai!/never lose the/high/I/eye/aye!/ LOVE/U/ewe/hue/yew/YOU/too/U2/to/two/whoo!/who?/hew/Hugh/ yoo hoo!/YOU!)*

It went on forever, for whole seconds, repeating and changing and building like a series of choruses in jazz without any of us ever forming a coherent sentence in words. And yet when the time came to speak, we found that we could—although we were one, we retained our individual voices and the personalities they represented.

No, put quotes around "speak" and "voices." If there'd been a stranger in the room, he would not have heard or seen or felt a thing. To him we would have been a roomful of strange and twisted people, standing around a snoring basketball player, smiling dementedly at nothing at all, in silence . . .

"All right, ladies and gents," Callahan said, his voice clear and strong in my skull, "let's get this show on the road. We need a plan. The floor is open."

"There ain't but the one plan," I said. "We get the Roaches on the phone and invite 'em over for a beer."

"*Here?*" two or three minds yelped.

"Sure. We badly lack data, and short of waking up Finn the only source is the Cockroaches themselves."

(A funny little thing happened then, entirely below the surface, that was over in an instant. I'm rather ashamed of it—but it's illustrative of something that was happening all around the room, so I'll tell it. A primitive ape who clings to my brainstorm still wanted Mary Callahan, still perceived Finn as a rival—worse, a successful rival—worst, a superior rival. That ape heard me calmly trying to cope with a problem that had Finn catatonic with fear . . . and smiled, displaying the kind of teeth that apes only have on Frazetta covers for Tarzan books. For an instant, it felt smug—*I* felt smug. For a picosecond or two, the ape fantasized outcomes in which all of us survived except Finn, in which—just for once, oh, Lord!—I ended up with the girl I wanted.

And then I saw Mary looking at Finn, and I beat that ape to death with a club. Maybe Finn was paralyzed by fear, not because he was more of a coward than I, but because he knew more about the situation. Or faced more stringent penalties than I did. My smugness rested on ego, my courage on ignorance.

Why I mention it is this: There were no unburied hatchets in Callahan's Place—there never had been for very long. But now even the buried hatchets were starting to decompose underground, to rust away to nothing. I would always want Mary—but the best I could ever hope for would be to help her get what *she* wanted. I guess I was learning to live with that. Similar mini-epiphanies were happening all around the room.)

"But why should they give us *any* data?" Mary asked. "What's our leverage?"

"We've got data *they* want."

"We do?"

"Locked up between Finn's ears, I'm sure of it. I don't know what it is he knows; apparently he doesn't know either. But the bugs came one Jesus long way to learn it. They're a cowardly race; they don't go in person to any place that a scout has failed to report back from without some powerful motivation; that's why Finn is so baffled. Well, they can't be that curious about *us* because they don't know us from pond scum, so it *has* to be Finn. Something in his memory tapes is worth the risk. Maybe we can cut a deal."

"I wouldn't bet on it," the Drink said.

"McGonnigle, you are going to have to. Right now."

"Jake's right," Callahan said. "Unless anybody here knows how to disable a bunch of invisible satellites and convince NORAD to go to Defcon One within the next half hour, we haven't got much choice." He frowned. A telepathic frown itches. "Another thing. We have to call the Cockroaches *right away,* and get them to come directly here from Mars, as quietly as possible. If they just come look over the whole planet, NORAD *is* going to spot them—and find out that its ICBMs don't work anymore."

"So what?" several people asked.

"Suppose we resolve this Cockroach situation somehow—but meanwhile the joint chiefs find out that all their warheads are worthless. So do the Soviets. Unstable situation. And it leaves the USSR dominating Europe. Finn was right: his scheme only works if the players don't know about it. It's too late to undo the scheme, so we've got to go with it. That means the defense of Earth has to be handled in this room."

That brought a buzz of voices so sharp that it spilled over into the thing that we were building with the other ninety percent of our minds, sending a small ripple of discord through the sonic tapestry, as though there was a printer's error in the sheet music. And then was felt the presence of Lady Sally McGee, a warm, competent, reassuringly strong and calm voice in our heads.

"Lighten up, darlings! This is a party—we're here to usher in the new year! It turns out we'll have to actually *do* something to accomplish that for a change, but there's no reason we can't enjoy ourselves, is there? This could be fun! Now, I think it would be a good idea if all those without concrete useful suggestions were to shut the hell up."

Fast Eddie spoke up in the silence. "De foist t'ing we gotta do is hide Finn."

Even Callahan blinked. "Hide Finn?"

"He's de only card we got—so we slip it up our sleeve. Den we dummy up."

In my head I saw (and therefore everybody saw) a little cartoon, with word balloons and borders and crosshatching and everything, in which a comic caricature of a cockroach in a pressure suit spoke to Callahan: "*Where is Txffu Mpwfs?*" "Never heard of him." "*An extremely powerful and dangerous scout; he would have fought valiantly.*" "Sorry, haven't seen him." "*Then how is it that you seem to know who I am?*" "Oh, I've made a study of lower life forms—"

It did seem like a gambit with some distinct possibilities.

"Eddie, you're a genius," I said. "There's one hitch. Jim, Paul—can you lie telepathically?"

They looked troubled. "We could lie to you; we've got years more experience. To a mind as trained and experienced as ours—possibly. It would be like playing forty-two chess games at once: there's so much to *keep track of* in a telepathic lie. To an alien critter that's never touched a human mind before—," their eyes met briefly, "—no sweat."

"Maybe," Tommy Janssen said, "we should tell the Roaches we spotted Finn before he got near us and annihilated him—make us look more powerful, like."

Callahan shook his head. "Just wrong, son. That would make us the equals of a Cockroach. We're *superior*—we never even *noticed* Finn. Some little automatic system swept him up and we paid no mind; interstellar invasion didn't even make the papers." He grinned. "Yeah, I think maybe we could pull this off—for a few minutes, anyway. We might just put them enough off-balance to find out what we need to know."

Doc Webster spoke for all of us. "You're our spokesman, Mike."

He kept grinning and quoted Lord Buckley. " 'Well if I ain't, I'm a great big fat groovy pole on a rough hill on the way there.' Okay, while I'm planning the con, you boys hide Finn somewheres."

Gee, that sounds easy, doesn't it? I mean, compared to trying to map out a strategy for outsmarting alien monsters, hiding a guy doesn't sound like a big deal.

A guy who stands damn near seven feet tall and weighs about the same as a Harley-Davidson . . .

The best thought we had was to lay him down on the floor behind the bar, but the Cockroaches might very well burn their way in from above—and besides, Finn *snored*. In three stages.

Then I happened to think of what Finn's physique had always reminded me of. It was a chilly January night; we had plenty of coats. What cinched it was that his shirt had two breast pockets that snapped closed: coats hung from that low reached to the floor. When we were done, you could hardly hear the muffled snore; it sounded like a failing fridge compressor somewhere in the next room.

"How do we know the Roaches will hear a telepathic call?" Doc Webster asked worriedly.

"They will," Jim and Paul assured him. "They're not telepaths any more than you folks are, but they'll hear just as you did. We got their 'address-code' from Finn before he went bye-bye.''

"Are you sure you can reach them? Last I heard your range was still pretty limited—''

"That was years ago, Doc. And this time we have twice as many minds around to help drive the signal. We're within . . . uh . . . Roach's Limit.''

The Doc glared at them. "Obviously you don't understand the gravity of the situation.''

Telepathy has its drawbacks. Ordinarily most of us would have missed puns that esoteric.

"All right,'' Mary said, "by now they've finished checking out Mars and they're shaping orbit for Earth. How do we do this?''

"It breaks down into three parts,'' her father told her. "Message, target location, and delivery. Me and Jim/Paul'll do the talking. Mary, you and Josie and Joe and Ben and Stan savvy planetary ballistics: you folks aim the beam—you're in charge, darlin', you're the only one of us that's actually been off Earth. Jake, you and the rest of the gang push the message where it's pointed—the way we did back when we first met Jim, get it? Any questions?''

There were none.

"Okay, let's do it.''

Our music grew, built, swelled, gathered energy from nameless places and expanded in all directions, churned itself to a mighty crescendo, began to throb and pulse and crackle with contained power. As it did so, vision faded. Reality faded. Physically impossible though it was, suddenly we were all *touching* each other at the same time. I had been to an orgy once, and found it disappointing; this was what I had wanted it to be. It felt like what the Sixties had tried, and failed, to be. Like my childhood conception of the Catholic Heaven. Like making love with God.

The last time I'd been on this plane, helping Jim MacDonald to find and reach his lost, tormented, terrified brother Paul, it had been pleasurable, but not nearly this ecstatic. On that occasion, we had all perceived ourselves as standing behind an imaginary truck, stuck in an imaginary ditch, and had put our shoulders and backs into helping get it unstuck. There was no truck now, and whatever was in its place was not stuck—but in some fashion we *strained* now as we had strained then, put all our strength behind a massive, convulsive common effort.

We tried to hide that. Have you ever lifted a very heavy object in front of a stranger you wanted to impress, and tried not merely to lift the crushing weight, but to make it look easy? In just that fashion, we drew figurative breath, fashioned a mighty Shout—and then tried to couch it in quiet, conversational tones, as though we could shout much louder than that if we wanted to.

"This time period (*) is a second," we bellowed calmly. **"You have thirty of them in which to bargain for your life."**

In the instant that contact was established, we knew just how flimsy our bluff was.

There was only one Master. We didn't even know then just what a break that was. The telepathic aspect of the creature was largely untranslatable, but you might think of it manifesting as a kind of giant space-going shark, a moving appetite, a vast, fast, terrible eating-machine which saw its purpose to be turning everything edible in the universe into shark shit. Like a shark it was implacable, remorseless, unreachable. What made it much more terrible than any shark was that it was highly intelligent and very learned.

This doesn't begin to convey it. The thing was *alien,* and nothing on Terra is as old or cold or deadly as it was. If I'd been alone, I think I'd have snapped like a twig and begged it to kill me quickly. But Mike Callahan was with me, legs planted wide, thumbs hooked over his apron, jaw out-thrust challengingly . . . I could see him through my eyelids . . .

It must have known telepathic races in the past; mental contact did not startle it. Its answering "voice" was no "louder" than ours, but it really *was* sending at the low end of its strength—it was much more powerful than we combined were. But it didn't know that— we bluffed it!

"WHO ARE YOU THAT A MASTER SHOULD BARGAIN WITH YOU FOR ITS LIFE?"

"—twenty-nine—" Callahan said for all of us.

"STATE YOUR ASKING PRICE."

"One: full and candid disclosure of your purpose and intentions here. Two: your promise not to disturb any sentient in this system. Three: your immediate departure. Four: your promise never to return unsummoned."

None of this was in English. That is, it left Callahan's mind as English but passed through the minds of Jim and Paul, who knew as much of the Masters' language as Finn did, and by hearing it through their "ears," we understood it independent of any grammar or vocabulary. The English of it doesn't begin to convey the monstrous arrogance of the bluff Mike was running.

"NO MASTER HAS EVER BEEN 'SUMMONED.' I GO WHERE I LIST, AND DISTURB ALL WHO PERCEIVE ME. WHAT—"

"Countdown resumes. Twenty-eight—," Mike interrupted— and a telepathic interruption is ruder than any other kind, I think.

I tried to imagine the situation from the creature's perspective. Humans were sufficiently advanced as a race to be able to hang out a telepathic No Trespassing sign for it, seemed completely unawed by its own majestic power—yet they restricted themselves to a single planet, of a single star system, and the only technology visible thereon seemed primitive. They were either suicidally brave—or they had something up their sleeves. The Masters were, as Finn had told us, remorselessly logical: its safest move was to play along until such time as it determined positively that we were bluffing, and *then* implode our planet, leaving no witnesses to its humiliation.

But it *hated* acknowledging any non-Master life form as an equal, even as a bargaining ploy. Mike got all the way down to twenty-five—and my heart got about three-quarters of the way up my esophagus—when it said:

"IT SUITS ME TO DIVULGE MY PURPOSE HERE. SUBSEQUENTLY, WE MAY DETERMINE TOGETHER WHETHER ITS FULFILLMENT WILL DISTURB LOCAL SENTIENTS AND THE PROBABLE TIME OF MY DEPARTURE."

"Speak. And make it snappy."

"I SEEK A MISSING SLAVE. SENT TO SCOUT THIS SYSTEM, IT FAILED TO REPORT BACK. I SEEK IT, OR ITS REMAINS. ONCE I HAVE IT, I HAVE NO FURTHER INTEREST IN REMAINING OR RE-TURNING HERE."

"Good-bye, then. Neither your slave nor its remains are here."

You might reasonably translate the Master's reply as "SHARK-SHIT." It had raised its "voice" slightly: it was getting angry.

We kept our tone level. "—Twenty-four—"

When I was a kid in school, I always sat in the back of the classroom. If things got too boring, I'd do a Slow Fade. You move your desk back and to the right imperceptibly slowly, about six inches per minute, toward the back door and out into the hall. If you do it slowly enough, the teacher never notices you leave. In a similar manner, Paul MacDonald began now to withdraw from the thing we had all built in Callahan's Place, without advertising his departure. It helped that his brother's telepathic aspect was so nearly identical to his own. I don't think anyone else noticed—maybe they never played Slow Fade—and I kept my own realization from the common awareness, did my best not to think about it even to myself. While we were talking to the front of the alien's mind, Paul was sneaking around the back . . .

"THE SLAVE WAS WELL-DEFENDED," it was saying. "I CAN BELIEVE YOU OVERCAME IT; BUT IF SO IT WOULD HAVE BEEN A MEMORABLE EVENT."

"Perhaps for one such as you," Callahan agreed. "Our automatic defenses are capable, and do not require our attention."

"THEN WHY ARE YOU SPEAKING TO *ME?*"

"AMUSED CURIOSITY. YOUR MIND IS SINGULARLY UGLY."

Oddly, it did not take offense. Every entity it had ever met in its centuries of existence had feared it; it did not know how to react to a direct insult. But it *did* get angrier—because we were wasting its time. "EVEN IF YOU HAD ANNIHILATED THE SLAVE, THERE WOULD HAVE BEEN A COMPONENT LEFT, INDESTRUCTIBLE BY ANY KNOWN FORCE. IT WOULD HAVE BEEN LOCATED HERE—" It sent a sort of three-dimensional X-ray picture of Finn's head, and clearly visible beneath and behind his right ear, between skull and brain, was a little nodule that looked like a marble. "IT IS A DATAFILE CONTAINING EVERYTHING PERCEIVED BY THE SLAVE SINCE ITS LAST MILKING. I REQUIRE IT IMMEDIATELY."

"You grow boring," Callahan said. "Countdown resumes—"

"I WILL TEAR APART YOUR STAR!"

Callahan made no reply. He made a throat-cutting gesture to us, and we broke the connection.

There was no chatter. Less than half a minute on the countdown, on our bluff.

"What did you get, Paul?" Callahan snapped, and I became aware for the first time that Paul MacDonald was back among us telepathically as well as physically. He tended to "blend in" with Jim's aspect, like an echo, which was why it had been possible for him to get away with a Slow Fade.

He made a convulsive mental effort, and did something like a file memory dump, sending information in a block rather than bit by bit, to all of us at once. In a matter of a second, we knew everything he had learned. Grasping it took me a few seconds more.

I have to put it in figurative terms. A lot of this stuff doesn't go into words; worse, the memories turn insubstantial as I try to translate them. Paul had sneaked in an unguarded back window of the creature's mind, while we occupied it at the front door. He had strolled around in some of the mustier back files of an immense storehouse of memories for a matter of whole seconds, teaching himself how to understand the operating language, the file-finder system, the retrieval commands—reconnoitering while keeping a low profile. He didn't get all he'd hoped for, he ran out of seconds, but Paul was a seasoned professional at tiptoeing through human minds, and he came away with more from this alien mind than I would have believed possible.

The majority of what he learned was incomprehensible or irrelevant or otherwise useless. The creature's name, to pick a basic example, was utterly untranslatable. We could no longer think of it as a Cockroach, and like Mary we refused to call it a Master. We reached an instant group consensus on what to call it: The Beast. (And hoped that we had its number.)

The Beast was a pervert. Don't ask me to describe what kind of pervert it was, or what constituted "normal" for its race. I don't want to think about either one. Please just take my word for it that it was, by its own lights, disgusting. It was *not* ashamed of itself. Shame is a kind of self-hatred, and no Master is capable of hating— or loving—itself. But it did wish strongly that it could be other than it was, and that is as close as such a being can come to shame. (Not close enough, in my opinion.)

Its perversion had recently become known to its kind. Social faux pas on a cosmic scale: it was now and forever an outcast, a renegade, to be slain on sight. Its slaves had been reprogrammed to others. It was alone. To one of its race this fate was simply intolerable. Masters cannot live in Coventry. This is weird, since they are not a gregarious race under the best of circumstances. They don't need each other's *attention*, the way humans do, but they positively require each other's *respect*. The Beast had exactly two psychologically feasible alternatives; to suicide, or declare war on its entire race.

In the billion or so years of Master-recorded history, only a very few of the very few outcasts had ever chosen the latter alternative, and their names were metaphoric symbols for evil itself. But The Beast was a *real* pervert.

It was also a logical pervert. No force or combination of forces it knew could seriously threaten its race. But it wasn't (The Beast was prepared, being a pervert, to admit to itself) strictly true that *everything* was known to the Masters. For instance, once in a very long time (even by Master standards), a scout slave failed to report back. Scouts were so heavily armed and defended that it was difficult to imagine anything capable of destroying one before it could get off a report. (No Master in the Universe was permitted to be as heavily armed as a typical scout, since a Master, unlike a slave, could bring himself to turn a weapon on another Master. I know that doesn't make sense in human terms. Very little about the Masters does.) An AWOL scout meant either that someone had destroyed it, someone who could perhaps be used, or that the scout had—incredibly—malfunctioned in some way, in which case its own weaponry might be salvageable.

The risk was horrible. A Master is not defended as well as a scout either.

It was a mad gamble, and The Beast knew it, but it was a pervert and doomed. Desperate and raging, it had followed the trail of Txffu Mpwfs across the big empty spaces to the place where he was known as Mickey Finn, hoping to find some terrorweapon it could use to avenge itself, and found . . . a bunch of barflies, a few time-traveling Micks, two telepathic psychiatrists and a talking dog. Callahan's Bar on New Year's Eve.

"All right," Callahan said in our heads as we finished assimilating the burst of largely useless data that included this, "we've got it right where we want it. At T-minus ten seconds, we tell it we've changed our minds: we're not going to kill it after all. It's too disgusting to kill. We're going to ignore it—and call the other Masters and demand that they come remove their garbage from our system at once. That should—"

He screamed then, with his mind and with his throat. I don't suppose I'd ever thought to hear Mike Callahan scream. I didn't hear the physical scream, of course, because sounds drown each other out and I and everyone else in the room were screaming, too, but mental screams *don't* drown each other out, each one registered with individual clarity. Amazing that I had time to register such trivia, with The Beast loose in my brain . . .

*　　*　　*

"ENTROPY!"

The beast was very angry; that was the strongest curse it knew.

"JUST AS I FEARED! IT WAS NOT A WEAPON WHICH DISABLED TXFFU MPWFS, BUT A DISEASE. THAT 'LOVE' FUNGUS. USELESS TO ME!"

Paul hadn't been as careful as he thought. We should have remembered: Finn thought faster than a human being; so would his Masters. Probably they thought even faster than him.

In the instant of opening communication we had told The Beast the rate at which we processed information—by establishing a second as a significant interval for us—and it had been outthinking us ever since. It had had plenty of time to spot Paul stumbling around in the back of its brain, without alerting him. It had learned a great deal about telepathy from him, and then had hidden in his pocket, as it were, and been brought back home by him. His data broadcast had opened us all up, allowed The Beast to access our files and study *us*. Our cover was blown sky-high. Jim and Paul MacDonald were effectively dead, their minds torn out, their personalities annihilated, their bodies and brains kept alive to serve The Beast as a telepathic transceiver.

I was caught. Swallowed by The Beast. Damn it, it was *just* like being swallowed by a Beast, the size of the one that got Pinocchio. My surroundings went away, my telepathic companions went away, my eyes and my mind found black nothingness in all directions—I tried to cast around with my arms and discovered that I could not find my body anymore. The audible screams, including my own, were now inaudible; so were the mental ones. There was just the Master and me. All my strings were cut.

"OR PERHAPS NOT *ENTIRELY* USELESS AFTER ALL," it went on thoughtfully. "I SEE POSSIBILITIES . . ."

I snapped, shrieked at him: "*Motherfucker!*" It seemed to echo.

"IT IS A MINOR COMPONENT OF MY PERVERSION THAT I AM NOT. YOU OUGHT TO TRY TO ENJOY YOUR CONSCIOUSNESS. THE ONE YOU CALL FINN WILL WAKE, AND THEN I WILL OWN IT AGAIN, AND THEN YOUR CONSCIOUSNESS WILL CEASE. SOON, AS YOU RECKON TIME: YOU HAVE NO TIME TO WASTE."

"When Mick wakes up you're gonna be the first Shark that ever got killed by his own Finn!" I only half-believed it, but I badly needed that half. My sanity hung from it.

"I CONCEDE THAT IT HAS DISOBEYED PROGRAMMING AN UN-PRECEDENTED NUMBER OF TIMES—ONCE, FOR AN INTERVAL MEASURABLE IN YOUR GREAT LONG SECONDS." Dimly I knew somehow that The Beast was not talking only to me, but talking privately to each of us, by time-sharing at a horrendous rate, the way a TV tube redraws each line of pixels so quickly that you never see them disappear. "IT WILL NOT DO SO AGAIN."

"Finn loves us!" I cried, while thinking, *Finn loves* one *of us*. "Even if he didn't, he'd fight you—because you're evil!"

"HOW AM I EVIL?"

"You're a murderer!"

"INCORRECT. I HAVE NEVER KILLED ANY SENTIENT ENTITY."

"You and your kind killed Finn's entire race!"

"INCORRECT. WE HAVE NEVER KILLED ANY RACE."

"Fuck you. Mick told us the truth."

"CORRECT. YOU MISUNDERSTOOD IT. ITS RACE IS NOT DEAD, MERELY IN STORAGE. IT TOLD YOU THAT EACH OF ITS PEOPLE HAS BEEN RECORDED ON A MOLECULE OF ITS OWN, DOWN TO THE LAST MEMORY. ALL WE KILLED WERE CELLS, AS YOU DO WHEN YOU PARE YOUR OWN FINGERNAILS. THE ESSENCE OF FINN'S PEOPLE, THEIR CONSCIOUSNESS AND MEMORIES AND GE-NETIC PATTERNS, ARE NOT ENDED. THEY COULD BE RECREATED AT ANY INSTANT, A TRIVIAL MATTER OF SYNTHESIZING ENOUGH PROTEIN. THEY ARE NOT DEAD, MERELY DISPLACED IN TIME. LIKE MICHAEL CALLAHAN."

Oof.

"IT IS A SHAME THAT THE METHOD HE USES TO TRAVEL IN TIME IS UNSUITABLE FOR MASTERS—THAT WOULD BE A MIGHTY WEAPON INDEED. I MUST GIVE THOUGHT TO ADAPTING IT—"

"You're worse than a murderer," I yelled. "You're a *slaver*, and an arrogant pervert!" Dimly it occurred to me that a videotape recording of the interior of Callahan's Place at this moment must look pretty strange: a roomful of people apparently hollering abuse at each other. Or was I actually yelling, with my throat? I tried to figure out how to regain control of my senses, groping around in the dark for the controls.

"DOES YOUR RACE NOT ENSLAVE CHIMPANZEES AND DOL-PHINS, THOUGH THEY ARE CLEARLY SENTIENT? AND WORSE, DO NOT MEMBERS OF YOUR SPECIES ROUTINELY ENSLAVE *EACH OTHER*? THIS IS PERVERTED ENOUGH TO REVOLT EVEN ME: IN ALL OF TIME, NO MASTER HAS EVER DONE SUCH A THING."

Damn him, he was getting to me, he kept poking little holes in all my postulates, undermining my moral position and turning my righteous anger into nothing more than the helpless rage of the victim. I tried to ignore him as I struggled to invest my body again.

"CAN YOU, INCIPIENT ALCOHOLIC WHO ARE ATTRACTED ONLY TO FAT WOMEN AND ARE COMFORTABLE ONLY HERE IN THIS ROOM WITH PSYCHOLOGICAL CRIPPLES LIKE YOURSELF, CALL ME A PERVERT? AS FOR ARROGANCE, CAN YOU, WHO KILLED YOUR FAMILY TO SAVE A FEW DOLLARS AND SHOW OFF IMAGINARY MECHANICAL COMPETENCE, CALL ME ARROGANT?"

My universe of blackness began spinning around me. Don't ask me how blackness can spin. I had to make it stop or I would go yammering insane, and the only way to do that was to get my eyes open. Damn it, I had lived in this goddamn skull all my life, navigated my way around it blind drunk, done a cold-restart of all systems after thousands of interludes of natural or unnatural unconsciousness—why the hell couldn't I tell where anything *was?*

Let's see. The ears should be the simplest; fewer bits of data to integrate than eyes. First get hearing back, then go for the big stuff. Sound off, ears, I can't see you.

"I HAVE NEARLY REACHED YOU NOW. SOON I WILL BE PHYSICALLY PRESENT, AND ABLE TO RESTART THE SLAVE FINN."

"He'll find a way to beat you. He won't let his wife down!"

There was a sort of far-off rumbling. Miles away up its alimentary canal, The Beast was grinning. "I WILL PROMISE HIM THAT IF HE HELPS ME TO . . . *RECORD* YOU ALL, AND FIGHTS MY WAR FOR ME, I WILL REVIVE HIS PEOPLE, AND GIVE THEM A PLANET TO USE AS THEY WISH. THIS ONE WILL DO ADMIRABLY. HE WILL COOPERATE."

No, damn it, it was *not* a faraway, metaphorical rumbling. It was close by, and real. My hearing was coming back—

—and The Beast was burning his way through the roof of Callahan's Place.

"I WILL GIVE YOU A RIDDLE," it went on conversationally. "THERE IS A RACE OF CREATURES ON THIS PLANET WHICH IS CLOSELY RELATED TO MY OWN, THOUGH MUCH DEGENERATED FROM THE PURE STOCK. A SMALL GROUP OF THESE CREATURES COULD EASILY KILL ONE OF YOU, YET NONE HAVE EVER DONE SO: THEIR WORST 'CRIME' IS THAT, LIKE EVERYTHING ELSE IN

YOUR ECOSYSTEM, THEY COMPETE WITH YOU FOR FOOD—AND LOSE IN THE COMPETITION, EVERY TIME. THESE CREATURES ARE CLEARLY AND UNMISTAKABLY SENTIENT. YET YOU SLAUGHTER THEM EVERY TIME YOU ENCOUNTER THEM, BY THE VILEST MEANS KNOWN TO YOU. CAN YOU NAME THESE ENTITIES? AND CAN YOU, IN LIGHT OF THIS INFORMATION, STILL CONSIDER *ME* EVIL?"

I heard scattered crashes, felt distant pain, understood that one of my friends had been hurt by a falling piece of burning ceiling.

"I AM HERE," The Beast said. "AH—YOU ARE EVEN UGLIER IN PERSON THAN YOU ARE IN YOUR MINDS. STRANGE THAT ONES SO AWKWARDLY AND PRECARIOUSLY CONSTRUCTED COULD BE SO COURAGEOUS. YOUR ATTEMPTED BLUFF WAS SPLENDID; IT MIGHT HAVE WORKED AGAINST ONE AS SLOW-WITTED AS YOUR-SELVES. I SHALL TREASURE YOUR RECORDINGS."

Dear God—how many minutes or seconds could there be left before the mickey finn wore off Mickey Finn and it was all over? Before the whole human race was *stopped*, recorded, frozen like six billion flies in amber for whatever portion of eternity pleased The Beast? Would we ever be revived? If so, would Terra still hold the resources to support technology, the food to support life? Would Sol still burn?

"NOW THAT I AM HERE, THERE IS NO NEED TO WAIT FOR THE SLAVE FINN TO REVIVE NATURALLY. I SHALL DO A SYSTEM FLUSH AND REBOOT IT MANUALLY . . ."

Dimly I heard several voices whimpering, realized that one of them was my own and therefore that my voice was working again.

"Mike!" I screamed. *"Mary! Sally! Help me!"*

And things happened very suddenly then.

Or rather, things had been happening very suddenly, and came to fruition all at once.

The Beast thought very fast, much faster than any of us could hope to, and it had that time-sharing thing down cold. But no one present in the room, including The Beast, knew as much about time as Mike Callahan. Callahan, who carried himself and his wife and daughter through time, without the support of any external hard-ware . . .

The Beast was carrying on over a hundred conversations at once, like a chess master playing a hundred opponents at once. Every few dozen picoseconds it got back to Mike's "table," and the big Irishman was always there. But in between, he was *elsewhen,* in a quiet, safe space-and-time where he could think things over and plan at his leisure. Leisure enough to work a lot of things out, and to come up with the swiftest and most elegant solution.

He restored our vision.

I saw my friends, and rejoiced. Seeing them, I could hear again in my head the vast thrumming music that we made, feel their support. I saw the far wall of Callahan's Place, the glass-strewn fireplace, flames dancing crazily, whipped by chilly winds that howled in through the space where the ceiling used to be. I knew I was looking at The Beast, we were all triangulating on its signal, but I could not see it anywhere. Was the damned thing invisible?

I blinked, and now I saw it. It had been there all along. Standing proud and arrogant before the fireplace, The Beast, the shark, the Master, the terrible entity that Mary Finn called a Cockroach.

It was a cockroach. In a little cockroach pressure suit . . .

The room exploded in laughter, the loudest, merriest belly laugh that had ever rung the rafters of Callahan's Place, back when the Place had still had rafters . . .

It was about twice the size of the biggest cockroach you've ever seen in your life—unless you live in New York; it would have aroused no comment at all on the Lower East Side. Now I understood the puzzle it had mentioned, and now I understood for the first time humanity's instinctive, unreasoned loathing of *periplaneta Americana,* one of the oldest life forms on Earth. Cockroaches were distant, long-lost cousins of a galactic obscenity . . .

We had to laugh at the true visage of the thing which had so terrified us, terrifying though it genuinely was, and our laughter momentarily undid the creature. For a subjective duration equivalent to that of a trillion-year-old human, it had ruled supreme over all the life forms it had ever encountered. We looked upon its awful majesty and roared and howled and hooted with uncontrollable mirth, and it stood rooted in place for an interval long enough to be perceptible by a human, paralyzed by mortified rage. (Through my head came a line from C. S. Lewis's *Screwtape Letters*: "The devil cannot abide to be mocked.") Its mental control over us snapped and was gone.

In the instant that we saw it, we laughed, and in the instant that we laughed, we stopped fearing it so much, and in the instant that our fear abated, our minds began working again, generating the obvious, logical question:

Why is it talking so much?

Why had the damned bug bothered to devote the attention and energy necessary for its time-sharing tour de force, merely to argue with us about the moral merits and deficiencies of our respective positions, insult us, and pose riddles?

It was trying to distract us from something.

Somewhere in our collective awareness were the tools we needed to defeat it. And realizing that much, we now knew what they were.

The solution was drastic, but it was the only one we had. Nothing good, they say, comes without sacrifice.

It was Noah Gonzalez who had been struck by a falling piece of ceiling; while that had not hurt him, the burning beam had knocked him sideways and then set his arm afire; it was on the rare side of medium rare and quite useless. That made me the nearest effective, and I knew what I needed to do. So did everyone else; as one they moved together and formed a screen between me and The Beast. Except Mary, who grabbed the coat rack and held on, and Callahan, who did the same with his Lady Sally. Our song rose to a final, indescribable hundred-note chord that rang in my skull and filled my heart with joy. We all closed our eyes.

And I reached into Noah's open airline bag and rolled the fuse-timer back to quadruple-zero.

Invisible hands slapped me, as hard as I've ever been slapped, over every inch of my body at once—including my eardrums, which went dead. At the same time someone kicked the world violently away from me and spun me end over end. My body was rigid as stone, petrified in the act of reaching into the airline bag. Even with my eyes closed I saw bright while light strobe as I rotated. Then I was slapped hard again, principally on the ass, and after a timeless interval I could see and hear and move again.

I sat up and looked around.

I was in deep woods, in the dark, surrounded by shattered branches. The bright white light must still be going on, but it was somewhere else, and the only illumination was feeble moonlight through the branches overhead.

I felt numb. Shell-shocked.

Branches rustled nearby. I got to my feet like a very old man made of cornflakes and roofing glue, and followed the sounds. Even before I reached him I knew who it was. I smelled the cigar.

"*Mike!*"

His deep merry chuckle came through the darkness. "Howdy, Jake. Nice work."

"Uh . . . thanks. Where's Sally?"

"Looking around for Mary and Mick. Listen: there's somebody else. *Hey—over here!*"

The newcomer was Noah. "Hey there, Mike. Good thing you had me go back for the bag. Hi, Jake—you did that great!"

"Thanks, Noah. Uh, how's the arm?" Even in my numbness I could grasp just how horrid it must be for a man who has lost a leg to watch his arm burn.

"I'd rather not think about it if you don't mind."

"C'mere," Callahan said. He examined Noah's broiled wing in the darkness somehow, then touched Noah on the shoulder in a complicated way. "It's fixable."

"Jesus," Noah exclaimed. "You fixed it, Mike."

"Hell no—that's just a nerve block. But don't worry—Sal'll fix it up for you as soon as things quiet down a little. C'mon, let's go find her."

"Mike," Noah asked, "how come a nuclear explosion didn't hurt us, but I got my arm burned?"

"Finn specifically protected you folks against blast forces and hard radiation. He never thought to include fire."

"Then why didn't the nuke *burn* us?"

"For the same reason straws got blown through brick walls at Hiroshima instead of burning up: they outran the heat."

Jesus Christ. And here I'd been thinking that I was invulnerable. I pictured myself trapped in a wrecked car—unharmed, conscious, and broiling slowly.

The way my wife and child had been . . .

We let Callahan lead us through the woods. Dimly I worked it out that this was the forest to the north of Callahan's Place. "Hey, Noah," I said as we walked, "aren't you going to get in trouble for borrowing that nuke?"

He chuckled in the dark. "Are you kidding? I saved 'em Police Headquarters, and cost 'em a roadside tavern—they'll probably give me a fucking medal."

At the edge of the forest we came upon Lady Sally McGee and

her daughter and son-in-law. Mickey Finn was awake now, surrounded by a large pile of coats. Mary, I recalled, had learned from The Beast how to manually revive Mick, something about an override bloodstream-flush—or perhaps he'd simply come out of it naturally. *You just can't get a better alarm clock than an atom bomb,* I thought dizzily. The moment they saw us, Mary came at a gallop, caught me up in her strong blacksmith's arms, and purely kissed the hell out of me. It was at least as disorienting as being at ground zero had been, but this time only a portion of my body went rigid . . .

"Oh, Jake, you *did* it! You were *beautiful!* My hero!"

I was banjaxed, out for luncheon, voiceless and mindless, for the first time in my life caught without a wisecrack behind which to take refuge.

She turned to her husband, now the most powerful being within several hundred light years. "Mick?"

"Of course, darling."

"Thanks, hon. Meantime, why don't you and Mom and Pop gather up the rest of the family? We'll meet you over there by the big power-tower."

"Yes, dear. Jake? Thank you. You have done something I could not have done. You have saved me, and Mary, and all our family. No, do not speak. I know it was mere chance that you were closest, that others here, perhaps all, would have done the same. But it was you who did it. I owe you everything."

He and the others took off vertically, like helicopters, and disappeared into the night. Along with them went all of the coats except for mine and Mary's.

And Mary began to undress me . . .

I am in a position to state categorically that a nuclear explosion at arm's length can be a comparatively trivial event.

". . . Mary?"

"Yes, Jake?"

"That was just like the last time."

She sighed contentedly and snuggled closer under my coat. "Yeah."

"No, I mean . . . that was a kind of good-bye."

"Yes, darling Jake. So was this. Our work is done here. Mom

and Pop and I will be leaving soon. We're needed elsewhen. And Mick needs maintenance he can't get in this era.''

To my surprise, I was unsurprised, and undismayed. ''I thought so. It was a great good-bye. They both were. You're never coming back?''

''Never is a long time.''

''I'll miss you.''

''Thank you. I'll miss you too, Jake. You really are a hero, you know. Triggering a nuclear explosion, on the unsubstantiated word of a time-traveling fat lady that it was safe—that took guts. We only had a second—if you'd frozen up, I would have had to self-destruct Mick . . . and *none* of us could have survived that. Let's join the others, now—it's time.''

''Yeah.'' I found my clothes and put them back on. Perhaps it had been her husband's brand of magic or something from her own time, but it was only when I was fully dressed again that I remembered it was January, and noticed how *cold* it was out here.

As we approached the LILCO power-tower around which all my friends were clustered, my attention was seized by the distant fading glow, and the heavy cloud that hung just above it. Contrary to my expectation, it was not mushroom-shaped—the bomb hadn't been big enough—but suddenly I was stopped in my tracks by the re-alization of what it represented. I'd known all along, of course, but I'd been too disoriented for it to sink in.

''Oh my God, no. Please—*no!*''

Callahan's Place was gone. Not a particle of it was left, not the fireplace or the cigar box or Fast Eddie's piano or Mary's beautiful spiral staircase.

God's golden gonads, *Lady Macbeth had been in there!*

Mary's hand was clutching mine. ''Jake, Jake! It's all *right*—truly it is!''

''Oh, Mary, you don't understand! I could stand losing you. I can survive—somehow—without Lady Macbeth. I could even stand a world without Mike Callahan in it. But a world that doesn't have Callahan's Place in it is a world I don't want to live in. I *can't.*''

''Yes, you can.''

''No, I can't!''

''Jake, listen to me now. Stop crying and *listen!* I know it's dark, but try to watch my lips.''

I tried to stop crying, and watched her lips.

''Jake, dear Jake, you don't need Callahan's Place anymore. And

I'll tell you why. I *couldn't* tell you before, or you might have stopped coming to the Place and Mom and Pop assured me you were going to be necessary. Jake, a lot of things about the past can't be changed, even by us time-travelers. I can't explain why in any terms you'd understand, so you'll just have to take my word for it. But many things we can at least *see*—see them happening, see them *have happened,* call it what you like." She paused and bit her lip.

"So what are you telling me?"

She hesitated, and blurted it out. "Jake, I've seen Barbara and Jessica die!"

"What?"

"I thought—there was just—I wanted to see if I couldn't find some way to save them for you. I knew there wasn't any way, but I just had to try—"

In my mind's eye I saw it all again, the little piece of film that I've rerun in my head a million times, the way it must have looked to an outside observer on the scene. The last minutes before the crash are gone from my memory, forever if God is kind, but I have read the police reconstruction and I have a very good imagination.

The car approaches the intersection at slightly higher than legal speed. The light is just going yellow, and the driver decides to beat it. Barely in time, he sees the sixteen-wheeler approaching the intersection from the left, realizes the trucker has decided to gamble too, and slams on his brakes. He has an instant to congratulate himself on his excellent peripheral vision and superb reflexes, before he realizes that the rear brakes he installed himself the day before are failing and he will not stop in time after all. Then the vehicles collide, and the engine block enters the passenger compartment at an angle, trapping the woman and child who sit beside the driver, drenching them in gasoline. The car spins crazily, trips itself and rolls end over end, comes to rest upright. All three occupants are unconscious, and two of them are on fire . . .

Mary was shaking me by the shoulders, hard enough to crack my neck, shouting something that ended with, "—by the crash, you skinny stupid son of a bitch!"

"Huh?"

"I *said,* the springs the accident report says were found hanging loose in the rear brakes were *snapped* loose by the crash. *It was the front brakes that failed*—I saw it with my own eyes! Did you hear me *that* time?"

I was baffled. "But I didn't put in front brakes, Mary," I said mildly.

"Ah, you did hear me. That's right, dopey, you didn't! The front brakes were done by the dealer who sold you the car."

I snorted. "Come on, Mary—the insurance investigator could never have missed something like that—"

"He missed it for two reasons. One, you were so damned insistent on hogging any guilt there was to be had. And two, he is related by marriage to the car dealer. That's something you can check on, if you don't believe me."

Enough is enough. Even a certified hero such as myself has limitations. I did the only sensible thing: I fainted.

When I woke, all my friends were gathered around me, and I was snug and warm beneath a scavenged tarp. It was still dark, but I made out Doc Webster, and Long-Drink McGonnigle, and Tommy Janssen and Tom Hauptman and the three Masers and Fast Eddie and the Cheerful Charlies and Ralph Von Wau Wau and all the rest of my family. For a moment there I swear I thought I saw Tom Flannery's ghost.

I felt more peaceful than I ever had in my life.

"It's time, Jake," Fast Eddie said. "Dey're leavin'."

"Sure thing, Eddie," I said. "Help me up."

Callahan and Sally and Mary and Finn were standing by the base of the tower. Josie Bauer was with them.

"Hi, Josie," I said. "You going too?"

"Hell yes," she said. "Us time-travelers have to stick together. I can't wait to find out how Mike's people do it without hardware."

Callahan cleared his throat. "Time to go," he rumbled. "If we get started on hugs and good-byes we'll all still be here when the universe winds down. There's no way, even in my time, to thank you all for all the good times. You know I love you, so let's just—"

"Just a second, Mike," I said.

"Sure, Jake. What is it?"

"Am I correct in guessing that Michael Callahan is not your real name?"

"Of course it is."

"Well, in this space-time, sure—but I mean, it isn't the name you were born with, is it?"

"Naw. My folks named me after a remote ancestor they admired—except that we don't use last names when I come from, so I only got half his name. But what's the difference, Jake? You told me once you never look at the corpse during a wake, because you prefer remembering folks the way they were when they were alive. This is like that: why would you want to remember me as anything but 'Mike Callahan'?"

"You're right. I guess I was just being nosy."

Suddenly he grinned. "Well, I shouldn't indulge you—but I believe I will. Leave you jokers with one last pun, as bad as any you ever laid in my bar. Now I think about it, it's too good to pass up."

He spat his cigar onto the frozen ground, squared his big broad shoulders and looked slowly round at all of us. His twinkling gaze rested longest on me and the Doc and the Drink.

"When I was born," he said, "I was known as Justin."

I blinked. "You mean," I said, "you were—?" and then I was laughing too hard to speak.

"You—" Doc Webster began, and then he lost it too.

Long-Drink McGonnigle never even got out the first syllable; his braying laugh reverberated in the chilly night air like the cackling of a lunatic.

And so it was left to Fast Eddie Costigan to say it.

"Jeez. You wuz Justin, de Mick o' Time."

And as the night rocked with laughter and cheers Mike Callahan and his family and Josie vanished. Gone to Harmony, somewhere up the line . . .

Even the greatest rocking, hooting, sidesplitting hundred-person good-bye-and-godspeed laugh has to end sometime, and when it did there was a silence that lasted nearly a full minute. We just stood there in the darkness, not ready to go yet, nothing to say, trying together to integrate the events of the evening. So much to encompass—too much.

Finally Doc Webster cleared his throat. "Ladies and gentlemen," he said in a more subdued voice than usual, "in the instant before the balloon went up, I did the best I could." He held up something that gurgled. "I clutched this here quart of Bushmill's to my belly, around on the side away from the blast, and held on. Fortunately, it seems I landed on my back.'' People started to work up a cheer, but the Doc silenced them with a raised hand and went on. ''I estimate that we could clear a sip apiece, and so I am proposing a toast. I drink to Paul and James MacDonald.'' He took a small sip and passed the bottle to me. ''Their bodies died when The Beast did. I saw Mick cremate 'em.''

I felt a pang. We all did, I guess. I had mourned the MacDonalds in the moment of their dying and had not thought of them since. I had come to know them impossibly well in an impossibly short time, and know I knew all there would ever be to know of them. They had been *good* men, had never once yielded to the temptation to exploit their freak gift for personal gain, had devoted their lives to healing hurt minds, and had fought valiantly on behalf of a race that would probably have torn them to pieces if it had known their secret. Now they were dead, and it had taken us the better part of half an hour to remember them.

''To Paul and Jim,'' I said, drank and gave the bottle to Eddie.

It went around the gathering, and every man and woman present toasted and drank, and by the time it reached the last man, Long-Drink McGonnigle, we pretty much all had tears frozen to our faces.

''To the MacDonalds,'' he said. Then he looked up past the drifting cloud of fallout to the stars and he said, solemnly and most respectfully, ''Lord, they deserve a break today.''

Those of us who were religious all chorused, ''Amen,'' and those of us who weren't wished, for that moment, that we were.

A few moments of silence. Then a few more. Most of us were poorly dressed for the cold, but no one complained. No one even shivered.

We were all, I knew, thinking back to—Jesus, less than an hour ago!—to long ago and far away in another universe, when we had all, for a timeless but all too short interval, been one. It didn't seem fair, somehow. We'd been on the trembling verge, at the threshold of something for which all the humans who ever lived have yearned in vain all their lives—it would have taken Armageddon to distract us, and sure enough that was what we had gotten.

So we had staved off Armageddon. Now the shining moment was past. The MacDonalds who had married us were dead. The Callahans who had raised us and given us away were gone. The nest, the brightly lit cave that had contained us, entertained us, and sustained us, was a radioactive hole in the ground.

We were still married. The thing we had forged while in telepathic rapport could not be undone—we knew each other too well, we *had* to be married. But like many newlyweds, we woke feeling oddly like strangers. Like many married people, we had gotten *so* close to one another that we had learned just how far apart we would always be.

I could no longer hear clearly in my head the music we had made . . .

"There'll never be another night like that," Tommy Janssen said wistfully.

Deep inside me somewhere, something that had been under strain for many years suddenly snapped clean through.

"The *hell* you say!"

"Jake," the Doc began, "all the boy means is—"

"I know what he means, Sam. I know what you mean. Do you know what *I* mean?"

I whirled and addressed the group, in a voice that may have been unnecessarily loud.

"All right. We're all locked back in our personal skulls again. We haven't got a pair of trained telepaths to make it easy for us this time. None of us has whatever genetic mutation made Jim and Paul's telepathic ability so powerful, made it so easy for them to access it—so easy that it nearly killed them before they got it under control, you may recall.

"But we know that we have telepathic potential too.

"We were one, damn it! Even after the MacDonalds died, right up until the instant the bomb went up, we were one. That wasn't the roach doing that, or the inside of my head would feel slimy. Jim and Paul led us to that place, but we were able to stay there without them, for a time at least. Maybe Callahan helped us, maybe Sally and Mary helped us, but we were doing some of it ourselves. The damned roach wasn't a telepath when it got here, but it sure-god learned the trick in less than twenty seconds. I know twenty seconds to it was like twenty years to us—but *I've got twenty years I'm not using.* What about you people?"

"How do you learn to be a telepath, Jake?" Marty Matthias asked.

"Hell, Marty, Callahan's been training us for years! Now we've got to start figuring it out for ourselves, that's all. To approach telepathy, you start with empathy and crank that up as high as you can. You care about each other. You feel each other's joy and pain. You make each other laugh, and help each other cry. You work hard at trusting each other, so that it's safe to dismantle the fortress around your ego. You forgive each other anything that stands between you, and try to bring out each other's best, you work very hard at hosing all the bullshit out of your head so that it's clean enough for guests, silencing all the demons in your subconscious so that it's quiet enough to hear somebody thinking at you, and most of all you find ways to make that work so much fun that you keep on working. You stick together and love each other and keep growing."

"How do we do that, Jake?" Isham Latimer asked.

"Everybody here makes enough money to get boozed regular, and some of us are flush. I say we pass the hat. Tomorrow night at my place—no, the night after, the banks won't be open tomorrow. Then we take what's in the hat, and we hunt us up a building, a big one back off the road somewhere where you have to look hard to find it, with a good fireplace and an upright piano, and we find out who you bribe to get a liquor license around here, and—"

I'm happy to report that at this point I was drowned out by cheers. A happy pandemonium took place under the stars, people shouting suggestions about buildings they knew, about how to appraise a building, about how the place should be furnished and how to get it done most cheaply. Finally Tom Hauptman shouted everybody down.

"Hold it, hold it! Brothers and sisters, we're going to need a place big enough to hold at least a hundred—I have the feeling we're going to have a full house pretty regularly from now on. Now, before we get to the logistical problems of all that, there's something I have to get straight. *My feet hurt.* Forty or fifty rummies a night, two or three nights a week, I could handle. But I am *not* going to take over full-time barkeeping. Who is?"

There was no hesitation at all. To my absolute astonishment, at least thirty voices chorused, in perfect synch, "Jake, of course."

I turned bright red and stammered. "Why—why me? Why not—"

And paused. Who? The Doc had a practice to maintain. Long-Drink was a bit too slaphappy. Tommy was too young yet. Noah had responsibilities. Ralph couldn't reach the fucking bottles. Eddie was needed at the piano, and Bill Gerrity could never get around fast enough in heels . . .

And while I was riffling the cards and coming up empty, Long-Drink answered the question I'd forgotten I'd asked.

"Because even in the times you were down, you were always the merriest of us, Jake."

And by God, there was a chorus of agreement.

I took a very deep breath, held it until my chest ached, then let it out all at once. "All right," I said. "I ain't a guitar player no more; I've got to do something with my hands. I'm in."

Cheers. "We'll call it 'Jake's Place'!" Tony Telasco yelled.

"Hell no," I yelled back. "We'll call it 'Mary's Place.' "

More cheers—then suddenly silence, as we all heard sirens approaching from both ends of Route 25A in the distance.

"What do we tell them?" Doc Webster asked.

"We'll discuss that together on the way to the highway," I said. "If this crowd can't come up with a suitable Tall Tale, no one can."

The Doc chuckled. "I believe you're right." We all began picking our way across the rough terrain between us and the road.

"Hey, everybody?" Fast Eddie called out softly.

"Yes, Eddie?" I said.

"I know dere's a couple hours ta go yet—but Happy New Year."

Halifax,
Easter 1985

PART IV

EARTH . . . AND BEYOND

POST TOAST

Jake Stonebender, proprietor of Mary's Place (spiritual successor to Callahan's Place), has been making music with Zoey and Fast Eddie for over an hour, and his fingers are shot. ''Tom,'' he calls out to the man behind the stick, ''bring me a double!''

Tom Hauptman grins. ''Sure thing, boss,'' he says. Then, oddly, he turns on his heel and leaves the room, walks through the bead curtain into the back—into Jake and Zoey's living quarters. Jake stares after him in puzzlement.

A moment later Tom emerges with a companion. Tall, unreasonably thin, long of hair and reasonably sanitary of beard, thick glasses, Beatle boots, otherwise clad in an odd mixture of L.L. Bean and The Gap, with long fingers, a splendid guitar around his neck and a vaguely alarming gleam in his eye. He is, in short, a reasonable facsimile of Jake.

''You *did* ask for a double,'' Tom says, straight-faced, and the bar bursts into thunderous laughter and applause.

''Spider Robinson!'' Jake cries. ''By da t'underin' Jesus, it's good to see you, mate!''

''Right back at you, bro,'' says Spider. ''Hi, Zoey. Hi, Eddy—Doc—Drink—everybody . . .''

There is a merry rumble of welcome. ''What brings you back to Long Island, pal?'' Long-Drink McGonnigle calls out. ''If you don't mind my asking,'' he adds hastily, as Fast Eddie stirs on his piano stool.

''I came to give you all a speech, and a toast, and a song,'' Spider says solemnly, and a respectful silence falls. Tom Hauptman is already pouring the Bushmill's 1608. Spider takes it, walks around the bar and strides up to the chalk line on the floor, faces the crackling hearth. He holds up his shot and looks through it at the fire for a long moment, seems lost in thought. Then he lowers it, untasted, and turns to the assembled witnesses.

''As most of you know,'' he says, ''I come from what Admiral Bob calls a different 'ficton'—a different dimension, a different reality—than this one. My reality is adjacent to and congruent to and very similar to yours, but different. For example, in the 1996 that I come from, the Beatles just put out two new singles.''

(rumbles of astonishment and profound envy from all sides)

''With help from Mike Callahan, I visit this ficton once every few years, and get Jake there stoned, and transmute what he tells me about you into stories that I publish as science fiction back in my own ficton. I get to support a family without owning a necktie, and Jake gets the free reefer and someone to listen to him talk: like breastfeeding, the relationship is mutually satisfactory, so much that it has endured for two dozen years.

''So in my ficton, there are a lot of people who have the preposterous idea that I *invented* all of you, that you are all just figments and figwoments of my imagination. To be honest, I haven't done much to dissuade them—because anybody who could think up people like *you* rummies would have to be one hell of a storyteller.''

(sounds of raucous agreement from the patrons)

''Well, I recently learned that, to humble me, God created yet another ficton, which is adjacent and congruent and similar to my own, yet different—called *Usenet*—and in *that* ficton, some people seem to have the idea that Spider Robinson is a fictional character *they* invented. They're apparently engaged in rewriting me as I speak, patting me into shape. I only recently got the word: some of them hipped me, and kept it up till I finally heard them.

''I'm not complaining: it serves me right. Talk about poetic justice! And they're not even doing a bad job, so far, if you ask me: they actually make me sound pretty interesting. Did you know, for instance, that Robert Heinlein once saved my life? I hadn't . . .

''But I didn't come here to boast. I came here to tell you all that the seed you used me to plant in my ficton has metastasized . . . to another.

''The denizens of this world called *Usenet*, see, were kind of like Jubal Harshaw's proverbial editor and his soup. Having invented a sci-fi writer named Spider, they decided they liked some of his stories enough to make them real. So, seven or eight years ago, they did.

''That's right, jadies and lentilmen: they whipped up their own Callahan's Place, out of thin air! It's called alt.callahans . . .''

(a *roar* of astonishment and confusion and glee and outrage and disbelief . . . which finally morphs into a long rolling wave of laughter . . . followed by another . . . and another)

''Now, I know what many of you want to hear about. You want me to tell you all the countless little ways their Callahan's Place is different from the one you lot used to drink in, and from Mary's Place here. And there are a lot of differences, and maybe we can talk about them another time. But the things I want to tell you first—the most important things—are the ways their Callahan's Place is *like* yours.''

''Do they make rotten puns there?'' Doc Webster calls.

''Do dey make music dere?'' Fast Eddie asks.

''Do they drink there?'' Long-Drink bellows.

''Do they smash their glasses in the fireplace?'' Tommy Janssen asks, and the rumble of the crowd indicates that he has come closest so far to a good question.

''None of that is really important,'' Jake Stonebender says, meeting Spider's eye. ''What about the *important* stuff, Spider? Did they get *that* right?''

The room falls silent.

Slowly, enjoying the suspense, Spider lets his poker face relax into a crooked smile.

''As far as I can tell, they *did*, Jake. At alt.callahans they believe that shared pain is diminished, and that shared joy is increased, just like here. They believe that a snoopy question merits a mild concussion. They help the ones that hurt and make merry with the ones that don't.''

(stunned silence in Mary's Place)

''They care about one another, there, 24-7. They don't make any magical claims, but they seem to have compassion by the carload, and they value kindness over hipness. And they use a system of communication that's startlingly like the telepathy you folks are shooting for here. Oh, there's a social disease rampant in their world with a horrid symptom called 'flaming' but they suffer far less from it than just about anywhere else in their ficton. First-time visitors are not called the 'N-word' there, for instance, as is customary elsewhere. Just like here, alt.callahans seems to be a place where it's All Right to Be Bright, where it's All Right to Be Dull, where it's all right to be any damn thing at all except a pain in the ass. You know the Invisible Protective Shield around this place? The magic force field that keeps out the bikers and dealers and predators and drinking alcoholics and kids looking to raise hell? Well, they've got one too, called a Sysop.

''And yes, they make exceedingly rotten puns there. And some splendid music. And they tell toxic jokes. Don't tell anybody, but I've already pinched a couple.''

Doc Webster clears his throat. ''Uh . . . how big a joint are we talking about, Spiderman?''

Spider grins. ''Nobody knows. This *Usenet* ficton is a truly weird universe, a snake's orgy of nodes and channels and webs and threads, and as far as I know there is no truly accurate census, and alt.callahans runs all through it like kudzu . . . and branches off from there to *another* ficton called—you won't believe this one! The Web. But the best guess I heard was, well in excess of 61,000 people are regular patrons. It's said to be in the top one percent of bars there, by size, and furthermore to be damn near the only one in the top two percent that doesn't have topless bottomless waitresses and a live donkey show. *This* Callahan's Place probably couldn't be destroyed by *fifty* nukes, all going off at once.''

(a vast collective intake of breath nearly extinguishes the fire in the hearth)

''Put it this way,'' Spider says. ''In January of 1995—their 1995—these people exchanged more words than I have written about you bozos in two dozen years of doing so for my living. Six and a half *megabytes*.''

''What kind of words?'' Jake asks.

Spider nods. ''Good question. I reached into a pile of their traffic at random and pulled out a message. Someone I didn't know was talking to someone else I didn't know, who was in the end stage of leukemia. He said, 'You are about to go on a wonderful journey through space and time with Mike Callahan and the gang.' He said, 'I envy you the trip.' He said, 'Save me a seat by the hearth, my friend . . . ' He . . . I . . . it was . . .'' Spider falls silent. His jaw muscles ripple, and he pokes around behind his glasses with a knuckle. ''Five deaths, so far,'' he manages. ''And some births . . . and God knows how many weddings . . .'' He shakes his head. ''And some of the *worst* goddamn jokes I ever . . .''

''Hully fuckin' Jesus Christ, *we done it!*'' Fast Eddie cries.

''We broke the membrane,'' Suzy Maser murmurs, thunder-struck.

''Through the Looking Glass . . .'' her co-wife Suzi breathes.

''Spider's right,'' Doc Webster rumbles. ''We've meta-stasized.''

''We're loose among the fictons,'' Long-Drink McGonnigle says with most uncharacteristic sobriety. ''We're fuck-ing literally out of this world!''

''All that pain diminishing,'' Zoey says softly.

''All dat joy increasin','' Fast Eddie adds just as softly.

Jake, with the air of someone quoting Scripture, says, '' 'God,' he cries, dying on Mars, 'we made it!' . . .'' and everyone in the room (recognizing the tagline of a Theodore Sturgeon story famous in nearly every ficton) nods.

Suddenly a spontaneous ovation occurs, a consensual roar of joy and glee and hope and pride that rocks the rafters, shakes the walls, rattles the glasses behind the bar, and makes a cloud of sawdust rise from the floor. People fall on each other and hug and laugh and sob and pound each other's back and pour beer over one another. Jake and Tom were off the mark the instant it began, from sheer instinct, and barely in time: as the blizzard of empty glasses begins to fall on the fireplace, they are busy passing out full ones.

Which reminds everybody that Spider said he has a toast to make. Which reminds them that maybe Spider has more on his mind than that just making them feel good. Slowly, hesi-tantly, the noise dwindles, until the room is more or less silent again.

''So,'' Zoey says, ''how do *you* feel about all this, Spi-der? If you don't mind my asking?''

''Well,'' Spider says slowly, ''I came here tonight because I didn't know the answer to that myself. I figured one of you would probably ask me sooner or later, and I know I can't lie to one of you, so I expected to get my answer here . . . and I have. The answer is, it beats the living shit out of me.''

''What do you *think* of the joint?'' Long-Drink asks.

''Dunno, Drink. I've never been there in my life.''

''Jump back!'' the Drink says. ''Why not?''

''Well, basically, you need a good Ficton-Twister to get there. A Ficton-Twister is a highly evolved descendant of the typewriter, and the one I own after twenty-three years of writing science fiction for a living, a Mac II, just isn't powerful enough to pierce the membrane, as the Doc puts it. I couldn't get to *Usenet* if I walked all day. The data I was given about alt.callahans amount to a time-lapse film of a couple of years that takes half an hour to watch: you can't evaluate a place on evidence like that.''

''But what's your first impression?'' Zoey prods. ''How does it make you *feel?*''

Spider is slow to answer. Slowly it dawns on those present that for the first time in memory, Spider Robinson is having difficulty finding the right words.

''I feel,'' he says finally, ''like a man who's just learned that he has a grown son he never knew existed, by a lady long-forgotten . . . no, a whole *herd* of grown children, with grown grandchildren with kids of their own. He can't claim the privileges of paternity, because he only meant to entertain the lady, and he wasn't there when the diapers were full, or the tuition was due but—nonetheless he feels warm and proud, whether he has any real right to or not.'' Jake and Zoey exchange a glance. ''I . . . put it this way: I feel less useless than usual, lately.''

''Does it bother you that some of them don't seem to know you from Adam's off ox—or care?'' Merry Moore asks.

Spider grins. ''That part fucking *delights* me. The only kind of church I'd be willing to duck into to get out of a driving rain would be one where some of the congregation are a little vague on the Prophet's actual name, and it's all right to call him an asshole out loud, but the goddamn *doctrine* itself somehow got preserved. I would rather those people remember 'Shared pain is lessened; shared joy is increased; thus do we refute entropy' than remember the name of the first idiot to say it. My interest in being worshipped approaches zero . . . from *beneath*.'' He looks thoughtful, and sights through his untouched drink at the dancing flames again. ''I admit I do feel just a tad like Moses, camped outside a suburb of the Promised Land, watching his name get misspelled in the history books.'' Suddenly he giggles and lowers his glass, rescued as always by his sense of humour. ''Then again, that happens in my *own* books, sometimes.''

''Hell, Spider,'' Jake says, ''I got an idea. You say somebody there hipped you to the place. So you can send them a letter, right?''

''Yeah, sort of. I can E-mail folks who can pass the file through the membrane.''

''So why don't you write and tell them all about your next Tor Books hardcover about us, *Callahan's Legacy?* You know, the one about the night Buck Rogers walked in and started setting hundred dollar bills on fire. Or tell 'em about the hardcover omnibus of your first three Callahan books that Tor will bring out shortly after that. Hell, tell them about the complete list of your books posted in the Compuserve SFLit Forum. If that many people bought a book or two apiece, you could afford a better Ficton-Twister, right?''

Spider shrugs. ''I'd like to, Jake. For one thing, I hear there's some confusion over there about the *non*-Callahanian book that just came out, the Baen paperback called *Deathkiller;* I'd like to tell them it's a combined reissue of two related out-of-print novels called *Mindkiller* and *Time Pressure*, slightly revised and updated; and I'd love to explain to them how the story ''God Is an Iron'' originally grew to become the former of those, and

why both books *belong* together; and I'd like to let them
know that I'm presently working on a third novel in that
ficton called *Lifehouse*. I could mention the computer-game
version of Callahan's Place coming soon from Legend Entertainment too. I might even remind them that anyone in
the world who wants to bother can, for less than the cost
of a single hardcover, become a nonattending member of the
World SF Convention, and nominate and vote for the annual
Hugo Award, thereby strongly influencing the course of
modern SF and the income of the winning writers . . . and
that even a man with three Hugos could always use a few
more. (Ask my friend Harlan.) But there are two problems . . .

''First, they might take all that for an attempt to 'post
a commercial message on *Usenet*.' This violates a stringent
ficton-wide taboo, roughly equivalent to defecating in
public after ingesting a prune stew, and punishable by
'public flaming' (which I will not describe, but I hear
it's worse than public phlegming) and 'spamming' (enough
said).

''And second of all, even if they *want* to hear about that
stuff . . . suppose I *did* clear enough to buy myself a
Ficton-Twister that'll run System 7, and a whole new whack
of compatible software . . . pardon me, I mean, 'enough
magic' . . . why, if that happened, I'd feel obliged to
visit alt.callahans with my new rig and say thanks, and
then they'd all know my interworld address. Have you ever
tried to answer mail from 61,000 people?''

(a rumble of apprehension as the magnitude of Spider's
problem begins to dawn)

''Even if one percent of 'em were interested enough to
bother,'' he goes on, ''that's enough man-hours to eat up
all the profit 61,000 sales would bring in, right there. Say
I only hear from one-*tenth* of one percent, and not one of
those is a chump: sixty-one interesting letters a day. The
nicest form-response I could design would disappoint or
offend many of them and that's not even the problem.

''The problem is that I would *love* to answer each one personally and at length, spend every waking minute of every

working day chatting with friendly strangers who believe
that shared pain is lessened and shared joy is increased,
who like to swap compassion and villainous puns, who tolerate the weird, who help each other through real life and
real death . . . and who in many cases happen to be familiar with and/or friendly toward my lifework. I had a friend
once named Milligram Mulligan, surely dead by now, who
said that the first time he heard the *term* 'speed freak,'
before he had any idea what that lifestyle entailed, he
knew It Was Him. Well, the drug alt.callahans was designed
to mate perfectly with my own endorphin receptors. I can
easily see myself disappearing up my own anus, (virtually)
partying away the hours . . .

''. . . and never publishing another fucking word. Not
the Callahan/Lady Sally/Mary's Place stuff, and not the
other fifty percent of what I write, alone and with Jeanne,
which is just as good and just as important to me and—hope-
fully to some percentage of the literate public.

''Even worse, the problem is not limited to *Usenet.* My sis-
ter-in-law Dolly tells me *another* Callahan's Place,
smaller but just as cool, recently coalesced in a ficton
called AOL . . .

''I hear the Siren call, and my heart aches to heed it
. . . but I have a family to feed, and rent to pay, and debt
to service, and a deep primordial completely eco-
irresponsible compulsion not to rest until the last tree
on my earth has been hacked down, sliced into strips, and
stained with graffitti of my composition. Gaea forgive
me . . .''

''I'm a vegetarian, myself,'' Long-Drink remarks. ''I
don't give a damn about animals.'' He grins sadistically.
''But I *hate* plants . . .''

Ignoring him magnificently, Jake says, ''Then there's only
one thing to do, Spider.''

Spider looks alert. (One of his better impressions.)

Zoey says it for her old man. ''You gotta write them one
long letter, with no return address. You gotta tell 'em

that you love 'em and that you're grateful to 'em and that
you wish 'em all well. Tell 'em they make you feel proud
and humble and awed and gratified all at the same time, and
make sure they know they're never gonna be far from your
thoughts as long as you live . . . and maybe ask 'em while
they're busy rewriting you to remember that you always
tried to be kind to your characters.''

(sustained rumble of agreement, at which Spider blushes)

''And you gotta tell them,'' Tanya Latimer says, ''that *we*
love them too, and that we thank them for making us all feel
just a little bit less superfluous . . . for making us feel
that all our struggles and trials have been *worth* something, have *meant* something . . . even if it's only to
people in another world. I don't know about anybody else
here, but I—'' She catches herself. ''No, I *do* know about
everybody else here. We're all gonna sleep *good* tonight . . .''

(louder rumble of agreement)

''You have to tell them everything you just told us,'' Doc
Webster said, ''and make them a quick toast or two . . .
and then tap-dance out the door and go back to work.''

(rumble graduates to table-thumping)

''He's right,'' Jake calls. ''Hell, you don't visit *us*
more than every other year or so, and you're always gone as
soon as you fill up a floppy. And God knows you're always welcome when you do show. You're the kind of pal, it's OK if a
few years slip by.''

(thumping becomes cheer)

Spider stands a little straighter, and for a moment looks
both older and younger than forty-seven. ''Thank you,
Jake. Thank you all. As it happens, your advice is exactly
my plan.'' He produces a tape recorder from thin air. ''All
this is going to be transcribed and sent to alt.callahans,
along with a sample chapter from *Callahan's Legacy*. I just
felt like it was time I connected you both, this ficton and

that one, directly—if only by proxy. Well, anyway, the job is done, so the only thing left to do is make my toast, and then—by way of thanking you and them for letting me pull on your coattail so long—to play you all out with a song.''

For the first time, he lifts his glass of Bushmill's, and every glass, mug, flask, and jelly jar in the room rises in unison with it. The silence is total.

''To all the Callahan's Places there ever were or ever will be,'' Spider Robinson says, ''whatever they may be called—and to all the merry maniacs and happy fools who are fortunate enough to stumble into one: may none of them arrive too late!'' And he drains his 1608 in a single draught, and hurls his glass into the precise center of the hearth, where it explodes with a sound rather like a Macintosh booting up.

''*To all the Callahan's Places!*'' everyone in the room choruses, and the fireplace begins to feel like Jupiter did when Shoemaker-Levy came to visit . . .

''Wait, one more,'' Spider calls. ''To the guy who found a manuscript called 'The Guy with the Eyes' in the *Analog* slushpile back in 1972, and decided to buy it, and mentor its author—to one of the best SF writers working today: Ben Bova, without whom all of this would not have been necessary . . .''

And another roar goes up from the throng. ''*To Ben Bova!*''

And Spider, both his hands free now, slings his guitar back up into combat configuration. ''Now I'll just sing you this quick one and go. Jeanne was out of town for a few weeks, and I missed her, so I wanted to write her a love song. The problem was, we've been married twenty years now: there just *isn't* any way to say 'I love you' that I haven't used already, often. So I produced a song called 'Belaboring the Obvious.'

He hits a bluesy A6 chord, and begins to sing . . . and one can't help but sense the words are more than a little apropos to Spider's situation in all *three* fictons:

BELABORING THE OBVIOUS

by

Spider Robinson

I want to tell you how I feel, love
 But it ain't exactly news
 Got no secrets to reveal, love
 But I'm gonna say it anyway,
  'cause I'm alone and you're away
   I haven't got a blessed thing to
 lose . . .

(so here goes:)

Water ain't dry, the sky goes up high,
 And a booger makes a pretty poor glue
 You can't herd cats, bacteria don't wear
 hats
 —and I love you

Sugar ain't sour, bread's good with flour
 And murder's a mean thing to do
 Trees got wood, and fuckin' is pretty good
 —and I love you

Yeah, I'm belaboring the obvious:
 You will have noticed all the good times
 This is as practical an exercise
 As taping twenty cents to my transmission
  so that any time I want to
   I can shift my pair o' dimes . . .

(but God knows:)

Goats don't vote, and iron don't float
 And a hippy don't turn down boo
 Dog bites man, the teacher don't understand
 —and I love you

Sickness sucks, it's nice to have bucks
* And the player on first base is Who*
* Kids grow up, most fellows pee standing up*
* —and I love you*

Guess I didn't need to say it
* Just a message that my heart sent*
* And I kinda like the way it's*
* More redundant than is absolutely*
*   necessary according to the Department*
*   of Redundancy Department . . .*
*   (Division of Unnecessary Repetition and*
* Pointless Redundancy Division)*

(I must close:)

Fun is nice, you can't fry ice,
* And the money will always be due*
* Bullshit stinks, and no one outsits the*
* Sphinx*
* —and I love you*

Livin' ain't bad, and dyin' is sad
* And little we know is true*
* But that's karma—baby, you can bet the farm*
* On this: I do love you.*

And with that, weeping with joy and giggling with sorrow, Spider vanishes back to what he calls reality (what a kidder, that guy), and to his best friend and co-author and oh yes, wife, Jeanne, and their sweet daughter Terri, and life goes on at Mary's Place.

And at alt.callahans, may their shadows be always bent at the elbow . . . And in

—Vancouver, B.C.

[posted to alt.callahans on 24 March 1996]

AUTHOR'S FINAL NOTE

I'd like to thank editors Ben Bova, Don Pfeil, and Stanley Schmidt, who bought the Callahan stories for magazines; editors Jim Frenkel, Ridley Enslow, Jim Baen and Susan Allison, who bought them in book form; agents Kirby McCauley, Eleanor Wood, and Ralph Vicinanza, who sold them in book form; Alfred Bester, who supplied the titles for all three books; and all of you who bought the books.

A (Limited) Callahan's Bibliography

Since the February 1973 publication of "The Guy with the Eyes" in *Analog* magazine, many stories about Callahan's Place have appeared in various magazines and books. For those among you who want to know just where and when the stories in this volume have previously appeared, we offer the (as far as we can tell) complete printing history of the stories in this book.

The one thing that won't appear in any other bibliography of these stories is a curious footnote to the publishing history of the first collection of Callahan's stories, *Callahan's Crosstime Saloon*. Only a very few people knew before now that before Ace Books published the book, it was actually under contract to be published by a not-yet-sister imprint, Tempo Books.

Tempo was an imprint of Grosset & Dunlap. In late 1975, planning to increase their publication of science fiction, Tempo bought the right to publish this book. Between that time and the book's publication in 1977, Ace Books was acquired by Grosset & Dunlap's parent company, Filmways, Inc. Tom Doherty, already the publisher of Tempo, was put in charge of Ace as well. Since these actions put Ace and Tempo under the same editorial direction, and Ace already had a long history of publishing science fiction, it seemed natural that *Callahan's* should become part of the Ace list.

In the years since then, the lives and fortunes of all involved have proceeded with the requisite numbers of corporate changes of ownership, job changes, and thankfully, more Callahan's tales created.

Now, twenty years later, Tom Doherty and I are entirely delighted to be reunited where we started, with Spider Robinson and Callahan's Place. It's been a long strange trip; here are the stops along the way.

Callahan's Crosstime Saloon:
  "The Guy with the Eyes" first published in *Analog*, February 1973;
  "The Time Traveler" first published in *Analog*, April 1974;
  "The Law of Conservation of Pain" first published in *Vertex*, December 1974;
  "Two Heads Are Better Than One" first published in *Analog*, May 1975;
  "Unnatural Causes" first published in *Analog*, October 1975;

" 'A Voice Is Heard in Ramah . . . ' " first published in *Analog*, November 1975;

"The Centipede's Dilemma," "Just Dessert," and "The Wonderful Conspiracy" were all first published in *Callahan's Crosstime Saloon*.

The collection *Callahan's Crosstime Saloon* was first published in June 1977 by Ace Books.

Time Travelers Strictly Cash:

"Dog Day Evening" first published in *Analog*, October 1977;

"Mirror/ютіM, off the Wall" first published in *Analog*, November 1977;

"Fivesight" first published in *Omni*, July 1979;

"Have You Heard the One . . . ?" first published in *Analog*, June 1980.

The collection *Time Travelers Strictly Cash* was first published in March 1981 by Ace Books. Note: That edition included some non-Callahan's material.

Callahan's Secret

"Pyotr's Story" first published in *Analog*, October 1981;

"Involuntary Man's Laughter" first published in *Analog*, December 1983;

"The Blacksmith's Tale" first published in *Analog*, December 1985;

"The Mick of Time" first published in *Analog*, May 1986.

The collection *Callahan's Secret* was first published in July 1986 by Ace Science Fiction.

An omnibus of the Callahan's stories from the three collections, *Callahan and Company; The Compleat Chronicles of the Crosstime Saloon*, was published in 1988 in a limited hardcover edition by Phantasia Press.

—JF

Callahan's in Cyberspace

As Spider noted in ''Post Toast,'' Callahan's Crosstime Saloon no longer exists merely in the pages of books and in the minds of its customers. Callahan's Place has become a real (or is it virtual?) part of cyberspace. Callahan's activity is rampant in chat groups on the Internet, and the Saloon has spread to the Worldwide Web. Following are current addresses for various sites on the Web. Bear in mind that chat groups come and go, websites change, and nothing is permanent. The addresses noted here are as accurate as we could determine as of press time (May 1997). We can't be responsible for sites that disappear, change, or are yet to be created, so when you read these words, please understand that this book is a print medium and stuck in time, unable to change to accomodate the fast changes of the electronic ether.

Callahan's on the Web

- The alt.callahans newsgroup is one of the most popular on the Internet, and there are several pages dedicated to it:
  http://www.ice.net/~kwalsh/callahans.html
  http://www.callahan's.org/
  http://www.vex.net/~leslie
- A page that supports the #callahans channel on IRC (Internet Relay Chat):
  http://www.voicenet.com/~jnork/callahan's
- The Internet webpage for the Callahan's Forum on Delphi:
  http://www.delphi.com/callahan
- Legend Entertainment's page about the *Callahan's Crosstime Saloon* computer game:
  http://www.kaizen.net/legend/gameinfo/callahan.html
- Steve Jackson Games's page about the role-playing game supplement *GURPS Callahan's Crosstime Saloon*:
  http://www.io.com/sjgames/gurps/books/Callahan
- The Tor Books homepage, with information on Spider Robinson and Callahan's:
  http://www.tor.com
- A page on the Baen Books website dedicated to Spider Robinson, including songs from Callahan's performed by Spider

in Real Audio and downloadable WAV formats:
    http://www.baen.com/blurbs/callahan.html
* A page dedicated to "The Crazy Years," Spider Robinson's regularly irregular column for the Toronto, Ontario *Globe and Mail*:
    http://www.theglobeandmail.com/docs/webextra/spider.html
* Last but not least, Spider Robinson's homepage, maintained by a friend:
    http://psg.com/~ted/spider/

ABOUT THE AUTHOR

SPIDER ROBINSON is the winner of many major SF awards, including three Hugos, one Nebula, and the John W. Campbell Award for Best New Writer. He is best known for his Callahan books: insightful, lighthearted science fiction stories centered around the most bizzare blend of barflies you're likely to meet in this or any other galaxy. He is also a singer/songwriter/guitarist; a CD-ROM based on Callahan's Place has been released, for which Spider recorded several original songs accompanied by blues guitarist Amos Garrett. His other works include three novels in the well-known Stardance sequence, *Stardance, Starseed*, and *Starmind*, all written in collaboration with his wife, writer/choreographer Jeanne Robinson. They currently reside in Vancouver, British Columbia, with their daughter Terri.